Dangerous PURSUIT

BETHANY ROSA

GALLATIN PUBLISHING

THE *pursuit* SERIES

AUTHOR NOTE

I want to take a moment to explain my thoughts on therapy, counseling, life coaching, and the like. Depression, mental illness, and life's general difficulties are not to be taken lightly. Unlike the views of my character, I am in full support of therapy. In fact, I love it. Whether you're as happy as can be or struggling in some way, I believe counseling can benefit everyone and am a big fan of self-coaches, counselors, therapists…etc.

I've frequented all three throughout my many years as a wife, mom, and individual working toward self-improvement. Please don't take my character's words to heart, but rather from a person who is struggling to find her way and doing her best.

If you've never been told how great counseling or self-coaching can be, let me be the first to do so. It's amazing. From self-discovery to working out issues, having an ear and some guidance can do wonders. Don't hesitate if you're on the fence. And know that there is always a light at the end of the tunnel.

There's no one more deserving than you, Michele.
Cheers to a new tomorrow.
Cheers to a new you.
Cheers to a lasting friendship.

Dangerous

PURSUIT

1

NEW BEGINNINGS

Jackson

"**Y**ou have got to be kidding me." I'm staring at my parents with my mouth open in shock.

"Jackson, Sofia's had a hard life, and if we can do something as simple as give her daughter a job to show some kindness, then that's what we're going to do. Her husband walked out on her and that poor girl five years ago. He just left them to gamble his life away." My mom has always had a bleeding heart.

"Mom, she's seventeen, for fuck's sake. She's barely out of diapers, and you expect her to be my assistant? Do you know what that entails?" I'm outraged. And that's putting it mildly. I knew Cindy, my executive assistant, was going on maternity leave soon, but I'd already talked to her about hiring someone from a temp agency to take her place until she returned. Instead, they want a high schooler to do her job.

Not only have I been managing the company alone since my sister, Cici, decided she wanted no part of the family business, but now I'm being forced to do it with an immature, inexperienced teenager. It's hard enough without the partner I thought I'd have with my sister. If it weren't for Cindy, my overly competent assistant, I might have run away like Cici.

As it is, my goal is to take us beyond anything they ever hoped for, which I've been doing a damn good job of so far. This, however, could be a significant setback. Since my parent's retirement, my focus has been on growth, having several deals in the works for sales and acquisitions of multiple properties, and now they're asking me to navigate it with inadequate help.

"I do know what it entails, Jackson. I stepped down a year ago, not long enough to forget. I'm also aware that Mia is a bright young lady who will do just fine after being trained by Cindy. You're overreacting. Young people are eager and make excellent employees. Don't be so dramatic." Mom is running the show on this one, while Dad has been uncharacteristically quiet, obviously making this her decision.

"Since you've already committed, it is what it is. But just so we're clear, I *will* make other arrangements if she can't keep up. I'm knee-deep in contract negotiations right now, and I need someone on top of their game. If she's not up to the task, I'll have to find someone who is." My mom can put her foot down on hiring her since this is still technically their company, but if I set my expectations up front, I'll have more firing power later.

My dad finally speaks up. "I agree, son. Give her a chance, and if she doesn't work out, we'll reevaluate the situation and find a different position for her."

"All right, one chance. When should I have Cindy start training her? She's still six weeks out, so a month from now?" Having my dad's back makes me more agreeable.

"I already made the arrangements, dear," Mom cuts in. "She starts on Monday. Even though Cindy's not due for another month and a half, she could go into labor before then. This way, Mia will be fully trained in case."

Fuck. My. Life.

I dial Braden as soon as I pull out of the driveway. "I need a drink. Meet me at the club?"

"Yeah, sure. What's got you so riled up?"

"Just leaving my parents'. I'll fill you in when I get there. See you soon." If anyone can talk me down, he can.

I don't have to tell him what club we're headed to. Ever since I helped our friend Eli with a business transaction he was doing, we've been on the VIP list at a local nightclub he owns. It's a nice perk: good service, prime tables, and plenty of hot women.

Braden is waiting on the sidewalk when I arrive. "Hey. What went down with your parents to put you in such a mood?"

"Fuck. This takes the cake, man. They have me running the company yet are insisting I replace Cindy with a fucking seventeen-year-old high schooler while she's on maternity leave. I'm livid." I run my hand through my hair and sigh in frustration. I'm so pissed I can't see straight.

"Dude, you can't even bang her. That sucks."

I laugh along with him. Leave it to Braden to lighten the mood. "You got that right. Come on, let's go find someone I can."

Mia

Glancing at the clock on the computer screen, I realize it's time to call it. Shoot. I'm on a winning streak, but oh well. Mom will be home soon, and I'd be in big trouble if she caught me playing online poker. I've made it this far with my secret; I'm not screwing up now.

If she knew this was what I did in my spare time, she'd probably take away all electronics, cancel Wi-Fi, and anything else she could think of to stop me. All thanks to my dad, who walked out five years ago because of his addiction, which just so happens to be gambling in the form of poker. The good news? He taught me everything he knew. I've played since I was old enough to count and surpassed my dad's talent at an early age. Being a whiz with numbers is handy, but my real strength is hiding emotions, which is crucial when playing live games.

When I saw how hard my mom was working to support us after he left, I decided to help. She thinks we get the extra money from a part-time job I made up. She'd keel over from shame if she found out the truth. I don't think she's recovered from my dad leaving us, even after all these years.

After an hour in the kitchen, I hear the front door close seconds before she walks in. "Ooh, what did you make tonight, honey? It smells delicious."

"Some pollo guisado tonight. It's almost finished. I figured you could take the leftovers to work with you tomorrow."

"Oh, mija, you're so good to me. I'll set the table. I have something exciting to tell you over dinner." She looks ecstatic, piquing my curiosity.

We dig in as soon as our butts hit the chairs. Cooking is something I picked up over the last few years. With the internet to provide recipes, I could probably make anything out there, and if groceries weren't so expensive, I'd be able to prove that theory.

"So, what's the exciting news?" I figured she'd get right to it, but we've been silent for the first five minutes, devouring our meals.

"Have I ever mentioned Jack and Hazel Soloman, the nice couple I clean for on Fridays? They were one of my first clients seven years ago."

"I think so. I don't remember for sure, but what about them?" Mom often comes home with stories from work.

"They're the nicest family—always making small talk while I'm there, and today, we were chatting about our kids, and I happened to mention that you finished your senior year early and needed a full-time job until fall, and guess what?" she asks, beaming. Her excitement is contagious, making me smile.

"What?"

"Well, their son, Jackson, who was already out of the house when I started for them, took over their property management company when they retired—Soloman Management or something. Their daughter, Cici, was supposed to run it with him but ended up moving away. I remember when she lived at home, she was such a sweetheart. I can't believe she left."

"Mom! Get to the point. What's the good news?" I interrupt her rambling, growing impatient. She tends to do this, drone on and on, taking forever to finish her stories. I'm honestly surprised to hear that the Solomans talk with her so much. My mom can be overwhelming at times. God bless her.

"Well, they mentioned that Jackson's assistant is going on maternity leave and that they needed a temporary replacement. I told them how smart and mature you are, graduating from high school early with all those advanced classes, and I can't believe it, but they offered you the job!"

"Like, they want me to interview for it?" This might be perfect, and I bet it would pay decent money.

She has the biggest smile on her face. "No, honey, they want you to start training on Monday. No interview necessary. They said any daughter of mine will be amazing, and with the drive you're showing, you'll be great."

I'm stunned. "Monday? Wow… that's just… wow…"

"That's good, right? I figured you needed something to do anyway since you won't have school anymore. Maybe it'll go so well that they keep you on until you start college in the fall." She's so happy, it's infectious.

My plan was to continue playing poker, but this way, I could make money guilt-free. Maybe it'll also give me time for a social life. If I work eight to five, I can go out at night like most people my age instead of playing tournaments. I'd still make meals and help around the house, but with my nights and weekends free, I'd have plenty of time for everything.

"It's great, Mom… just crazy that I start on Monday with no interview, but with the timing, it's like it was meant to be. They know I have no office experience, though, right?" The doubt is seeping in.

"Sweetheart, you'll do great. I'm sure you'll pick it up in no time. You have nothing to worry about with how smart and responsible you are. Why don't you go up to start picking your outfits for next week and let me clean up."

"Mom, you worked all day. I can do it. I have all weekend to decide what to wear, but nice try. You should take a bath and relax. I don't mind." I refuse to let her clean when she gets home.

"Mia, I don't know what I did to deserve you, but I sure am lucky. I love you, honey. Come say good night when you're done."

"All right, I'll be up in a few."

I ruminate over my new job while putting away dinner and tidying up the kitchen. I'll be an assistant to the owner—well, the owner's son. I know nothing about him or Soloman Management, so I'll have to do some research over the weekend. The last thing I want is to walk in unprepared and clueless.

After saying one more thank you and final good night to Mom, I rush to get ready for bed so I can call my best friend, Walker, and tell him the good news. He knows how much it bothers me to lie about the extra income. Another positive is that I'll have something to keep me busy during the day since, unlike me, he's still in school until graduation.

I'm a nervous wreck getting ready for my first day. I played my last poker games over the weekend, even declining an invite to a live tournament this week. Since I'm taking this job, I've decided to go legit. Being full-time should cover the extra expenses I take care of and still allow me to save for a car. Poker is lucrative, so it's hard to give up, but knowing how upset Mom would be if she knew is enough motivation to quit.

Pairing my classiest black skirt with a fitted purple ribbed V-neck is the best I came up with from my limited selection. Clothes have been at the bottom of my list for the past few years. Gold hoop earrings complete the look with my favorite necklace, a nightingale spreading its wings. It was a graduation present from my mom, a tribute to my middle name, which happens to be Nightingale. Finishing up with two sprays of my favorite scent and my only pair of heels, a wedge sandal, I'm as ready as I can be for a first impression.

I enter the kitchen but don't dare eat with the butterflies in my stomach. Puking at work on day one is not on my to-do list. Instead, I grab a cup of coffee and try to stay calm.

"You look great, sweetie. Are you excited?" My mom appears from around the corner.

"More nervous, but what are you still doing here? I thought you had a job at seven."

"I couldn't miss my baby's first day of work. I'll just be home an hour later tonight. Do you want to order pizza for dinner since we'll probably both be tired?"

"That's perfect. Sorry you have to work late, but I'm glad you're here now. What do you think?" I spin around.

"Very professional. I can't believe how grown-up you look. You're going to do amazing. I know it. Be confident and remember how wonderful you are, mija." She leans in to hug me.

"I love you, Mom. Thanks again for getting me this job."

"Of course. You're going to have a great first day. I can't wait to hear all about it," she says before grabbing her things and heading out the door.

After a few more minutes, I force myself to follow and make my way to the bus. It's not a long commute, but it's enough to ponder all my research from the weekend. I learned that Soloman Management Group is a pretty big deal. They not only do property management for numerous places but own many of the buildings they manage. Even more impressive is that they started from nothing and grew their business to become one of the largest in southern California.

I tried to look up Jackson but only saw his business profile and some family bio regarding their company. I found an article that said Mr. and Mrs. Soloman retired, entrusting their son, Jackson, to carry on, but that sums it up. He exists on Instagram but hasn't posted in years, so he's not on social media much. I couldn't find anything else regarding Jackson or the company. From the few old pictures I did see, he's hot. But being that he's a decade older, attraction shouldn't be an issue.

From the sidewalk, I study the building before me. It's not pretentious, just an ordinary, one-level office building. It's large, though, with only one sign above the main entrance, indicating they occupy the whole thing. With as many buildings in their portfolio, it makes sense that they need ample space.

Taking a deep breath, I walk in and see a large reception desk. "Hi, I'm Mia Marcos. I start training today as the temporary assistant for Jackson Soloman."

"Oh yeah, great. Let's start with your paperwork, and then I'll take you back to Cindy." She hands me a clipboard and directs me to the chairs. "Have a seat and take your time. Come see me when you're done."

My nerves are skyrocketing as I fill out the forms with shaky hands. Once I'm finished, my palms sweat as I'm led back to meet Jackson's current assistant, Cindy. Her desk is in an open area toward the back corner of the building with a large office behind it. The office, which I assume is

Jackson's, has two massive windows on each side of the closed door with blinds that are shut, preventing a glimpse of my new boss.

When Cindy stands to greet me, my eyes immediately gravitate to her protruding belly. I can't believe she's still working.

"Mia, I'm so happy to meet you. I was excited when Hazel called to tell me you'd be training. You'll be a perfect fit while I'm gone."

"Thanks. I, uh, well, I'll just be upfront and tell you I have no experience, but I'm a fast learner." She's still standing, and I wonder how she's managing. "Please, sit down. I feel like you could have a baby any minute." *Crap, did I say that out loud?*

She laughs. "I wish, but I still have six weeks. It looks worse than it is, I promise. It's all the popcorn and chocolate over the last seven months. Advice for the future: Don't use pregnancy as an excuse to eat whatever you want. It doesn't work out in the end."

I like her already. Laughing, I respond, "I'll try to remember that in about ten years. But seriously, let's sit down." A chair has already been placed beside hers, so we both take a seat.

She shows me how to do some morning tasks, supervising while I work. The next time I glance at the clock, I see we've been at it for a couple of hours already, and things are going great. She'd prepared everything for an easy transition.

While we wait for a program to boot up, I take the opportunity to ask about the boss. "So… what's Jackson like? I tried to do some research, but nothing came up."

Instead of answering, I see her eyes dart past my shoulder.

"Good to know my new assistant is cyberstalking me," comes a deep voice from behind.

Seriously? The man is stealthy.

I swivel in my chair to get my first look at Jackson, towering behind me with a scowl. That answers one question—not so warm and fuzzy, then. But, wow, the last few years have been good to him. He's built like a beast and could probably snap me in half. Does he live at the gym or what? I mean, seriously, his muscles look like they're about to bust the seams of his long-sleeved dress shirt. After you get past his biceps, those bright blue eyes draw you in immediately. But it's his casually styled blond hair hanging slightly over his forehead that gives him a boyish charm. He's gorgeous, even with the asshole vibes he's radiating.

"I… I was trying to research the company I'd be working for. My mom didn't give much information besides the business name and the fact that the owners are nice."

For some reason, that earns me another scowl. I can tell he's going to be tough to win over.

"Yeah, they're the nicest. I'll be in my office. Message me if you need anything, Cindy. Good luck." With that, he walks straight into his office and slams the door.

Okay, he's not happy I'm here. Which is rude, considering he doesn't even know me. Screw him.

Although he is my boss, so I'd like to start off on the right foot.

"So… I feel like that wasn't a great first impression." I look to Cindy for advice.

"He's usually a softy, but he's under a lot of stress lately with all our restructuring. Why don't you try that again and introduce yourself properly? Maybe offer to get him some coffee." She gives me a look of encouragement as I stand.

Pulling my skirt down and smoothing my shirt, I rap lightly on the door before entering. Walking forward with slow, unsure steps, I approach his desk while he stares with venom.

Whoa, talk about intimidating. Strangely, it's kind of sexy, which hits me out of nowhere and is so out of character.

"Um, I just wanted to introduce myself and thank you properly. I'm Mia, and I'm truly grateful for the opportunity to be here and eager to learn. I'm prepared to do whatever it takes, sir."

Could that have sounded any worse?

Jackson

I peruse her up and down in silence, and what I see is unexpected. Her thick black hair is pulled back, showcasing her slim neckline and gorgeous face. Her darker skin tone is attractive; I remember it was mentioned that her mom is Puerto Rican. It's her large round eyes that do it, though.

They're soft and innocent, with defiance lurking just beneath the surface. She's stunning is what she is, which only pisses me off more. But apparently, she is eager to learn.

It must be my lucky day.

"You're eager to learn, huh? Well, here's your first lesson. Knock and wait until I answer before you step into my office. And don't thank me. Thank my parents. You wouldn't be here if it were up to me, little girl. Now… Mia, is it?" She nods in stunned silence. "Get out and shut the door behind you."

Her jaw drops. Usually, I'd take that open mouth as an invitation. Unfortunately, she's off the table unless I want to be in cuffs.

Finally coming out of her stupor, she swivels and tries to walk out calmly with all the dignity she can muster. She gets props for keeping it together… she might be more of a challenge than I thought. Still, I give her a week—tops.

On the other hand, I could certainly get used to the view she gives me on the way out. That's the finest ass I've seen in a while, plump and perfect on her slim little frame. I could do some damage to that body of hers, that's for sure.

Fuuuuck. What am I thinking? I cannot possibly be attracted to a girl her age.

This week is going to be long as fuck.

My door opens once again, and Cindy comes barreling toward my desk. "What did you say to her? She was white as a ghost when she came out."

"Only the truth. She wouldn't be here if my parents hadn't insisted. She's seventeen, Cindy. There's no way she's qualified to fill your shoes."

"You don't know that. I can already tell she has a good head on her shoulders. You were young once, remember? Did you like being treated like a child? At least give her a chance, Jackson. You've scared the crap out of her, and I won't always be here to run interference."

Cindy is the only reason my head stays above water. She's been my right hand ever since I started full-time after college. She deals with my excessive demands and doesn't complain about my blunt communication skills. She also puts up with random office visits from my flavors of the month. I would have paid her not to have kids had I known I'd be without her for so long. She asked to be home with the baby for the first six months, and it wasn't difficult to acquiesce rather than risk losing her for good.

"Look, she won't last the week. Don't worry. We'll find someone else for you to train before it's too late. Just indulge her for now, but don't waste much effort."

"We'll see about that. She might surprise you, you know. In the meantime, be nicer. She's darling, and I think she'll work out great if you let her." Cindy always sees the good in people, that's for sure.

"I'll leave her alone for the rest of the day. Satisfied?"

"It'll do for now." She leaves, closing the door behind her.

Damn, that woman is relentless sometimes. It sounds like she's already got a soft spot for the girl. That didn't take long.

It puts a damper on my plan, but I'll figure something out. That girl cannot walk around here for the next eight months, that's for sure. She's way too fucking tempting. Although, I wonder if she enjoys an occasional hookup.

For Christ's sake, what am I thinking? She might not even have *hooked up* yet. Nah, no way. Kids are doing it early these days. Fuck, I'm going down a rabbit hole.

On that note, I grab my phone to respond to Jessica, last weekend's conquest. She texted me this morning that she'd love to stop by and say hi. The eggplant emoji was all I needed to know her intention. She couldn't have picked a better day. Satisfied that she's on her way, I distract myself with work while impatiently waiting.

It's not long before the phone intercom beeps. "There's a Jessica here to see you, sir."

Damn Cindy for having Mia make the announcement. She's the last thing I need on my mind right now.

"Send her in," I reply curtly before a soft "Yes, sir" sounds in reply. *Fuck. Me.*

It's hard and over quickly, just the way I needed it, and judging from her eagerness, she did too.

Alone once more, I drop my head into my hands, feeling no better than I did fifteen minutes ago. I cannot believe I just fucked a woman while imagining she was my new, hot little assistant. What the hell is wrong with me? Mia is a child—I should not be fantasizing about her. Women have always been a weakness, but this is a new low. I need to get out of here, stat.

After hitting the gym for a couple of hours, I call it a day because there's no convincing myself to return to the office. Having already texted Eli and Braden, I head to the bar where we meet when it's too early for the club scene.

There's no traffic this afternoon, so getting there takes minutes. I spot them immediately and make my way over, feeling the tension I've been holding begin to release.

"Hey, guys. Thanks for meeting so early. I needed out of the office." I run my hand down my face and blow the air from my lungs, grateful to see a beer waiting for me.

"She's that bad, huh?" Braden knows why I'm on edge, having heard about it over the weekend.

"She's that hot is more like it. I wasn't expecting her to be total eye candy. I can't have her running around there, tempting me with those fucking curves. Especially not when she's a minor, for fuck's sake." I won't be able to handle it.

"Whoa, whoa, whoa, back up. You're lusting over a kid?" This from Eli, who's not been clued in.

So, I bring him up to date.

"That's fucked up. When does she turn eighteen?" Eli might be more of a womanizer than I am if that question is any indication.

"Dude, she's almost a decade younger. That's a lifetime at our age. It's not happening. She's a baby, for fuck's sake," I say.

"Doesn't sound like a baby if she gets your dick hard, dude. Plus, girls have always matured faster than us, so maybe you two are on the same level," Braden says, laughing.

Fucking Braden.

"A couple of months," I say, ignoring him and answering Eli's question. "It was the first thing I looked at after she left my office. There's no way I can go two months with that ass parading around my office and not fuck up."

My beer is already empty. Signaling the server for another, I sigh, exasperated.

"Well, it sounds like you're gonna have to. Hopefully, you have someone to keep you occupied. If not, it'll be a long couple of months, buddy." Braden, ever the realist.

I raise my refilled glass in a toast. "Then here's to keeping myself sufficiently occupied."

2

GAME ON

Jackson

THE REST OF THE WEEK GOES NO BETTER. I'M ANGRY AND SICK OF hiding in my office to avoid the brat and bear witness to any more of Cindy's fawning over the girl. I've been as cruel as possible without earning more tongue-lashing from Cindy, who seems to like Mia more than she does me. I can't blame her with the mood I've been in.

However, my tactics aren't working—I've produced no tears and no snarky attitude by the end of the week, thus giving me no reason to write her up. Moreover, she hasn't quit. She doesn't even seem bothered by my demeanor and continues to lay on the eager employee act. There's no way she can be this unaffected; she's either oblivious to moods around her, or she's a damn good actress. I'm going with the latter, which means I'm not giving up. I'll break her down eventually.

In the meantime, I have the weekend to regroup, decompress, and deliberate how to up my game. I'm planning to get my fill in the bedroom over the next couple of days, so maybe I'll stop fantasizing about taking Mia over my desk every time she walks in.

Speaking of… "Come in," I say after the second knock on my office door—because why would I make it easy on her? And I know it's her because Cindy doesn't knock.

"Did you need anything else handled before the weekend, sir?" I'm sure Cindy put her up to this. She still thinks I'll come around eventually and be nice to the girl. She couldn't be further from the truth. In fact, an idea just popped into my head.

"I do, but it requires your services over the weekend. Our cleaning company had something come up and can't make their usual rounds to clean the common areas. I'll need you to handle that," I tell her curtly without further instruction. The longer I draw it out, the more reaction I expect to get.

"Do you need me to call and find a replacement company for the weekend?" she asks as she writes on her notepad, trying not to make eye contact.

"No, as in, you need to do it yourself. Your mom is a house cleaner, right? This shouldn't be much of a stretch for you." With that comment, I see the slightest tic of her jaw—finally, something.

"You want me to clean over the weekend?" She looks a little taken aback. This is more fun than anticipated.

"I expect you to do your job, and right now, that entails handling a problem by whatever means necessary. Are you unwilling to perform the duties required?" I sit back in my chair and thread my fingers behind my head.

"How many buildings need to be cleaned? Will I be paid overtime?" At least she's got a head on her shoulders to consider that.

"Does this look like the payroll department? You can direct your questions there. I'll have maintenance provide you with a list of buildings, locations, and requirements for each one. That's all."

She pastes on the biggest smile before saying, "Great, I'll get it done, sir. See you Monday."

On her way out the door, I get the last word in. "Enjoy your weekend, Mia."

She doesn't turn around, and I'd give anything to see the eye roll I'm sure she did.

When the door closes, I pick up my phone and dial maintenance. "Hey, buddy, it's Jackson. I need you to do something for me. I'm having

Mia, my assistant in training, clean our buildings this weekend to familiarize herself with our properties. Can you print off the cleaning schedule and task list we provide our crew and get it to her? Let the team know they have the weekend off, and I'll pay as scheduled."

"Can do. I'm sure they'll appreciate it. Thanks, boss."

"You bet. Have a good weekend and say hi to the missus."

"Will do."

Okay, that felt way too good. It's my first genuine smile all week. Who knew being an asshole could be so much fun. I think it calls for a celebration.

> Me: Club tonight?

> Braden: Does someone have some pent-up sexual tension?

> Eli: How many times have you jacked off this week?

> Me: Fuck off. I'll see you bastards later, and I won't be jerking off tonight.

Mia

What a prick. It's not the request that bothers me, it's the fricking delivery. Other than not going out with Walker and Ben tonight, I'm not upset about it. And hopefully, I'll be getting paid extra. It sucks that I'll have to tell my mom another white lie in addition to the ones I've been feeding her all week about how great my boss is. If I were to say what my job was this weekend, she'd insist on helping, and that's not happening. I'll use Walker as my cover and say I'm hanging at his place since that's what used to happen before he got serious with Ben.

"How did it go in there? He didn't give you a hard time, did he?" Cindy has been a godsend this week. Things could have been worse if she hadn't stepped in to defend me. She's become my haven and the only bright spot in this place. I don't know what I'll do when she's gone. Luckily, I still have plenty of time.

"He was as pleasant as always. The cleaning company had some emergency, so I'm cleaning the buildings over the weekend. I could use the extra cash anyway." What sucks is that I'm using public transportation between each building. It's going to be a long weekend.

"That's unfortunate. I hope it didn't ruin any big plans you had." Cindy makes up for Jackson's rudeness.

My email pings, and I see that the information has arrived. I open the file as I answer. "No, nothing important. I'm here to learn and make money, so it's fine. But looking at this list, I think it might take all weekend. Do you mind if I cut out now and get a head start?"

"Not at all. I'll see you Monday, Mia."

"Thanks. See you next week." I wave before walking away.

I'm out the door after a quick stop in payroll to ask about weekend hours. Reading the instructions as I go, I'm relieved to see that each location has its own supply closet with supplies. Good thing I didn't wear a skirt today, so I can hit a few of these on my way home.

It's a perfect time to call Walker en route to the first stop.

"How was the asshat today?" he answers with no pretenses. Walker has been my outlet all week. I usually have most of it out of my system when Mom comes home, thanks to him.

"Miserable as usual, if not more. You'd think it would be getting better by now, but I swear it seems to be going in the opposite direction, especially after this. He gave me extra work over the weekend, so I won't be able to go with you guys tonight." I'm expecting an argument.

"Bullshit. What did he ask you to do, take notes while he jerks off staring at your chest?"

"Ew, gross. He doesn't stare at my chest." Not that I'd know because I try not to make eye contact. "He thinks I'm a child, not to mention despises me. Anyway, I'm cleaning some of the buildings they manage. Their cleaning crew couldn't make it for some reason."

"So now you're his personal bitch. It's getting worse, Mia. And just so you know, he's male. All males think you're gorgeous and stare at your chest. It's the nature of the beast. Also, I hate to break it to you, but your age does not prohibit your boss from having dirty thoughts about you."

"Gee, thanks for putting that in my head."

"That's what friends are for. Now, why are you putting up with this crap? And more importantly, why can't you come tonight? You have all day tomorrow and Sunday to clean if you insist on doing his dirty work."

Walker wouldn't know what it's like to need a job and the money that goes with it because it grows on trees in his family. It's never been an issue with us, but he doesn't always get it.

"Walker, I love you, but we've talked about this. I need the money, and my mom got me this job. It means a lot to her, and I want to prove I can do it. I won't let some bosshole scare me away from a good job. He may be the first one I have to deal with, but I'm sure he won't be the last, so I might as well learn how to handle it now."

"You're probably right, but remember, there are other jobs out there. Anyway, what about tonight? Come with us, and I'll help you for half the day tomorrow—the second half once my hangover goes away."

"In that case, fine. Pick me up on your way. Also, I'm staying over this weekend. I don't want my mom to know I'm working." Thank goodness I have Walker for things like this.

"You got it. I'll see you tonight."

Before he can hang up, I shout, "I'm holding you to helping me tomorrow!" It'll be nice having a ride for part of it. And I miss spending time with my best friend.

I'm glad Walker made me go out with them last night. He was right; I had fun, and it was seriously needed after the week from hell. But I'm currently paying the price. I wish I had the luxury of staying in bed half the day and nursing my hangover like Walker, but duty calls, which means I'm dealing with the headache from hell as I work.

While dusting an area of the lobby in the current building, I hear someone enter, stopping behind me instead of proceeding to the elevator, raising my hackles. Turning around, I see my least favorite person on the planet.

"Did you come to check up on me?" I ask the man responsible for my presence.

"I live here, but glad to see you're following orders."

"I aim to please, sir." I give him my megawatt smile through gritted teeth when a sudden sharp head pain makes me wince.

"Are you okay?" he asks, concern lacing his voice.

"Yeah, I'm fine. Just one drink too many last night."

"You're way too young to be drinking."

Seriously? He's going to lecture me about my private life?

"Right, and I'm sure you never drank at this age. You don't strike me as the golden child." I shouldn't engage, but I can't help it.

"Oh yeah? What type do I strike you as then?"

Damn, it's hard focusing on the conversation when his muscular bronze chest, on display from a few undone buttons, is right in front of my eyes due to his considerable height.

"The wild child who started drinking and having sex in middle school. Rebellious, defiant, and still hasn't grown out of it."

"That's quite the assessment. And you derived all this how?" His left eyebrow rises.

"Well, you don't like that your parents gave me this job, thus defiant, and you're acting rebellious by treating me like shit. You had some skank come to your office for sex, so I'm assuming you've been around the block. As for the drinking, I suppose it goes with everything else. How did I do?" I ask, cocking my head to the side and wincing again from another shooting head pain.

"I guess you've got me all figured out. Not to step outside the box, but do you need some medicine for your headache?"

I just got whiplash.

Shaking my head, I respond, "Uh, no. I already took some. I'm just waiting for them to set in. Thanks, though."

"All right, I'll let you get back to work. Bye, Mia."

"See you Monday," I say with a smile as he walks into the elevator, then immediately drop it and sigh in relief when the doors shut.

I was doing such a good job of hiding how much he gets under my skin, but it's exhausting, and I don't have the energy this morning. I can't believe I said all that, but dammit if he didn't egg me on with the jab about my age. And what was with his nonengagement? He didn't even argue, so maybe I was spot on.

He lives in a nice place, that's for sure. So far, this is the swankiest building I've been in. Judging from his clothes, it looks like he didn't stay here last night, and I can't help but wonder if he was with the girl who visited the office or if he has a different one for each day of the week.

Ugh, who cares? It's not my concern and nothing I should be thinking about anyway. But dang, it's hard not to when he looks so good. His blond hair was casually messed up from an obvious overnighter, and as always, I could see the contour of his thick muscular arms under the shirt. A tiny part of me wonders what it would feel like to have them wrapped around me. And that's what occupies my thoughts the rest of the day.

That was seriously one of the most exhausting weekends of my life. But being familiar with their properties will be good for the job, so I suppose it was worth it. I'm just glad Walker came through; otherwise, finishing would have been a stretch. I don't know how my mom has done it all these years. Thank goodness for the full scholarship to San Diego State because I don't have it in me to follow in her footsteps.

After this weekend and last week's training, I'd be fine taking over now if I had to. Cindy did a great job getting things ready for her to leave. The situation with Jackson, however, needs improvement. He's beyond rude and practically refuses to deal with me, talking to Cindy like I'm not even present most of the time. His plan to get me to quit last week was obvious, but he doesn't know how stubborn I am. Plus, I'm familiar with chauvinistic assholes like him from the poker table, and I love winning while being underestimated.

I'm surprised Cindy isn't in when I get to her desk. Instead of twiddling my thumbs while I wait, I get right to it, working down the list she made. She had the foresight to create a spreadsheet with staff names, their corresponding departments, and responsibilities, along with daily tasks. I've gone through voicemails, returned a few calls, made a couple of appointments, and printed out today's agenda all by the time Jackson walks in. When I look up, I forget for a moment what a complete ass he is. As far as looks go, he takes the cake. If only he had the personality to go with it.

Pasting on a smile, I greet him with as much enthusiasm as possible. "Good morning, sir. Do you need anything right away, or would you like me to go over the agenda for today?"

"Cut the crap. Where's Cindy?"

Aaand we're off to a great start.

"She hasn't arrived yet, so I dove right in. Does she have the day off?" I ask.

"No, she doesn't have the day off. Fuck… just… keep doing whatever you're doing. I'll figure it out." He stomps into his office and slams the door.

Okay then… that went well. Cue eyeroll.

I continue with the voicemails from the weekend. Everyone and their dog must decide to call after hours so they don't have to speak to an actual person. Most people want to be rude and complain to a machine so they won't get talked back to. Luckily, most everything is delegated to other departments in the company—it's just a matter of getting it to the right person.

I've finally run out of things I can do on my own and, unfortunately, need Jackson's assistance with the rest. I have no choice but to ask for guidance on things requiring his attention. I'm not looking forward to interacting with the bosshole, but it's a necessary evil. I'll have to fake it 'til I make it.

This should be fun.

I pause outside the door, remembering his warning from my first day, and knock lightly. Nothing. I knock again. Nothing. By the third attempt, I pound on the door, earning me a curt reply to enter. Bracing myself, I stand tall and straighten my shoulders before opening the door. He doesn't even look up while typing away.

"What?" he asks gruffly while still not looking at me. At least he knows I'm here.

"I've finished with everything I can from this morning," I say as I walk toward the desk. "Here's a list of items that require your review, along with today's agenda. Is there anything you need me for, sir?"

He finally looks up with a smirk before shaking his head like he remembered his rule of only scowling at me.

"What do you mean, you've finished everything? Do you even know how to use the computer?" His tone is as condescending as can be.

This week is shaping up to be no different than the last. I think it's time to give him a taste of his own medicine. I'm done backing down. "You might be too old to know this, but we use computers in high school these days, and I was already familiar with most of the programs Cindy showed me." The look on his face is furious. Oh well, nothing new. "Where is Cindy, by the way?"

"She unexpectedly went into labor this morning, and I just found out. She and the baby are doing well, but she's officially on maternity leave starting today. That means you're on your own. Can you handle it, or should I make other arrangements?"

Oh, wouldn't that make his day. Sorry to disappoint—not. "I can handle whatever you give me." It takes all my willpower not to be snarky now that I'm taking the gloves off, but I decide it's not worth getting fired on my first day without Cindy.

"I highly doubt that, but challenge accepted. For now, just answer the phone. I'll let you know when I need you."

Asshole. Damn that he's such a handsome one.

He won't need me, as he clearly thinks I'm an imbecile. Now, if he needed me in other ways…

Oh my God, where did that come from? I cannot fantasize about my boss. I swear it's Walker's fault for putting thoughts in my head.

Jackson

Challenge accepted? When I need you? Where the fuck is my head at?

The answer is obvious but highly inappropriate. She's in another form-fitting skirt today that hugs her voluptuous ass that I can't get enough of. Why I don't call her in more often just to watch her walk away is a shame. Then there's the low-cut shirt that cuts right across the top of her breasts. With the words that come from her mouth along with that body, she's killing me. My dirty thoughts shot through the roof when she asked if I needed her for anything. *Fuck yeah, I need you to bend over my desk and give me a better look.*

I grab the back of my neck and forcefully blow out air. I've got to get my mind out of the gutter. There's no fucking way this is going to work. Picking up the phone, I dial my parents.

"Hi, honey. To what do we owe the pleasure?" Mom answers. I can tell I'm on speaker.

"Cindy had her baby this morning. They're both doing well, but because it was early, they'll need to stay in the hospital for a couple of weeks. I told her I'd give her a few days before visiting."

"That's great news, son. Thanks for letting us know. We'll be sure to send our congratulations," Dad says from the background.

"The bad news is that I now have an assistant with one week of training and no clue what she's doing. I want to bring someone in from a temp agency." This favor they made without my involvement pisses me off.

Apparently, Dad had a sip of the Mia Kool-Aid, judging by his response. "Jackson, we made a commitment. It may be tough for a few days, but she'll catch on. Look at the positive. This way, you can teach her the ropes and show her exactly how you want things."

And my mind is right back in the gutter. "How do you not see that I need someone with more experience? It's a busy time for the company. She's too young to keep up." And too young for me to be in lust with.

"We're done with this conversation, Jackson. Mia is your new assistant, and you'll have to accept that. Make it work. Cindy will be back before you know it." Mom's final words.

Fuck, why did I even try?

> Me: Cindy went into labor today. My parents won't let me get rid of the girl. What the fuck am I supposed to do?

> Braden: Jerk off…

> Eli: Give her a birthday present she'll remember… in two months.

> Braden: A lot…

> Me: Assholes.

> Eli: There's a cash game this Friday. You guys in? It'll be a good distraction.

> Me: Yeah, I'm in. Send me the info.

> Braden: Next time. I have a date.

> Me: Sucker.

> Braden: I hope she is. At least I'm not using my hand. Good luck with that.

> Me: Fuck you.

I can't avoid her forever; I need a fucking assistant. "We need to go over a few things. Come in and plan to take notes," I say over the intercom.

She answers with her typical response. "Yes, sir."

Sighing in frustration, I run a hand through my hair. If I don't solve this problem, it's going to be a long six months.

She enters seconds later.

"Have a seat." She doesn't look afraid. I keep underestimating her. She seems to have nerves of steel, or she's damn good at hiding fear. Either way, it's time to move forward.

"I'm sure it's apparent that I'm less than thrilled to have you here. No offense, but you're young, and you lack experience. If it weren't for my parents, you'd already be gone. That being said, we have to make this work for now. Cindy must've done a good job training you last week since you've managed this far into the day without her."

"She had me do everything with minimal assistance. She also created a company directory and a list of daily tasks. If you give me a chance, I'll prove I'm not too young for this. I can do the job, I swear. Since you seem pretty hung up on my age, you'll be happy to know I'll be eighteen soon. Then you can stop treating me like a child."

Sweetheart, if you knew why your age is a problem for me, you might not want your birthday to come so soon.

I narrow my eyes at her. "I'll stop treating you like a child when I see proof that you aren't one. Until then, just do your job."

"Will do, sir." Her face is earnest.

Fuck, if this is going to work, I need to set some ground rules.

"You need to stop calling me sir. I'm not fifty."

"Would you prefer Mr. Soloman?"

"I'm also not my dad. Just use my name."

"Okay… Jackson."

Hearing my name from her lips gives me an unexpected desire to hear it more, wondering what it would sound like while she's begging for my dick. *Fuuuuck.*

"And you need to start wearing more appropriate clothing," I add, frustrated at my drifting thoughts.

"What's wrong with my clothes?" She looks affronted. Shit. Why did she pick today to let her guard down? I can't tell her to wear sweats to work. I just pinned myself up against a wall.

"Nothing, never mind."

"What? Are they not expensive enough to be acceptable? Sorry, I don't shop in designer stores like you." She's offended, which wasn't what I meant to do. "At least I'm not in rags."

I'm not fast enough to stop my next words from tumbling out. "I'd rather you be in rags," I mutter.

"What is that supposed to mean?" She doesn't get it at all; that's how naïve she is.

"I said never mind. Forget I mentioned anything."

"No, tell me. I need to know if there's some sort of dress code around here." She's not going to let this go.

"Fuck. You want an explanation? Here it is. I meant that I'd rather you walk around in sweats than have you tempting me while you're completely off-limits. Is that clear enough for you, little girl?" Goddammit. Did I just admit my attraction to her? I watch as her face goes red, and that alone makes my confession worth it.

"Oh… okay… I'll take that into consideration." She pauses and then continues with an adorable pout on her face. "And I am not a child, so stop referring to me like one." Of course that's what has her irritated over all else.

"You are until your age says otherwise." She rolls her eyes, proving that she's done pretending to be immune to my attitude, which might make this situation a little more entertaining if nothing else. "Moving on. Order flowers to be delivered to Cindy's room at the hospital—no price limit. Go extravagant, and I'll email you what to put on the card. Also, get an update from our attorneys on the Bryer Building and Delaware transaction. That's it for now. You can go."

"Thank you, sir… I mean Jackson." She didn't even try hiding that she did that on purpose. This damn girl is playing with fire.

I watch her strut out of the office, and I swear she has a little more sway to her hips—fucking tease. My situation just became a lot more complicated. Shit.

Needing a distraction, I pick up the phone and dial my sister, Cici, as soon as the door shuts. She answers on the second ring. "Hey, Jackson!" It's good to hear her voice.

"I just want you to know I'm still pissed at you for leaving, and with the latest development, I'm never forgiving you," I tell her.

"What's got you so cranky?"

I catch her up on the situation.

"Okay, well, how is she doing so far?"

"She's been here a week. Who the fuck knows? Today's the first day she's been on her own, and I've been dealing with the weekend's bullshit all morning, not paying attention to what she's doing." Not completely true; I've been paying plenty of attention to her sweet ass as it exits my office each time. Okay—and I'll admit this to no one—she did handle the morning way better than I expected and *maybe* knows what she's doing.

"Snap out of it and figure shit out. She's there, so you might as well use her." She lectures.

Fuck, everything sounds like an innuendo about Mia right now. That's the main problem, one I'm not sharing with Cici.

"Did you not hear me? She's a high school student. There's no way she should be taking over Cindy's job. I'm so fucking frustrated."

"I get it, Jackson. But just because Mom and Dad are digging their heels in doesn't make it this girl's fault. What's her name?" It comes out of my lips with venom before she continues. "It's not Mia's fault you're in this position, so don't take it out on her. Trust me, I know what you can be like when you're mad. Be nice. At least it's only temporary, right?" She knows how it is when our parents make demands, but that doesn't mean she gets this particular situation.

"Easy for you to say, runner."

"Yeah, yeah. Miss you too. Keep me posted. And seriously, *be nice.*"

I chuckle as I hang up the phone after we say goodbye. I love my sister, and I get why she left, but I'm not going to stop giving her shit for it, even though I'm proud of her. She never liked being under our parents' control and knew early on that she wanted to make her own way, even though doing so got her cut off. It took balls for her to leave, but she's thriving now, and unbeknownst to her, I check on her frequently. I can't say I'd have made the same decision if this wasn't what I wanted to do, but luckily it is.

She wants me to be nice to Mia, but if that happens, we'll have a different problem altogether. Better stick with the plan.

3

EVEN LOWER

Mia

’M NOT SURE HOW I’VE SURVIVED MY FIRST WEEK WITHOUT CINDY. It was hard enough to put up with Jackson’s crap when I rarely had to interact with him. Now that our barrier is gone, it’s taken everything I’ve got. If he treated me half as nice as he did Cindy, we’d probably be just fine. I still can’t get over the message he sent with her flowers. It was so incredibly sweet that I may have developed a slight crush on the man— until our next interaction, that is.

I let my guard down for one minute, and we ended up going for each other’s throats. It won’t happen again. Getting a response out of me only seems to encourage him further. It’s best to maintain appearances and squash his attempts to provoke me. If he’d stop behaving like an ass, maybe he would notice that I’m great at this job.

I admit, it’s been fun messing with him by wearing the most sug-gestive clothing I can get away with since his confession last week. It was worth splurging on a few items from the thrift store, even adding a pair of heels. Walker was spot-on—age has no bearing when it comes to physical attraction. At least I’m the only one who knows it goes both ways. Jackson and I have two things in common: attraction and scorn for each other. Hopefully, scorn will continue to win out, or there might be a problem.

So far, the job itself is a piece of cake. Jackson, on the other hand, is like dealing with a grizzly. Speaking of which, it's time to poke the bear again. Though it's not my intention, my mere presence seems to have that effect.

I knock on the door and wait. I'm certain I have a mild case of PTSD from his *lesson* on day one.

"Come in," he calls through the door.

We're making headway; that was only one knock. I fist-pump internally and school my features as I enter.

"I have the updates you asked for. Would you like me to go over them or leave my notes for your review?" I remain inside the door, waiting for a response, cringing at my fake ass-kissing.

After several beats of silence, he finally answers—or so I thought. "I hope you realize this job is more than just sitting at a desk, answering phones, and checking items off a list. It's whatever I deem necessary as my—*personal*—assistant. Meaning, you're expected to perform any task given, whether work-related or not."

Where is he going with this, and why do the implications excite me? *Oh my God, Mia, stop.*

"For example, today, I'll need you to pick up my dry cleaning and deliver it to my condo. A list of groceries is on the kitchen counter to shop for and put away. You'll find a credit card in your desk's top right-hand drawer, and I'll email the dry cleaner's information along with my address and door code. Any questions?"

Relieved at not having to question my morals, I genuinely smile, relaxing the fake one I'd pasted on, and release the breath I was holding. That is not what I expected to hear after his opening speech. *Phew.*

"It sounds simple enough, but I use public transportation, which isn't a problem, but I may not make it back in. Also, can I get your number to text in case I have any questions or need to substitute any items?"

He's looking at me in a way I can't decipher, like he's irritated but smug at the same time. My responses never seem to satisfy him.

"Here." He hands me his phone. "Text yourself."

I do as instructed. "Okay, I'll get going, then." I smile and return the phone.

Grabbing my things, I head out while texting Walker the latest. He's not impressed. But hey, at least it gets me out of the office and away from the bosshole. It isn't so bad, other than I'm learning nothing. I was told "Jackson's assistant"—my fault for assuming executive over personal. However, if I had to place a bet, this is probably another tactic to get me to quit. Well, too bad.

Unfortunately—or fortunately, depending on how you look at it—I don't make it back to the office. With public transportation, you aren't always in control of your time. Today was one of those. It seemed I was always just missing the trolley or bus each time and waiting for the next one. Then, since this was the first time at Jackson's, it took a while to find where everything went. If this becomes a regular thing, it'll go faster next time. His place was clean, decorated nicely, and seemed comfortable. I was tempted to look around but left his dry cleaning on a doorknob in the foyer instead of searching for the bedroom, fearing he'd somehow turn it against me.

After messaging Jackson that I'll see him tomorrow, I call Walker on the way home. He was already fired up, so I expected the outcome.

"So you *are* his personal bitch. You're really going to put up with this crap, Mia? Come on, you're better than that."

"I don't see what the problem is. At least I don't have to deal with him while I'm out. I'd call it a win-win. Neither of us wants to be around the other. I'm surprised he hasn't demanded to replace me yet." Though he's probably tried.

I hear the sigh before he speaks. "Look, I know you're trying to do the right thing, but there's no harm in playing poker. You're good at it, and you're not your dad. Fuck this asshole and do that instead. Your mom would understand if you told her the truth." *Yeah, not happening.*

"I've already made my decision to stick it out. I'm not letting the bosshole win. Besides, what's six months in the rest of my life?" Is this my stubbornness talking or my rationality? I'm undecided but going with rationale for now.

"I've said my piece—it's your call, but I'm not guaranteeing I won't try again. So… did you at least get some good snooping in?" Of course Walker would ask me this.

"Hell no. He probably has cameras, and then he'd have a reason to fire me. Come on, Walker, I thought you were smarter than that."

"Yeah, you're probably right. But you could've just peeked in his nightstand really quick and told me the size of his condoms."

"You're awful. I didn't even step foot in his room. And who cares what size his condoms are? I won't be anywhere near that thing."

He chuckles. "Oh, Mia, we need to get you laid so you're more fun."

"You have plenty of fun for both of us. Bye, Walker."

"Bye, babe."

He might be right that this isn't worth it, but now it's become a challenge that I'm determined to beat.

Jackson

I've been happy in my job since taking over for my parents a year ago—until now. It's been weeks since Cindy left, and while I can admit that her replacement doesn't suck, she doesn't *suck*. Not that Cindy ever did, but I also never wanted her to.

All joking aside, Mia's more capable than I'll ever admit out loud. She's kept her composure through all my rants, strange requests, and asshole behavior over the last month. I'll give her props for the mask, but I can only imagine the things running through her mind while she smiles through gritted teeth.

Her work is impressive; she has a natural common sense that enables her to do anything asked with minimal direction and produce the answers I need without telling her how to find them. I stopped trying to get rid of her shortly after Cindy's departure, and I'm thankful it's working out so well. Unfortunately, my attraction hasn't faded, and she's still as off-limits as before, which is a problem today.

This week began no differently from the last. A typical Monday morning with tons of bullshit from the weekend to handle—which she's doing like a pro, I might add. So, what's the issue? *She* is, or rather, her goddamn body is. I should have made some bullshit dress code when I had the chance. Now, I'm forced to deal with all the filthy thoughts running through my mind because of her attire.

Heels. Need I say more? A tight-ass fucking skirt I've never seen before that barely reaches midthigh. Topping it off is the low-cut blouse, accentuating her perky tits that are pushed up to create a luscious mound of soft flesh begging for my tongue. Listen, I'm male. I get laid—a lot. I get who I want when I want, save for the one who can't be touched, and it's killing me. Not to mention, I'm fucking crazy for having these thoughts about a girl ten years my junior. Fuck this.

Making it through today is not possible. Finding someone to fill in for my fantasy is. Relief sets in after a one-minute phone call to my last hookup, knowing I'll be sated soon. Now I need to create enough work to keep Mia busy. I'd send her to do my grocery shopping, but I learned my lesson last time. All I did that night was fantasize about her in my space. Thank God she didn't put my dry cleaning in the closet. Fuck, imagining her in my bedroom would have been the death of me.

"Mia, could you come in for a minute?" I ask through the intercom, apparently feeling better with my solution on the way. I'm not usually so nice in my tone, nor do I typically ask. The habit developed early on and was ingrained by the time I decided to keep her on. Oh well… it works for us.

She knocks, as always, with my new practice of keeping the door shut—anything to maintain distance.

"Come in," I call out.

"What can I do for you, Jackson?"

I can't wait for her to ask that question in three weeks. God, she kills me. Her voice is my kryptonite. Her neck is my weakness, with her hair pulled back in a slick ponytail. She appears more sophisticated today, like there's someone to impress, making the following words pop out of my mouth for no reason other than curiosity but taste an awful lot like jealousy.

"Do you have plans after work today?"

"I do, sorry." She sounds nervous.

"Why are you sorry?" I ask, abstaining from the burning question of what those plans are.

"Well, I assume you asked because you had something for me to do." She's confused.

"If I had something for you to do, I wouldn't care about your plans. My question was because you look ready to go somewhere."

"Oh, well… I'm going to some fundraiser tonight." She waves her hand in the air.

So, she has a social life. Interesting. I've never wondered about it until now, and I'm dying to know more. Like, does she have a boyfriend, and how do I not know that by now?

"What was it you needed then?" she asks impatiently.

Good question. It's time to move on rather than get myself in trouble by continuing down that dangerous road.

I hand her a paper. "Here's a list of things I need you to follow up on. I'll also need you to stop by the maintenance department and deliver this to Jeb. Have him print off the monthly reports while you're there. You can do that before you get my regular order from the deli and bring it all to me at one o'clock. That's all for now." It should be enough to keep her busy and conveniently out while my guest is here.

"Will do. See you this afternoon." She turns around, utterly oblivious to my penetrating gaze on her backside.

Fuck. Is it noon yet?

It's twelve-thirty, and I'm getting impatient. Mia's left to run the errands I gave her, and if Valerie doesn't show up soon, I'm going to lose it. My door stands open to welcome her arrival, and I'm deep in an email when I finally hear her approach. I look up to see the door closed as she saunters toward me, giving me the green light.

"Thank fuck you're here. I'd be lying if I said this'll be a fair exchange, but you did beg to suck my dick last time. Are you ready to come show me what you can do with that mouth of yours?" I push my chair back slightly from the desk and point to the floor before me.

She sashays over with a seductive look on her face. "I thought you'd never ask." She kneels as I undo my belt and unzip. My dick's been at half-mast all day, and now it's ready. I pull it out and stroke myself as I reach around her head to pull her down.

"Open up for me," I say, angling the head toward her mouth. I feel the first lick and moan. "Oh, yeah. Show me what you've got. Don't hold back, baby. There's not much time."

She takes me in slowly as I look toward the ceiling and close my eyes.

What comes straight to mind is none other than a sexy little assistant with black hair in a high ponytail and her full lips wrapped around my cock. I grab her hair, gripping it tight while she works me up and down.

"Fuck yeah." Shit, I almost called her Mia but caught myself and said it silently instead. The thought is all it takes to make my balls tighten, practically ready to explode. "Suck harder. Yeah, just like that."

I open my eyes, overcome with sensation, and catch movement in my periphery. Bringing my head down, I see Mia frozen in the doorway, holding my lunch with her mouth open in shock. Our gazes collide. I've hit a new low because this right here… it's happening.

"Take it all in, little girl," I say as I grip Valerie's head, staring into Mia's wide brown eyes. "You like that, don't you?" I ask, talking straight to Mia, noticing the flush in her cheeks and the visible gulp she makes in return. "Yeah, you do. That's right, baby."

"I bet you're soaking from this." Her mouth parts and her chest starts to move quickly. Knowing she's as turned on by this as I am is all I need to put me over the edge. I tighten my grip, flex my hips, and hold Valerie's head down as I explode down her throat, all while watching Mia's heated reaction.

"Fuck… fuck… fuuuck." It seems to last forever while I'm fixed on the sight before me: Mia's rapid breaths, the lustful slack in her jaw, and the haze in her eyes. I'm mesmerized as my climax finishes while my girl soaks in the scene before her. Suddenly, she breaks the spell, abruptly turning and closing the door.

Holy fuck, that was the orgasm of all orgasms.

"Did someone just walk in?" Valerie asks as she rises, wiping her mouth.

"No, I think someone slammed a door down the hall." I tilt her chin up and brush my thumb across her cheek. "Hey, thank you. I needed that. Unfortunately, I don't have time for an equal exchange, but maybe I can return the favor sometime." I tuck myself in as she stands and leans down to kiss me goodbye.

"That's okay. You warned me, Jackson. I'll hold you to it because that was hella hot." She blows me a kiss before leaving, shutting the door behind her.

She has no idea just how hot that was.

A few minutes later, I hear the faint knock of my naughty little assistant.

Mia

I'm panicking as I stand at the door waiting. Oh my God. What am I going to say? How should I act? He's going to fire me. Maybe I should quit first. Shit, why did I stand there? I mean, seriously, what the hell was I thinking? Okay, I know the answer to that, but oh God, it's so bad.

Things were going so well, too. He was finally getting used to me as I proved myself capable. He wasn't consistently trying to break me down anymore, and we seemed to have found a rhythm. His initial reaction to me was justified when I realized how busy he was running the business alone. Sure, he has a team of people that handle the day-to-day stuff, but with the new acquisitions and everything they entail, it's a lot to handle for one person. He still has his moments, but they're tolerable. We were at least moving in the right direction, but now I feel like I've hit the reset button.

"Come in." He doesn't sound angry, not even as cranky as he typically does. I suppose it makes sense for him to be relaxed now. *Gross, Mia.*

There's no way I can go in there. My hand is on the doorknob, but it refuses to move.

"Come in." Crap. It's louder this time, more demanding.

Taking one last deep breath, I open the door, bracing myself for whatever follows. Each step feels as if my feet are made of lead. While looking anywhere but in front of me, I propel myself forward and place his lunch on the desk before him.

"Have you learned your lesson in knocking?" He raises one eyebrow.

I'm not sure where his mind is as he stares straight-faced, waiting for an answer. There's no indication of anger, but he must be after that, right? Crap, I don't think I'll ever look at him the same.

I tilt my head down in shame. "I'm so sorry. The door wasn't shut completely, and I knew you were waiting for your lunch. I had it early, so I started to come in and heard you say yes and misunderstood the tone... obviously. I don't know what else to say. There's no excuse. I was shocked and then just froze, but it was so inappropriate. I don't know what happened." I finally look up from my rambling and am shocked to see the first smile I've ever seen from him.

He draws out my anguish and doesn't speak for what seems like forever. "I know exactly what happened. I was in a similar situation once. You were thinking deep down that you wished it were you. Your body reacted and compelled you to watch—so turned on that your desire won over rationality. It's natural. But I bet you won't be walking into my office without knocking any time soon, will you, Mia?" He raises that eyebrow again, and if I didn't know any better, I'd think he was teasing me.

"N-No. Even if the door is ajar, I'll wait for your response." *That's for damn sure.*

"All right then, let's move on. Where is the maintenance report I requested?" He's back. This is the Jackson I'm familiar with—the one I can handle.

Realizing my mistake immediately, I slap my forehead and groan. "Crap. That's why I was early. I completely forgot about that. I'm so sorry. It won't happen again. From now on, I'll be more prepared with pen and paper to take notes if necessary. I'll go get it right now if that's okay?" *Please let me leave.* I need a minute to regroup after this fiasco.

"Be quick about it. I need it before my next meeting." I'm dismissed as he starts unpacking the lunch I brought in. Thank God.

As soon as I close the door, my body sags back against it, and I drop my face in my hands for a moment. My heart has been hammering since I walked in on him, and it hasn't slowed down. How can he be so calm and nonchalant about this? He said he'd been in the same situation and understood, but that's crazy. I intruded on a private moment. There's no way he's okay with it. Although, I swear, at one point, it seemed like he was talking to me and not whoever the woman was under the desk.

Did that really happen, or will I wake up any minute now?

Propelling myself to move, I head toward maintenance to drop off the file I was given earlier and get the report. Dammit, I can't believe I forgot. This whole thing could have been avoided had I just written it down. This was all my fault.

Wait. What am I thinking? It's Jackson's fault for doing it in the first place. Who does that at work? He's the boss for crying out loud. That is so unprofessional.

The rest of the day goes to shit. My mind won't shut up about what I saw. The worst thing is that Jackson was right about all those thoughts in my mind, and I'm so ashamed. As I stood frozen, my muscles clenched, and I could feel the wetness between my legs. I haven't experienced that kind of desire before and can't believe it happened while watching my boss get a fricking blow job. Seriously, what is wrong with me? I need some significant therapy, but Walker will have to do for now.

Thank God we already have plans for tonight. Ben is busy, so I'm his date for some fundraiser his parents are making him attend. I know he'll talk me through this. We may not be at the same level, but he's as advanced as it gets and can help sort through this mess in my head. God, how embarrassing.

"Hey, Mia. You on your way?" Walker picks up within the first ring.

"Yeah. Do we have time to chill at your place before we go to this thing?" *Please say yes.*

"Of course. But what's wrong? Did the bosshole fire you?" My calm tone didn't fool him for a second.

"No, but I don't want to talk about it over the phone. I'll be there soon." He allows me to hang up by promising I'll spill the second I get there.

Twenty minutes later, I'm crying in Walker's arms, having a pity party from my mortification and shame. He insists it's not my fault, although he disagrees that it was a dick move on Jackson's part. Walker said he'd probably do the same thing since it is his office and he owns the company. The only problem, according to him, was that the door wasn't shut.

"Walker, I just stood there, paralyzed. Our eyes were locked when he… when he finished. How gross is that?" Now that my tears are dry, we're sitting on his bed cross-legged, facing each other.

"That's not the word I'd use. I'm more along the lines of *fucking hot.* Mia, I think it's time for you to move past the kissing phase so you have a different perspective. Damn, girl, I'm sorta jealous. People pay for shows like that, and from what you told me, it was a good one."

"God, you're such a perv. I mean, yes, it was… hot." I shiver. "Ugh, even saying that out loud makes me cringe. Maybe now that I'm not studying all the time or playing poker, I do need to get out more."

High school boys always annoyed me with their constant drama and new girlfriends every week. I've only had three boyfriends, if you could even call them that, and all we did was kiss. After that, I usually pulled back from lack of chemistry.

"But even if I wanted to start dating, how do you find people outside of school and work when the only coworker you see is your boss, who's not an option?" Not that I would ever consider that. I am not lusting over my boss. Nope.

"Let me help you set up a dating profile. That's what everyone in college does." He holds his hand out for my phone.

"I am not doing that. I've heard of those, and they're just hook-up sites. I'm not looking for sex. I just want to find one guy to date. Plus, I'm not in college yet."

"Close enough, and it's not just for hookups. You won't find someone if you don't get out there, Mia. We'll be specific in your profile on what you're looking for and what you're not, and if someone's interested in more than sex, they'll reach out. Yeah, you'll still get some assholes, but you decline them. Come on, what can it hurt?"

He reaches for my phone again, and this time, I give it to him.

4

DISTRACTION

Jackson

MY FOCUS HAS BEEN ABSOLUTE CRAP AFTER WHAT HAPPENED three days ago. Sure, I was attracted to Mia before, but now that that shit's gone down, it's intense. My dick certainly has a new obsession because it springs to attention whenever she's around. I want this girl like I've never wanted anyone. Which means I've become even more of an asshole recently out of frustration. What happened hasn't come up since, nor will it, other than being the only thing on my mind when she walks into the room.

And speaking of… "Come in," I call out upon hearing her faint knock.

My eyes take her in from my peripheral vision as my head remains turned toward my computer. A dress today. And not a modest calf-length dress. No—that would be too tame. It's a mid-thigh summer dress with a loose flap to conceal her braless breasts. *Fuck me.* I shouldn't be surprised since this has been the norm after our conversation about her clothes. She's been relentless in her attire since. Taunting me with tight-fitting clothes, low-cut necklines, short skirts… and now this.

"Good morning. I have the report you asked for with attrition rates for each property, along with a summary of each building's condition and other factors that may affect the numbers. I took the liberty to include information regarding the nearest transportation stops and walkability to local services and parks." She sets the file on my desk and waits for my reply.

Screwing with her has become habit, so instead of responding, I stay silent and slowly pick up the file to review the documents. I'm impressed. She not only provided the data I asked for but went above and beyond with additional considerations.

"I know you didn't ask for all that, but I assumed with the reorganization you're doing, you were looking for which buildings might be worth turning over, and I figured it would help to be aware of what may be affecting their performance, especially as you find new properties." She's composed and confident in her speech. The only sign of trepidation is her slight blush, which I see when I finally raise my head.

And if I weren't already hard for the girl, witnessing her competence and sharp mind, not to mention that blush, I'd be right there. As it is, I'm busting at the seams. She's gorgeous and brilliant, and fuck… if I don't snap out of this stupor, I might as well get down on my knees and bow.

"I realize we've had this discussion before, but you are aware this is a professional office, not the beach?" Time to get my head on straight with the only way I know how—rudeness.

She looks down only to look me in the eye a second later. "I'm sorry, I assumed a dress was appropriate office attire. Personally, I usually wear a swimsuit when I go to the beach, and I wouldn't dream of wearing that to the office—unless you'd like to do swimsuit Fridays?" She smiles, baiting me.

This is the most she's said since our encounter earlier this week. Maybe it's time to shake things up a little and see if I can get to her the way she does me.

"The problem with that idea, Mia, is that there's a good chance you'd be naked on my desk by the end of the day, and then I'd have to write you up for violating the dress code. As for the *dress*…" My eyes travel down her body. "You're treading in dangerous water, little girl, and in three weeks, you may not have anyone to save you." The clench of her thighs and the heat in her stare are apparent.

"In three weeks, I might not want to be saved." Bold.

She turns without another word and starts toward the door.

"Mia?"

She stops and looks over her shoulder.

I lift the file. "You did well on this. I appreciate the extra information you gathered. You're right that it'll be useful. Thank you."

The shock in her eyes says everything before she continues out the door.

By three o'clock in the afternoon, I call the guys to meet me for an early happy hour after a long day of pent-up frustration. I just need to get out of my head and away from the girl on the other side of the door.

"So, let me get this straight. You have a bombshell on her knees in front of you, and your assistant is the one you get off to?" Braden asks.

"Yep, that sums it up. I mean, I was already imagining it was her, so when she appeared, it was like a dream come true—except she wasn't the one sucking my dick, though she might as well have been with how fast I blew once I saw her." I'm hard again just thinking about it.

"Dude, that's some sick shit. As in, I want an assistant like that." I'm pretty sure Braden's already had an assistant like that.

"Trust me, you don't." *Not one you can't have.*

"Besides being the bane of your desire, how is she doing as your assistant these days? You still trying to get her to quit?" Eli chimes in.

"Hell no. I gave up on that weeks ago. Two reasons: A, I swear she's made of steel—couldn't crack her for the life of me. B, she's fucking amazing. It's no wonder she graduated early. I've never seen anyone as capable as her other than Cindy. She's on top of shit, save for the one damn time she forgot to do something, resulting in this mess."

"That's on you, man. Ever heard of a lock? It's a thing that prevents people from walking in at inappropriate times." Braden's on a roll tonight.

"Yeah, yeah. Since when are you a comedian?" I shake my head at him. "Look, I was out of my mind at the time. It was a lapse of judgment, a moment of weakness, and possibly worth it." I smirk and take a sip of beer.

"Right. That's obvious by how tormented you are. So, what's your plan? How are you going to get through five more months lusting after this girl?" Braden asks, in pure lawyer form. It's a good question but one I have no answer for.

"I don't fucking know. More daytime visitors?"

"Yeah, because that worked out so well the last time. How long until she's legal again?" Eli is fixated on her birthday. He should have it memorized by now since he brings it up every time we're together.

"Too long. Three more weeks, but even then, it's not happening. She's almost a decade younger than me, naïve, and starting college in the fall. She's also my employee—not to mention, thinks I'm an ass." There are so many reasons it's a bad idea.

"I didn't hear any solid argument there. She's going to have sex with someone regardless of how old she is. She can't be that naïve if she stayed to watch, and your college excuse is just pitiful. Do you have a policy against interoffice dating?" I shake my head in response, only to have him continue. "Christ, man, you don't have to marry the girl to quench your thirst." Braden will find a way around any argument. As an attorney, it happens to be his specialty.

"Don't bother trying to convince him. He's into self-torture. I've seen it before, right, man?" Eli taps his bottle to mine and takes a drink.

"You're an asshole. And a hypocrite. You think I don't know about you and my sister?" He scowls back at me. "Yeah, so fuck off." I'm pretty sure my parents weren't the only reason Cici took off.

His jab about my past with Lily, his brother's fiancée, doesn't get to me like it once did. She was Cici's best friend growing up and the only person I've ever wanted for more than sex. Too bad I realized it *after* she'd met my competition, who made it clear I was too late the night I walked in on him claiming her innocence.

And that's where shit got weird. Instead of walking back out, I decided to stay and watch the show. It was too tempting to pass up, so I jerked off while the one girl I wanted a future with gave herself to someone else. Not one of my proudest moments, but it was the hottest. Keyword being *was*—until Monday.

Mia

I'm so glad Jackson's gone for the rest of the day. I can't concentrate when he's here, especially since this morning and the obvious flirting going on. I'm in a constant state of arousal after what happened on Monday. It might not affect him since he probably gets more action than a dog in heat. However, I have nothing to replace it with, and it's killing me.

Which is exactly why I'm excited about my date for tomorrow. Walker's been helping me sort through prospects, weeding out the bad ones and responding to the guys with potential. This one seems like a nice guy who's not just out to get laid.

The bottom line is that I need someone other than my boss to make me feel things. I've deprived myself a little too long if what I witnessed is having this much effect on me, meaning I can't stop myself from visualizing it along with my accompanying dirty thoughts. Plenty of guys out there can give me what I need—not that I know what that is yet, other than to get my mind off Jackson for now.

When I leave the office for the day, I'm feeling better. The two hours I spent focused on work instead of the man on the other side of the door were necessary to get ahead on the transactions I'd been helping with. The extra work will allow me to walk away worry-free tomorrow.

I'm relieved to be home, putting another day of tension behind me. I make it two feet in before someone steps out from behind the door, gripping my neck with one hand while covering my mouth with the other. At the same time, another guy appears in front and grabs my arms roughly, securing them to my sides. I kick out and begin twisting furiously, trying to break free, which only results in the hand around my neck tightening.

"This'll go a hell of a lot easier if you just calm the fuck down," the guy in front says. He's slimy looking, with greasy, messed-up hair and what resembles a beard, though it just looks like he's too lazy to shave. He has a gold chain around his neck and smells like he smokes a pack a day. I don't even want to know what the one behind me looks like, but I imagine a version of the same. All I know is he's way too close, holding me tight to his body. I'm trembling with fear.

"I'll uncover yer mouth now, darlin', but if you scream, things'll get a whole lot worse." This comes from the guy behind me, who leans in, forcing me to feel his breath on my skin. "Nod if you feel me, sweet cheeks."

I do as he said, wanting his hand off my mouth. The smell of stale cigarettes from his fingers makes me want to puke.

The hand drops, but his hold around my neck barely loosens, making it hard to breathe. The guy holding my arms relieves no pressure. I'm going to have bruises tomorrow—if I'm still alive.

"What do you want?" I choke out as best I can.

"Why don't we sit down and have ourselves a little chat? Zip-tie her wrists," he says to the guy in front. I struggle once more before my neck is squeezed tighter, cutting off my breath and causing me to go slack.

"What I tell ya about calmin' the fuck down? Don't make me hurt ya more than I have to. I might enjoy it." This time, he licks my ear. I almost gag in disgust.

A whimper escapes as the zip tie around my wrists is tightened, cutting into my skin. "That'll teach ya to put up a fight. Remember that next time we come by."

Next time? Does that mean they're not going to kill me?

"Why are you here?" I ask.

"You keep quiet. We do the talkin'," he says as he shoves me onto the couch, forcing my cheek to hit the armrest. Damn, that hurt. My eyes are tearing up, though I'm not sure whether it's from pain or fear at this point. "Sit there and don't try to run, or this'll get real ugly. You sure are a pretty little thing, just like yer daddy said. It's too bad our orders aren't to hurt ya too much. We could've had some fun together. Maybe next time I'll have to sweet-talk the boss."

I'm frozen in place at the mention of my dad. I'm too scared to speak, though, so I wait for him to continue.

The one who held me from behind appears to be the leader. He looks more put together with a leather jacket and biker boots. His hair is black and thick, with a beard that's more filled in. He's also the one who's done most of the talking. They're standing before me, looking down, arms crossed over their chests, trying to intimidate me. It's working.

"So, let's get to the point, shall we? Your daddy's in a lot of trouble with the boss. See, he borrowed a whole lotta dough and decided to skip town with it instead of payin' it back. As you can imagine, the boss don't take too well to losin' money. Good thing we remembered him braggin' about his pretty little daughter. Well, surprise, darlin', we've come to collect."

"I don't have any money," I blurt, earning myself a slap to the face. I immediately feel the sting, bringing a fresh set of tears.

"Shut up now, ya hear? If I want ya to speak, you'll know. We'll get to whether ya have money soon enough, and don't think about lyin'. We'll find out, trust me. The fact of the matter is, you're gonna earn the money, sweet cheeks."

My breathing is erratic, and I choke on a sob. My life is over. This can't be happening. How could my dad do this? Did he know they planned on coming after me?

It doesn't matter. That he even told them about me is bad enough.

"Now, now, don't cry. Yer daddy told us how good he taught ya to play cards, bragged about you bein' some prodigy. So, here's what's gonna happen. You'll earn the money back, same way yer daddy lost it. And let me tell ya what'll happen if yer not good enough to win. You'll work it off in other ways, darlin'. Do you pick up what I'm puttin' down? Yes or no, sweet cheeks."

I nod. There's snot running down my lips, tears streaking my face, and the ties are cutting my skin, but all I can think about is what will happen if I don't win enough.

"So, let's get a few things straight. Some ground rules, darlin'. First, you love yer momma, don't you?" Immediately, I panic, nodding while my tears get thicker. "That's what we thought. Pay close attention, then. If you tell anyone about this, you can say bye to yer Momma. If you even think about callin' the cops, you can say bye to Momma. And just to be clear, if you so much as breathe the wrong way, you'll be sayin' bye to Momma. You following? Nod yer head, yes. Good," he says when I do.

"Now, here's how it's gonna go. You play whatever games we tell ya, when we tell ya, and where we tell ya, and all yer winnings go to Daddy's debt. Sound like a plan?"

There's nothing I can do but nod.

"Glad you agree. We're almost done here, darlin'. But first, let's go back to you not havin' money. We've been watchin' you, seein' yer one of the best damn players out there, and you expect us to believe you haven't saved any of those hard-earned dollars? Huh?"

I don't know what to do. That's our safety net if something happens, maybe for a car eventually, but not to bail out my dad. Would they find it? What if I give them half?

"That's a lotta thinkin' for a simple question, darlin'. If I were you, I'd do a little less thinkin' and a lot more talkin' right about now unless you want yer left cheek to match the other."

"I have some," I say quickly.

"Good answer. How 'bout this? You figure out how much you have, round up all the spare change from those cushions, and plan on havin' that for us next time. We got places to be, and ya know what?" He leans down and gets right in my face. "I trust ya. I do. I think you'll do the right thing. Ya know why? I don't think yer ready to say bye to yer momma just yet." He wipes my tears with his thumb on the side he slapped, making me wince from the sting.

"There, there. You're okay now. If ya do as yer told, there won't be any problems. Isn't that right, Frank?" He grabs my chin hard as he stands, tilting my head in his direction.

"That's right, Jay. All she has to do is follow directions. If not, though, we get to have some fun, and boy, would I like that. She's a looker." The other man stares at me, licking his lips.

This can't be happening.

"I couldn't agree more. For now, darlin', we're givin' ya a chance to do right. Put your number in my phone here, and we'll be in touch." He goes to hand me his phone and stops. "Well, shit. Ya can't very well do that now, can ya? Cut the tie, Frank. And don't you get any ideas, girl. Just sit there and be good."

Frank pulls out a pocketknife, and I gasp at the sharp pain from the tie digging in as he pulls on the blade to cut through. The guy named Jay holds his phone out again. "Here."

With shaky hands, I enter my name and number, then hand it back.

"Well, there ya have it. We're all set, darlin'. You'll be hearin' from us real soon. We'll be thinkin' about you and all those things we're lookin' forward to if ya don't do as yer told. You have a good evenin' now."

Before they reach the door, I call out, "Wait," making them pause and turn. "Can I ask a question?"

"Well, now, that was mighty rude of me. Sure, darlin', ask away, and I'll see about answerin.'"

"H-How much does he owe?"

"Ah shucks, I forgot to tell ya. He owes boss two hundred grand, sweet cheeks. Looks like you're gonna be playin' our games for a while." He winks at me before they walk out the door.

5

WHAT THE FUCK?

Jackson

SOMETHING'S OFF. MIA'S BEEN JUMPY ALL DAY. SHE'S NOT HOLDING herself like she usually does, confident and poised. Instead, she's hunched and withdrawn. I notice because, despite my best efforts, I'm constantly paying attention to her even when she thinks I'm not, and I know something's wrong.

The problem is that I'm her asshole boss who shouldn't care, but I do. She doesn't know that, though, and as it stands, has no reason to confide in me, but it's been plaguing me all afternoon. Since I can't let it go, I need to get to the bottom of this, and I'll do it the only way I know how.

"Mia, can I see you for a minute? Don't knock, just come in," I say through the intercom.

"Sure, I'll be right there." A minute later, the door opens, and she approaches my desk. "What can I do for you?" There it is, the hunch, the head down, the meekness. It's not her.

"Well, for starters, you can tell me what the hell is going on." The flinch further proves something isn't right. She never reacts to my harshness.

"I… what do you mean? Did I do something wrong?"

"Is there anything I should know about?"

"No!" she practically shouts. "I mean, there's nothing, sir. I mean Jackson. I just… I didn't get much sleep last night and must be tired. I'm sorry. I'll snap out of it, I'm sure." She's fidgeting with her hands, rubbing her wrists—something else she never does—and that's when I see the marks.

"What the fuck? Mia, hold out your hands." I'm seething.

"What? No, I'll just get back to work, okay?" She's pleading.

"Hands, now. I won't ask again."

She slowly raises her arms and reaches out. I grab one and barely push the sleeve up to confirm what I saw. Sure enough, a gnarly mark around the outside of her wrist looks like it's from a rope or zip tie. I rub my thumb over it, and she flinches. I inspect her other hand and find the same.

"Do you want to explain why it looks like your wrists were bound? Does that have anything to do with why you're so skittish today?"

She yanks her hands away and steels herself. "No. I said I was fine, and I meant it. It's nothing. And it's none of your business what I do in my private time." This is the Mia I'm used to. Strong and defiant with her head up—which is how I catch sight of the faint bruising around her neck that looks like she did a cover-up job to hide. Seriously, what the fuck happened?

"The bruising around your neck and the wounds on your wrists say otherwise, so again, is there something I need to know about?"

"Like I said, my private life is not your concern, nor is it your business. Can I get back to work now? I have a lot to do before the weekend." She stands tall, ready to retreat.

"Mia, I can help if you're in trouble. I can't have my assistant distracted, so if I need to eliminate that distraction, I will. Do you understand?"

"Yes, but I don't need help. I'm not discussing my personal affairs and what goes on during my time away from the office. What I choose to partake in is my choice. And that's all I'll be saying on the matter. May I be excused?" So, that's what she's going with. Unbelievable. Anything else may have been more believable than the bullshit she's implying.

"If that's the direction you're taking, then yes, you're excused. But, Mia, I don't believe you for a second. If you had a proclivity of that nature, you wouldn't be scared of your own shadow today. I'll find out the truth, one way or another." *I'm not letting this go.*

"It's the truth. In fact, I have another date tonight, but I won't let my personal life interfere with work again. Don't bother wasting your time searching for answers that aren't there. Just let it go." She doesn't wait for a response but turns around and walks out.

I know she's lying. Something is going on, and she's too scared to tell me. Granted, she has no reason to trust me. I'm her boss who treats her like shit, not someone she can talk to. Does she have anyone who can help?

Realizing I know nothing about her life outside work, besides her mom cleaning for my parents and her dad being out of the picture, I decide it's time to learn more about Mia Marcos—and I know just the person to ask for help.

> Me: Can I get the name of the private investigator you use?
>
> Eli: I'll send you the contact. Need any help?
>
> Me: Not at the moment. Thanks, man.
>
> Eli: You bet. There's a game this Saturday, want in?
>
> Me: Sure, another thing to keep my mind out of the gutter.
>
> Eli: Is that possible?
>
> Me: Probably not. Shoot me the details.

After I finish my call with the investigator, I do something way out of character and call my parents for dinner on Sunday. They may know more about her private life by seeing her mom weekly. In the meantime, the investigator can check into Mia's background to fill in the blanks. And I might be crazy, but I'll be accompanying Mia on her date tonight; she just won't know. We'll see if this is the type of hookup she's making it out to be or simply a cover like I think it is.

I feel better about setting the wheels in motion, but I can't shake off my anxiousness and this strange new draw to protect the girl I have no business getting involved with. I'm sure it's just concern over her safety and nothing more. That's what I'm telling myself anyway.

It looks like we both might be liars.

Mia

Crap, crap, crap. The last thing I need is someone getting suspicious right out of the gate. Whether I like it or not, I'm in this, and with the amount owed, it'll be for a while. Why did I have to fidget? I did such a good job covering my neck, keeping my head down, and wearing a blouse with flouncy sleeves covering my wrists, only to screw it up by fricking fidgeting.

I still can't get over what happened last night. After taking a minute to calm down once they left, I went to clean myself up but took one look in the mirror and broke down again. I only had so long to pull myself together before Mom got home. Making it through dinner was draining, and by the time the kitchen was clean and my bed suddenly appeared in front of me, I climbed in like a zombie and crashed. The night was filled with bad dreams amidst minimal sleep, so I'd told Jackson the truth, saying I was tired.

He can't find out what happened—thus, my brilliant idea to act like it was from a night of kinky sex. It was the only thing that came to mind. I'm sure that can make a girl tired. Seriously, what was I thinking? He didn't fall for the lie in the slightest, and then I dug myself deeper by blabbing about my date tonight. I figured it would make the story more believable even though I'd planned to cancel the damn thing because, hello… how can I think about dating with all this?

Now I realize it's exactly what I need. Not only will it make everything appear normal, but it'll be a good distraction. If I were to cancel, Walker would never let it go, pestering me until I changed my mind or told him the truth. If I keep up the ruse, it'll kill two birds with one stone. Walker will have no reason to question me, and Jackson has no way of knowing what happens behind closed doors. I'll just fake it 'til I make it.

This is so fricking complicated. Not only do I have to worry about the shit I'm involved in but Jackson's meddling along with it. When he offered to "eliminate my distraction," I almost caved at the authority and determination in his voice, making me believe for a moment that he could do it. I know better than to mess with these guys, though. I need Jackson to let it go, but I have a feeling he won't be giving up easily. If he were to learn the truth, he'd more than likely force me to go to the police, and then my mom's life would be on the line. I *won't* let that happen.

That's why, from this moment on, I'm shaking this shit off. I'll put my poker face on and pay my dad's debt. They didn't say I couldn't play more games, only that I had to play the ones they told me to. It just means I may have to put school on hold for a year, since I'll be a walking zombie until this is over. I'm sure there's some kind of deferral I can do. *God, what a mess.*

Now I need to figure out what I'm going to do about handing over the money I've saved. How would they know how much I have if it's hidden away? I'll have to decide what amount I'm willing to give that seems believable.

My phone buzzes in the drawer. Instinctively, my head snaps toward Jackson's office, which does no good since I can't see through the closed door or blinds. I don't get many texts, so I'm curious as I reach to grab it. Didn't they say curiosity killed the cat? It's an unknown number, but not hard to decipher who it's from.

> Unknown: Tomorrow night, sweet cheeks. Seven sharp, $2K buy-in. Let's see if Daddy was right about you. Address tomorrow.

My eyes go wide, and my mouth opens in shock. Thankfully, my first paycheck was deposited today because the whole thing is going to the buy-in. Even though the situation scares me, I can't deny the excitement of playing again. Not only do I love it, but I'm damn good, and it gives me a sense of satisfaction. And this time, I'm not deceiving my mom by choice. Though it does suck that the money won't be going in my pocket.

Jackson's door opens abruptly, making me fumble and drop my phone.

"Not skittish at all, huh?" he asks rhetorically.

Scowling, I bend, but he beats me to it, picking my phone up off the floor. I panic as he looks at the screen before handing it over. Thank God it's locked.

"You startled me. I'm not usually on my phone during work, I swear." Why is he standing here looking like there's more to say?

"What was so important that you had to take care of during working hours?" he asks sternly.

God, he is such a jerk.

"I was confirming my plans for later," I say, the lie rolling convincingly off my tongue.

"For your *date*, huh? Tell me, is he the guy you were with last night?" He's not buying it.

"Not that it's any of your business, but no. It's someone new." This might work out in my favor. I can play off the "insatiable sex fiend" angle since I have the marks to prove it. *Yeah right…*

"And how did you meet this new guy? Is there a secret club or something?" He's smirking at me as if calling me out.

"Online. There are these things called dating apps. You're probably too old for them," I snap back. My cool façade isn't staying in place today based on what I've dealt with in the last twenty-four hours.

"Nice try. You're not old enough to be on those, so how did you manage that?"

I scoff. "Are you the dating app police now? Everyone my age has an account. It's just a way to find people, you know… who might be looking for the same *things*." The implication is evident in my tone. "Age isn't an issue."

"Age is most certainly an issue when you're a minor and shouldn't be fucking someone who could go to jail for it." He looks at me with raised eyebrows like he's got the upper hand.

"I'm literally of age in under three weeks. Chill out. Not to mention, half the girls in high school are having sex with someone who could get in trouble for it. Are we all supposed to stay celibate until we're eighteen or just date underclassmen?"

"Not my problem to solve. But back to the point. You're telling me you went on an app to find some random guy you know nothing about, who could be some psycho or turn out not to be who he said he was." He runs his hand through his hair in evident frustration. "You do know you're vulnerable, not to mention naïve, and could easily be taken advantage of or worse. Does that not worry you?"

I'm screaming inside at the condescending remarks. "I am not naïve, for your information. Walker helped me choose a few guys I've been texting and getting to know, and we picked safe, public places to meet."

He blows a huff of air out like all of this is crazy. "How nice of Walker to help you. Who the fuck *is* Walker, and where the hell are you going that is so public and safe?"

"You're acting like a lunatic. You know this is how most people meet these days, right? Walker happens to be my best friend, and he was the one who suggested I do this. Mason and I are having dinner at Beach Hut. It's a good location with a lot of people around. Why do you care anyway?"

"Good question. I don't. I'm wasting too much time trying to talk sense into someone who clearly doesn't have any. You're right. Your choices are your business. Have fun with *Mason*." He stomps off, spewing the last words as he walks away.

What is his problem?

Jackson

What the fuck is my problem? I'm letting this girl get to my head. Why couldn't I keep my mouth shut and thoughts to myself? Dammit. I don't want to care about her.

Wait. Caring for her is *not* the issue. I simply want to make sure she's okay, just as I would for anybody.

That's the only reason I'm walking into the Beach Hut Deli right after work to scope out a table. I know all about dating apps. I'm a guy who likes to get laid, and there was no better way to find a willing girl than one of those sites back in the day. If I believed that was really what she was doing, then whatever, but something's not adding up, and I intend to figure it out.

Twenty minutes into my brooding, I catch sight of a guy standing at the entrance, scanning the place. He stays there, not finding who he's looking for. This could be Mason. He's young, maybe a couple of years older than Mia, and doesn't look like a total creep, but who knows? He also doesn't look capable of what she's supposedly into—but again, you never know.

Not that I'm buying that crap. Not when I've seen her almost every day for nearly two months and haven't seen a single sign of it. Plus, it's not proper to leave visible marks if you *are* into that type of thing. She's full of shit. So what is the truth? She could have been attacked, though would she be going on a date right after if that were the case? Not knowing is killing me.

Braden: Up for drinks?

Me: Can't, busy.

Braden: With what? You don't have a life.

Me: And you do?

Braden: Did you find some pussy for the night?

Me: No, just doing some recon. I'll explain later. Enjoy yours tomorrow.

Braden: I will. She's a hot one.

Me: Dinner with my parents again on Sunday. Meet after?

Braden: Yeah, good luck, see you then.

Two minutes later, Mia walks in, and the guy recognizes her immediately. How could he not? She's fucking beautiful. They awkwardly greet each other, proving this is, in fact, a first date. At least she was telling the truth about that. Luckily, they're seated where I can watch easily out of their line of sight. I chose my location well.

I watch intently as they interact, trying to decipher as much as I can through their body language. I'm mesmerized watching Mia outside the office in a casual setting. She's cute. Her laugh, which I now realize I've never heard, is music to my ears. Enough that it makes me want to change my tune in the office and try a new approach. I don't know when I went from trying to get her to quit to trying to get in her life, but my sudden determination is fierce.

It's obvious the guy is already infatuated with her. Who wouldn't be? He's made her laugh quite a bit, pissing me off on one hand while also wanting him to do it more. They're paying now, and I quickly signal my waitress to do the same. I'm pretty sure she thinks I'm a total stalker, noticing where my attention has been all evening. Funny how she'd be right. It wouldn't be surprising if the cops show up any minute from an anonymous tip.

I wait until they're out the front door to head in their direction. *Let's see if she makes good on her intention to find someone with the same interests.* What a joke.

When they start walking, it's safe for me to exit, and since there are plenty of people out, I'm unconcerned about being spotted. I'll give this Walker guy props for picking a busy place.

They walk along the Embarcadero, apparently not ready to call it an evening, and I'm not prepared to let her out of my sight. Fifteen minutes have passed, and they stop for ice cream at Seaport Village. Fuck, could this date go any longer? At this point, I'm ready to interrupt this thing and not-so-casually end it for them. I'm getting increasingly irritated as I continue watching from the shadows, feeling much like the creeper I am as he makes his move.

After tossing their garbage, he reaches for her hand to help her up and pulls her into his body, steadying her with his hand on her hip. She doesn't seem to mind as she looks up at him and smiles. *Fuck me.* How is it that suddenly, I want that smile directed at me? The guy says something, and she nods before he cups her cheek and leans down to kiss her. It's chaste at first—*wimpy fucker*—but then he goes in for more, and soon they're standing there with their tongues down each other's throats.

Christ, this is torture.

Thankfully, they pull apart shortly after, and I see her shyness from here. There's no fucking way she's into what she says she is, so where does this date come in, and how the fuck could she be okay with it the night after an attack? I'm more lost than I was before and determined to find answers—not to mention putting the kibosh on any future date with this fucker.

Following the pair as he walks her to the bus stop, I watch them awkwardly hug each other before she gets on alone. Perfect. I wait until the bus is out of sight.

"Hey, Mason. That was Mia, right?" I ask, coming up behind him.

He turns around, studying me. "Yeah. Do I know you?" He's caught off guard hearing his name.

"Let me give you a little tip. She's off-limits. She may act all sweet and innocent, but she's involved in some shit you don't want to mess with. Stay away from her, or you might not like the consequences."

He holds up his hands in defense. "What the fuck, man? I don't want any trouble. That was our first date. If she's with someone, she didn't tell me, I swear."

"I'll let it slide and keep this to myself for now, but if you mention this to her or try seeing her again, there's no guarantee you won't be paid a little visit, understand?"

"Yeah, man, we're good. She's all yours or… whoever's. I don't need this shit. I'm out."

"Good choice, Mason. Glad we're on the same page." I turn and walk away, feeling damn satisfied with the evening.

6

DANGEROUS

Mia

COMMUTING TO THE POKER GAME TONIGHT GIVES ME PLENTY OF time to reflect on my conversation with Walker this afternoon. Apparently, describing last night's kiss as "nice" wasn't good enough. It wasn't terrible, but it certainly wasn't a mind-blowing "take me back to your place" kind of kiss. Although, I suppose it doesn't matter since he ghosted me. He told me to let him know I made it home safely and then never responded. Walker told me to give it another day before losing hope, but we'll see.

I'm sure we'll talk more about it since I'm staying at his place tonight. I told my mom we were going out and then crashing there. Walker was surprised to hear I was taking up poker again, making withholding the truth difficult. But I can't risk these guys finding out I told someone, so the less he knows, the better.

I'm starting to get nervous as the bus approaches my stop. Then again, I'm always a little anxious before an in-person tournament. Most players don't take me seriously. Not only am I female, the minority at these things, but I'm always the youngest. Condescending remarks are common until I prove myself. I've gotten good at pulling off indifference, but inside, I'm not as calm as it seems. I started branching out into live games just over a year ago, and it's gotten better since those early days, but still nerve-racking.

Stepping off, I look at my phone to see where I'm going. The address arrived an hour ago, with instructions to send my results after. It came with barely enough time to get here, and had it been any later, I would have had to Uber. As it is, I'll arrive right on time without a minute to spare. You never want to be late, or you'll start with fewer chips, which is fair but not a great way to begin.

I dress more maturely at live tournaments, but with a game in this neighborhood, I stepped it up, wearing black slacks and a sexy low-cut shirt that doubles as a distraction tactic. We ladies should use what God gave us for something other than sex. Men have strength, and we have beauty, which is helpful in certain circumstances.

The large house in front of me has a circular driveway lined with expensive cars along the edge. No other details were given besides the time, address, and buy-in, but this looks like a big game. I hope there are no issues, and I'm on a list because you don't just show up to these things; they're by invitation only. Stopping before an enormous wooden front door, I take a deep breath and knock.

It swings open to reveal a staff member who asks my name while looking down at his clipboard. My heart is pounding as he skims the list, but he finds it quickly before standing aside and motioning for me to enter. Once inside the foyer, he takes my coat and leads me to a table to take care of the buy-in. This is the most money I've ever paid for a game, and I'm shaking a little as I hand it over. It's a month's worth of wages, but much more than that is at stake.

Once he's finished securing it, he holds out a playing card. "Here you are, dear. Find the seat with the matching card, although that won't be hard to do with everyone else here. I'll show you the way." I look down to see the Queen of Hearts. Is it fate that it's my lucky card? I hope so, because here goes nothing.

He motions me to follow before leading me down a set of stairs, where the sounds of conversation can be heard below. The voices get louder as we descend, and after reaching the bottom, he steps aside for me to pass. All eyes immediately turn in my direction. Three large oval tables with ten chairs at each tells me twenty-nine other people are already here. As I scan the room, my eyes land on a familiar face, and I blanch.

Holy shit, what is Jackson doing here?

Jackson

"What the hell?" I realize I've said that out loud as all eyes target the stairway.

"What's up, man?" Eli asks from the table over, hearing my expletive. We didn't end up at the same one tonight, which is good and bad. While we don't get to fuck with each other all night, it does prevent us from potentially taking a friend out of the game.

"That's Mia," I say in his direction, quieter this time.

He looks at me with shock. "From the office?"

I nod, watching him mouth the word 'fuck', which is my thought exactly. This is no place for her. What the hell is she doing here?

"Do you know her?" Cole asks from across the table. I barely know the guy and don't feel like answering but decide to satisfy his curiosity in hopes of ending the conversation.

"She works for me. I didn't know she played poker." Her presence takes me off guard, and my answer comes out harsher than intended.

"Well, this should be interesting. She looks about twelve. Are you violating any child labor laws?" The table chuckles at his jab, and I ball my fists. I see Mia's head turn toward our table and know she heard his comment.

"Keep talking shit, and we'll see what laws I can break. Why don't you worry about whether she'll kick your ass in poker and not how old she is." This shuts him up, and he doesn't respond. The subtle lift at the corner of Mia's mouth tells me she heard my response.

My eyes follow as she makes her way to the only empty seat, which happens to be at Eli's table. Great. He better keep his mouth shut. He knows I'm attracted to her, but that's all. I haven't told him about my recent stalking tendencies or that I may have discovered that I'm interested in more than just her body.

Damn, the surprises keep coming. How did she get invited to this, anyway? It's a big money pot, and I know she doesn't have a lot to spare.

She made that clear early on when she was insulted by the comments about her clothes. That was when I first showed my cards, so to speak, and alluded to my attraction.

Speaking of which, what the fuck is she wearing? I swear she keeps throwing curveballs. Her black slacks are fine, but waist up, I want to walk over and cover her with my jacket. She's wearing a mesh blouse with a sexy bra underneath that manages to push her cleavage up over the low-cut neckline more provocatively than I've seen before. Is this her typical style or a ploy to keep the attention on her chest instead of her cards? She dressed more conservatively for her date, so I assume the latter.

"Ah, the Queen of Hearts has arrived," Eli says as she reaches her seat.

"I have. I'm Mia," she responds, sitting and organizing her chips. It's apparent that she's familiar with the motions, digging right in with no hesitation.

"Very nice to meet you, Mia. I'm Eli. Good luck tonight." His back is to me, but I have a clear view of Mia and her steely demeanor, which she put in place the minute she sat down.

"Thanks. You too," is the only thing she gives in return.

My eyes rarely stray from their table as the game gets underway. It's fascinating to watch. This isn't her first rodeo with how comfortable and capable she is. And it's sexy as hell, prompting an uncomfortable situation under the table.

The game progresses as blinds are raised and people are starting to bust. Thank fuck I've been blessed with good cards because I'm too mesmerized by Mia to focus on playing. Between listening to the conversation and watching their progression, I've discovered that Mia's a fucking shark. And suddenly, I'm desperate to know more about the girl who has consumed my thoughts for weeks, leaving no room for anyone else.

I want to learn everything there is—but first and foremost, why the fuck she's here, subjecting herself to so many scumbags and putting herself in danger.

When the tenth guy busts, we're given a ten-minute break before consolidating to two tables.

Time to get some answers.

I'm the first out of my chair, reaching a still-seated Mia to lean down and whisper from behind. "Follow me." I catch Eli in the background, raising his eyebrows in question. Ignoring him, I turn around and hope to God she follows. I'd hate to make a scene, but I will if necessary. Luckily, it's not, since the sound of her footsteps indicates she's behind me.

On the main level, a hallway leads to a library, which I discovered upon arrival while using the restroom. I go in that direction and step inside, shutting the door after she enters. "Want to explain what the fuck you're doing here, spending an entire month's salary on a game of poker? How did you even get an invite?" Okay, maybe that wasn't the best way to start, but I'm so pent-up that it was inevitable.

"I have just as much right to be here as you do. You're not my dad, nor do I owe you an explanation." She takes a step closer with her last sentence, displaying strength.

I move forward, putting myself mere inches from her. She leans back but doesn't retreat. "Maybe what you need *is* a daddy to answer to. Seriously, Mia, what the fuck are you thinking? Some of these men are dangerous. This is no place for someone like you. And in case you forgot, you are not an adult."

"You don't know anything about me or what kind of person I am. And stop with the adult comments. I'm eighteen in nearly two weeks. Just drop the age thing already. You do not get to tell me what to do. You may be my boss, but we are not at work. As far as I'm concerned, you're the most dangerous one here." She leans forward in anger.

I close the gap by another inch, and this time, she steps back. I do it again and again until her back hits the wall, then cage her in with my hands on either side of her and look down menacingly.

"You want me to overlook your age? Are you sure about that, *little girl*? Would you like to see how dangerous I am?" My dick is rock-hard in my pants, busting at the seams and dying for friction.

"I… I want you to stop thinking of me as a child, that's all." The last words are practically a whisper as she licks her lips, begging to be kissed.

I press my body into hers. "Does it feel like I think of you as a child… or does it feel like I wish more than anything you weren't? The fact of the matter is this: You. Are. Off. Limits. No matter how I see you." I press harder into her, and she lets out the tiniest moan. Fuuuck, I'm torturing myself.

I push off the wall and shake my head. "Look, you don't belong here.

Why are you putting two thousand dollars on the line in the first place?" That's the real reason I pulled her away—to question her, not to rub my dick on her. Although, now that I have, it's all I want to do.

"I'm here because I enjoy playing, which I'm assuming is the same reason you're here. Speaking of, we need to get back." She starts toward the door.

"Don't think I'm letting this go," I warn.

"Ugh, just… whatever." She throws her hands up and walks out with me trailing behind like the puppy dog I am.

Mia

Now that's the feeling I wanted from my kiss last night. Yet here I am getting it from my boss—again. Dammit, why does my body keep responding to him like this? The minute he caged me in, my breath became erratic, and I couldn't focus. I wanted him to kiss me so badly; it was all I could think about. Then, when he pressed into me… holy hell, all coherent thought was lost. The feel of his firmness was such a turn-on that a moan came out. How embarrassing.

He's such an ass, treating me like a child. Well… not entirely. But he's acting like I can't take care of myself, which is infuriating when I've been doing it for longer than most. I mean, yes, I live at home with my mom, but we take care of each other. We're a team. I'm not the helpless little girl he thinks I am. I have every right to be here, and I'll prove it by playing the best damn game ever.

We choose cards for our seats after walking in and end up at the same fricking table. *Just great.* Oh well, I need to stop letting him get to me. While I'm slightly distracted by the memory of his body pressed against mine, as soon as my ass hits the chair, my poker face comes on.

"Did you enjoy the break?" The question comes from Eli, whom I met earlier, and is directed toward Jackson, so they must know each other.

Jackson looks at him and scowls.

"How about you, Mia? This guy didn't harass you too much, I hope," Eli addresses me, nodding in Jackson's direction.

"Eli," Jackson says, sounding like a threat.

"Relax, I'm just trying to rile you up. It's good for my game, and you're making it way too easy, man."

The others at the table chuckle, but Jackson just mutters something that sounds a lot like "motherfucker."

"So, Mia, do you come to these games often?" Eli asks nonchalantly while someone else is taking time to consider their bet.

"Every now and then. I took a break for a while with my new job, but I figure I can still pick up a game here and there in the evenings. How about you?" I ask in return, noticing how Jackson's jaw ticks as he follows our conversation.

"A couple times a month for fun." Eli shrugs. "How do you like working for this guy? You had some big shoes to fill with Cindy. I'm sure it hasn't been easy."

They must be good friends then.

"Cindy planned for an easy transition that I'd say has gone well. Wouldn't you agree, Jackson?"

He nods.

"As far as working for him goes…" Do I screw with Jackson or give a real answer? I'm not sure if there's anyone who Jackson wouldn't want to see his employee give him shit, so I think I'll play it safe and go with the truth. "He runs the company incredibly well, which makes my job easy. He's so organized that sometimes I wonder if he actually needs me, but I'm glad he thinks so because I'm learning a lot."

Jackson's gaze is unreadable but intense, and the ability to look away escapes me.

"Well, whether he needs you or not, it looks like he's lucky to have you," Eli says finally, breaking the moment.

"I am lucky to have her," Jackson says, surprising me before focusing back on the game.

Our conversation ceases after that, and Eli busts a few hands later. He stands from the table, says his goodbyes, and comes around to shake my hand. "Mia, it was a pleasure to meet you. I hope we see each other again." Then he looks at a scowling Jackson and chuckles. "I'm headed to the club. Join me if you end up going out soon."

"You won't be seeing me even if I do."

"Ah… well, then, good luck. I'll look forward to catching up tomorrow," Eli says cryptically.

"Don't," Jackson states angrily, making Eli laugh harder as he walks away.

"I take it you two are good friends?" I ask Jackson casually as the cards are dealt for the next hand.

"We're friends. I'm questioning the 'good' part."

"I'm just surprised you have any," I say, jumping right back into our enmity and earning a few chuckles and curious glances from the other players.

"I'm surprised you can talk and play cards simultaneously. That's impressive for someone your age," he says with a straight face. *Jerk.*

"You'd be amazed what someone my age is capable of."

We stay silent for the rest of this round and then break for ten minutes before consolidating to one table. This time, I don't leave the main room, preventing another encounter alone with Jackson. Jumping between animosity, lust, and niceness is throwing me off-kilter, and there's no telling what will come next. So, instead, I choose to stand back and study the remaining nine opponents.

My cards have been decent, though nothing to write home about like the hands Jackson's lucked out with. You don't need to be a great player with the cards he's getting tonight. I, on the other hand, have worked hard for my wins. I've had no-brainer hands a few times, which allowed me to control the table, but otherwise, it's been more about bluffing and strategy. Jackson can spout off about my age all he wants, but it certainly helps at live games since no one expects what's coming.

By this time in the game, though, people start to think they have everyone figured out, which is right when I switch it up, going in for the kill. Two guys are trying to bully the table, but we'll see how they do when the role's reversed. My chip count is high enough to make bold moves and press harder, and that's what I plan to do. If it doesn't work, I have other things up my sleeve to keep them guessing.

Poker is not just the cards dealt, but strategy—which I learned from my dad. You can memorize all the probabilities for the different hands and still not know how to win. It certainly helps to understand the odds of your hand, but it's not the most crucial factor. Other players' tells, betting habits, and tactics are what it comes down to. And then, of course, there's the name of the game. If you're not willing to gamble, then you won't win in the end.

Tonight, the top five players will walk away with money. For me, fifth place isn't an option, as it's only double the buy-in, and after playing for six or more hours, it's not worth it. A third- or fourth-place finish means I'll be indebted for a lot longer than I want, so I need to finish in first or second place if I want my freedom any time soon.

Three of us with larger chip stacks and four more stragglers aren't out of the game yet. This is about time when the smaller guys start going all-in when they see a top pair in their hand. They're tired, already thinking they're done for, and willing to make bold moves. Stupid, in my opinion, but when you're already down, it doesn't matter and sometimes pays off. To these guys, two thousand dollars is nothing; to me, it's everything.

We get down to four players, and the chips are in my favor. It's a good sign, but as the saying goes, the game isn't over until it's over. Never assume the win. Jackson was the last to bet on this hand, and it's my turn to call. I'm not sure what the protocol is for taking your boss out. It's not like he won't walk away a winner, just a few grand less than the next spot.

"What's it going to be, Mia? You've seen my cards all night, right? Call me if you think I'm bluffing."

"Who says I think you're bluffing? Maybe I'm just wondering if my hand is better than yours." Oh my God… I can't say anything without it sounding like an innuendo—this sexual tension is killing me.

"I'd be happy to find out, but we should finish the game first." This earns a few snickers. "Pay to play, little girl."

Okay, that's it. Taking the boss out is no longer a concern. I already knew I had him beat, but I wasn't last on the button, so my contemplation was not on his hand at all but on how to maximize my take from the other players.

"Well, in that case, by all means. And you know what? I'm all-in. How about you? Are *you* willing to go all-in?" I ask the last question with a slow drawl, deliberately implying more to the statement than the game at hand. I know I'm flirting with disaster when his eyes darken. It's the same look he had a couple of hours ago when pressed against me.

The entire table folds, not wanting to get involved in whatever this is between me and Jackson, who's staring me down. I could have been a little more strategic, keeping one or two guys in, taking a larger pot, but damn, he pushes my buttons. He'll figure out soon that this *little girl* doesn't back down.

He throws his cards on the table, folding his hand. "I'll go all-in when I'm confident there's no risk. Until then, I think I'll keep playing."

"That's the thing, Jackson, the risk never goes away. You're just prolonging the inevitable."

What have I gotten myself into?

Jackson

She's probably right. I like this bolder side of Mia—it's sexy as fuck. This girl is a force to be reckoned with, not the complacent one from the office.

I go all-in not much later and lose out to another player. There's a part of me that wishes I'd just gone against her when I knew I'd lose, adding to her stack, but honestly, she doesn't need the charity; she's holding her own just fine. It's down to her and just two others.

My dick has been strained all night, hard as a rock and dying to break free. The incident upstairs has been on constant replay, and if it weren't for the great cards I've been dealt tonight, I'd have been out a long time ago from being distracted. With only three players left, I'm sticking around. There's no way I'm letting her leave alone when I still don't know the story behind the marks on her body. Until I do, I'll be keeping an eye on her. I end up hanging around the table, watching as if I'm interested in the game when all I'm truly interested in is the girl whom my eyes rarely stray from.

She's an amazing player. How she's this talented at such a young age leads to more questions. If she's this good, why the hell has she put up with me for so long instead of doing this for income? Her finish tonight isn't a fluke. She earned it and could be a professional player if she pursued it, although that could be dangerous for someone like her.

Although I love the game, I'm not serious about it. It's a hobby, not an income source, and certainly not an addiction. Socializing is why I do it more than anything, and it breaks the monotony of going to the club and hooking up.

The evening proceeds with normal trash talk, however no insults are directed toward Mia. I'm sure everyone caught on to some type of connection between us and wouldn't have risked an offensive remark while I was here. I'm a big guy. After playing football all through college, the discipline to care for my body has stuck, and I lift daily to keep my physique in top shape. I could take anyone in this room and barely break a sweat.

Mia is quiet while she plays, only speaking when she places her bet or calls. The most she's said all night was when we bantered with each other. Other than that, she's been impossible to rile up, remaining calm throughout. It's unnerving, and I've noticed it gets under the skin of the other players when they can't get a reaction from her.

The third player finally goes out, leaving only Mia and Bill. "Mia, you're quite the player. Where did you learn?" he asks during the next shuffle.

"Here and there. Online. You know." It's a short answer and a complete cop-out. She's obviously hiding something.

"Well, you must be a natural, then, because it took me years to master the art of poker." He looks at her until she lifts her eyes to meet his. "So, Mia, we've been playing for hours, and we're equally stacked. What do you say we split the pot and call it a night? I'd like to get home to the missus, but I'll play until the end if that's what you want."

She's quiet as she contemplates for a few minutes before answering. "Yeah, we can do that. Who knows how long we'd be here if we didn't, and I'm getting tired anyway. Thanks for offering."

"The thanks are all mine. You're a challenging opponent. It's been a real pleasure. Do you need help getting home?"

"That won't be necessary, Bill. I've got her. Nice of you to ask, though," I interject. I can tell she's dying to argue, but she *is* smart enough to wait until we don't have an audience.

"Well, in that case, you enjoy the rest of your weekend. Jackson, it was good to see you." He walks upstairs, leaving the two of us alone.

I knew it wouldn't take her long. "I don't need help getting home. Can you believe I made it here like a big girl? And now I'll get home like one—by myself." Sarcasm is dripping from her voice. She drives me fucking crazy.

"It wasn't dark then or two in the morning. There's no way I'm letting you go alone." I stand inches away, staring down at her, looking formidable with my arms crossed, giving my best "don't fuck with me" vibe.

"Jackson, you are not the boss outside of work. I can take care of myself." Same argument I've heard before, and quite unimpressive at this point.

"Come on, get your winnings, and we'll discuss it upstairs."

She shakes her head and rolls her eyes as she starts toward the stairs.

Following, I get an eye-level view of her juicy rear end. I wish we had further to go, but unfortunately, we arrive on the main level too soon. Once the money is tucked into her pocket, we head for the exit.

Stepping outside, I cut her off at the first sound of her voice. "Cut the crap, Mia. I'm here, I have a car, and I'm not letting you out of my sight. You can go the hard way, over my shoulder, or the easy way and walk. I have a preference, and it's not what you think." I pause, letting that sink in. "So, what's it going to be?"

She stares at me with a clenched jaw before walking toward the driveway. *Good girl*, although not what I was hoping for.

"Put the address here." I point to the touch screen. She enters it, and it's not what I would expect, knowing what little I do about her. Her mom cleans for my parents, and her dad's out of the picture. Could she live in that part of town?

"Is that your address?" I ask casually, not wanting to offend her with the reason behind the question.

"No, it's Walker's house. I'm staying there tonight." She's looking out the window, avoiding my gaze.

"I see. Are you two more than friends?" I ask with a clenched jaw, not sure I want the answer. Is there a chance he was the one who did that to her? Maybe I need to pay this fucker a visit.

"I don't think that's any of your business." She's right, but I don't give a shit.

"Is he the one who marked you up like that? Say the word, Mia, and I'll kick his ass."

"No! He would never hurt me. He'd be just as mad as you if he knew. Shit." She shuts her mouth, growls, and shakes her head, frustrated at giving that away.

If he doesn't know about the abuse she received, then she's hiding it from everyone. Why?

"Listen, I know you don't trust or particularly like me. I've given you no reason to, but seriously, I can help you, Mia. Whatever it is, I can take care of it if you just tell me what happened." God, I'm practically begging her at this point. I sound pathetic.

"I told you. It's nothing I wasn't looking for."

"Bullshit!" I bang the steering wheel, making her flinch. "There's no fucking way that's true. Why are you lying? If someone took advantage of you, it's not your fault. Let someone help you. Let *me* help you," I plead.

She seems to soften at my last statement. "Jackson, I appreciate your concern, but I don't have a different answer. I'm not who you think I am. Just let it go and forget it. I don't want to keep arguing with you about it, okay?"

"I'll drop it for now, but I won't stop until I have the truth, Mia. Whether I get it from you or by other means is your decision."

She raises her brows. "What is that supposed to mean? What other means?"

"I have my resources. Don't think I'll just let this go, not when I saw the evidence that you've been hurt with my own eyes." I sigh. "Look, I know your dad is out of the picture. You're not confiding in this Walker guy either, so that leaves your mom, who I'm assuming you're also not coming clean to." Her lack of response is all the confirmation I need.

We're pulling up to the address she punched in my GPS. The car rolls to a stop at the curb, and I put it in Park before facing her. I grab her chin and turn her face to look at me. "You need someone on your side, and whether you want it or not, I'm making that person me. You'll have to accept it sooner or later." I rub my thumb along her jaw and then across her bottom lip before reluctantly bringing my hand down and sitting back. I was too close to pulling her in and devouring those lips.

She sighs and shakes her head in denial. "Thanks for the ride, Jackson. I'll see you Monday." She exits the car, and I watch as she stops, typing something on her phone before going in.

I pull away with more questions than answers.

7

CATCHING FEELINGS

Mia

WALKER WAKES ME UP AT NOON. "HEY, SLEEPYHEAD, IT'S TIME to get up. You're late for work."

Grabbing my phone in a panic, I look at the time before noticing laughter spewing from Walker's mouth and remember what day it is.

"You jerk, it's Sunday!" I flop back down on the pillow.

"That was priceless. You should've seen the look on your face. God, I wish I was filming that shit." He's still laughing. Meanwhile, my heart is racing.

"That was not nice. You know I got in after two in the morning. Geez, cut me some slack, would you?"

"How'd it go? Did you rake the table?" he asks.

"I split for first. It was late, and we were evenly stacked. Ready for the crazy part?"

"Shoot." He climbs on the bed beside me, eager for the story.

"Jackson was there." I pause for effect.

"No fucking way. What the hell? How?"

"I don't know, it was random. He was as surprised to see me as I was him."

"So, how was it?"

"Condescending, as usual. Then he dragged me upstairs away from the others and said I was too young to be there and blah, blah, blah. He finished fourth, stayed to watch, and insisted on giving me a ride. He drives me crazy."

"He *dragged* you? Was he rough with you, Mia?" Protective Walker is in the house. I love that he cares and would probably do anything for me, making me wish more than ever that I could confide in him about my shitty situation.

"No, he wasn't rough. He… God, Walker… I shouldn't feel this way, but dang it, I was so turned on by him. He caged me up against the wall, and when he pressed his body into me, I almost combusted. I practically eye fucked him, begging him to kiss me. He's a total dick, Walker. How am I attracted to him?" I drop my head and cover my face with my hands in embarrassment.

"Because he's hot as shit. I have a boyfriend, and I'm attracted to the man. So, he didn't kiss you, then?"

"No. He pushed away, stuck on the fact that I'm still seventeen. He won't touch me with a ten-foot pole." I close my eyes and blow out a breath of frustration at myself for being upset. "For a minute, when we pulled up to the house, it looked like he was going to. He was staring at my mouth and rubbed my lip with his thumb, but then he just dropped his hand and turned forward again." Ugh! I remember the feel of his hand on my face, the soft caress of his thumb, and how I wanted nothing more than his lips on mine.

"He's a lot older than you, so you can't blame him for holding back. But look at the bright side." I open my eyes and see the smile plastered on his face as he wags his eyebrows. "You're eighteen in a couple of weeks, and then what is there to stop him?"

"My dislike for him, that's what. I don't even want him to kiss me," I huff, hoping I sound believable.

"Riiiight. You're saying you would've stopped him if he tried last night?" He looks at me knowingly.

"Shut up. It was a moment of weakness. Now that I've experienced it once, I can control myself next time."

"Sure you can, honey. I can't wait to hear how that goes. In the meantime, what about Mason? Did he ever text back?"

Another crappy situation I don't need reminding of. "He definitely ghosted me. I texted him again, like you said, and got nothing. I don't like this dating thing," I say disparagingly.

"Don't give up yet. At least not until we get you some action." He winks.

"Ugh, whatever. I need to get home. Want to be my chauffeur?" I say, giving him my best puppy dog eyes.

"Your chariot awaits." He hops to his feet and holds his hand out to help me up.

During the drive, I recap what it was like playing against Jackson and meeting his friend Eli, finishing as he pulls up to the curb outside my house. Opening the front door, I spot my mom in the kitchen preparing dinner. She loves cooking but is usually too tired during the week after a full day of cleaning. Her meals are my favorite, and my stomach growls from the smell.

"Mmmm. What are you making?" I ask as I kiss her cheek in greeting.

"Hi, sweetie. We're having *asopao de pollo* for dinner. Did you have fun last night? You look tired."

"I did, and yeah, I'm exhausted."

"Why don't you go rest, and I'll wake you up in a bit."

"Thanks, Mom, I think I will."

Alone in my room, I can finally check for a response to the text I sent from Walker's last night. I didn't want to look in front of anyone in case my reaction gave something away, raising questions that are best avoided. Sure enough, there's a message waiting.

> Unknown: Looks like Daddy was right about you. That's too bad. I was looking forward to a different form of payment. See you soon, sweet cheeks. And don't forget about the savings. Unless you want to work some off, we'll expect more than the winnings.

That's all there is. Nothing about when or where. They're just fucking with me. Are they going to be waiting inside one night after work again? The last thing I want is for them to show up when my mom is here.

I hate this. I'm so mad at my dad. How could he put us in this position if he cared about us? Obviously, he doesn't, and the hope I've been holding on to the last few years has truly died. It's best to just get this debt paid off and move on.

Calculating how long it'll take to pay them off is impossible. The problem is that not all games have that large a payout. Two thousand dollars was a steep buy-in, plus there were thirty players. Most games aren't so big, not to mention smaller dollars. If these guys keep sending me to high-dollar tournaments, I'll need to keep a bigger cushion.

I'm also not guaranteed to pull off a top finish every time. The minute you start thinking that highly of yourself, you get in trouble like my dad did. You start losing, getting in your head, and it's a downhill battle from there. I should know because I watched it happen firsthand. Now, here I am, paying the price for his demise.

Jackson

"So, that's the girl you're hung up on. I mean, I can see why. She's gorgeous. Then add in those mad poker skills, and man, she'd be a catch if she wasn't so damn young. I'd ask if she's legal, but we all know she isn't." Eli laughs as he takes a swig of his beer.

We're meeting at the club on Sunday night after dinner with my parents, who were happy to hear that I was settling in with Mia and not obsessing about getting rid of her. Little do they know I'm forming a much more inappropriate obsession with her. I'm sure they wouldn't be so happy about that.

The only information I garnered was the same I'd already heard—except while paying closer attention, it clicked why her dad was out of the picture. He left them because of his gambling addiction, which would explain where Mia more than likely learned to play. The only other beneficial tidbit was what restaurant Mia's mom decided on for her birthday dinner, which I'll use to my benefit. Everyone loves a birthday surprise, right?

"Seriously, enough already. I've got blue balls like you wouldn't believe. I don't need you rubbing it in." I'm never going to hear the end of this.

"By the way, what happened during the first break when you two disappeared upstairs?" I knew it was killing him to find out.

"I just questioned why she was there. There's no way she should be spending two thousand dollars on a poker game. Although seeing how good she is, I'm curious why she isn't doing it full-time instead of putting up with my bullshit. She gave me some lame excuse, but I don't buy it. She's hiding something."

"It didn't look like all you did was talk. You were sporting quite the boner when you came back down, and her face was flushed as hell. Did you do something you shouldn't have? You know she's a dangerous pursuit for you," Eli warns me.

"I'd think it was right up your alley with your adrenaline-chasing tendencies." I retort, his accusation irritating.

"I've got your back, Jackson. We'll handle it if shit comes back to bite you. It's not ideal, but you'll be okay with her being so close to eighteen," states Braden, who's in full attorney mode now.

"Fuck, I didn't do anything, all right? I won't touch her until she's legal, and even then, I'm not sure I will. I haven't told you what's happening, but there's more to the story." I fill them in on the last couple of days, including the marks I noticed, the private investigator I hired, and my new stalker status.

"Dude, are you the same guy who tormented this girl a few weeks ago? You sound like there's a little more going on than just concern if you're scaring her dates away. Did you catch feelings for this chick?" Braden hasn't had an interest in anything but a good lay since he was dumped by the woman he almost proposed to and decided love was overrated. He also saw what I went through with Lily, further proving it's not worth it.

"I don't know. One minute, I want to strangle her. The next, I want to learn everything there is about her, and during both of those, I want to fuck her brains out. If that sounds like catching feelings, then maybe I have. Shit." I take a long drink of my beer and slam it down.

"From what I saw, you already have it bad, man. You weren't

focused on anything but her the entire night. Your eyes were glued, and everyone there could see it." Eli chuckles. "So, when will the PI have a report back? Are you putting protection on her until you figure this shit out? You saw what happened to Lily. You can't be too careful these days—there are way too many psychos out there." Lily, Eli's future sister-in-law, was kidnapped by an all-too-eager admirer last year, and if it wasn't for her security, it could've been worse.

"I know, I just haven't thought that far out. I don't know what the fuck I'm doing. That's why I'm talking to you guys. Wouldn't I be overstepping by having her followed?" I'm so out of my league here. It's okay if I follow her like a creeper, but don't hire someone to protect her. What the fuck am I thinking?

"Not if it's for her safety. Look, if she was someone I cared about, and I saw marks like the ones you described, and you're sure they're not consensual, then fuck yeah, I'd put security on her. Especially since she's not coming clean and won't tell you what's going on. She might be in some deep shit. Though that begs the question, do you want to get caught up in something for a girl you know nothing about and aren't involved with beyond an eye-contact orgasm?" I know Eli means well, but Christ, way to put it out there.

"Fuck you. She doesn't have anyone else. I think I'm the only one who knows there's a problem, and yeah, I do fucking care about her. I don't know why or when it happened, but it did, and it's too late to turn back, so tell me what to do."

"I agree with Eli." Braden cuts in. "Fuck overstepping and hire someone to watch her. If something worse happens, you'll never forgive yourself. Second, you've gone this long, so keep your dick to yourself until she's of age. Take a two-week vacation if that's what it takes. It'll make my job a lot easier if shit hits the fan."

"Jesus, Braden, I can keep it in my pants for two weeks. But you did just give me a great idea. Eli, will you send me the contact for the security company Sebastian used for Lily?" At that, I call it a night and head home to start planning.

First, I followed their advice to set up protection for Mia. Although, they said it would be impossible to cover her adequately without her knowing since she uses public transportation. They suggested putting a device in the battery compartment of her phone to make it doable. It gives me creeper vibes, but as Eli said, it's this or risk something worse happening until she comes clean about what she's involved in. With security tailing her, I'll find out what shit she's gotten herself into one way or another.

The second part of my plan is a little more complicated and conniving. It also means involving someone else as an unwitting accomplice. Picking up the phone, I dial, hoping the idea Braden unknowingly gave me turns out to be a good one.

She answers on the first ring. "Jackson?"

"Hey, sis."

"What are you doing calling me on a Sunday night? I'm surprised you're not too busy with your flavor of the week."

"If that isn't the pot calling the kettle black, I don't know what is." My sister made it clear long ago there was no room for the tough big brother act in her life. She likes her men the same way I like my women: horizontal, perpetual, and varietal.

"Yeah, yeah. So, what's up? Last we talked, you were pissed about some new assistant the parentals made you keep. Has the big bad wolf scared her away yet?"

"Nah, she turned out to be okay and managed to suffer through my bullshit to come out the other side. We're making it work. Anyway, there's a reason I'm calling. You keep hounding me to visit and check out all the great opportunities there, so I figured I'd take you up on it." She's screeching in excitement while I'm still talking.

Cici chose real estate as her career path after college and decided Bozeman, Montana, was the city to do it in. They were experiencing a growth influx, and it's far enough away from here to escape our parents without being on the opposite side of the country. That she chose a profession so closely linked to what she was running away from did not escape me.

"*What?* Seriously? I'm so excited! Oh my gosh, Jackson, I can't wait to show you everything." Shit, if I'd known it would make her this happy, I might have visited sooner.

"Don't get too excited yet. I want you to find some deals to look at first. Give me a few to consider, and let's narrow it down before I come out. I'm making it a business trip."

If I go under the guise of looking at properties, it makes sense to bring an assistant—to take notes, of course. When Braden suggested I take a vacation, the idea came to me. The difference is that he was trying to keep me away from temptation, and here I am, planning to bring it with me.

"There are so many, Jackson. I'm going to flood your inbox. But you better come out here to have some fun, too. Oh my gosh, I'm so excited. We don't have clubs like San Diego, but there are some great restaurants and bars. You're going to love it."

"I'm sure I will with you as my guide. I'll start making arrangements if you get me some stuff to look at this week. Let me know what hotel to book that's close to you." I hope she doesn't balk at that, but I know better.

"You're not staying in a hotel. I have plenty of room," she argues.

"I'm bringing Mia along. I'd like her there to keep track of my questions and the documentation needed for each property. I'm sure she'd be more comfortable in a hotel. It's a small town, right? It can't be that far from you." I'm hoping this explanation puts any suspicion to rest.

"Jackson…" she says suspiciously. "Why would you bring your assistant? You've never brought Cindy on a *business* trip. Is there something going on between you two? Wait. Isn't she still in high school? What the actual?" I should have known better, but I forgot how perceptive my sister is.

"No, nothing is going on. She's hot, but I'm not stupid. I wouldn't jeopardize jail time for a sweet piece of ass. I get plenty, thank you very much. I just think it would do her good to get out of town."

"Why? What's in it for you?" I can hear in her voice that she knows there's more. I might as well come clean enough to satisfy her curiosity.

I sigh. "Look, I think something's going on with her, and I'm trying to earn her trust because I think she needs help. Maybe if she's forced to spend time with me, she'll let her guard down and open up." I didn't want to get into this with Cici, but I know her, and she wouldn't have let it go. But I'm not spilling anything about my deeper attraction to Mia. She's not ready for that. Or maybe it's me who's not ready.

"You seem to be taking a big interest in her. Are you sure it's only out of concern and not something more? Not that you'd tell me if it was, and since I'm so glad you're coming, I'll let you off the hook for now. You'll have an email with prospective properties by tomorrow afternoon." I'm sure she'll see that it's more while we're there—if Eli's observations from last night are correct.

"Thanks, sis. I'll let you know which ones I'm interested in and send you my itinerary so you can make appointments. Don't forget to let me know which hotel."

"I won't. Bye, Jackson." She hangs up, and her excitement brings a smile to my face—but also makes me think that maybe she's lonelier than I thought.

8

THE NICE APPROACH

Mia

'M STILL FULL FROM DINNER LAST NIGHT AS I WALK TOWARD MY DESK. Since I took a nap earlier in the day, it was late after searching for the best hiding spot for my money while contemplating how much to give them. With the last buy-in at two thousand, I've determined that's the amount I'm keeping for my poker fund.

I've saved ten thousand dollars and certainly don't want to hand them all of it, but I'm not sure what the chances are that they'll ransack my house to look for more if I don't. I'm torn, but I also need to decide soon since I still have no idea when they'll show up and need to be prepared. The unknown is killing me, which is part of their plan, I'm sure.

Last I saw Jackson, he was bringing me to Walker's house. It didn't go unnoticed that he waited to drive away until I went inside, even though it took me a minute to send the text first. I'm still shocked at falling for his charm and wanting him to kiss me, but I've come to my senses, thank God. Hopefully, he'll turn back into a bosshole today and further my resolve to put that fantasy out of my head since replacing it with someone else didn't work. Well, not yet anyway.

Walker is coming over after dinner later to help me sift through some of the other guys I've been chatting with and see if there's anyone else worth seeing. I told him I'd give it one last chance. It really would be nice to have someone to take my mind off lusting over my boss.

Which I realize is damn near impossible when I look up and see him walking in. How is he so damn gorgeous? He looks like he just came from a photo shoot for *Muscle & Fitness* magazine's "Muscles Undercover" edition. And something about his hands makes me wonder what it would feel like to have them roam over my body. Unlike the small, spindly guys I'm accustomed to from high school, Jackson's are big and manly, just like the rest of him.

Shit, why does my mind keep going down this path?

"Good morning, Mia. Did you enjoy the rest of your weekend? That was a big pot you took home. Splurge on anything fun?" Whoa, did aliens take over his body since I last saw him? He doesn't usually talk to me unless it's related to work.

"I slept the rest of my weekend, and some of us can't afford to be frivolous." The snarkiness comes out naturally.

"Yeah, that was a late one," he says, ignoring my dig, furthering my suspicion of an alien invasion. "By the way, in case I forgot to tell you, you're a damn good player. Impressive even. I've never seen Bill split a pot before. Where'd you learn to play like that?"

Is he fishing for information or just making small talk? Ugh, I'm being paranoid—it's normal for him to be curious about it, and it doesn't hurt to tell him, especially since I'm sure this isn't Jackson. Are the Men in Black almost here?

"My dad taught me. I knew the rules of poker before I could add and subtract. It probably had something to do with me becoming a math nerd." I laugh at that. The memories are fond, even though thinking of my dad makes me cringe now.

"That explains a lot. He must've coached you well. I imagine he's good if you're any indication. Wonder if I've played with him. What's his name?" He's for sure fishing now.

"He's not good. That's why he left us—to chase the wins he wasn't having. He probably plays in seedier games than you're used to, so I'm sure you haven't seen him. He's also no longer part of my life, so I'd rather not talk about him. My skills surpassed his long ago, and what he did teach me isn't what makes me a good player." I hope that ends his questioning because I'm done with this conversation.

"You're right. Most things are gained from experience. I can't say I've mastered any of them, but now and then, I get the cards to keep me going like the other night. It was fun to watch you play, that's all." He leans in a bit and lowers his voice. "But just because you *can* play, doesn't mean you should. I don't think pursuing tournaments like that is smart. Some of those men are dangerous and wouldn't hesitate to take advantage of you in that situation." He's suddenly concerned about my well-being? Yeah, right.

"Good thing it's not your concern then. I don't need a father figure, Jackson. I've been fine the last few years without one."

"Dammit, Mia. Stop with the defensive crap. Can't someone worry about you? You're not even old enough to be there. What would've happened if I informed them of your age?" The alien has vacated his body. Bosshole is back.

I scoff. "Seriously? This isn't about caring. This is yet again about you thinking I'm too young. I'm eighteen in two weeks, so don't bother *informing* anyone. It wouldn't matter anyway—I pay to play, and I'm damn good. Don't mess with something you have no business getting involved in. I mean it." I'm shaking mad. He cannot screw this up for me. I get queasy thinking about the consequences of not being able to play and what I'd be forced to do instead.

"Or what, Mia? You can't stop me from digging, so why don't you just tell me what the fuck is going on?" His voice sounds more like a low growl now.

We stare at each other for a minute, neither backing down, before I decide to respond. "I'm done with this, Jackson. I've gone through this weekend's messages, and here's a list of the ones you'll need to handle." I thrust a piece of paper at him. "Let me know if you need anything else. Otherwise, I'll go through the agenda for the week and be in shortly."

He won't break me.

Jackson

She dismisses me by angling her head toward her computer like I'm not there. I stay for another half minute, contemplating whether to continue lecturing her or walk away. Choosing option two, I stomp off, slamming the door to my office like a child. *Great.* I'm now acting less mature than the adolescent herself. The infuriating female has me inside out.

I find myself replaying our conversation in my head. Seeing her smile made me want to stand there all day and pull more from her. But then I went and blew it by trying to lecture her again. Dammit.

Opening my email to sign the contract with the security firm I hired makes me feel slightly better since she won't let me help. What she doesn't know won't hurt her. I have her scheduled for protection on weeknights after work and over the weekend. She doesn't ever leave for lunch unless I send her out on an errand, so there's no need for anyone during the day because I'll be keeping her in from now on.

My only problem is planting the device on her phone. The firm is sending someone to do it this morning and will text me when they're here so I can call her into the office. I've already let reception know to allow them back.

While I wait, I finish reviewing the messages from the weekend. Mia does a great job filtering everything out, making sure I only deal with what needs my attention. She's excellent at her job all around.

My phone buzzes with a text telling me they're in position around the corner. I use the intercom to request her presence, and seconds later, Mia knocks lightly on the door. After responding, she steps inside, sitting in front of my desk. I get up and shut the door as if it's completely normal, wishing it was for a better reason involving less clothing.

"Here's the overview of your agenda for the week. You have a meeting with the attorney this afternoon to discuss the next steps in the Delaware transaction," she says, back to her calm and collected self.

"Mia, I'm trying to be helpful here. I know you haven't seen the nice side of me very much, but I'm working on it. Please, if there's anything you need…" Here I am, trying to be empathetic, and what my mind immediately strays to is that what I'd like her to need has nothing to do with her current situation. I never said I was perfect.

"Thank you, Jackson. I appreciate the effort, but we both know we're only tolerating each other because we have to. I've come to terms with that. My personal life will stay out of the office, and I'd appreciate you not interfering. We've never run into each other before this weekend, and it probably won't happen again, so let it go." She rises to leave, but they might not be done yet, and I panic.

"Mia, wait! I don't just tolerate you. I realize I've made you feel that way, but you've repeatedly proven you're great at this job. Let me make it up to you and help with whatever you're involved in." The look on her face is a bit of shock and awe combined, showing she's caught off guard. Hopefully, I didn't play my cards too soon.

"Thank you, Jackson, but I don't need help."

Goddammit. I thought I was getting somewhere.

"Mia, I'm trying to approach this nicely, but you're making it very difficult." The string holding my patience is ready to snap.

"I'm a whole can of difficult, Jackson, so just stop trying," she says before walking out the door. Luckily, I received the text seconds earlier indicating they were finished.

I growl out loud as the door closes behind her. Boy, did she just challenge the bear in me. Taking the high road didn't work, so it's time to move forward with my plan.

Opening my email, I see that Cici came through for me. There's a file waiting there with at least a dozen opportunities in and around Bozeman. It wasn't necessarily at the top of my list to invest there, but she's been on me about it for some time, so the possibility was already brewing; this circumstance simply kicked it up a notch.

When Cici left San Diego after college, I swear she had to have closed her eyes and pointed to the map, ending up in a small town in the middle of the Rocky Mountains. It couldn't be any more different from here. However, she chose well because she's been thriving ever since. I give her crap about going into real estate since it's a stone's throw from what she could have been doing, but it's so much more suited for her. She's social, bubbly, and loves interacting with people. I can't say property management is a fun business, but it is lucrative.

That's why it makes sense to branch out into another growing market, and with Cici able to keep an eye on things, it's a good opportunity. She's been nagging me for months about getting up there to take a look. What she doesn't know is that I've already researched the area to see if she was blowing smoke up my ass or if there truly was potential there.

Turns out, there is—a lot. But I've been so busy with all the transactions in the works that I couldn't make it happen.

With the current situation, I can kill two birds with one stone. Mia's birthday is in two weeks, which happens to be perfect timing for a trip to Bozeman and allows me to research available properties before we go. Mia just lost a battle she didn't know she was part of.

Mia

The rest of the day was spent avoiding Jackson like the plague, saving myself from any more crazy. Where did that conversation come from? He was still condescending, but the genuine concern came out of nowhere. Did he just wake up this morning and decide to give a damn, or what? No part of me would ever confide in Jackson about this, and he's not at the top of my list to ask for help, either. In fact, I'm pretty sure he doesn't make the list at all.

Part of me wants to tell someone what's happening, but the more sensible half wins. It's too dangerous to drag anyone into this, and I can't even think about what would happen to my mom if these guys found out I'd told someone. I'll be okay if I just follow their orders and play along.

I'm glad Walker is coming over soon to look at my dating matches again. A distraction is exactly what I need right now. If I had a dollar for every negative thought that ran through my head these days, I'd be able to pay my dad's debt off.

I'm shaking my head at the absurdity of my life as I walk up the front steps, open my front door, and freeze. The worst of my negative thoughts is in my living room.

"Well, look who made it home. We missed ya, darlin'," Jay says as he sits back casually on our sofa like he owns the place while Frank stands beside him.

"Can you give me some sort of heads-up next time?" I ask as I close the door and set my purse and phone down. I'm not as scared as I was last time since I know they won't kill me until they have their money.

"Now, what'd be the fun in that? Besides, we had a nice look around, familiarizin' ourselves with yer humble abode and all the nooks and crannies. Yer not very good at hidin' stuff, darlin', but we appreciate ya makin' it easy on us." He holds up a wad of cash—*my* wad of cash. "This here is a nice chunk'a change to get ya started. Keep it up and you'll be done in no time."

Shit, I'm instantly panicking. Did they find it all? "How do I know you're keeping track? And how will I have enough to enter the next game if you take it all?"

"Don't worry, sweet cheeks. We'll make sure not to miss a penny. You'll figure out yer buy-in, I'm sure. Yer workin' every damn day, aren't ya? Seems like that should cover it." He's still sitting with his arm slung over the couch, legs spread, one bent at the knee and the other straight out. "Or maybe I'd be inclined to leave ya a bit if ya give me somethin' in return, huh? Ya want to come here and work for it?" He grabs his crotch and squeezes while Frank stands there with a sneer on his face.

"Thanks, but I'll figure something else out. How long until the next game?" As disgusted as they make me, I won't let it show. I learned my lesson last time not to get worked up. They're like dogs, feeding on my fear.

"You'll just have to wait and see, darlin'." He gets up and walks toward me, making me brace myself. I'm still standing in the entryway and don't want any more marks on my body for Jackson to question.

Stopping within inches, he grabs my chin firmly. "Now, if you'd like to play a little nicer, I'm sure we could be more accommodatin'." He leans close and whispers in my ear as I freeze. "You might even like it." He licks my ear, and I cringe, closing my eyes in disgust.

"I'm fine waiting" is all I manage, hoping he accepts it. If he decides to go further, there's not much I can do to defend myself against two strong men. I'm silently praying he backs off.

He does, thank God. I inhale deeply as he lets go. Frank is right behind him and continues to stare at me like he's visualizing me naked. It's disgusting.

"Well, then, I guess we'll leave ya to it. You'll be hearin' from us again soon, darlin'. Be sure to call if ya change yer mind about the workin' arrangement." He snickers before opening the door, and both men walk out.

My shoulders immediately cave, and I take a few deep breaths to steady my nerves when I suddenly remember he just walked out with all my cash. I bolt up the stairs and freeze in the doorway to my room. It's trashed. Everything's out of my drawers, the mattress is half on the floor, and all the shelves are empty. They left no stone unturned. Thank God it was enough to satisfy them, or they probably would have done this to the entire house.

Crap, there's no way Walker can come over with this mess, and I'll never get it cleaned up in time. Remembering my phone is still in the entryway, I shut the door and go back downstairs to grab it, dialing as I head into the kitchen to start dinner.

"Hey, girl, what's up? Are you ready for some man shopping tonight?" Leave it to Walker to put a smile on my face at a time like this.

"Sadly, no. It's been such a long day that I'm exhausted. I was actually looking forward to it, if you can believe it, but I'm barely going to make it through dinner. Can we meet tomorrow instead?"

"Yeah, I'm free tomorrow. You sound like you got hit by a Mack truck, so I know you're not lying just to get out of it. Did something happen today with Jackson?" he asks suspiciously.

"Nothing out of the ordinary. Well, unless you put being nice in that category. He was trying to be all protective about me playing poker, which he has no business doing. I swear he acts like my dad at times."

"Maybe he *wants* to be your daddy." He chuckles, and even though I'm naïve, I'm not that clueless.

"You're gross. He does not. He wants to criticize me and treat me like a child. It's annoying. He said he was worried about me, but come on—a few weeks ago, he couldn't stand the sight of me, and now he expects me to believe he cares? Whatever."

"I don't know, but that sounds like a daddy to me." He laughs. "Seriously, though, maybe he finally sees the awesome person you are and feels differently. You did say he stopped trying to get you to quit a few weeks ago, right?" Walker is constantly searching for the bright side of things.

"Tolerating and liking are two different things, and I don't know that we've passed the tolerating stage. What I do know is that I don't care. Anyway, thanks for switching to tomorrow. I won't bail, I promise."

"Sounds good. Get some sleep, and I'll see you tomorrow night. Bye, babe."

"Bye." I hang up with a heavy dread settling over me. I need to make it through dinner before a long night of putting my room back together and figuring out what to do now that my nest egg is completely depleted.

9

PLANTING THE SEED

Jackson

I'M CASUALLY LOOKING AT TODAY'S REPORT FROM THE SECURITY FIRM
with no expectation of anything new. It's been a week and a half since I
put protection on Mia, and I'm no closer to the truth than I was then.
But at least I know I'm not imagining things. The first day they were on
duty, two shady-looking men were spotted coming out of the house after
Mia had been home for twenty minutes but weren't seen going in, which
means they were already inside waiting.

For the briefest second, after initially reading the report, I wondered
if Mia had been telling the truth about her special interests, but common
sense wiped that notion out quickly. She's too naïve for that to be the case,
and twenty minutes wasn't long enough for anything. Plus, the report
from two other dates she went on proves she likes her boys vanilla, judging from the pictures. I instructed security to warn off the potential suit-
ors after each date concluded. I'm an asshole for interfering, but for some
reason I've yet to name; I can't stand the thought of her with anyone else.

I've backed off from trying to talk to her, returned to our simple
boss-employee relationship, and given up prying for the truth. We're doing
better this way and are more cordial with each other. I hoped security

would fill in the blanks, allowing me to take it from there, but that's not happening. I'm starting to get impatient, and my restraint is waning. The question of who these guys are and why they're showing up are answers I want now since the report I'm reviewing details another visit yesterday.

The only good news is the lack of more brutality. I've been watching closely for it unless it's been in places I can't see, and I don't think that's the case since she hasn't been skittish again. But because I've been watching her, I've also noticed how tired she's been. And since I'm not getting any answers, it might be time to attempt the nice-guy approach again. Not that it worked before, but with the past few weeks going smoothly, maybe she's warmed up to me.

God knows, my attraction hasn't cooled down. The more I'm around her, the more it grows. She's gorgeous, number one, but after witnessing her competence at work and discovering her incredible poker skills, she's enough to make any man fall at her feet. And therein lies the problem— she's not old enough for any man, let alone me. I'm counting the days until she will be, with the date already highlighted on my calendar. As for now, it's time for round two of Operation Nice Guy.

"Mia, can I see you for a minute?" I say over the intercom and hear the responding, 'Be right there.'

We never did recover from the 'eye-contact orgasm' incident, as Braden calls it, with the door staying closed since—albeit unnecessarily, because I've had no more office visits of that nature. In fact, I haven't had much of anything because nothing seems to satisfy me anymore. I've gotten off to that memory more times than I can count, whether by my hand or someone else—which, as I said, hasn't been often. In hindsight, it's probably a good thing the door remains closed; otherwise, I'd be tuned in to her every move and never get a damn thing done.

"Come in," I respond to a light knock on the door.

My physical reaction when she walks toward me never lessens. If it weren't for the desk to hide the erection I get every time, she'd know just how strong my attraction is.

"What can I do for you?" And then there's that—the way my dick wants to manipulate everything out of her mouth into something sexual.

I clear my throat before replying. "I need you to gather information for a few properties I'll be looking at in Montana. I made a list for each one. It might take some digging to track everything down, but I'm sure you'll figure it out."

"Will do. I'll let you know if I hit any roadblocks. Anything else?" She takes the list I hand her, ready to retreat.

"Yeah. I'm heading to Bozeman next weekend to view the buildings in person, and I booked you a ticket to go with me."

"You what?" Her eyes go wide.

"I'd like you to be there so you can take notes and keep track of questions, concerns, pros, cons, and anything else relevant. Are you good with that?"

"You didn't think to ask me first? I… I can't just leave. I have responsibilities." She's practically panicking. I expected surprise, but not this. I figured she'd be thrilled to go on a business trip. Most assistants would jump at the chance.

"What kind of responsibilities? It's summer, and this is your only job, right?" I'm curious to hear what she comes up with.

"Well, I make dinner for my mom every night. I have a date next weekend. And Walker and I are going out to celebrate my birthday." She's grasping for excuses.

"I'm sure your best friend and *date* would understand rescheduling for a work commitment. As for dinners, I'd be happy to pay for a service if that's the sticking point. Like I said, it would be nice for you to be there so I don't have to reiterate everything when I get back. Can you make it happen?"

The contemplative look on her face as she turns her head to the side to think lets me know I'm making headway. "If it's that important to you, let me see what I can do. The meal service isn't necessary. I'll make extra in advance if I go."

"Why do you make dinners? Does your mom not cook?"

This question brings her straight from annoyed to downright angry, causing her to lay into me before I can backtrack. So much for the nice approach.

"My mom works her butt off cleaning all day to support us. She shouldn't have to shoulder that alone, but she does. The last thing I want is for her to come home to cook and clean more. It's called caring for someone else, in case you aren't familiar with the sentiment." She's fierce when she's pissed. I like it.

"Are you as talented at cooking as playing poker and being an executive assistant?" I need to get back on track with her. Mr. Nice Guy has some ground to cover.

"Uhhh…" I've finally rendered her speechless.

"I'm just trying to find out if there's anything you're *not* good at." I smile, imagining other things we could check off that list.

"Well, it's pretty easy to follow a recipe, so if that's all it takes, then sure."

"You're talented and modest then. Listen, Mia, I'd like you to join me on this trip. Will you please try to make it happen?" I ask earnestly.

She's thinking, and I can practically see the debate taking place in her mind before she sighs dramatically. "Okay, fine. Send me the itinerary so I can let my mom know and plan ahead. I'll try to reschedule the other stuff. When do you want all this information?" She holds up the list.

"Have it by the time we leave to review during the flight. That'll give you plenty of time to find everything. I'll forward you the ticket right away so you have the details. And Mia, thank you… I promise I'll make it worth your while." I wink—might as well start planting the seed.

"Uh… the experience alone is worth it. I'm sorry I reacted the way I did. I know this is a good opportunity, and you don't have to thank me since you really didn't give me much choice. I'll get started on this list." She takes her leave after that and shuts the door behind her.

Happy to have that settled, I go online to book our tickets. I told her I'd already booked, thinking she'd be more likely to say yes. Next, I call the hotel Cici suggested and make sure to request adjoining rooms. With Mia turning eighteen right before we leave, nothing prevents me from making a move. She must be aware of my attraction from my behavior over the past couple of months. From grinding into her at poker to climaxing while staring at her, I'd say it's pretty obvious.

Next on the list is taking care of Mia's birthday dinner next week. I call the restaurant my parents told me about to verify they have the reservation and leave my card on file to pay for everything. And because I know the owner, I request someone to text me when they're finishing the main course.

Eli: TGIF, plan for tonight?

Braden: Club?

Me: Sure.

Eli: Jackson, cool if Sebastian comes? Lily has some girl thing.

Me: That's fine. Surprised she's allowed…

Eli: Be sure to tell him that. See you there.

Braden: I can't wait to see that. Later, bitches.

Mia

Hours of research later, I'm still replaying the conversation with Jackson and wondering if the wink, along with his final comment, was part of my imagination. God knows I've imagined some things lately involving Jackson that I certainly should not be. But if I'm reading things correctly, Jackson's thoughts might not be far from mine. And that right there is a problem.

Things have been going so smoothly between us. It's been strictly professional—outside my imagination, of course. But honestly, we've come a long way. We work well together, and when he's not hounding me about my personal life, we get along just fine. I'm amazed at how competent he is in running the business. The day-to-day operations have an entire staff to handle, but the property transactions he's initiating to increase their portfolio are all on him. Not only is he talented… but sexy as hell while he's at it.

Grrrr. I need to get my head out of the gutter. Especially with this trip we're taking. *Business trip.* I'll need to remind myself often if I'm going to get through it with my virginity—I mean sanity. I haven't felt anything like what Jackson has made me feel with any of the dates I've had, and a couple of them have ended with pretty good make-out sessions. How can someone I've never even touched get me more worked up than everyone else?

There's his body, of course, which is fricking built. From his broad shoulders to the biceps bulging under his shirt, who wouldn't want to strip him down and lick each muscle? Then, when he shows his megawatt smile, like he did earlier, with dimples to drown in and pearly white teeth… holy crap, Batman, no one stands a chance. But I cannot be hot for my boss. My decade-older boss, who has a new bed partner every night of the week, and is so far out of my league it's insane. My boss who knows about my secret hobby, and could ruin me if he found out the reason behind it.

Basically, this trip is a disaster waiting to happen, and I'll need to be on my game to stay on track because if the heat between us isn't just my imagination, then I'm in trouble.

Wait until Walker hears about this new development. I'm just now calling him on my way home from work to let him know I'm staying at his house since I have another live game tonight.

He picks up on the first ring. "Hey, babe. What's cookin', good-lookin'?"

"Nothing yet, but I'm going home to start dinner." I laugh as I picture him rolling his eyes. "There's actually a lot cooking, but first things first, can I crash at your place tonight? I have another game."

"You don't need to ask every time. Just give me a heads-up so you don't end up walking into something you'd rather not see." I hear his smirk in those words.

"Ew, gross." I make a gagging noise. "I for sure don't want to see that. No offense, just not my thing."

"You mean it wouldn't be as good as watching your boss get off in front of you?" He laughs.

"Ha ha, asshole. But, speaking of—"

"Oh my God, did it happen again?"

"*No!* No, thank God. I don't know if I'd survive another show. But here's the thing. He wants me to go to Montana with him next weekend to look at some real estate he's interested in. He wants me there to take notes and keep track of everything, and he already bought my ticket, so we'll have to postpone my birthday celebration." I press my lips together, dreading his reaction.

"Get the fuck out. Seriously? Oh, Mia, this guy is *so* hot for you. Take notes, my ass. You realize it'll be perfectly legal for you to do the nasty while you're there since it's after your birthday. I bet I'm not the only one to think of that."

"We will not be doing anything, I can assure you."

"Care to make a wager?" He asks confidently.

"I don't gamble unless there are cards involved." *Nor do I make un-sure bets.*

"Well, either way, it's time for me to meet this guy. You're not going on that trip until I do." Whoa, that is not what I expected to hear.

"I already said I'd go, and you can't make a judgment call after meeting someone for five minutes anyway. How would you even get the chance to meet him?" He can't be serious, can he?

"You seem to forget I have a car. So here's the plan. Since I don't get to take you out for your birthday as planned, I'm taking you to lunch on Wednesday instead. I'll come in when I pick you up so you can introduce us."

"But—"

"I'm not taking no for an answer—deal with it. Text me when you're on your way tonight, and not that you need it, but good luck."

I roll my eyes and groan. "Thanks, I'll keep you posted. Bye."

I hang up before walking into the house. Even though the assholes were here yesterday to collect money from a couple of online tournaments I'd won and have no reason to be here today, I'm in the habit of being on edge every time I get home. They've shown up three times so far.

Luckily, they're not monitoring my every move and have no idea I've been burning the candle at both ends, playing way more online games to try and build a nest egg back up. I'm being smart this time by keeping the money hidden in my desk at work. Hopefully, I'll be done with this mess before Cindy comes back.

I'm exhausted between my day job and sometimes staying up half the night playing in online tournaments. I might be heading toward a major crash if I don't take a break soon, but I'm determined to pay this debt off as quickly as possible so I can return to normal. Although, I may have forgotten what normal *is* at this point.

I'm a zombie as I make dinner, but manage to keep from falling asleep during dinner. Mom insisted on doing the dishes, giving me extra time to get ready for tonight's tournament. This game is in the industrial part of town, so I don't feel like I need to dress as nice as the last one, but a distraction is still a distraction, so I choose one of my low-cut tops with a pair of jeans and flats. It's at least comfortable. Knowing the evening is chilly, I grab a jacket and head downstairs.

"Hey, Mom, I'm staying at Walker's tonight, so don't wait up," I say, walking over to hug her goodbye.

"All right, mija, I'll see you tomorrow, then. Be safe, especially at night, and pay attention to your surroundings. I hate you taking public transportation when it's dark. It makes me nervous. Will you text me when you're in for the night?" She's wrapped in a blanket on the couch with one of her romance novels. I wish she'd get out and date instead of just reading about it. Although, who am I to judge?

"Yeah, I can do that."

"Thank you, mija. I love you." She goes back to her book.

"Love you, too, Mom. Bye."

Locking the door behind me, I head toward the bus stop. There's a blue sedan-type car down the street that I've been noticing for a couple of weeks now. It's always parked in the same spot and reminds me of a cop car. I'm probably being paranoid, but some part of me wonders if they're keeping their eye on me or if someone else could be. I don't even know who these guys are, whether they're some big mafia-type organization or a gambling outfit. What if they're being investigated, and they've been seen at my house?

My mind races with thoughts and theories, making the commute go quickly. Before I know it, I'm getting off the bus as close to the location as possible when I notice how seedy the area is. Great. I keep my phone in hand on the walk there, ready to dial 911 if needed. Luckily, I arrive without incident, but looking at the warehouse I've stopped in front of, my unease is far from over.

10

HANDS FULL

Jackson

AFTER SPENDING A COUPLE OF HOURS AT THE GYM, I'M MORE THAN ready to unwind at the club. I walk straight up the stairs to the VIP section, where we have a regular table. Everyone's already there, including Sebastian. Not my favorite guy in the world after he flew in and stole the girl I'd had my eye on, but it was my fault for not making a move sooner. A mistake I don't plan on making again.

We buried the hatchet when we came together to rescue Lily from an overzealous admirer who thought kidnapping her was the way to make his intentions clear. Luckily, Sebastian had the resources to find her, and we made it there in time, but it was close. It's why Eli gave me the advice he did, and why I took it. It would have been unforgivable if something happened that could have been prevented.

"Hey, buddy, it's about time you show up. Did you double your routine today or what? I think your muscles might be protesting." Braden loves to razz me about my gym time.

"Dude, you wish you had half this going for you." I go to the gym as much for my mind as I do for my body. It's my outlet—time to think, plan, and reflect.

"Hell, I'd take a quarter," Braden says.

"You're full of shit, Braden. I see you at the gym every day. Jackson's just in a league of his own. It's unattainable for us non-Hulk types," Eli interjects.

"Hey, Sebastian, I haven't seen you in a while. Aren't you and Lily joined at the hip?" I get the inevitable out of the way and acknowledge his presence.

He chuckles. "Now and then, I let her out of my sight. She'll be here after dinner with some other ladies from the office. So, what's this I hear about some underage girl you're hung up on?"

I'm sure Eli's told him all about it. They're tight, being twins and all. "Four more days until she's legal, and so far I haven't touched her. She is a fucking bombshell, though. My discipline has been remarkable considering, but I suppose the risk of bars makes it easier." I say, hearing snickers from Braden and Eli.

Sebastian continues, "I hear she's in trouble."

"I'm not sure, but something's up. I'm hoping to figure it out next week when we visit Cici and investigate some properties there."

"You're visiting Cici? How is she?" Eli never divulged, but I knew there was more to him and my sister than they let on.

"Yeah, finally. She seems to be thriving there. She's been begging me to visit for months, dangling investment opportunities to entice me. It's good timing." *Impeccable* timing.

"I bet it is since your travel buddy will be legal, huh?" Braden lifts his beer to cheers.

"I can't deny it won't suck to finally get my hands on her, but I'm also trying to help, not just fuck her."

"Fucking… helping." Braden lifts both his hands in a pendulum-scale motion. "I'd say both are equally important. You've been pining over this girl for two months now. Might as well go for it already." He's the biggest manwhore of the group, thoroughly enjoying his single status over the last year.

Not that I have room to talk. Hell, weeks ago, I'd been making the rounds myself. Now, I'm just biding my time until I can satisfy my fantasy without the use of my hand and imagination. If her reaction to me caging her in at poker was any indication, it won't be a hard sell.

"We'll see. But I need to figure out what's going on with her first. My gut tells me something's up even though she insists there isn't. She's always tired and hasn't been her usual self since I caught sight of those marks."

My phone rings as I finish my comment. When I pull it out of my pocket, the security firm lights up the screen. Speak of the devil.

"Hello?" I answer immediately.

"Good evening, Mr. Soloman. I've just tracked Mia to an industrial building in the warehouse district. There are no windows at ground level, so I can't see what's happening without going in. A few nicer cars are parked outside, so there are a handful of people already here. I don't have a problem checking it out, but I didn't want to put you in a bad spot by blowing my cover and thought I'd get your thoughts first."

Well, fuck. "Are you sure it's not just some teenage rager? That seems typical for a Friday night." I offer.

"There's no loud music coming from inside, and I'd expect more teenagers to show up if that were the case. So far, I've only seen two other males enter, casually dressed in their mid-thirties. It's your call, boss. We can go in or wait it out."

"How did she look going in? Was she hesitant or scared?" If that's the case, he should have started with that information.

"She appeared normal, cautious of her surroundings, but nothing out of the ordinary. She hesitated before going in, possibly from fear, but nothing I could make out from where I was standing."

"Text me the address, and I'll get back to you in five minutes with my decision. I have an idea what we're dealing with. Thank you for the call," I say before hanging up.

"Goddammit. Mia's at another tournament, and it's a lot seedier than the last one. What should I do? She doesn't know I'm having her followed, so I'm reluctant to send security in. Any chance you have a connection to this one?" I show the address to Eli, who's usually the one to hook us up when a good game comes up. I'm assuming this one is not, which is why we didn't hear about it.

"Let me check." He looks down and starts scrolling on his phone.

"Why don't you just go there yourself and pull her out?" Sebastian asks. He wouldn't hesitate to do just that, consequences be damned.

"Because there's no reason for me to know she's there. I'd have to tell her I've been having her followed, and I'm pretty sure that won't go over well."

"I agree with Sebastian. Fuck it. If she'll end up mad eventually, why does it matter if it's today or some other day?" Braden gives his two cents.

I scowl at him, telling him exactly what I don't say aloud—he's supposed to be on my side.

"Did you find anything?" I ask Eli, still not sure what the right move is.

"There's a reason I didn't suggest we go to this one," he replies. "The guys putting it on aren't ones you or I want to be involved with. It's a bad idea for Mia to be hanging around this group. If I were you, I'd meet your guy and go in together. You don't want to stir up trouble, but getting her out of there is probably worth the risk."

"Fuck. How is she even getting into this shit? Maybe that's where I need to start. How do you end up on the list for a game like this?" I direct my question toward Eli since he seems to be in the know.

"Sorry, man, knowing criminals is the only way to get into these kinds of tournaments, which means she's somehow connected to the wrong people." Eli shakes his head and sips his beer.

"Sounds like you've got your hands full with this one. Good luck with that," Sebastian says.

"Yeah, I think I'll need it. Could you contact the host and let him know I'll be stopping by without causing any problems?" If Eli was able to find the game, I'm hoping he can make a connection.

"I don't know, but I'll try. I can't guarantee anything, so tread lightly when you get there."

"Be careful, man, and remember—four more days. Don't do anything stupid," Braden says. *As if I could forget.*

"Yeah, yeah, I get it. You guys enjoy. It looks like I'm out of here."

I text my guy on the way out with instructions to wait and that I'll be there soon.

Mia

This is nothing like the last tournament they sent me to. This one is filled with sleazy men who keep leering, making me uncomfortable. And because they only have one table for twelve, I'm sandwiched between two creepers who keep brushing against me too frequently to be considered accidental. It doesn't help my anxiety that the last text instructed me to be extra nice and not cause any problems with these guys—that there would be consequences otherwise.

We're already down to eight players after an hour, with a couple more about to go out. It takes thirty minutes to knock out the next three players, leaving five, including myself. The good news is that I won't be here all night, but the bad news is that the last guy who went out didn't leave and is trying to make a move on me. He's standing behind me, and my anxiety skyrockets when he starts brushing my cheek while making lewd comments, causing the other guys at the table to laugh at his tactics.

The host, or whoever is at the entrance, calls for a ten-minute break at the absolute worst time, giving this guy the perfect window of opportunity.

He grabs me under my armpit and lifts me out of my chair. "Come here, baby, let's get to know each other a little better." The others just sit back and watch as he pulls me into him.

"I have a boyfriend," I say, trying to stop him before he goes further.

"What he doesn't know won't hurt him. Come on now, you give me what I want, and I'll let you finish the game. Or are you shy and want me to take you somewhere private?" He's holding me tight and starting to lean in.

"No, I don't." I'm not sure what "causing problems" looks like, but I'd say it might be when I try to shove him away only to receive a slap in the face for my efforts. It's so hard that my eyes instantly tear up from the pain.

"Listen, bitch, we were told you'd be good to us if we let you in. Now prove it. I was only going to have a taste, but I think I want the whole meal now."

He spins me around sharply and bends me over the table, holding my back down while he fumbles with my button and zipper, ignoring my protests. He starts grinding into me with his crotch, and panic sets in as the tears start while I struggle to get free.

When I almost lose hope, shouting can be heard from the entrance. All heads swivel, and even though I can't move mine, I recognize one of the voices. I never thought I'd be as happy as I am right now to hear it.

"You want to take your hands off my girl, motherfucker?"

I'm released immediately, and from over my shoulder, see the guy stepping back with his hands up. *His girl?*

"No harm done, man. We didn't know she was taken—we thought she was here for some fun, is all."

I turn to see Jackson walking toward us in utter rage. I'm afraid he might kill someone when I notice there's a guy behind him who looks just as intimidating. He steps forward, pushing the guy who held me down away before Jackson has a chance to get his hands on him.

He pauses for a few heartbeats, taking in the sight of me before enveloping me into his chest. Without any hesitation, I wrap my arms around his waist and cling to him, letting the tears flow while I catch my breath.

That was too close. What is he doing here? What if Frank and Jay find out? What if he *hadn't* shown up? What do I do now? I'm going into panic mode.

"Breathe, Mia. I've got you. You're okay, now." His whispered words calm me as he holds me tight and caresses my hair, rubbing my back with soothing strokes. I hear the others talking in the background but am too unhinged to pay attention to anything being said.

"What are you doing here?" I mumble into his chest, realizing this is the one question burning above all others.

He continues to hold me, running his hand over my back. "Shhh. We'll talk when we get you out of here. How are you doing?"

I lift my head to look around. The guy who shoved me down and the man who came in with Jackson are gone. The others are waiting to play, and I'm not sure what to do. All I want is to go home, crawl into bed, and forget this night ever happened.

"I… I don't know what to do." A whisper is all I manage, but Jackson hears me. He's staring down at me, rubbing my cheek, where I'm sure it's red, and wiping the tears from my eyes.

"Can I get you out of here?" he asks gently.

"I guess so. Or… I don't know. There are only four players left. I could just finish. I don't want to lose my money." It's not an option to lose it after the rest was taken.

"Do you want me to get your buy-in back so you can leave, or do you want to finish? I'll stay if that's what you want." Why is he being so nice to me? And because I'm half delusional, I ended up asking that out loud.

"Answer my question first, Mia. Do you want to stay?" I'm not sure how he manages, but somehow, his question is both soft and firm at the same time, compelling me to respond.

I shake my head.

He doesn't hesitate. "What do you guys think about giving Mia here her money back to make up for the trouble and finish your game without her?" They start to balk, but he adds, "Unless you've already forgotten that she's a better player than all of you combined and will no doubt be taking all your money if she stays."

At that, they shut up and agree to his suggestion.

Jackson stays glued to my side, his arm wrapped protectively around me as he walks us to the entrance, where I'm given my money back. We step outside, and I recoil into Jackson at seeing another man waiting on the sidewalk. He squeezes me in reassurance.

"I got it from here. Thanks for waiting," Jackson tells him. I look up and recognize the man who arrived with him.

"You got it. I'll follow up in the morning." He salutes, then stands in place as he watches Jackson lead me to his car.

I'm not sure what to say or how to act, and I can't wrap my brain around what just happened or is currently happening. My mind is numb as he opens the passenger door and helps me in before walking to the other side. I take a deep breath before he enters, still trying to calm my nerves. He gets in and does the same. We sit in silence as I stare down at my hands, one squeezing the fingers of the other.

He turns toward me and pries them apart, slowly bringing one to his lips and holding it there with his eyes closed. He remains that way, taking deep breaths before finally opening and looking at me. My heart is pounding from the intensity of his stare.

He breaks the silence. "We can't talk about what happened yet because I'm too angry about what I walked into. I just need to get you home." An instant ache forms in my chest at the thought of being without him before he continues. "Can I take you to my place to make sure you're okay? I'd like you with me right now."

I'm too shocked to respond. *Where is this coming from?*

"Please," he pleads.

"Um… sure? I'll just need to text my mom and Walker."

He doesn't say anything, just nods and kisses my fingers before lowering our hands to the console, still not releasing mine from his grip. He drives the whole way using his left hand, unwilling to let me go, forcing me to make do with one hand as well.

I text my mom that I'm in for the night because I know I'll be safe with Jackson. Next, I text Walker and let him know where I'm going and that I'll explain later, but not to worry. His response, "You go, girl!" makes me smile for the first time tonight.

I could lie and tell myself that I'm only going to get answers, like how he knew I was there and who that man was, or I can be honest and admit that I feel safe and was relieved when he suggested taking me home with him. I don't know what this means or why things suddenly feel different between us, but I do know I need him right now as much as he seems to need me.

11

STAY

Jackson

T HE IMAGES KEEP REPLAYING IN MY HEAD. THE MINUTE I SAW THAT fucker holding Mia face down on the table, pressed into her with his hands on her body, I saw red. It's a good thing I didn't stop at my place first and grab my gun, or else I'd probably be in jail right now, which is ironic considering the girl I saved could easily put me there.

All I want to do right now is wrap her in my arms and keep her safe. She's too good a person to be around men like that. Why is she risking her safety to play at those types of poker tournaments? What exactly is she involved in? I need answers one way or another, but right now, that isn't my priority; ensuring she's okay is.

I'm silent on the way to my place, too afraid to speak about what happened and scare her any more than she already is because I'm too angry. Angry that I took so long to get there. Angry at the asshole who thought it was okay to take advantage of a woman. Angry at whatever she's caught up in that put her in this situation, and angry that she won't confide in me so I can help her out of it.

I've decided it's best to remain quiet for the time being until I can calm down and manage a civil conversation. In the meantime, I'm not letting her out of my sight, refusing to take her anywhere other than my condo, which, thank fuck she agreed to. Now that I have her, I'm not letting her go.

The minute I held her, my feelings hit me like a tsunami. I knew there was no going back to the way things were before. Fighting my attraction is one thing, but fighting the feelings bubbling up to the surface is damn near impossible. I want to protect her, care for her—I want to make her mine.

I'm relieved to finally pull into the parking garage from what felt like the longest drive in history. After pulling into my space, the short time it takes to get from my door to hers is long enough to realize that I'm powerless from the need to touch her. Reaching for her hand, I help her out and lead us into the building, refusing to let go. She was silent the entire way here, and I have no idea how she's feeling.

Once inside, I pull her into my arms, and after one deep breath, she breaks down sobbing, giving me the answer. Picking her up and carrying her bridal style, I walk into the living room and sink onto the couch with her head in the crook of my neck while she cries. All I can do is hold her as I caress her hair, moving it off her neck and then rubbing her back while whispering words of comfort. At the same time I console her, I'm trying to erase the earlier images from my mind but failing. I want to hunt that asshole down and make him pay for causing Mia's anguish. I'm lost to this girl.

"I'm sorry. I just can't stop thinking about what would've happened if you hadn't shown up." She sucks in air as she tries to speak.

"Shhhh. Mia, I've got you. Let's not think about what could've happened and just be grateful it didn't. I'm here now. I won't let anyone hurt you, I promise."

"You can't promise that. Oh my God, I'm so stupid. What was I thinking?" Well, at least she's admitting to that.

"I don't think you're ready for that conversation. I'm certainly not." I give the softest chuckle to make light of the statement and not freak her out, but fuck no, I'm not ready for it yet. She'll need to be in a better state of mind because I have a few choice words I won't be able to hold back.

"I'm not sure I'll ever be ready. Why did you bring me here? I just… I don't know why you're being so nice. What's going on?" She's still cradled in my lap with her head resting on my chest. The tears have stopped, and she's beginning to breathe normally.

"I brought you here because… fuck, Mia, I had to. The thought of taking you somewhere else… it just wasn't an option. This need to hold you, keep you safe, is too damn strong to do anything else." I think it's time to come clean about how I feel about her.

"Mia, I'm sorry. I know I've been a complete asshole. It's the only thing I could do to keep my distance. The truth is, I'm so fucking attracted to you that it's killing me. I know I'm too old for you, not to mention your boss, but the worst part is that I can't even legally touch you, and I'm not used to keeping my hands to myself. Making you the enemy was to prevent me from taking what I really wanted. And, Mia, I want you. In the worst way possible."

Mia

Am I in the twilight zone? Is something wrong with my hearing? My body just became hyperaware that I was sitting in Jackson's lap while he admitted to wanting me. *Oh. My. God.* I'm tingling between my legs, muscles clenching of their own accord, and I know I should not be feeling this way after all that's happened, but I can't help it.

"Mia, please… don't do that." His words are almost pleading.

Oh… ohhhh… I feel his erection growing under me. Holy… Should I move over, or do I just stay still? What if my body clenches again by accident? Oh crap, it just did. Thinking about it obviously isn't helping. He's the only one who makes me feel this way, and there's no denying my thoughts are *very* inappropriate at the moment. And now I'm making it worse as the images running through my mind cause me to clench again. This is going downhill fast.

"How about we move you over so we can talk?" His voice comes out gravelly as he lifts me easily, setting me on the couch beside him with zero space between us. He chuckles. "There, that's better. Now, tell me what you're thinking… other than the obvious." My panties melt at the cheeky smile he flashes. Good thing I'm not on his lap anymore.

Our fingers are entwined while his other arm keeps me pinned to his side. I don't think he's let go since the moment he showed up tonight, other than getting in and out of the car. I guess he wasn't kidding about needing to hold me.

"I don't know what to say. I'm obviously attracted to you, but you've pretty much treated me like crap from day one. And yeah, you've been better recently and even nice this week, but I still feel sort of blindsided."

"So, you're attracted to me, huh?" He smirks.

"That's all you got out of that?" I ask in disbelief.

"I was focusing on the positive." He chuckles.

"Seriously, Jackson, you've been a jerk. I don't get it. You've treated me like a child, acted like I wasn't capable, and have basically demeaned me for the past two months. I'll give you credit for getting better the last few weeks, but before that, you were horrible. You're telling me that was all just an act the entire time?" I'm shocked by his confession, but I'm also irritated that I had to put up with him, all because he couldn't handle it.

"Okay, maybe not the *entire* time. Yes, I was attracted to you from day one. I mean, you're beautiful. How could anyone not be? But my resentment toward you was stronger. Not only were you completely off-limits, frustratingly so, but I also didn't think you were qualified." I tense at that, and he sighs. "Look, I'm under a lot of pressure. Running this company alone while trying to take it to the next level puts a lot on my plate. And through it all, Cindy's been my rock, keeping me going day in and day out, and then suddenly you're forced on me by the same people I'm trying to prove myself to. I expected the worst when they told me."

"Gee, thanks," I say sarcastically. Although his perspective *is* understandable, and I understand why he felt the way he did.

"But when Cindy went into labor early, and I saw you in action that first day, I could tell you were more than I gave you credit for. But I was too stubborn to let go of your age. I was at war with myself, one side wanting to prove you'd fail and the other realizing how amazing you were. I'm so sorry I put you through hell, and I hope you'll forgive me so we can move forward." He ends his explanation with a kiss on my head, which is resting on his shoulder.

He doesn't press me to respond immediately, and I don't, staying silent while I process his words and internalize this new reality. What does he mean by "move forward"? As in, getting along in the office? Or something more? And what do *I* want? Can I overlook the fact that he's been a jerk to me over the last two months? And then there's this screwed-up situation I'm in. I can't involve him—though he's already more involved than I thought if he found me tonight. Maybe we should have that conversation before we dive further into what his intention is.

"Jackson, I think we need to talk about tonight first. How did you know where I was?" I sit up, extracting myself from his hold to face him.

Instead of answering, he reaches up to caress my cheek, concern reflected in his eyes. "First, how are you feeling? Do you hurt anywhere?" I can hear the anger underneath the surface of his words.

"I'm doing better." Surprisingly, I'm not as weirded out as I should be. Being here with Jackson makes me feel safe... comfortable even.

"What about your pain, Mia? Did he hurt you anywhere other than your face?" He grimaces.

"I'm okay." He gives me a stern look. "All right, I have a slight headache, and my cheek hurts. He didn't have a chance to do anything else. He was just rough, is all."

Upon hearing my last words, he closes his eyes, and his chest slowly expands before deflating. "Come on, let's go get you something to drink and a couple of aspirin. Then we'll talk." He stands up and tugs my hand.

Heading to the kitchen, he guides me to the island with my back up against it and stops before me, caging me in against the counter. Looking directly into my eyes, he says, "I'm so damn sorry I didn't get there sooner." He presses his lips to my forehead before he backs away to get a glass of water and two pain pills out of the cupboard, handing them to me expectantly.

After I down the entire thing, along with the medicine, he leads me back to the couch, positioning us so we're facing each other, our hands clasped in his lap.

"Are you going to tell me how you knew where I was?" I ask before he has a chance to speak.

He smirks. "How about an answer for an answer?" His right eyebrow rises in question before I turn my head to look away.

Shit. Why didn't I see this coming?

"Don't you want to play this game, Mia? If you'll recall, I have quite a few unanswered questions myself."

"I answered all your questions. You just didn't like the answers," I say defiantly.

"Is that how you'd like this to go, then? Because I'd be happy to give you some answers that *you* won't like." He smirks, and I growl in response.

I'm not sure where to go from here. I don't want to lie anymore, but the truth can't come out. And I can't expect him to come clean if I'm unwilling to do the same. It's frustrating that he's right and has me backed into a corner.

"Are you ready to tell me what's going on and why the hell you were at a game like that? Because I have a lot to say on the matter. Or are we at an impasse for now?" He brings my hand to his mouth and kisses it.

His lips on my skin cause flutters in my belly, making me wonder how much better they would feel on my mouth. Maybe we should return to that topic since we probably won't get anywhere on this one.

"What did you mean earlier when you said you wanted to move forward? Do you mean, start being nice to each other in the office or…?" I leave the question unfinished, unsure how to phrase it.

"Nice change of subject, but I'll take the bait. What I meant is that I don't want to hide my attraction to you anymore. And to finally admit that ever since that day you walked in on me, I've been imagining *you* on your knees, your mouth around my dick, until you're swallowing every… last… drop."

My breath catches as the image comes to mind, and I'm trying hard to control the response from my body. Is it possible to orgasm from words alone?

"Oh." I try to normalize my breathing, which could currently be labeled as panting.

He smirks. "If your reaction is any indication, I think you're just as interested in my fantasy as I am. Unfortunately, neither of us can give in yet. I'm warning you now, though, when you're old enough to be fucked by a man and not a boy, I'll be the first in line. Does that clear up any confusion about how I'd like to move forward?"

"Yep. All clear." *Holy shit. Is it boiling in here, or is it just me?*

"Your blushing is adorable. I can't wait to make you blush with more than just my words." He runs his finger down my arm, causing goose bumps to rise in its wake.

"I also want you to know that this isn't just sexual attraction. That did come first, but I hope you were listening earlier when I said you were special. You're the full package, Mia. You blow me away with your drive, your common sense, and the way you carry yourself so assuredly. I tried to fight my feelings, lying to myself that it was just physical, but it's so much more. Can we start over so I can prove it and make up for being such a prick?" He's looking at me expectantly, wanting a response this time.

"Well, you're making a good case, I'll give you that. There's no doubt that the physical attraction is mutual. As far as the other stuff goes, I'd say you're off to a good start. So, I'm not opposed to the idea. And we'll definitely have to start over… because it'll take me a while to forget what a bosshole you are." I smile up at him and am met with laughter.

"I earned that and more. I promise I won't be deserving of that title anymore. I'll even do one better and work toward earning the title of boyfriend if that's okay with you."

Swoon.

"You don't need my permission to work toward it, just my acceptance if it's earned." I can't believe this is the same Jackson as yesterday. If I didn't know better, I'd think the aliens were back for good.

"Fair enough. I'll take that as a win for now. Will you stay with me tonight?" He sees my shock. "Not for anything but sleeping… in my arms. I swear I won't make a move on you." He gives me the Scout salute, making me giggle. However, I'm not sure if I'm relieved or disappointed.

"I'll stay, but I need to text Walker and tell him I won't be there tonight."

Jackson

When she pulls her phone out and starts texting, I catch sight of the previous message and grin.

"I take it he approves?" I ask as I raise my eyebrows and tilt my head toward her screen. She blushes again, which I've now become addicted to seeing.

"Yeah, he's been on your side since the office incident. He thought it was hot. Then, when you cornered me at poker, he tried to get me to admit I wanted you. And by the way—" She bites her lip and looks down. She's so fucking sexy, and she doesn't even know it. "—he's insisting to meet you before I go to Montana." Her hesitance is adorable.

"Is that so? And when will this be happening?" I'm glad to hear she has someone in her corner, although I wonder if he's aware of what's really going on with her. I'd like to have a private conversation with him, so I'd say his insistence on meeting me works out in my favor.

"On Wednesday. He's coming to pick me up for my birthday lunch since our previous plan was canceled because of a certain bosshole."

"Oh really?" I reach over and tickle her, causing her to erupt in laughter. It's music to my ears. She's beautiful when she smiles, and my heart feels like it grows larger with each one I earn. She almost manages to escape, but I pull her in tight before she's out of reach.

As soon as she's back in my lap, her arms fling around my neck, hugging me tightly. "Thank you for coming to my rescue. I don't think I said it earlier, and I… I know you don't want to think about it, but if you didn't come when you did… I might not be the same person sitting here. So, thank you."

I squeeze her tighter, knowing how right she is, and start to feel the anger bubbling up again. Before it gets too out of control, I frame her face with my hands, holding it inches from mine. "I won't let anyone hurt you, I promise you that. I'll protect you no matter what." Our lips are so close, and my resistance is wavering. "God, you have no idea how bad I want to kiss you right now."

"Why don't you, then?" she challenges me.

"You're not old enough yet," I say matter-of-factly, purposefully riling her up. She rolls her eyes, making me grin and plant my lips on the tip of her nose. "But also because I want you to see the real me before I start making moves on you. Let's take a few days to get to know each other in a new light and see if you're still interested in kissing me on your birthday. And maybe I'll even have a surprise for you." I bring her in and kiss her forehead.

"I don't like surprises." She's cute when she pouts. Tonight, I'm discovering the many sides of Mia.

"I think you'll like this one." I scoot out from under her and stand, reaching my hand out. "Are you ready for bed? It's been a long day for both of us."

"Bed sounds good—I mean sleep… in the bed." Her blush is fierce.

"I knew what you meant, Mia. Don't worry, I'll keep my hands to myself… mostly," I say, wagging my brows in her direction while leading her down the hallway.

After escorting her through my bedroom to the master bath, I place a hairbrush, along with a brand-new toothbrush, on the counter.

"I picked up the habit of keeping extras from my parents. Get ready for bed, and I'll set some clothes out for you." Squeezing her hand before letting go, I walk out, shutting the door behind me.

To distract myself, I grab two water bottles, place one on each nightstand, and plug my phone in next to the bed.

When she's finished, we trade places so I can get ready and give her time to change. Usually, I sleep naked, but for Mia's sake—and mine, I leave my boxers and undershirt on. For now, the more layers between us, the better.

My dick wakes up at the sight of Mia lying in my bed. However, I can't help but smirk when I notice that she's stiff as a log with the covers pulled up to her neck. It's like she's never been in a man's bed before. Well, I suppose she hasn't, only boys'. Or maybe she's just nervous to be in *my* bed. Normally, I wouldn't blame her, but I did promise not to make a move tonight.

"Nervous, Mia?" I tease.

"No! Why would I be? I just didn't know which side to take, and I was worried I picked the wrong one."

I give her a skeptical look while pointing to my phone. "Riiight. Hmm, it should've been obvious since I already plugged my phone in. You sure you're not nervous?"

"I'm sure." She's still clutching the covers in a death grip, motionless save for her head turned my way, nodding.

I climb in and move toward the middle. "Then you, little girl, better get over here and let me hold you."

"You did *not* just call me that." She makes no move to join me.

"I did, and I'm going to until your birthday because I know how much you love it. Isn't that nice of me?" I smile.

"Oh my God, you're pathetic. You're seriously going to, just to piss me off, aren't you?" She shakes her head in frustration and rolls her eyes. I love messing with her. That won't ever change.

Turning off the light, I lie on my back and pull her over to me. "Maybe, or maybe I like calling you that because it gets me hot. What gets you hot, Mia?" I probably shouldn't be going down this path, but I'm having too much fun pushing her buttons.

"Ummm, I don't know," she squeaks.

"Hmmm, we'll have to figure that out together, then—after your birthday." If only my dick would get that memo because he's been fighting to be let loose all night.

I nuzzle her into me, caressing her back and running my fingers through her hair. She's tucked into my side with her head on my chest, and I can feel her rapid heartbeat. I'm glad we're on the same page sexually, but it would be nice if she actually liked me first.

"Get some rest, little girl. I'll keep you safe." I smile as I kiss her forehead, and she groans in response. Within minutes, her breathing turns heavy, telling me she's already succumbed to her exhaustion.

It's nice having her in my bed, snuggled up to me as if it's the most normal thing in the world. Having her in my arms feels right, like it's where she belongs. Never in a million years did I think this was how my day would end. I didn't plan on making my intentions known until her birthday but couldn't stop myself after what happened.

It's crazy what a difference a day makes when, just this morning, we were arguing as usual. And what a day it was. The fury I felt at seeing her about to be—I can't even fathom the word—is inexpressible. It would never have happened if she'd simply told me what was going on so I could help her. I'm beyond frustrated that she won't confide in me and more determined than ever to earn her trust until she does. I just pray nothing else happens until then.

How she'll react when she finds out I've been having her followed has me equally concerned. Sure, it's for her safety, but will she see it that way? When the time comes, I anticipate it to be a battle of wills, and if I'm lucky, I'll come out the winner. Until then, I'm not changing anything other than beefing up security, starting tomorrow. It's worth the risk of her anger rather than any harm coming to her. I just hope she sees it that way in the end.

12

SEDUCTION

Mia

Before I fully come to, I notice the heat from a body behind me and something hard pressing into my backside. As evidenced by his breathing, Jackson is still asleep, so I remain as motionless as possible. I'm afraid that any movement might wake him, and given our current position, I'm not sure I'm ready for that this morning.

I must have passed out immediately because I had zero time to process everything that happened yesterday. My mind is bombarded with thoughts as they rush into my brain all at once. Such as, what will Frank and Jay do when they catch wind of what happened last night? I don't think it'll matter that I was assaulted, and now I'm freaked out over what their supposed consequences will be. The fact of the matter is, I'm a sitting duck until they show up since I don't want to bring any unnecessary attention by texting them first.

If only I could stay at Walker's to hide out for a while, but then they'd end up going after my mom as threatened. I know Jackson wants to help, but no part of me would pass on my problems to someone else. He also has no idea what he's asking for. It's not like he can just hand over the remaining $180,000, and even if he could, these aren't the kind of guys you want on your radar. I can't let him get involved; he has too much to lose and nothing to gain.

Which brings me to my next concern—how do I come to terms with this new side of Jackson? Maybe he's had these feelings for a while now, but I certainly haven't. In my reality, he went from tolerating me to trying to date me in the span of one day and is more likely to bite my head off rather than kiss it. There's no denying the physical attraction, but so far, that's all it's been. Had I spent time with last night's version of Jackson over the last two months, hell, I'd probably be in love by now.

And even though Walker might be all for giving this a go, what will my mom think about the age difference? What do *I* think about it? Then there are his parents, who I doubt would be okay with their son dating the cleaner's daughter, who also happens to be an employee.

I would say my lack of experience also makes the list of concerns, judging by his erection at full mast behind me. He's made it clear where he wants this to go, and it's apparent from certain comments that he assumes I've been with other guys. It doesn't seem like something to randomly blurt out: "Oh hey, by the way, this sex thing, yeah, I've never done it."

He's the guy with a different girl every week, and booty calls to the office for crying out loud. I wonder if he'd change his mind about wanting me if he knew how inexperienced I am. A guy like Jackson doesn't want to deal with some girl who has no idea what she's doing. This could be over before it gets started with everything stacked against us, and likely won't go anywhere. However, our current sleeping arrangement indicates otherwise.

"Good morning, gorgeous. What's on your mind?" He must've been awake for a minute if he caught my huff of frustration.

He squeezes me and nuzzles the back of my neck, breathing me in. Whatever had me concerned flies out the window when I feel his lips on my skin, and his hips press forward. My body's reaction is instantaneous, and I get that delicious sensation down *there* again. It's crazy how easily he brings these feelings to the surface. Does he know what he's doing to me? I'm so turned on right now, and I'm not sure how to handle it.

A second later, my body takes over by arching into him, and I find myself tilting my head for more. I'm overcome with lust, and he's not even touching me—not with his hands, anyway. His lips are on my skin, and his dick is rubbing against me, but there are two layers of clothing between us. How in the world does this feel so good?

Oh shit, I think I just moaned.

"Fuck, Mia, you smell so good." He nuzzles further into my neck and thrusts his groin, and oh… my… God… He's killing me. Grabbing his hand on my hip, I try bringing it to where I'm aching, only for his muscles to bulge in resistance.

"Mia, I'd like nothing else than to feel your sweet pussy right now, but we're not going there yet. You're my little girl, remember? Or should I say… my dirty little girl." His filthy words whisper against my ear while his lips graze my skin.

Oh shit. My walls clench even harder. I think I might climax from this alone.

"Mmm, Jackson, please." It comes out unbidden, not sure what I'm asking for, but the pleas won't stop while my body writhes in desire.

"Jesus, Mia, I'm sorry. I need to get up before I do something stupid." He scrambles from the bed. "Fuck, I didn't mean to get carried away." He's facing away from me, running his hand through his hair, panting.

"Uh, I'm pretty sure it wasn't all your fault. *I'm* sorry. I don't know what got into me." I'm not exactly sure what I'm apologizing for, but I certainly didn't help the situation.

He turns back toward me with a sly grin. "Well, thankfully, *nothing* got into you—no thanks to your begging. I get an A-plus in willpower."

"You did *not* just say that." I groan and sink back into the bed.

I'm toast.

Jackson

She turns beet red, and it's fucking adorable. Does she have any idea of the effect she has on me? I was way too close to giving us what we both wanted. One more plea out of her mouth or push of her hand and I might have caved. Thankfully, I came to my senses before that happened.

"Seriously, though, I'll behave. Are you okay if I get back in bed?" The urge to be close to her is overwhelming.

"You're the one who got up. Why are you asking me?"

"I don't know, maybe because I just about took advantage of you a minute ago?" Even though I have myself under control now, she doesn't know that, and if the boner I'm sporting is any indication, she has no reason to. Unfortunately, it's not going anywhere for a while after that nice wake-up.

"You were not taking advantage of me. Like you said, I was the one begging. I'm not a damsel in distress."

"Actually, you are, remember? You're here to be protected and feel safe, not to be mauled. I shouldn't be trying to seduce you. You're just too goddamn tempting."

"There was no trying involved—I was thoroughly seduced. It looks like you get an A-plus in seduction, but I think you should retake the test to be sure."

And that's when I know I am well and truly fucked.

"You're going to be the literal death of me." I climb back in, propping myself on my elbow, and look her straight in the eyes. "When you're not off-limits anymore, and you find yourself back in my bed, I can assure you—I won't be stopping."

"Okay…" Damn… That response alone… What I wouldn't do to fast-forward time by a few days. This is ridiculous. Why am I waiting again?

I groan and fall back, staring up at the ceiling. "Fuck, Mia, if I'm going to do this, I'm going to do it right, and that means waiting not only for your birthday but making sure you know what you're getting into and that you want to go down this road with me." I put my arm up in an invitation for her to get closer.

"Come here, let's start over." She does, and I can't help but notice how perfectly she fits against me. My arm drops down around her, and we both settle in, taking a deep breath of contentment. "How about you tell me what was on your mind this morning? I could tell it was going a million miles a minute."

"Just… everything. The whole situation last night. You show up as my knight in shining armor, and instead of being angry, you throw me a curveball. One minute, I'm your nemesis, and the next, you're trying to date me, I think. See, I don't even know. Is that what you're doing?" I love her frankness. I wish she could be this honest about everything.

"Yes, Mia, I'm trying to date you. Can you take my behavior over the last couple of months and wipe it from your memory? I'm not usually like that. Just give me a chance to win you over, and I'll prove I'm the type of guy you deserve." Her head rests on my chest while she casually grazes her hand over my abs. Thankfully, it's through my shirt, or we might be right back where we were minutes ago.

"I'll try. We'll just have to take it one day at a time."

"How about we start today, and I take you to breakfast?"

"Are you asking me on our first date?" She lifts her head and looks at me.

The fact that she used the words "first date" tells me she's already invested in this more than she'll admit—she knows we're happening. And that knowledge is all I need for now.

I gently caress her cheek. "Yeah, I am. Mia, will you go out to breakfast with me this morning?"

"I would love to, Jackson," she says, rewarding me with a massive smile.

My chest swells, and I feel something I'm not sure I'm prepared for.

Breakfast with Mia was more than I could've hoped for. She truly saw me from a new perspective, and it felt like we made a year's worth of progress in two hours. She shared details about her life, allowing me to experience a more personal side of her, and with each new facet, I'm more and more enamored. In turn, I talked about my family, friends, and work, explaining the dynamics of my parents' retirement and how it affected my role at the office, giving her an even better understanding of my previous behavior.

After bringing her home, I hit the gym for a couple of hours to release some of the built-up sexual tension. Unfortunately, I'll be taking care of that myself for a while. There's no doubt our time together has left me pent up. I'm glad I'm holding out to kiss her, though, because when it finally happens, it'll be worth the wait—and impossible to stop there.

I need to make plans for another date before Wednesday so she has more time to experience the real Jackson. It might have to be tomorrow since I know she makes dinner for her mom throughout the week. I'll surprise her with something. But before I do anything else, I need to call Cici to confirm our plans and make sure everything is set for the trip.

"Hey, Jackson. Are you getting excited for Friday?" Cici asks excitedly, making me chuckle.

"Yeah, how could I not be? You've been talking up the place forever. Is everything set for next weekend??"

"Yep, all the showings are scheduled for Friday. We're getting an early start, so we have time for dinner. I made reservations already and assumed Mia would join?"

"She will. And I should probably give you a heads-up before we get there. I'm sort of… seeing her."

"I *knew* it. I knew right when you said she was coming. Wait… I thought she was seventeen. What the hell are you thinking?"

"Cool your jets. I haven't touched her. Well… I haven't kissed her… anywhere other than her neck—barely. Anyway, that's beside the point. She turns eighteen Wednesday, and until then, I'm keeping my hands off… for the most part." She tries interrupting again, but I don't let her. "Listen, I like her, okay? A lot. Just save your judgment until you meet her. She's special. Fuck, I know she's young, but at the same time she's not. You'll understand what I mean soon enough."

"Jesus, Jackson, how did you go from hating the girl to being in love?"

What the fuck?

"I didn't say anything about love. I've just managed to convince her to give me a chance for Christ's sake. She still thinks of me as her asshole of a boss. It's a new development for now. Maybe I'll have made some headway by the time we get there. Can you just wait to give me shit until after our visit?" I ask in earnest.

"I can't believe you're bringing a girlfriend for me to meet the first time you visit. I feel so special. I bet Mom and Dad don't know, do they?"

"Cici, no one does. This is brand-fucking-new. Hell, *I* don't even know. I'm just seeing where it goes, and you're the first one I've said anything to, so there's nothing for Mom and Dad to know, and if there were, who cares? They're responsible for this in the first place. Anyway, moving on, I just wanted to make sure everything's set. Other than that, I'll see you Friday morning. We get in late Thursday and can just Uber to the hotel. You have Uber there?" I need to get her off the Mia topic already.

"Yes, we have Uber, dumbass. I'll pick you up at seven thirty Friday morning, then. Text me your room number because I'm at least coming to your door for a real greeting and a proper introduction to your future wife." Damn her.

"Fuck, I knew telling you was a mistake. Please don't make it awkward. Just act like she's my assistant."

"Wow, Jackson, I thought you were smarter than that. If you're trying to win her over, I'm pretty sure playing the 'only my assistant' card when you introduce her to your sister won't win any points, but if that's what you want…"

"I'm seriously reconsidering this trip." Not.

"Sure you are. I'd say this trip was your way to close the deal, and I'm not talking about one of the deals you're coming to look at."

"God, you drive me nuts. I'm hanging up now. I'll see you Friday." I end the call before she gets another word in. I can't take any more of her insufferableness.

With that settled, it's time to plan a date.

Mia

While getting ready for bed, I reflect on the day. Brunch with Jackson this morning was fun… and weird. It was surprisingly the best of all four dates I've been on over the last couple of weeks, which is good since the others all slighted me. I was starting to wonder if I just repelled men, but I hope that's not the case because I really like Jackson. To put it simply, we click. The chemistry between us is undeniable, and the conversation flows seamlessly. We have a lot in common—we're both overachievers, enjoy poker, and strive to please our parents, just to name a few.

It was nice to hear about his family, especially his little sister, Cici, who I'll be meeting in a few days. She sounds great, and I can tell by how he speaks of her that they're close. Jackson seems sure about this, but what if she doesn't like me? It could be an easy way out of things becoming more serious… if that's what I want, but I think a big part of me already knows it isn't.

He's sweet when he's not intentionally trying to be an ass. I would even say he's a catch. He's stable, hot, knows how to treat a woman, and he makes me laugh. Honestly, I wish my birthday was tomorrow because I'm ready for that kiss—and, embarrassingly, way more than that. My body seems to light up from his touch. I can't help but imagine what it will feel like when there are no clothes between us and his hands explore more… forbidden places.

I expected him to cave and kiss me when he brought me home after brunch, but he stayed true to his word with only a hug and kiss on my forehead. I even leaned in and licked my lips, but he ended up shaking his head, chuckling, telling me I was dangerous. Hopefully, I can get him to make a move during this trip to Montana, which, in hindsight, I'm now excited about.

What I'm not excited over is the text I got from Jay informing me that after some deliberation, the boss (whoever that is) decided to add fifteen grand to my debt for the complaints about my behavior and that I should be grateful that's all I got. If this is how it continues to go, I'll never pay them off. They're fining me for being sexually assaulted. How that's fair is beyond me, but apparently, this boss of theirs makes the rules.

They sent details for two online tournaments next week, and luckily, they're not on my birthday or during the trip with Jackson. I decided not to tell them I'm leaving town, so they won't know my mom is alone, but I'm screwed if they send me to a live game next weekend. The problem is, they never tell me in advance.

My phone lights up with Walker's name. "Hey, Walker, what's up?" I answer as I pull back the covers and crawl into bed, having just finished my nighttime routine.

"You tell me. The last text I got from you said you were staying at Jackson's. You better tell me everything and start with why *I* had to call instead of hearing from you earlier."

"Sorry. I know I should've at least told you I was home. I just wasn't ready to talk about it. I'm still trying to wrap my head around everything. I swear I was about to call you."

"Well, then, start talking. What's going on? Did you do the dirty?" I knew this was coming.

"No. I already told you he won't touch me until my birthday. Well, not completely. We were kind of grinding on each other while spooning this morning, and he was nuzzling my neck, but that's all."

"Whoa, I need details, but back up and start at the beginning. How did you end up with him in the first place? I thought you were going to play poker. There's no way he could've been at another game again when this has never happened before." I can hear the suspicion in his voice.

This was the part I was worried about explaining. I'm still clueless as to how Jackson found me, and I'm not sure whether to tell Walker about the assault or not. I don't want to worry him for no reason, but I also don't want to lie to my best friend more than necessary.

I describe the situation that led me to his house, glossing over how he knew where I was, finishing up with something to distract him.

"The important part is that he wants to date me, so we started by going to breakfast this morning."

"Right after you dry-humped each other in bed… that's not considered keeping his hands off, you know."

"Hence the 'not completely' part. I didn't exactly help the matter. If I'd had my way, he would've bypassed first and second and gone straight to third base, but he stopped when I tried to move his hand down. His willpower is annoying."

"Holy shit, way to finally take the plunge. Do you seriously like this guy? Because other than the fact that he's hot, he's been a total prick. What changed?"

"Well, last night was insane, and then breakfast… wow. He's the full package, Walker. He's funny, sweet, a gentleman who opens doors, and he asks questions while actually listening to the answers. We hadn't had any real conversation until last night, but it's weird—he seems to know me. It's like he's been paying attention to everything since day one. Which may sound a little creepy, or it could prove that he really was interested this whole time but resisted."

"Huh, so what? You're in love now?" It sounds like Walker's not as sold on the idea as I thought.

"Heck no, it'll take more than a little chivalry and a few words for that. But if he's for real, then I want to see where it leads."

He sighs. "I can't say I'm surprised. I saw it coming a mile away. Plus, he wouldn't be taking you to Montana with him if he couldn't stand you, which means he probably has ulterior motives. I'm glad I'll meet him on Wednesday so I can check this guy out."

"So, tell me this. He thinks I've been with other guys already. Do I say anything or just leave him in the dark? It's not like he needs to know, right?"

"This might be one of those times when having a guy for a best friend isn't very helpful, but *as* a guy, I'd want to know. It may be no big deal to you, but there are things he can do to make it better for you. And as your gay best friend, I can tell you that that's important. If Ben had assumed I'd done it before, I may have never done it again. Do you need a clearer picture, or do you want me to leave it at that?"

"Please stop there. And I get what you're saying, but what if I tell him, and he decides it's too much hassle and changes his mind?"

"Then he's not worth it anyway. If the guy is really into you the way he says he is, it shouldn't matter. It'll just change the way he goes about things."

"But I don't want him to change anything. I like how he is and don't want to be treated with kid gloves. I want the raw version. Can't I just tell him right before it happens? If it even does happen."

"Mia, it's going to happen. It's just a matter of when, and if you want to wait until you're right there, that's up to you, as long as you give him some sort of heads-up before he rips you in two and then feels like a jerk about it. And if I were you, I'd be packing some sexy lingerie for your *business trip*."

My eyes widen. I hadn't thought of that. "Crap, you're right. New plan, then. Can you take me shopping instead of lunch on Wednesday? Pleeeaaase?"

"Hell yeah. Shopping's my specialty, baby. I'll leave after third period and come straight to pick you up. See you at noon on Wednesday?"

"I can't wait! Okay, I'll see you then. Bye."

He chuckles. "Bye, Mia."

When I hang up the phone, I close my eyes, laying my arm over my face. I can't believe I just had a conversation about having sex with Jackson. That I'm even *thinking* about sex with Jackson is crazy. My mind goes straight to the scene from his office that day—which happens more often than I'd like to admit—and my hand moves down my body of its own accord.

Picturing his climax makes my body clench with need. God… I

want to feel his hands on me, his body on mine, feel him inside of me. My hand pushes under the waistband of my shorts and then into my panties before my fingers graze my clit. A quiet moan escapes as I move them in a circular motion over that sensitive area. I've never done this before and can't believe how good it feels.

The more I picture Jackson, the faster my fingers move, making my breaths become hurried. "Oh God, Jackson. Yes, please," I whisper.

The pressure is building, and I know something is coming. When I picture him telling me to *take it all in* like he did the day in his office, it gets closer. And when I take it up a notch by imagining him calling me *his little girl*, I erupt. The explosion hits me with a delicious clenching of my core, repeating over and over again. My fingers slow, and my breathing calms as it fades, and I slowly come back to earth.

How have I never done that before? That was a-maz-ing. My body is humming and more relaxed than it's ever been. My mind is reeling with thoughts of how much better it will be with Jackson as I fade into the deepest sleep I've had in a long time.

13

SURPRISES

Jackson

"**H**ey, beautiful." I greet Mia by bringing her hand to my lips for a kiss.

Technically, this is our second date, but the first that I'm picking her up for, so I'm going to do it right. Although, with everything we've experienced together already, it feels like we've been dating for weeks at this point. It's unsettling how much I missed her during the less than twenty-four-hour span we've been apart for and that every minute of it was spent with her occupying all corners of my mind.

"Are you going to tell me where we're going now?" She tried hard to get it out of me on the phone, but I'm not giving in.

"No. I told you, it's a surprise."

"And I told you, I don't like surprises."

"That's too bad because I like giving them. So much so that I'm keeping you in the dark until we get there. Do you trust me?"

She laughs. "That's a loaded question. Do I trust you? For now, yes."

"Then close your eyes, sweetheart." She complies, and I reach into the console to grab the scarf I stashed there earlier. "I'm blindfolding you to keep the suspense," I say, as I bring it to her eyes and tie it around her head while she protests.

"You're literally keeping me in the dark? People will see, and they'll think you're kidnapping me or something. This is embarrassing. You can't—"

She stops talking when I turn her face toward mine and put my thumb over her mouth to quiet her. I move it back and forth slowly, relishing the feel of her plump lips. As I caress down her neck, her lips part, and it takes everything in me not to lean forward and taste them.

"Don't worry, Mia. The windows are tinted, so no one can see inside, I promise. It's only you and me. Are you good?"

She nods in response.

"That's my girl. Now buckle up, buttercup."

She fumbles for her seat belt, which, in hindsight, I should have had her do before I blindfolded her, but it gives me a great excuse to get close and breathe her in as I lean over to help.

She was surprised when I called her this morning, forgetting that I had her number from when she'd entered it all those weeks ago. She didn't hesitate when I asked her out today, but she did protest to the surprise part of it. She tried telling me she needed to know what to wear, but I didn't take the bait and instead gave her some options. The idea was spontaneous and hit me out of nowhere yesterday.

"So, why wouldn't you let me come to the door to get you? Are you hiding me?" I ask as I pull away from the curb. It was her one condition for picking her up—she made me promise to stay in the car and text when I got there.

"No, I'm just not ready to tell my mom and have that conversation. I don't know how she'll react to hearing that I'm dating my much older boss. Plus, this is new. It might not even go anywhere." Hearing her say that creates an uncomfortable sensation in my chest.

"Do you really think this isn't going anywhere? Because I feel like this is going somewhere pretty fucking good. Actually, how about this— don't answer until I ask you again, okay?"

"I'm sorry, it's just… I'm not ready to face questions about us."

"Fair enough. For now, let's have some fun. How was the rest of your day after I dropped you off?" She blushes as soon as I ask the question, making me wonder if she thought of me as much as I did her.

"Um… not much. Did some laundry, had dinner with my mom, and chatted with Walker before I went to bed. That's all." She croaks the last part, as if the words were bitter on her tongue.

"That's all, huh? Are you sure, Mia? It looks like you're hiding something." A deep red creeps up now, compelling me to reach over and caress her cheek.

Her breathing immediately goes shallow. Her response to me is out of this world. I've never been with someone so sensitive to a simple touch, and I can't wait to see her reaction when my hands can finally reach the places I've been fantasizing about. With the tightening of my pants, it's safe to say we're equal in our hunger for each other. I feel like she's prompted more erections out of me in the last couple months than I've had my entire life.

"No. I mean, yes. I mean, I'm not hiding anything." I can see her thighs clench, confessing what she won't.

"Tell me, Mia, did my little girl do something last night that only big girls do?" Shit, I feel like I just opened Pandora's box, and I'm too weak to shut it.

She bites her lip in response and squeezes her thighs even tighter. "Jackson, don't."

"Don't what? Don't ask if you touched yourself last night? Don't ask if you made yourself come? Don't ask what you were thinking about while you brought yourself to orgasm?" I pause, enjoying the sounds of her desire. "What *were* you thinking about while you stroked yourself last night, Mia?" I want to hear it out loud.

She's squirming in her seat now, gripping the armrest tight in one hand and squeezing my fingers with the other.

"Tell me what you were thinking, Mia," I say more firmly, demanding the answer. Apparently, I'm into self-torture by going down this path.

"You, all right? I was thinking of you… what you looked like that day in your office. And…" Fuck, she does want me just as badly.

"And what, Mia? Say it."

"What it would be like if you were on top of me… in me." She squeezes my hand tighter, in a death grip, making my dick jerk in my pants.

"Fuck, Mia. I want that more than you can imagine. But right now, I think you should touch yourself. Show me what you did last night." I'll beg if that's what it takes.

"No! I can't do that here. You're crazy."

"What's crazy is how much I'm dying to watch. Come on, Mia, you're aching for it. No one can see. It's only you and me here." The pressure in my pants is bordering on excruciating.

I can't take it anymore and make a split-second decision to pull off the highway. Since it's a Sunday afternoon, I quickly find a deserted parking lot and park where the chance of someone walking by is unlikely. Having Mia blindfolded worked out better than I thought. We can both enjoy the moment without her seeing a thing. Now it's up to me to keep my no-touching rule in place.

"Where are we? What are you doing?"

"Shhhh. We're somewhere private, I swear. You're not the only one worked up here, and I need a release just as badly as you. If I don't take care of this, it's going to be one hell of a long day. Lay your seat back and undo your pants for me, Mia. That's it. Let me watch as you finger that swollen pussy for me."

She's putting the seat back as I work my pants open and gasps at the sound. "What are you doing?"

I laugh. "What do you want me to be doing?"

She licks her lips. Her seat is back, and she slowly undoes her pants.

"Since it's not fair that you can't see, and I can, I'll talk you through it. I'm pulling my dick out of my pants right now. It's rock-hard for you, Mia. There's precum already leaking out to make it slick for me. I'm gripping it now, rubbing my thumb over the top, spreading my come all over."

Her hand slides into her pants. "That's it, Mia. Show me how you touch yourself. I want to see you come apart."

Her hand is on her pussy now. I can't see it, but I can see her fingers moving, and hell… I could probably blow right now.

"Keep talking. I like it," she tells me, and fuck if that's not the sexiest thing I've heard.

Holy hell, this girl—what she does to me. I put my seat back a little more and close my eyes.

"I'm pumping my dick now, squeezing it hard, imagining it's your tight little pussy. Fuck, Mia, you're so wet, I can hear it. Dip your finger in for me." She does, and I ease up so I don't come right here and now.

"Good girl. Now take your hand out and show it to me." When she does, I immediately bring it to my mouth, sucking and savoring her juices.

She bucks her hips and moans. "Jackson."

"I needed a taste, Mia—something to look forward to." I put her hand back. "Finish yourself off for me. Let me see you come."

She reaches in, and we continue together, getting closer and closer.

"That's it, Mia. Give me a show. Let me see you come undone." I'm jerking myself fast and hard, the noise loud in the quiet car. Her moans tell me she's close.

"That's right, pretend I'm fucking you. Imagine my dick stretching your tight little pussy. Do you feel how big it is? Feel how hard I'm fucking you right now?"

She's so close. Her mouth is wide, breathing shallow.

"Be my good little girl, Mia, and come for me." That tips us both over the edge, exploding simultaneously.

"Jackson! Oh my God."

"Fuck, that's it. You're milking my dick, aren't you?" I let myself go as she whimpers through her own climax. I come onto my stomach in long spurts that seem to go on forever.

Half a minute later, we're silent and sated, still catching our breaths.

"That was the sexiest fucking experience I've ever had." I chuckle. Here I am at twenty-seven, with more sexual partners than I can count, having the best orgasm of my life without even touching the girl. That's some crazy shit.

Mia

There's not much I can say to that considering it was the *only* experience of my life. *Holy crap.* Did that seriously just happen? Thank God I'm blindfolded right now, or else I'd die from mortification.

I hear the click of the glove box before something soft is placed in my hand. "Here's a napkin, in case you need it. I'll clean up and get back on the road. We're almost there."

"Where?" I ask super casually, earning a chuckle.

"Nice try. You'll see soon enough." After a moment, he says, "Hey, Mia?"

I turn my head in his direction. "Yeah?"

"Thank you. That was… surprising. And I like surprises."

I can't stop the massive smile that forms. "I'm starting to," I respond, making him laugh again.

"Good, 'cause I'm just getting started." He brings my hand to his mouth and kisses it, causing butterflies in my belly for no reason other than he makes me happy.

After less than ten minutes of driving, we're parked once more.

"Can I take the blindfold off now?" I ask as soon as the car turns off.

"Impatient much?"

"Well, I just figured I'd be able to since we're here. It's not like you can make me walk around with it on. That would be weird."

"I'm pretty sure I can do whatever I want, and if you keep it up, I'll make you keep it on just to mess with you. Now, what's your favorite animal?"

"Huh? Why?"

"Because it's part of my quest to know everything about you. Just answer the question."

"You're insane." I think for a moment before answering. "Koalas. What's yours?"

I'm met with a minute of silence, and then he answers. "Wolves."

"Why wolves?" I ask.

"Because they're strong, protective, and care for their women. Why do you like koalas?"

Could his answer be any more perfect? Is this guy for real?

"Because they're cute. I did a report on them in middle school and fell in love. They look like big cuddlers, and the mom carries her baby in a pouch. I know they're wild animals and can be aggressive, but how can you think badly of something so adorable?"

"Am I adorable?"

"I wouldn't put you in the adorable category. More along the lines of… charming."

"I'll take it. Okay, so here's the deal. I'll remove the blindfold if you keep your eyes closed until I say. I brought a pair of sunglasses so no one will know, and I won't steer you into danger, I promise."

"You sure make a lot of promises, you know that?"

"I mean every one of them."

Sometimes, he just takes my breath away. I swear he's too good to be true. How did he pull off being an asshole for so long?

"Ugh, fine, I *promise* to keep my eyes closed."

"Good girl." I feel his hand on my cheek, and then his thumb runs over my lips before moving to the scarf. *Maybe we should have a round two first…*

"Close your eyes, Mia. I mean it, no peeking," he says before removing the blindfold and replacing it with sunglasses.

"All right, are you ready?" he asks.

"Not really, since I have no idea what we're doing. This is killing me." I pout, causing him to chuckle.

"You'll survive, I'm sure. One more thing. Here, put these in your ears so you can't hear where we are." He places a pair of earplugs in my hand.

I scoff. "You've got to be kidding me. You're taking away my sight *and* my hearing? I don't know, Jackson."

"Pretty please? It'll ruin the surprise if you hear where we are before it's time. It'll be worth it, I swear. Just trust me."

"You're asking a lot for our first date."

"Technically, it's our second date. I took you out to breakfast yesterday, remember? Not to mention the fact that you did sleep over." I can hear the smirk in his voice.

"Yeah, but that was sort of a product of the situation. This is official." I groan. "Ugh, whatever, let's do this." I put the earplugs in and reach for the door handle but stop when he tells me to wait.

A few seconds later, my door opens, and he guides me out of the car, once again reminding me to keep my eyes closed, threatening me with the blindfold if I cheat. It's hard not to take a quick peek, but I don't because, honestly, I'm excited for the surprise.

I was shocked to see "Bosshole" on my caller ID this morning, forgetting that we already had each other's numbers. My finger hesitated over the Answer button, assuming he was calling for work. I'm still not used to this. At the last minute, I decided to pick it up and was greeted in a very non-work-related way.

"Good morning, sunshine. Are you ready to spend the day with me so I can sweep you off your feet?" He said he didn't want to take up an evening this week for a date so I could spend time with my mom before our trip. Did this guy step off the pages of a romance novel or what?

Now here I am, still with no clue as to what's happening, but I'd say my feet have already been swept.

We finally come to a stop, and he guides me to sit before speaking into my ear. "Wait right here for a few minutes while I check in. I'm not going far, and I'll be able to see you from where I'm at. I'll keep my eyes on you the entire time, okay?"

After nodding in response, I sit and wait. I can hear background noise, but nothing specific other than what sounds like a lot of kids. I literally have no clue where we are.

A few minutes later, I startle at the feel of a hand on my shoulder before Jackson's voice sounds in my ear once more. "We're all set. Keep your eyes closed while we get to our final destination. Not much longer, I promise."

He then helps me up and leads me forward, keeping my arm tucked in his. I catch snippets of things through the earplugs, which must be industrial with how well they work, and I hear Jackson laugh, telling me there's another person with us.

I'm ushered into what seems like a golf cart and he gets in beside me. Shoot, I hope we're not golfing. I never have, and it doesn't seem all that fun, to be honest. But the kids don't make sense for that idea unless it's some sort of golf camp. If that's his idea of a date, then shoot me now. I'm planning the next one.

After driving for a few minutes, he helps me out, and we walk until we enter a building, coming to a stop. He removes the sunglasses and earplugs and tells me to keep my eyes closed until he says. All I know so far is that some funky smells are going on wherever we are.

"Are you ready, gorgeous?" I nod. "You can open your eyes now."

My eyes reluctantly open, sensitive from being closed so long, and blink a few times before focusing in on the scene before me. I gasp. There's a fricking koala sitting on a small treelike structure, happily munching on a leaf while a man in a zookeeper's uniform stands by. Turning my head back and forth, I take in the surroundings of some sort of lab or veterinary room.

"Surprise, Mia. We're spending the day at the zoo, and this is our first stop." He's smiling down at me with a big grin lighting up his face.

"Wait, how did you plan this so fast? You only found out about my favorite animal minutes ago." I'm in awe. Seriously, I feel… I don't know exactly, but *this moment…* feels special.

"I booked it yesterday, but they let me wait until today to pick which experience we wanted, and lucky for me, you picked an animal they had. It was just meant to be, I guess." He shrugs, still looking at me with that goofy grin, causing me to giggle.

"I can't believe you did this. He's so cute," I say, returning my attention to the koala. I've been to the zoo before—everyone growing up in San Diego has at some point—but I've never done anything like this.

"Feel free to come closer and interact with him. We just don't let you hold them anymore. We'll show you how to feed him, and you'll be able to get some pictures. Would you like to get started?" The zookeeper asks, ready to begin.

I nod enthusiastically as Jackson and I move in closer, his hand resting affectionately on my back.

Jackson

Fascination and excitement flit across Mia's face the entire time we spend with the koala, and I'm more enraptured by watching her than the animal. My sudden infatuation is intense, taking me by storm—a category five that I'm not sure I'll survive. I went from merely being sexually frustrated to all-around enamored in the span of two days, and now I can't get enough of her. The floodgates are open, and I'm worried my heart is filling too quickly, but slowing it down seems impossible.

After the behind-the-scenes experience, we enjoyed our private tour for the next two hours and then proceeded to act like kids for the afternoon, wandering around, holding hands, and gawking at the animals while taking silly pictures and laughing hysterically. The gorilla who sat in front of the window, picking his nose and eating it as two more were getting it on in the background, took the award for the day. We were wiping the tears at that point.

Not only was this the best date in history, but it was by far the most fun I've ever had with anyone. There's no denying my feelings that seem to be growing stronger every minute we're together. My only hope is that I've made progress making up for my terrible behavior over the last couple of months so she can catch up to my level.

Both of us are still giddy from the afternoon as we walk out hand in hand, with Mia hugging the enormous stuffed koala I insisted on buying for her. Making our way to the car with matching smiles, I don't remember the last time I was this happy, and I'm not ready to call it a day.

I stop abruptly and turn to face her. "Will you go to dinner with me? I'm enjoying this too much for it to come to an end," I say honestly.

"Me too. I'm glad you asked." Her smile widens more before she unexpectedly throws her arms around me and wraps me in a hug. "Jackson, that was the best day I've had in a long time. Thank you so much. I'll never think of the zoo the same."

"I'm glad you liked it. It's at the top of my list too." Holding her feels so good that I never want to let go, and I'm hoping there'll be plenty of time for more in the days and weeks to follow.

I reluctantly release my hold as she pulls back. "Let me just call my mom to make sure she didn't plan dinner already."

"Go for it. I'll make a call myself." Stepping away, I pull up my favorite Italian restaurant to make sure they have room for two, anticipating the thumbs up from her mom.

"We're good to go. She's so caught up in her book that she was just going to order in any way."

I grab her hand as we walk the rest of the way to the car. "Great. Do you like Italian?" I probably should have asked before I chose the place. If she doesn't, I'll just cancel, and she can choose somewhere else.

"It's my favorite. What's not to like about pizza and pasta?"

"God, I love you—shit… sorry… what I meant is that I love that you're so real. You're not fake like the girls I'm used to being with." I'm glad she's smiling after the initial look of panic, which is exactly what I did at hearing the words that came out of my mouth.

"Nope, you get what you get with me whether you like it or not.

I'm good at keeping a game face on, but I choose not to most of the time. Unless I'm around a certain bosshole." She smirks up at me and nudges me with her shoulder.

"Damn, you're not gonna let me live that down for a while, are you?"

"I'm thinking more like never, so don't hold your breath." She grins at me, then climbs into her seat, and I shake my head with a smile to match as I close her door.

We continue to laugh the whole way to dinner, recounting the gorilla exhibit. I honestly don't remember the last time I laughed this much. She's like the breath of fresh air I didn't know my lungs were dying for.

Once we're seated at our table, a question pops into my head. "I'm just curious. What did you tell Walker about Friday night?" I ask, looking up from my menu.

She lifts her head with a contemplative look. "Hm, well, I told him that you showed up right as I was being manhandled and saved the day, then wanted to bring me to your place to declare your undying love to me."

I choke on my drink and immediately reach for my napkin to wipe up as Mia laughs across the table.

"Just kidding. The first part's true, and then I told him you're interested in seeing me. I also said you won't touch me until my birthday, other than grinding on me that morning." Her eyebrows go up mockingly.

"God, he must think I'm an asshole trying to take advantage of you, doesn't he?"

"No. He knows me, and if you think you could take advantage of me? Well, then, *you* obviously don't. I let him know that you were the one to put the kibosh on things and wouldn't let me taint your morals." She smirks, making me chuckle.

"I'd say they're pretty flimsy morals after what happened on the way to the zoo. You're too tempting to resist. Just thinking about it now… let's just say it's a good thing there's a tablecloth." She giggles as the waiter approaches to take our order.

After he leaves, I ask her what I've been dying to know all afternoon. "So tell me, do you like what we did?"

"I'd say that was obvious, wouldn't you?" she says sarcastically—such a tease.

"You gotta give me more than that. Was there anything you didn't like, anything you'd change?" Maybe I'm looking for reassurance, but I also want to make sure she's pleased and gets what she needs from me.

"I would have rather had *your* hand in my pants instead of mine." She's so blunt.

"Fuck, Mia. You're killing me over here." I reach down to adjust myself.

"You asked." She shrugs. "Seriously, though, I like it when you talk. It's a big turn-on. And when you grabbed my hand and… you know… I almost orgasmed from that alone."

Thank God we're in public, or we wouldn't make it to Wednesday with my no-touching rule. Fuck, this girl is driving me insane. I know what I'll be doing later. Who am I kidding? I'll be doing it every night until I make her mine.

"I'm glad you feel comfortable being honest." She puts her head down at that statement and presses her lips together. I'm sure that has to do with the secrets we both know she's keeping from me, but I'm not bringing it up while we're having such a good time.

"So, tell me about school and what you're going for." My dick needed a change of subject before it ended up snapping in half. Maybe the rest of the meal will be slightly more comfortable.

We stay on safer topics, and the conversation flows freely without any awkward pauses or moments for the remainder of the meal. After paying, there's no excuse remaining not to take her home. During the drive, I hold her hand, caressing it as I pull up to her house. Then I turn and bring it to my lips, one of my favorite things to do until I can kiss everywhere else I'm dying to.

"Thank you, Jackson. That was an amazing first—I mean second date. I think you're ruining me for all others."

"I would hope so. I'm not seeing anyone else, Mia, and I haven't for a while. I'm serious about this, and I know I'm in no position to tell you what to do, but I'd like it if you weren't dating anyone else while we explore the possibility of a relationship."

"Funny, you've never shied away from telling me what to do before," she sasses.

"Like I said, I'll go as long as it takes to prove I'm not that guy. How am I doing so far?" I raise my eyebrows up and down in question, pulling a laugh from her.

"Too good. I have to say, I like this new version much better. Jackson 2.0. I can't wait to see what the next upgrade brings."

"I think you have an idea what that upgrade looks like after this morning," I say suggestively.

Her cheeks turn pink, and she presses her lips together while her thighs tense. "Well, I have no intention to see anyone else while we're dating. I was only trying to distract myself anyway. I was having inappropriate thoughts about my boss at the time."

I smirk. "Is that so? Were you successful in distracting yourself?"

"Not in the slightest. So I'm glad I don't have to anymore."

"Me too." I grab her hand and hold it while we sit quietly, staring at each other, both in our own heads.

I've never had this kind of connection with anyone before. It's exhilarating and unnerving at the same time. I don't know what the future looks like, but I know I want her in it.

I reach for the back of her neck and slowly pull her toward me, bringing my lips to her forehead. Lingering there, I breathe her in, savoring the moment.

"I'd offer to walk you to the door, but I won't in case your mom is watching. I'm looking forward to meeting her, though, to tell her what an amazing daughter she has."

"Ugh, seriously, you can't make me like you this much." She sits back in her seat and closes her eyes for a moment.

"It's only fair since you've already captivated me. It's time for the question from earlier, do you still think this isn't going anywhere?"

Turning her head to look at me, she says, "No, I think we've already made it somewhere. And if I'm being honest, I'm excited to see where we go." She reaches for the door handle, ready to retreat after her confession, but I grab her hand and kiss it one last time.

"I'm happy to hear that. I had a great time, Mia. Thank you for spending the day with me. I'll see you tomorrow morning?"

"Is that a question? Because I'm pretty sure I still work for you unless you're firing me to make this ethical."

I chuckle. "There's no rule against interoffice dating, just my rule—before you came along. Now go before I break another one and kiss you good night."

"Yes, sir." She opens the door while laughing, making me shake my head as she walks away.

I haven't forgotten about the elephant in the room but decide to let it rest for now. With security in place, until she trusts me with the truth, there's not much more I can do. I plan on bringing it up again while we're in Montana, but I may need to increase security and implement more invasive measures until then. I'd prefer not to go that route and jeopardize whatever we're building, but her safety is more important, and I'll just have to pray she'll forgive me.

14

PROMISES

Mia

'M AN OFFICIAL ADULT. THE SMILE ON MY FACE AS SOON AS I OPEN my eyes may have to do with a certain someone who wouldn't touch me until I was eighteen. He said if I still wanted to kiss him on my birthday, he'd have a surprise for me. I've never been more excited for a surprise in my life. Will he call me into his office and kiss the living daylights out of me? Because that, I've decided, is my birthday wish.

When I get downstairs to the kitchen, my mom is setting a plate of chocolate chip pancakes on the table. A cup of coffee is already waiting, and there's a present next to my plate. Mom looks up to see me and beams.

"Happy birthday, mija! I can't believe this is it. And look at you—I swear you look ten years older today. It's like you blossomed overnight." Good thing I wasn't sipping my coffee; I might have choked at the reference to ten years older.

She comes over and envelops me in a huge hug.

"I'm pretty sure I look the same as yesterday, but thanks, Mom."

"Not to me, you don't. Knowing you're not my baby anymore is hard to grasp." She holds me at arm's length and looks me up and down, tearing up.

"Don't cry. Nothing is different than yesterday."

"Well, I don't know about that. You seem, I don't know, older somehow. I'm glad to see you dressing up on your birthday. Now come, sit down. I made your favorite breakfast, and I want you to open your present."

I wonder if she's just being a typical mom or if I really do look older today with the clothes I'm wearing and the extra bit of makeup I did—not a lot, just a hint more to freshen up my look. I want Jackson to see me as an adult and let go of all the ways he's been holding back.

"Thank you, Mom. I kind of figured that once I finished school, you'd stop making birthday breakfasts."

"It's tradition, and as long as you're home, I'll never stop. Let's eat so you can open your present."

We serve up and start digging in, but I can't help but ask, "Do you think my outfit or makeup is too much?"

I'm in a blush cotton wrap dress that cuts low in the front and ends midthigh. It's professional but also transitions to dinner, which I was going for since I'll probably meet my mom at the restaurant after work.

"I think you look beautiful, Mia. That color goes great with your skin tone, and I don't think your makeup is overdone at all. It makes you look more mature. I'd tell you if I thought otherwise." She smiles at me, and I know she's telling the truth.

"Okay, I just don't want to look like I'm trying too hard."

"Mia, honey, you don't have to try. You're beautiful just the way you are, but there's nothing wrong with adding a little oomph. Just don't get carried away."

"You know I wouldn't. So, what time are we meeting at the restaurant for dinner tonight, or do you want me to come home first?" My mom made reservations weeks ago at one of the best steakhouses in town. I told her not to pick somewhere so pricey, but she insisted. It came highly recommended by none other than Jackson's parents.

"I'll meet you there. I'm finishing up early today to come home and get ready. I'm so excited to celebrate your big day. All right, open your present now, honey."

Picking up the small square box, I remove the bow and slowly unwrap it, lifting the lid to a pair of gold nightingale earrings with blue gemstones for the eyes. "Mom, they're beautiful."

"They match the necklace I got you for graduation. Aren't you glad they're not M&M earrings? It crossed my mind, but I figured you'd like something more mature with your new adult status." She's smiling playfully, making me laugh. When I was younger, she and Dad always found fun M&M things for me. The memory gives me a moment of sadness, remembering when my dad was still with us, but I shake it off for Mom's sake.

"Thank you. And yes, I much prefer the nightingales. They're perfect. I'll go upstairs and switch mine out. They're so pretty." I stand to hug her. "Thank you for breakfast. I can't wait for dinner tonight. I love you," I say as she squeezes me tight.

"Oh, mija, I love you too. I hope you have a wonderful day. You deserve it, since you're the best daughter a mom could ask for."

I pull away and see her eyes are glassy. She's so sentimental.

"Well, the best mom in the world raised me, so that makes sense." I smile at her. "Okay, I'll go change my earrings and then head out. I'll say goodbye before I leave."

"Okay, sweetie."

Standing in front of the mirror, I take another long look at myself. I'm excited to see if Jackson notices any difference. Even though we had the best time this weekend, he's still holding back, and I hope it's just technicalities and not his perception of me that's doing it. Either way, both bases are covered today, so if he doesn't make a move, I plan on doing it for him.

I still can't get over how amazing our date was this weekend—like unbelievably amazing. He's more mature than anyone I've been with and still knows how to relax and just have fun. We laughed more than I have in a long time. Being with him wasn't only comfortable, but I truly enjoyed every second we were together. The thought he put into the date was over the top, and the spontaneity on the way there was icing on the cake. My desire meter about blew a gasket in the car, and it's still hovering at the top as I walk into the office.

Although, this is the third morning I've woken up with doubt, thinking it's too good to be true. I'm nervous, wondering if he's come to his senses and changed his mind about me or if I imagined the whole thing. I'm a big girl; I can take it, but I don't want to at this point, since I'm head over heels already.

When I reach the desk, my phone buzzes in my purse, and I pull it out to look.

Walker: Happy birthday! Have a good morning, birthday girl. I'll see you at noon!

Mia: Thanks, Walker. Can't wait!

I send my text with a bra and underwear emoji and get a laughing emoji in return, which makes me giggle.

"Is that my giggling little girl?"

My belly dips at hearing his sexy voice, and I look up to see Jackson wearing a sultry smile. Okay, it wasn't my imagination.

"Try that again since I'm an adult today."

"We can always pretend." *Damn.* How can four words make me so hot? "Happy birthday, beautiful. I missed you last night." He leans down to kiss my forehead. "Did you have a good morning?"

It would be better if you'd kiss my lips instead.

However, I keep my thoughts to myself. "I did. My mom made my favorite breakfast and gave me a pair of earrings." I turn my head to show him.

Pushing my hair back, he runs his fingers along the skin behind my ear, continuing to my neck, and then farther down my chest along the top of my dress, ending at the V between my breasts before pulling back.

For crying out loud, kiss me already.

"They're beautiful, just like you," he says while staring at my chest.

All I manage is a gulp in between the panting I can't seem to control. That desire meter is about to blow.

"Do you like birds?" he asks, jolting me from my stupor.

"Huh?"

He smirks. "Your earrings?"

"Oh… right. They're for my middle name, Nightingale."

"Mia Nightingale Marcos. I like it."

"Yeah, well, my initials are MNM, so there's that." He laughs heartily. "My parents thought it was cute and would get me M&M trinkets all the time when I was little. I'm glad I've graduated to nightingales."

He laughs some more. "That's great. I love it. M&M, huh? Should I start calling you that?"

"Don't you dare. I will hurt you in your sleep."

He grins mischievously. "I like the sound of that. I might just have to try it."

One sentence and I'm back to my dirty thoughts. He's not playing fair. Maybe I need to give him a taste of his own medicine and see how far I can push him before he breaks.

"Are you looking for trouble, Jackson?" I stick my leg out and rub my heeled foot up his calf.

"You've been giving me trouble since the day you got here, Mia, and I have a feeling there's more to come." With that, he retreats to his office, shutting the door behind him.

What the hell? That's all? I'm eighteen, dammit. Isn't he supposed to grab me and unleash the passion he's been holding back? That's how I imagined it, anyway.

Argh! If he wants to play this game, fine by me. But I play to win.

Jackson

I shut the door like always, but this time, it's not about maintaining distance; it's about keeping my remaining willpower intact. I'm waiting until tonight to make my move and hope she ends up a fraction as pent up as I've been for the last several weeks. Her attempt at provoking me was adorable and didn't go unnoticed, which was why walking away before the current bulge in my pants became any more visible was necessary.

It's going to be a long day. I'll have to get out of the office for some of it if I want half a chance at keeping my hands to myself. That dress she's wearing... fuck. It would be so easy to undo the tie around it and unveil what's underneath. And Christ, those heels? She's making this more difficult than I expected. I already have a plan, though, and I'll be damned not to see it through.

I'm barely through last night's emails when there's a soft knock on my door. "Come in," I call out.

Mia enters holding a file and shuts the door, giving me pause, but I'm too distracted while checking her out from top to bottom to over-think it. Not a day goes by that I don't find her attractive, but today she shines. From the dress, heels, and something else I can't quite place, she looks different, which is probably a figment of my imagination since it's finally the day I've been waiting weeks for.

"We need to review your schedule and go over a few messages," she says.

"Sounds good, shoot."

She sets the file on the desk and then continues around it.

"Mia, what are you doing?" I sit back and turn to face her.

She doesn't answer. Instead, she climbs onto my lap and straddles me with her knees on the chair. *Fuck. Me.* I am a dead man. My hands can't help but reach for her hips, squeezing them.

"I thought you said you'd have a surprise for me on my birthday. I'm sick of waiting." She gives me the most adorable pout.

"You told me you didn't like surprises, remember?"

"I've decided I like your surprises." Her smile… God, I'm in so much trouble.

"Mia, I'm hanging on by a thread here. This wasn't how I planned to do things." It's taking all my willpower to refrain from mauling her.

"What will it take to snap that thread? Because I think your plan needs revising." She reaches around and tugs my hair as she whispers in my ear. "I'm still your little girl, Jackson."

"Fuck it." I grab her face and slam my mouth to hers.

It's explosive. We're both so hungry for this, devouring each other hard and fast, our mouths melding together, fighting for more. Our collective moans fill my office as I grab the back of her hair while my other hand moves to palm her breast. God, it feels fucking amazing, but it's not enough.

I reach inside her dress, under her bra to come skin to skin, and my dick jerks at the feel of pure perfection. The moan she releases is music to my ears. I rub her nipple with the pad of my thumb over the hard pebble before pinching it.

"Jackson," she squeals. Her hips begin to grind back and forth over my throbbing erection.

Fuck. For the love of everything holy.

"Mia. Wait." I pull my hand from her dress and lean back to look at her. She's a siren with glassy eyes and swollen lips parted from panting, her hair disheveled from my grip. "You have no idea how long I've wanted to do that, and I swear, I wouldn't take it back for the world. But let's take it easy. I'm afraid if we keep this up"—I draw her attention downward to the bulge she's sitting on—"I won't be able to stop."

"I'm sorry. I shouldn't have done that," she says in shame and tries to rise, but I hold her in place and tip her chin up with my finger.

"You did nothing wrong. The problem is that everything you do is perfect. Your noises, your touch, your body… fuck, Mia, it's incredible. *You* are incredible." I lean forward and give her a chaste kiss on her lips. "And that's why I want to do this right. I promise you won't be disappointed if you'll just be patient."

She gives me a slight smile. "There's another one of your promises."

"And I told you I don't break my promises, so will you trust me?"

She groans and leans her head on mine. "I guess so, but it's *my* birthday, which means *I'm* supposed to get what *I* want."

I laugh at her petulance. "Ah, there's my little girl. Remember, sweetheart, all good things come to those who wait."

"Screw you and your words of wisdom." She climbs off my lap, and I slap her ass as she turns to walk away.

"Screwing is for later, Mia."

"Ugh. I take it back—your surprises suck." She's about to leave but stops at the threshold. "Don't forget, Walker will be here at noon to meet you," she says over her shoulder before stomping out and slamming the door, causing me to bark out in laughter.

Where the hell did that wildcat come from? Apparently, I made some headway this weekend, but I still need to make sure she knows I'm not just in this for the sex. If that were the case, I would have had her bent over the minute she came around the desk. And although I'm planning for that in the near future, it's not where I want us to start. She means more to me than just a quick fuck.

It was almost impossible to stop, but I've waited this long; what's a little longer? I certainly wasn't expecting Mia to make the first move. She took me by surprise, and damn did she bring out the big guns, saying she's my little girl. Fuck, I'm hard just thinking about it.

A text lights up my screen, snapping me from my thoughts.

Braden: We still on for tonight?

Me: Yeah, see you at six.

Eli: I'll be there.

Braden: See you fools later.

Dinner with the guys will keep me occupied while Mia celebrates with her mom tonight. The wait would've been difficult as it was, but now that I've had a taste, every minute is going to be torture. I'll probably get a ton of shit, but fuck it, I don't care. I'm officially whipped, and I'm on board with that.

Looking at my watch after going through the list from this morning, I see that Walker will be here in ten minutes. I've been looking forward to this visit to discuss what's happening with Mia and whether he knows anything or not. It's doubtful, but one can hope.

Mia's voice sounds through the intercom. "Walker just got here. Is it a good time, or are you busy?"

"I'm good, Mia. Come on in." I chuckle at hearing the hopefulness that I was too busy. Is she worried I won't like Walker or that he won't like me?

I'm coming around the desk when the door opens to Mia with Walker trailing behind. I meet them halfway, noticing the look of trepidation on Mia's face, and reach out to shake his hand.

"You must be Walker. I'm Jackson. It's good to finally meet you. I've heard a lot about you."

His grip is firm in return as he looks me in the eyes. "Yeah, likewise."

"Mia, would you mind giving Walker and I a few minutes to talk? Man to man."

She scrunches her eyes as if my request is crazy and then narrows them in accusation like she's got me figured out.

"I'll be good. Just thought I'd give him a chance to grill me without you here."

"It's fine, Mia. I'll only be a few minutes, and then we'll go," Walker says and gives her a wink. If I didn't already know he was gay from my prior conversation with Mia, we'd be having a different kind of talk.

"Fine. Hurry up, though. I'm hungry. And you," she points to me, "be nice." I give her the Scout's honor sign before she leaves.

"So, you and Mia, huh?" Walker starts in right away.

"Yeah, I guess it sort of snuck up on us."

"Well, from what I've heard, you've treated her like shit until last week. What's your angle? She's eighteen today, so what? You think you're free to get in her pants now?" He stands with his arms crossed, accusation written all over his face.

"That's a fair question, and I deserve it," I said, then proceeded to explain the same as I did for Mia.

I sigh before continuing. "Listen, Walker, I like her a lot. As in, I'm all in at this point. I've been fighting it for weeks, but everything seemed to fall into place when I finally stopped resisting. I'm not just trying to get laid. Hell, I've been trying not to." I laugh at my internal joke. "I'll do whatever Mia wants, and if that's to take things slow, then that's what we'll do."

"Look, Mia's my best friend, and I don't want to see her taken advantage of. I haven't seen her this into anyone, so I'm only going to say this once: if you hurt her, I'll hurt you." That's as good an opening as any.

"Glad to hear she has someone in her corner, but it won't come to that. Speaking of hurting her, do you know about anyone who might be trying to do that?"

He narrows his eyes. "No. Why?"

"I don't know exactly, but I've been noticing things. Like the poker games she's attending. They're not safe. Why is she putting herself in those situations when she has a good-paying job?"

"Mia's been playing poker for as long as I remember, but only online until last year when she started with live ones. That's for her to say why she's playing. I haven't noticed anything unusual other than what happened on Friday. She was lucky you were there to step in. So, how *did* you know where she was?"

Mia opens the door, halting our conversation. "Seriously, can we go now? Geez, you've been in here forever. Are you all caught up on the last eighteen years or what?"

Walker turns back to me. "We'll have to finish that conversation next time," he says pointedly.

Or we won't. "Sure. It was nice meeting you, Walker. Enjoy lunch, you two."

"Oh yeah, can I steal Mia for an extra half hour today? We have some *shopping* to do." He smirks as she punches him in the arm.

"Sure, don't rush. Take all the time you need. Mia, I may be out when you get back, but I'll leave a note if I need anything."

"Oh. Okay. I guess I'll see you tomorrow," she says dejectedly. Her disappointment kills me, but I remind myself it'll be worth it later.

"Happy birthday, Mia. Enjoy dinner with your mom. Oh, and text me if anything comes up this afternoon?" I say, half tempted to give in and tell her that I'll see her later.

"Yeah, okay," she says before walking out.

Walker's eyeing me curiously, and I smirk, giving him a wink to indicate there's something up my sleeve.

With a dawn of understanding and a nod of his head, he follows her out.

As soon as they leave, I clean up my desk and grab my keys to head out. After a meeting with some potential investors, I'm picking up a few more things for tonight. I want it to be perfect—not only because it's her birthday but because tonight is important. It's time to take this to the next level but also prove how special she is.

We're wrapping up dinner, and I'm waiting for the text signaling that Mia and her mom are almost finished with their meals. I was able to get everything ready to bring her back to my place tonight, but first, I'm stopping by for a surprise visit to introduce myself to her mom. Conveniently, the restaurant I'm at is around the block from theirs.

"So, tonight's the big night, huh?" Braden asks, clinking his drink against mine. I indulge him in the mock toast, with Eli joining in.

"It is. I'm just not sure how big it'll be," I respond, knowing we may not end up in bed tonight. I won't pressure her, no matter how badly I want it.

"Ah, buddy, I didn't know you had a size problem. Too bad it doesn't match up to the rest of you," Eli jests.

"Fuck you, man. Look at my hands. I guarantee it does. I'm just not sure we'll end up there tonight, that's all."

"Seriously, dude? You've been hard for this girl for months, and now that you can have her, you're gonna keep it in your pants? Who are you, and what have you done with Jackson?" Braden wouldn't know how to keep it in his pants if his life depended on it.

"She means a lot to me. I'm not just in it for the sex, so if it doesn't happen tonight, that's okay. Hopefully, there'll be plenty more opportunity."

"Shit, so we've lost you, then. Well, here's to you and me, Eli. Looks like we're the last holdouts." Braden and Eli tap their beers together and take a drink.

Perfect timing for my phone to buzz, signaling it's time to go.

"All right, guys, I'm outta here."

"Good luck, man. We'll see you on the other side," Eli quips.

"Don't do anything I wouldn't do," Braden says.

"Yeah, okay. See you guys later," I say and turn to go, but Braden keeps talking.

"Meaning, I wouldn't leave a girl hanging. Go get yourself laid, man."

I flip him the bird on my way out.

15

BIRTHDAY GIRL

Mia

M OM AND I ARE TAKING A BREAK FROM CONVERSATION TO SAVOR our meals, giving me too much time to think. It's been such a great day that I should be happier. Walker treated me to lunch this afternoon *and* paid for all the lingerie. We had so much fun. It was like old times, hanging out during the day like we used to. I didn't realize how much I'd missed him since being out of school.

That's part of my melancholy, but I know it's not the main reason. Jackson told me to trust him, but how can I? I'm disappointed with the way things ended today. It gave me an unsettled feeling, and I don't like it. Hearing that he was leaving for the afternoon gutted me. I figured things would be different after our connection this weekend. I thought… well, I'm not sure what I thought, but I know not seeing him for the rest of the day felt wrong. Especially after that kiss—that unbelievable, "take me to your place and finish what you started" kind of kiss.

"Mia, honey, what's wrong? You look upset. Do you not like your dinner?"

"No, it's amazing. I get why places like this charge so much. It's more than worth it."

"Then what are you thinking about so hard over there? I can tell something is bothering you. What is it, mija?"

I'm already keeping so much from my mom; maybe I should just get this off my chest since it's not terrible. I hope.

Here goes nothing. "Mom, I haven't said anything because it's new, but I'm sort of seeing Jackson. You know, from the office. The Soloman's son?" I clarify at seeing her confusion.

"You mean the man you're working for? Why haven't you said anything? How long have you been dating?" She doesn't sound angry, just surprised and maybe a little hurt that she didn't know.

"We had a rough start because he thought I was too inexperienced for the job, but after proving otherwise, he came around, and the last few weeks have been going well. Recently, we ran into each other outside the office, and one thing led to another. He said he'd been attracted to me for a while but held back because of my age."

"How serious are you?" she asks.

"That's why I'm upset. I thought things were moving forward. But maybe I read too much into it because today, he left for the afternoon… and he didn't do anything for my birthday." *That sounded so vain.* "I sound like a brat, don't I?"

"Not at all. It's a special day, and if someone cares about another person, it should be special for them too. I'm sorry, sweetie. Did something come up? Maybe it was a busy day."

"No, that's the thing. He only had one appointment. It's almost like he was trying to avoid me." I groan. "Ugh, maybe he was. I sort of made a fool of myself this morning and practically threw myself at him." I rest my elbow on the table and put my forehead into the palm of my hand, mortified at the memory.

"You must really like him, then. I bet it will work itself out. Did he give you any reason to think he was upset?"

"No, and it's driving me crazy." I look at her and frown. "I'm sorry, Mom. I don't want to ruin dinner with this. It doesn't matter."

She pats my hand. "It matters to you. And you're not ruining dinner. Maybe wait and see what happens before jumping to conclusions. You could always call him later and ask what's going on."

The server comes to clear our plates since we finished dinner while talking.

"I don't know. I don't want to be that girl. It's still new, and I don't want to seem clingy. Ugh, I didn't even see this coming. I mean, I was always attracted to him, but I never thought—"

"Well, if it isn't the two most beautiful ladies in San Diego."

I whip my head sideways to see Jackson striding to our table with two roses. My eyes widen in shock. *What is he doing here?*

He stops before my mom, bending slightly to present her with a rose. "You must be Sofia, Mia's mom. I'm glad to finally meet you. I'm Jackson, Mia's boyfriend." He holds his hand out to shake, and if possible, my eyes get even bigger at his use of the word "boyfriend."

She smiles at him. "Jackson, it's so nice to meet you. What perfect timing. We were just talking about you. Mia, he should join us for dessert, right?"

What?

"I'm sure he has other plans, Mom."

"Actually, I don't. But only if you're sure, Mrs. Marcos. I don't want to intrude," he says seriously.

"Call me Sofia. And I'm positive. You two should be together on Mia's special day." Her grin and teasing tone finally prompt a smile of my own.

"Well, in that case, Sofia, I'd love to. Thank you for the invite." Jackson finally turns to me. "Happy birthday, sweetheart." He hands me a rose, cups my cheek, and bends down to place a chaste kiss on my lips—in front of my mom. My cheeks flame at his show of affection.

A waiter appears with another chair, and Jackson sits down while reaching for my hand. He proceeds to order one of each dessert on the menu before the waiter departs.

"How was dinner, ladies? This is one of my family's favorites. I hope it lived up to expectations," Jackson says, giving my hand a squeeze.

"It was delicious. I'm so glad your parents recommended it. I'll be sure to let them know next week." I bet his parents told him where we were going. And then it dawns on me… he must've planned this.

Mom continues, "So, Jackson, how long have you and Mia been dating? She was just telling me about it before you arrived. It sounds like a fairly recent development." I never knew Mom was so sly.

"It is, and it's not. I've been into Mia for quite some time but didn't say anything until last week. I was waiting for the right moment, and it worked out since we had a chance to get to know each other over the last few months. Although, I think last week is when I really won her over." He smirks at me.

Oh, he's good—and so full of shit. *Do you mean last week was when you decided to stop being an ass?*

"That's sweet. Mia was telling me that you were holding back because of her age. Does it bother you being with someone so much younger?"

Kill me now.

"Not at all, ma'am. I was more concerned about Mia and if she would be okay with it." *Liar.* "I've been around her long enough to know how easy it is to forget her age. Her maturity level surpasses mine at times." He laughs, and my mom beams, already won over. He's charming the heck out of her.

When dessert arrives, we take a few moments to taste each one, oohing and aahing as we go.

"How did the rest of your day go, Jackson?" I ask casually, trying not to sound desperate.

"My meeting went well, and then I ran some errands before having dinner with friends. Now I'm hoping to convince you to go out with me after this. I planned something special for your birthday." He turns to my mom. "If it's okay with you, of course."

"Well, it's not up to me anymore. Mia can decide—not that she couldn't before, but now it's official. If she's okay with it, then I am." She smiles, both sets of eyes looking to me for an answer.

I'm relieved that my fears were all for nothing, the ache in my chest gone. "Well, it is a work night"—I smirk—"but I could probably manage to go out for a little bit." He smiles in response, making my heart pound.

"I won't keep you out too long, and if I do, you can start late tomorrow." He winks and squeezes my hand. *How is he so perfect?*

"A benefit of dating the boss, huh?" I raise my eyebrows at him, making him chuckle.

"I suppose so," he answers.

I look at my mom, and she's practically glowing while staring at us. Shoot, I hope this was a good idea. She might be reading too much into it and seeing more than what's there. I don't want her to be disappointed if this doesn't last, but I can tell she's over the moon already.

The waiter comes to clear the table, and my mom asks for the check. "Your dinner has already been taken care of, ma'am. Happy birthday, Mia. We hope you enjoyed your evening and come back soon."

I look right at Jackson. "Did you do this?"

"Maybe." He shrugs nonchalantly.

Mom takes it from there. "Thank you, Jackson. That was very nice of you and a lovely surprise. I'll get going and let you two enjoy your evening. Mia, happy birthday, honey." She stands and comes over to give me a hug.

"Thank you, Mom. You don't need to wait up," I say quietly in her ear.

Jackson stands. "Sofia, it was so nice to meet you. You've raised an amazing daughter." *He just hugged my mom. This is so weird.* "Why don't we walk you out." He reaches for my hand, not letting go as we follow her to the exit.

On the sidewalk, Mom turns to us. "Thank you again, Jackson. I'm glad we had a chance to visit. I'd tell you to take care of my girl, but something tells me I don't have to." She smiles up at him, completely smitten.

"You sure don't. She's my top priority," he states matter-of-factly.

"I'll see you tomorrow, Mia," Mom says before walking to her car.

It doesn't go unnoticed that she didn't say "tomorrow morning."

Jackson

I turn Mia so she's facing me. "Hey, birthday girl," I say softly before cupping her cheeks and leaning down to kiss her until she's melting.

Pulling back, I look her in the eyes. "God, you're beautiful. So, before we leave here, I'd like to make sure you're okay with what I have planned."

"And what is that?" she asks, still dazed from the kiss.

"I wanted to bring you to my place and give you your birthday presents… then take it from there. How does that sound? And before you answer, I want you to know I have no expectations. Where this night goes is completely in your hands."

"In my hands, huh?" She snickers and raises her eyebrow.

"Oh my God, that's not what I meant. Christ woman. You're in control tonight—as in nothing happens you don't want. Would you like to come over?" Her face gets serious, and I'm nervous as she considers.

I held back today when she basically served herself up on a platter, but I won't be holding back from going as far as she'll allow tonight. My willpower has reached its limit.

"Well, you did mention presents." She grins up at me, raising her eyebrows and making me laugh at her playfulness.

"Oh, Mia, don't ever stop being my little girl." I kiss her forehead. "You ready to get out of here?"

She nods and I waste no time leading her to the car, excited to have her alone at last.

It made me happy that her mom already knew about me. I didn't think Mia would have told her about us, but the fact that she did means she might be as serious about this as I am. I'm glad I didn't upset her by crashing dinner or introducing myself as her boyfriend—not that I'd feel too bad if it had. The sooner she realizes where my head's at, the better.

We're both settled in our seats as I pull onto the road. As always, I'm holding her hand and bring it to my lips for a kiss. "Tell me what you're thinking."

"You showing up was a surprise tonight."

"Good surprise or bad surprise?" I ask.

"A good one. I'm thinking I already like you way too much, and I was upset when you left today. The fact that it affected me so much scares the crap out of me."

I don't know what to say. While I'm deliriously happy to hear those words, I don't want her to be scared. But damn, I can't say that those aren't the same thoughts running through my own mind. Then it hits me—that's exactly what I need to tell her.

"Would it make you feel better to know that you took the words right out of my mouth? I had my plan in place, but when I told you I'd be out the rest of the day and saw the look in your eyes, I almost backpedaled. I scheduled dinner with my friends to keep me away until it was time. Mia, the intensity of my feelings scares me too. I can assure you, you're not alone in that." I squeeze her hand.

"Thank you, that does make me feel better. I just don't want something one-sided. Your reputation might take some time to shake off. I'd rather not end up being one of the girls you call for an office quickie."

"Why do you think I stopped us today? That's exactly what I don't want. I didn't want our first time together to be at work. But more importantly, I don't want it to be anything other than special because that's what you are."

"Wait, does that mean we can't fool around in the office?" she asks coyly, making me laugh and lightening the mood.

"Fuck no. I'll be bending you over my desk daily. But only after you know, without a doubt, that that's not all I want from you."

"Well, hurry up and prove it because a certain scenario keeps replaying in my mind that I'd like to try."

"Fuck." I adjust myself, trying to relieve the pressure thanks to the little vixen beside me, and decide to give the car more gas to shorten the drive.

Arriving home faster than ever, I unlock the front door and waste no time leading Mia straight to the couch.

"Wait here for a minute," I tell her.

She nods.

I start to walk away but pause and turn around. "Do you want anything to drink first?" I ask, setting my excitement aside and remembering my manners.

Mia laughs. "No, I'll be fine."

"Okay." I lean down to kiss her and then head into the bedroom. Everything is already set, but I need to light the candles. Making quick work of it, I return to the living room with two wrapped presents in hand and sit next to her.

"Hey. I did lure you here with presents, so we better do that first." She smiles brightly as I hand her the smaller box. "Open this one first."

She tears the paper off, lifts the lid, and moves the tissue paper aside. She giggles immediately, bringing her hand to her mouth and covering it.

"I couldn't pass them up once you told me," I say, chuckling.

Smiling, she lifts the G-string panties and spins them around to look at the M&M prints all over. "They're adorable, thank you."

"I'm sure they'll look better on," I tell her.

She bumps me with her shoulder, and I pull her into me, kissing the top of her head.

"And I can't wait to see if I'm right," I add. She ducks her head shyly, which is funny considering her forwardness in the office this morning.

"Okay, now this one." I hand her the second box. My nerves start to fire, anticipating her reaction.

She opens the box to the latest iPad and keyboard with a gasp.

"Jackson, no, this is way too much." She shakes her head and hands it back.

I set it on the coffee table and pull her in for a kiss. It quickly deepens, our mouths fusing together. But before it gets too carried away, I pull back, smirking at her sigh of frustration.

"Mia, let me spoil you. I put a lot of thought into what to get and figured this would be perfect for school. Please accept it," I plead with her.

"Who are you, and what have you done with my bosshole?" She smiles up at me, and my heart pounds.

"I pulled his head out of his ass. Now come here." I reach my arm around her waist and pull her over, lifting her onto my lap to straddle me.

"Is this all right?" I ask before making the next move.

"It's about time."

"Is that so? What else is it about time for?" I ask, hoping her answer will tell me how far she wants to go.

"I'm pretty sure I showed my cards earlier and lost, so now it's your turn," she says shyly.

"Listen, I'll gladly take the lead, but you have the upper hand here, okay? If it's too much too fast, just say the word, and I'll stop."

"Okay. Can we stop talking now?"

"Demanding little girl, aren't you? Well, I wouldn't want to cause a tantrum."

I grip her head and claim her mouth. It's rough and hard, our tongues warring with each other, exploring every space. Her eagerness lets me know she's ready for this. My hand reaches her chest while I grip her ass and pull her close, thrusting my hips to find the friction I so desperately need.

"The only thing I want coming out of your mouth from now on are sounds of satisfaction." My mouth travels from her lips to the sweet spot below her ear, licking and kissing before I move to taste every inch of her luscious neck. Her head goes back, and she pulls my hair while rocking into my swollen dick, making me growl.

"You need it so bad, don't you, sweet girl? Let's see what you've been hiding from me. You're such a brat, teasing me with all your low-cut shirts."

My mouth travels farther as I yank her dress and bra down, popping her breasts out. They're more beautiful than I imagined. She's fucking perfect. My mouth finds her tight bud, sucking and flicking it with my tongue, resulting in the sexiest sounds I've heard yet while she shoves her chest out for more.

I'm not sure how much more of this I can handle until my willpower snaps, and I take this to the next level. I'm ready. She seems ready, and my dick is about to burst with how ready it is. The question is, to what level are we taking it?

Mia

I've been so wound up ever since this morning that I want more. I'm nervous about making a move after what happened in his office, but not enough to stop me from doing what I've dreamed of since a certain scene two months ago created a permanent fantasy in my mind.

Pulling my bra and dress back up, I slowly crawl backward until my knees are on the edge of the couch. My hand roams down his chest until I get to the bulge in his pants and rub it through his jeans.

"God, that feels good."

That's all the encouragement needed. My knees drop to the ground between his legs, and I reach for his pants, both nervous and excited at once. I've wanted to know what it's like to make him go crazy ever since that day in the office. But before I make any progress, he places his hands over mine.

"No, Mia, tonight is about you."

"Please, you have no idea how bad I want this. It *is* about me, I swear." I look into his eyes, pleading.

"Goddamn, Mia, how am I supposed to say no to that?"

"You're not."

He caresses my bottom lip and tugs it down before relaxing back. Deciding I need a better view, I lean forward to open his shirt button by button. Holy shit, he's seriously ripped. It's always been evident from the muscles that bulge underneath, but it's nothing like seeing the real thing and the six-pack—hmmm, maybe eight—that he's been hiding. His body is a work of art.

It's impossible to stop myself from roaming over his chest before finally making my way back to his pants. This time, he doesn't stop me and even helps me when I slide them down to reveal what's underneath.

Whoa! The minute it springs free, my eyes go wide. I don't think I was prepared for this. I'm not sure if it's possible to have been prepared for this. Maybe I should have spent a little more time watching porn. I saw a few different videos—I mean, come on, it's great research—but he's a heck of a lot bigger than any of those ones.

"Breathe, Mia. You gonna be okay there?"

"Yeah… yes. Um, you're really big. Is that normal?" He chuckles in response. Am I just being naïve? Are there a lot of guys this… massive?

"Sometimes I forget how young you are. I'm hoping that means you haven't seen many of these. But to answer your question, judging from what I see in the locker rooms, it's bigger than most."

"Okay. 'Cause whoa." I tentatively reach out and slowly wrap my hand around it, feeling how hard it is—but soft at the same time. It's silky and smooth, and it twitches as I squeeze my fist and rub my thumb over the top, causing me to loosen my grip, fearing I did something wrong. Although, if the groan from Jackson is any indication, I didn't.

"You don't have to be afraid of it, Mia. I promise it won't hurt you." He smirks at me.

"Be careful with those promises. I'm pretty sure you'll be breaking that one when the time comes."

"Sweetheart, I'll have you so wet and ready for me before we get there that I guarantee your pussy'll be begging for it." His words immediately cause my thighs to clench, triggering me to take the next step.

My head lowers, and I lick the moisture leaking from the top, wanting a taste. It's salty. The tip is velvety, prompting me to kiss it and feel it against my lips. I lick at his precum again, and Jackson groans, tipping his head back.

Oh my God, I really like this so far.

"Fuck, you're a tease. Are you trying to kill me here?"

Hmmm. I guess that means I should do less exploring and more doing. I squeeze my hand around the steel rod and move it up and down, pulling more sounds from him.

Deciding it's time to just go for it, I open wide to take him in. His responding moan urges me on. I know I'm supposed to be sucking at some point since I've watched enough to know the basics, so I try that and immediately feel it jerk inside my mouth. Getting bolder, I rise to better the angle so I can take him deeper while moving my hand simultaneously since there's no way I'll be able to get him all the way in.

"Fuck, Mia, that feels so good. You have no idea how many times I've imagined this. The real thing is so much better."

His words make me moan, eliciting a guttural sound from Jackson, encouraging me. Suddenly, I feel his hands on my head, grabbing my hair, causing butterflies in my belly with what I hope is coming next. He doesn't disappoint and takes charge, controlling my movements, just like he was doing that day in the office. It's not long before I end up gagging, and I'm immediately embarrassed.

"Oh, fuck yeah, Mia. You sound so good choking on my dick. Do it again for me." Okay… so he likes that.

He pushes my head harder, and I'm choking again whether I want to or not. He doesn't pull back right away this time, causing spit to run down his shaft. It makes it slippery and easier to move my hand up and down under my mouth.

"Fuck, Mia. I'm so close. Squeeze it hard, baby." He looks down at me. "That's it, just like that."

He keeps watching with a carnal look in his eyes. His hips start moving now, thrusting up, pushing it to the back of my throat. "You're taking me so good. You're my filthy little girl, aren't you?" Holy crap, I could orgasm with his dirty talk alone. "Are you gonna drink me down, 'cause if not, you better finish with your hand. I'm right there, baby."

I look at him intently, telling him exactly what I'm ready for… what I want.

"Uhhhh… *fuck. Mia…*" He holds my head down and stills as he grunts out his release. It's not unpleasant, but it's a lot, lasting longer than I expected. I don't even come close to getting it all, the rest running down his shaft as he pulls me up and looks me in the eyes. *Apparently, I did just fine.*

"Holy shit, Mia. You're fucking amazing. Come here, sweetheart." He pulls me up, kissing me passionately. I'm sure he can taste himself, which is so weird to me, but what do I know? And seriously, this man can kiss, so who cares?

He leans back, tucking himself into his jeans. "How did I get so lucky when it's *your* birthday? It's definitely your turn to be treated, but first, I want you in my bed."

Yes, please.

16

PROCESSING

Jackson

THE LOOK ON MIA'S FACE IS PRICELESS. WHO KNEW I'D GET THAT reaction at the mention of taking her to bed? I'm not sure if it completely freaked her out or got her excited, but there's only one way to find out. I stand up, pull her to her feet, and kiss the living daylights out of her. I can't get enough of her, and judging from her response, she feels the same.

"Come on, let's get you comfortable so I can finally get my mouth on you." I anxiously lead her down the hallway toward my room, eager for more.

"Your mouth *has* been on me," she states, and I laugh at her joke, although there's a niggling part of me that's wondering if she was serious.

"Yeah, but not where I want it." I smirk and kiss her once more before opening the door to another surprise.

"Jackson, what… what is this?" She looks around, taking in the scene before her. The only light comes from the twenty candles around the room, with vases containing a single red rose placed between each one, and soft music playing in the background.

"Happy birthday, Mia. I wanted this to be special for you."

"It's beautiful. What if I said no to coming over?"

"Then I'd have left it all until you did."

"You're… really sweet."

"I bet you are too. Now come on, baby, don't make me wait any longer to find out." She blushes furiously as I lead her to the bed.

I'm dying for a taste of her, to sink my fingers deep inside, stretching her open while she begs for more. My dick twitches in anticipation, but unfortunately won't be participating. I've already decided to wait until we're in Montana, giving her plenty of time to want me as badly as I do her.

When we reach the bed, I turn her so her back is to the mattress, then lean down and seal my lips to hers. She seems apprehensive now, and I'd like to bring back her previous state of passion. Moving my mouth to her ear, I whisper, "Are you ready for me to blow your mind, little girl? Do you want my tongue on your tight little pussy?" I know I've accomplished the goal when her knees go weak and her breath hitches. "You like the sound of that, don't you, Mia?"

Straightening, I reach for the tie to the wrap dress that I've been dying to get her out of all night. I pull slowly. "You have no idea how many times I thought about doing this today. From the moment I walked in this morning, all I've wanted is to unwrap you for your birthday." I'm rewarded with her laugh.

"I'm the one who's supposed to be unwrapping presents." She slides my already unbuttoned shirt from my shoulders and drags it down my arms, grazing every inch before pushing my cuffs off and letting the shirt drop to the floor. Her touch feels so fucking good. She returns back up, caressing each muscle on her way to my jeans, but before she gets any farther, I grab both arms and move them to her side.

"Those are staying on. I'm walking a fine line of resistance here, Mia, and if my dick comes anywhere near where it desperately wants to go, I'm not sure I'll be able to reason with it. You're my priority, and right now, I want nothing more than to feast my eyes on your body before laying you down and burying my face between those luscious thighs." I grab her ass and pull her up against me so she feels just how hard I am for her.

Her reaction makes me want to say fuck it and sink into her right here and now. The whimpers that escape are sexy as fuck, and if I wasn't holding her up with my arm around her, I swear she'd fall to the ground.

"I'm ready to finish unwrapping my present now, which means you need to stand on your own, sweetheart." I chuckle as I slowly release her and lean back.

"Okay." She stands up straight and steels herself.

"That's my good little girl."

"Jackson, you can't say that after you just told me to stand on my own," she says as she falls forward with her hands and head on my chest.

I laugh, loving that she's so affected by my words alone. I can't wait to make her body come alive with what's next.

I let her lean on me while I finish untying her dress and then find another string holding it together underneath. Her silky skin is incredible as I feel my way to the knot. Goose bumps appear everywhere I touch, and I know she's enjoying this as much as I am. After I finish, I open the dress, excited to stand back and get my first look at her. I can feel her reluctance to move but can't fathom how she could be shy about her body. She's gorgeous; there's no reason she should be hesitant.

"Come on, sweetheart, I've waited all day for this. Let me see how beautiful you are," I encourage her.

She slowly peels herself from my torso, looking down shyly. Her dress hangs at her sides, giving me my first view of what's underneath, and holy fuck. She's exquisite. Her modest bra and underwear only add to the allure of her beauty.

I tip her chin up, looking her in the eyes. "You are absolute perfection. What in the world do you have to be shy about? Because from what I see, you should be proud to show off this body."

"I don't know. I guess… I'm not sure. I haven't had anyone stare at me like this." Her cheeks turn crimson at the admission.

"Then whoever you've been with hasn't been worthy of you if they didn't make you feel like the most beautiful thing in the world." Jesus, what kind of guys has she been with to give her this lack of confidence?

"Well, so… that's the thing. I wasn't going to say anything, but I don't want you to think I'm crazy, so now I feel like I should, or you're just going to keep wondering why I'm acting like this, but it's just…" She fades off and goes silent, afraid to say whatever it is.

I pull her into me and kiss her forehead. "Mia, you can tell me anything. I promise I won't judge you. Did something happen that makes you uncomfortable with this? I can take it slower. Whatever you need, just tell me."

"No, it's nothing like that. It's just… Ugh, this is so embarrassing." She looks to the ceiling, blows the air out of her lungs, then looks at me with resolve. "Okay, here it is. I haven't exactly been with anyone before." I can't keep the shock from my face, and she turns her head to the side when she sees it.

Gripping her chin, I turn it right back to me. Some clarification is in order because there's no way she meant what it sounded like. "So, when you say you haven't been with anyone, what does that entail? You just delivered a damn good blow job downstairs, so I'm thinking you mean you haven't been completely naked with someone? Maybe you kept some of your clothes on?"

"Uh, no, I meant what it sounded like. You're the first person I've ever done that with. I've never been interested in anyone enough to go past making out. I guess I was just waiting to feel… I don't know… turned on." She shrugs. "And you make me feel that, so I'm ready." Finishing, she lifts her head in assuredness.

I blow out the breath I'd been holding. *Fuck me.*

I must stand in shock for too long, giving her the wrong idea. "You said you wouldn't judge me. In fact, you promised you wouldn't. I knew you'd break one of those eventually," she says as she wraps her dress around her again, crossing her arms to hold it in place.

"Wait a minute. I'm not judging you. I'm processing. How about this—why don't you tell me what you mean when you say you're ready now that you're *turned on*? What exactly are you ready for?"

"Everything."

Holy shit, what am I supposed to say to that?

Mia

I'm mortified. "You know what? Never mind. You don't have to feel bad for changing your mind. It's fine, really. I'll just go." Why do I feel like I want to cry right now?

I move to leave, but he grabs my shoulders, holding me in place.

"You're not going anywhere but on top of that bed. Does it look like I changed my mind?" He looks down, and my eyes follow, catching sight of his massive erection.

"Let me clear this up for you. I don't want you any less than I did five minutes ago, and a part of me wants you even more because honestly? The thought of popping your cherry gets me hard as fuck. What it does change are the steps I'll take to make sure you can handle me because… well, you saw what's coming." His dirty talk never fails to light me on fire. I don't want him doing anything different.

"I shouldn't have told you. I don't want to be treated with kid gloves. I'd rather you act like you don't know and not change anything."

"I wasn't going to. But I also wasn't planning to fuck you tonight prior to this knowledge. I'd already decided earlier to wait—so don't think you screwed up by telling me because I promise I'll be screwing you soon enough."

My head drops in disappointment, but he lifts it right back up. "Don't worry. That doesn't mean we're not doing other things that will have you screaming my name just as loudly. Got it?"

I nod. "Can we stop talking now?"

He shakes his head and chuckles. "There's my sassy little girl. What am I going to do with you? How 'bout this…" he says as he steps back from me. "Remove the dress," he demands.

"Wh… what? I—"

"Uh, uh, uh. No more talking, Mia. You don't want me treating you differently, right?" I nod. "Then take it off—now."

Okay, yes, this is what I want. I like this dominant side of him, maybe even more than his sweet one; I know my body does. My dress falls open when I uncross my arms, and it's on the ground within seconds. This will be the first time I've been naked in front of a guy.

"Bra," he demands after gazing at my body for a minute. No other words are needed. I can see the lust in his eyes, the want—the need.

This is really happening. Reaching around with both hands, I undo the clasp but leave it in place, too nervous to remove it.

"Off."

His eyes go molten with lust before my bra even hits the floor.

"Fuck, Mia, your body is a work of art. I'm the luckiest man alive." He reaches down to adjust himself.

"Are you just going to stand there?" I ask him, starting to feel awkward.

"There's that smart mouth again. I think I need to do something about that, and since you already had my dick in your mouth, we'll have to use something else."

He closes the distance, wraps his hand around my neck, and reclaims my mouth. I could kiss him forever. He palms my breast and squeezes, making me moan, and then pinches the nipple.

"Jackson!" The zing of pain causes my core to tighten.

"You like that, don't you, sweetheart? Let's see what else you like."

He continues kissing me while his hand moves lower, sliding over my panties. He groans when his fingers push at my entrance over the thin fabric, and I can't help the whimper that escapes from the pressure of his palm on my clit.

"Fuck, Mia, you're soaking. I'll take care of you soon, but first I need to take care of that mouth of yours."

His hands go to the top of my panties. "If these don't give away your innocence, I don't know what does, but fuck do I like the look on you. They're coming off now, though… okay?" He's asking this time.

I nod, ready to do anything he tells me at this point. Plus, I'm at a loss for words, trying to focus on the act of breathing while hoping he'll be taking care of my mouth by kissing me all night.

"Good girl."

Why, oh why, do I clench any time he says that?

He slowly lowers himself, kissing my body along the way, and when his head is in front of my panties, he slides them down even slower, like he's savoring the moment. I can't believe he's right there, and I'm naked. When they're completely down, he inhales deeply.

That did not just happen.

"Jackson! What are you doing?" I try to step back, but I can't because his hands are holding my ankles.

"God, woman, you smell delicious. I need you on that bed." He motions for me to lift each foot, taking my underwear off before standing and kissing me into oblivion once again.

"Now, about that mouth. Since this is all new to you, some things I do might be shocking, and I don't need you questioning my every move, do I, little girl?"

Again, no words are registering.

"Open wide, Mia."

What? But instead of asking, I simply comply. The next thing I know, he stuffs my panties between my parted lips. I try to argue but only succeed at making garbled sounds.

"Shhh. This way, you won't get to interrupt every few seconds. Everything I'm about to do will make you feel good. Do you trust me?"

Holy shit, is this for real? My head nods, my body reacting of its own accord. He can put whatever he wants in my mouth as long as he delivers on his promise to make me feel good. And let me just say, fuck is this turning me on.

"That's a good little girl. Now climb up on the bed and spread your legs for me. I need to feast my eyes on that pretty pussy you've been hiding from the world. It's begging for some attention."

Oh. My. God. I'm going to die a slow and painful death from dirty talk.

Once I'm lying back on the pillows, Jackson raises his eyebrows, giving me a look that says he's waiting. I can't believe what I'm about to do. It feels so weird.

"Mia," he says sternly.

That's all it takes for me to comply. I slowly open my legs, mortification permeating my mind.

"That's it. Now bend your knees and plant your feet on the bed. I want a good look at you, sweetheart. Show me what no one else has had the privilege of seeing." I do what he says and immediately ache with need.

"Damn, Mia. I'd die a happy man if I could stare at that pussy the rest of my life." He stands there looking between my legs as my heart pounds in my chest.

He walks forward and grabs my breast, kneading it and rubbing his thumb over my nipple. "These are equally beautiful. I can't say there's anything about you that isn't, but what I've been salivating over the past few months is that ass you've paraded around the office. I haven't even had a look yet. Why don't you be a good little girl and flip over for a proper introduction?"

My pussy clenches as I turn over and feel his hand caress my butt before squeezing it.

"Perfect, just like the rest of you. Get up on your knees and bring that sweet ass to the edge of the bed."

I comply, maneuvering myself so it's directly in front of him. Once I'm situated, I look over my shoulder to see what he's doing.

"Good girl. Now spread your legs. That's it, Mia. You know I can see that uncertainty in your eyes, and I bet if you didn't have your mouth full, you'd have plenty to say right now. But fuck me if this isn't the prettiest view I've ever had. There's nothing to be embarrassed about, sweetheart, and in just a minute, you won't be able to think of anything except how good I'm making you feel."

Holy shit. I'm in way over my head here. First off, the fact that I was upset when he told me we weren't having sex tonight speaks volumes, and now here I am, dying for him to touch me. And I don't mean caressing my butt like he's currently doing, but where I'm aching between my legs.

I feel like I should be freaking out about being in this position and what he plans on doing back there, but I don't have time because he drops to his knees and starts kissing my inner thighs. Oh my God, he's licking the juices running down my legs.

"Mmm. Fuck, you're delicious."

His mouth continues going back and forth to each side all the way up to my center when I suddenly feel his tongue at my core, making me flinch.

Wait, I thought oral sex was supposed to be from the front. His face is in my ass. This feels so wrong. I start to pull away, but he grabs my hips to hold me in place.

"No way are you taking this away from me now that I've finally got it. You're soaking back here, sweetheart, and I'm not leaving until I get every drop."

He travels farther until his tongue is on my clit, flicking it, making me cry out. It feels soooo good. His hands are spreading my cheeks, giving him better access, which is somehow adding to the pleasure. He's relentless, and I can feel the pressure building. But all too soon, his mouth is gone.

"This might be my new favorite place to be," he says before diving in once more, shoving his tongue deep inside while his hand comes around to my clit, and I'm about to come undone. But he retreats again, placing a kiss where his tongue has left me empty.

"I don't think I'll ever get my fill of this sweet pussy. Fuck, I could do this all night, baby."

Then he licks from my core up to the hole he should certainly not be touching. Shocked, I try pulling away again, but when he holds me in place, my mind catches up to realize how fricking good it feels as I moan and push back.

"See how nice it is not to question what's happening, Mia? All you have to do is enjoy it, sweetheart. You taste amazing, just like I knew you would. I'll take this for dessert any day," he says before diving back in fervently.

The sounds escaping me are uncontrollable as he continues to penetrate my forbidden hole with his tongue while still giving attention to my clit. I'm seconds from exploding when he suddenly stops.

Again? Is he serious right now? But my groan of frustration only causes him to laugh.

Jackson

Not sure what I did to deserve this, but I'm the luckiest bastard alive. She's amazing. I never expected her to be this open and receptive. Holy fuck, I'm in actual heaven right now. But as much as I've enjoyed my time back here—I could stay all night—I want more. The need to see her face while she comes undone is too great to have her turned away from me.

"Ahhh, don't be upset, sweetheart. I'll get you there soon. It's the journey, not the destination, Mia." She makes some sort of angry jumble of sounds since she still can't talk, but I know exactly what she's saying.

"What's that?" I ask, trying to rile her up. "You don't like my words of wisdom?" As she starts spewing more sounds, trying to yell at me, I swat her lightly on the ass before flipping her onto her back, making her squeal. She gives me a death stare as I stand there and smirk.

"Hmmm, is there something you want to say? Should I let you talk yet, or will you be a sassy brat?"

She glares but then starts pleading with her eyes.

I climb onto the bed and straddle her legs, holding her wrists above her head. "You know what? I think you've been a good little girl and deserve to talk now." Lowering my head, I grab the underwear with my teeth to pull them from her mouth and drop them onto the bed next to her, then immediately silence her with a kiss before she gets a word out.

I love her enthusiasm, the thrusting of her hips, searching for more. She's on edge and could probably come any second.

Her mouth is so luscious I could kiss her for days. "Are you ready for more? You need me to finish you off, sweetheart?"

"Yes… please… you promised," she begs between kisses.

"I believe my promise earlier today was that you won't be disappointed. Are you disappointed?"

She pulls back with a glare. "Jackson, you're killing me. I'm going to be disappointed in a minute if you don't finish what you started."

"Well, we can't have that now, can we? I'm a man of my word." I move to the side and bring my fingers to her clit. "Is this where you need it, sweetheart?"

"Yes, please, Jackson. More."

"Scoot back and prop your head on the pillows. You're going to watch me eat your pussy, and I need to see your face when you come undone." I can feel her clench from my words, and damn, I can't wait until I feel that around my dick.

When she's situated, my mouth instantly finds her tits because these babies have been seriously neglected. She whimpers and presses into my mouth as I take one in, squeezing and pinching the other. Her breasts are a thing to worship, perfect handfuls and soft as fuck. Her dark nipples scream to be toyed with, not to mention the sounds she makes when I do.

"You like when I pinch these, huh? Should I see how wet you are from it? Do you have more dessert for me down there?" I start moving lower, kissing and licking her stomach on the way. When I dip my tongue into her belly button, she moans and bucks her hips.

I grab her knees and press them out as far as they'll go, opening her wide for me. She's staring in anticipation of my next move. I look down to see her tight little cunt glistening. Oh damn, she's so wet and ready. Why did I tell myself I was waiting to fuck her again?

"You're dripping, sweetheart. Literally dripping." I dip down and lick right over her hole, lapping up the moisture. My dick jolts in response. "Mmm, tastes so good."

She closes her eyes. "Uh uh, Mia. You're going to watch. If you close them again, I'll stop."

"You can't do that. It's not fair."

"What's not fair is that I had to wait over two goddamn months for this, and now I want the full package. Do we have a deal, or should we call it a night?" Okay, maybe I'm not being fair, but fuck it, I want to watch her come apart. I want her to see the pure ecstasy on my face while I deliver her pleasure. I also want to watch her reaction when she feels me inside for the first time.

"Fine. But I still think you're making a lot of demands for it being *my* birthday."

I chuckle. "Let's see if you still feel that way when I'm finished." Then I lower my mouth and plunge my tongue in, flicking as much as I can in her tight channel. Holding her hips in place while I savor everything I can, my head travels higher to make room for my hand. Touching her virgin pussy for the first time is something that won't soon be forgotten.

"Jackson, what are you doing?" She asks in a panic as I rim her tight hole.

"I'm about to blow your mind, baby. It's nothing you can't handle and if it's too much, tell me, but I know you can take it, Mia. You need it so bad."

"Oh God," she moans as I insert my middle finger.

Holy shit, she's so fucking tight. My dick is aching for her.

"Your pussy's squeezing the life out of my finger, Mia. My dick can't wait to get inside you." I'm slowly moving in and out of her, getting her used to the feeling. I'm so turned on that my hips are thrusting into the bed, creating enough friction that I might be joining her at the finish.

"Jackson, that feels so good. I need more."

"Sweetheart, I'll give you anything you want." I pull my hand out and slowly press in again with two fingers. They slide in easily with the amount of moisture there.

"Oh my God," she exclaims, her eyes rolling to the back of her head.

At this point, I move my mouth to her clit and give it the attention it needs, making her call out my name in ecstasy, just what I like to hear. She's moments away from climax, and frankly, so am I. I'm humping the bed like a fucking teenager, chasing my release. Watching her writhe and moan is better than any porn I've seen, and making her watch me is the cherry on top.

My next move is twofold. I bring my free hand down to her ass and find her hole to apply pressure while curling my fingers inside her pussy. In less than five seconds, she's screaming, flooding me with her release. Unable to stop myself, I explode inside my jeans as I continue thrusting into the mattress while I watch her come unglued.

"That's it, Mia. Give me everything you've got." I replace my hand with my mouth once more and lap her up, taking it all as she rides out her orgasm. Eventually, her screams die down and turn into labored breathing.

"Oh. My. God. That was…" She shakes her head, at a loss for words.

"Yeah…" I don't have many words myself because she's right. That was… something else. I crawl up and lie beside her, reluctant to leave her even though I should probably clean up.

"I mean, is that normal? Because if so, I've been missing out." She's so candid, I love it.

"Hell, Mia, that was the hottest thing in the world, and I didn't even get my dick into you, so that's saying something. You're so damn responsive, that watching you gets me off. I came in my fucking pants, Mia. That's never happened before."

"Really?" she asks, shocked.

"Really," I respond, and she beams. I think I just fell in love. *What the hell?*

"And to think we're just getting started." She snuggles into me.

"You have no idea."

17

ARE YOU MINE?

Mia

I'M STARING OUT THE WINDOW OF MY HOTEL ROOM, TOO EXCITED TO sleep anymore, watching the sun rise over the mountains of Montana, sipping my coffee. This is insane. I can't believe I'm in another state after flying for the first time yesterday. Not only that, but I'm here with my boyfriend.

The only problem is that we're in separate rooms, but he insisted, saying he wanted me to have my own space so I didn't feel pressured. He must've missed the memo when I said I was ready. It's time to be more persuasive. That's my plan when we come back to the hotel tonight because I'm tired of waiting.

He ended up taking me home on my birthday two nights ago, worried what my mom would think if I stayed over. Which I think is funny, considering she knew we were taking this business trip together, but whatever. He's trying to be considerate, and it's sweet, but it's also why I didn't want him to know about my virgin status. I want the real Jackson, and after that first incredible night, I want him now.

In hindsight, going home did give me time to process everything. It's certainly been eventful. Having Jackson go from the bosshole from hell to my knight in shining armor to my boyfriend is a lot to wrap my head around. But even my mom has noticed that I'm happier than I've been in a long time, and that speaks volumes considering the stress I've been under. The debt hanging over my head has been rough, although it does seem to be going smoother lately.

I did two online tournaments earlier this week, and they seem to be appeased by the money I've paid so far. We made an arrangement to put an envelope of cash behind the bushes for them to pick up. It's been refreshing not to worry about them showing up with this new system. They didn't text me about any tournaments this weekend, so I'm in the clear, and I didn't have to leave my mom vulnerable by saying anything about being gone. It worked out perfectly. I still have a long way to go, but it's manageable. Plus, Jackson has backed off trying to figure out what's going on, and if I can maintain this steady pace of payback, I'll be able to coast through. That's what I'm telling myself anyway.

I'm nervous to meet his sister. We're booked all day to view investment properties in the area. Jackson and I went over everything I found for each one on the flight last night. We were both spent by the time we made it to the hotel after busting our asses all day to prepare for our absence, so I guess I can't be too upset that he just kissed me good night and sent me to my room.

I'm not sure if he wants Cici to know about us—I need to ask him before meeting her this morning. There was no time yesterday since we were so busy. But not too busy to keep him from touching me the entire way and stealing kisses whenever he leaned in to look at something. It feels natural, as if we've been together for months, not days.

Finally peeling myself from the window, I notice I have an hour until it's time. Shoot, I'd better get going. My plan for tonight means extra prep time in the shower. I can't wait to see his reaction at each stage of undress. First, when he gets my dress off to reveal my new lingerie and then when he sees what'll be waiting underneath. I'm giddy just thinking about it.

Between that and the nerves around meeting his sister, I'm all sorts of flustered as I'm pulling my dress on. The butterflies in my stomach are flapping uncontrollably when there's a knock on the door. Pausing at the full-length mirror to make sure everything is in place, I inhale one last deep breath before opening the door.

"Hey," I say breathlessly before stopping in my tracks. He's not alone.

"Good morning, beautiful," he says before the firecracker beside him steals the show.

"Yay! I'm so happy you're here. I'm Cici, Jackson's way better sibling." She steps in to hug me, then keeps on going. "I'm excited to hang out today and get to know each other. Although I feel like I know you already with all I've heard. Whereas you probably only know me as the selfish brat who left my brother to fend for himself, but don't worry. I'll change your mind by the end of the day, I promise."

Whoa. She's like the Energizer Bunny—so different from Jackson's calm and collected demeanor, although, making promises must run in the family. She's the epitome of perfection, with beautiful blonde hair and bright blue eyes, just like Jackson, and looks even more gorgeous in person than she does in the pictures adorning his walls. How did these two get so lucky in the gene pool? *Come on, God, spread the love a little.*

"Jesus, Cici, take a breath. Sorry, Mia. She came early because she's the most impatient person on the planet—" He gives Cici a look of exasperation. "—and then she wouldn't wait in the lobby. Sorry to bombard you."

"No, it's fine. Come in. I just need to grab my shoes and purse before we go. Cici, I'm excited to meet you too. Thank you for letting me crash your weekend." I step back so they can enter. "And Jackson hasn't said one bad thing about you." I see him shake his head and smirk.

On the way in, he cups my cheek and kisses me before whispering, "Not that you know about, anyway," loud enough for Cici to hear.

"I heard that."

"Good," he states.

"You love me, and you know it," she quips.

"Love and like are two different things."

"Ugh, you're such an oaf. I hope Mia knows what she's getting into."

"Getting into or already in?" Jackson says with a raised brow.

Okay, so I've gathered that she knows about us. He's being very open about touching me, not to mention the kiss.

"Potayto, potahto. See what a pain in the ass he is, Mia?"

I'm laughing at their hysterical banter. They're a force to be reckoned with. "Not sure if he told you, but I only knew him as a pain in the ass until a week ago. He's working his way up the ladder," I reply.

She laughs. "Hmmm, what a strategy. Maybe I should try that. Hell, maybe we should coin the method and make millions coaching people on it."

"If anyone could do it, you could." His respect for his sister is evident. Their jesting is fun, but he obviously adores her.

"All right, I forgive you. Now, let's get going. We're due at our first stop soon. It's going to be a long day," Cici says, propelling me into motion.

And right she was. We spent all morning going from location to location fast enough to make my head spin. We're only halfway through the day, and I'm already experiencing information overload. It's fun looking at the different units, but with all the technical information associated with investment properties, I'm ready for a break. Luckily, she scheduled lunch, because not only am I spent but starving, only now remembering that I was too nervous to eat anything this morning.

We end up at a restaurant in the middle of town, a busy lunch spot tucked inside their mall, which I'm surprised they even have for a city this size. Bozeman is so different from San Diego that I feel like I'm in another country. We have skyscrapers, and they have mountains. The tallest building in their downtown—one street, I might add—isn't even half as tall as ours. And they have pine trees instead of palm trees. The air smells fresher, and the people are extremely friendly. It's like they have happy drops in the water here.

"So, what do you guys think of Bozeman so far?" Cici asks, practically reading my thoughts. I can tell by her enthusiasm that she loves it here. Or maybe she's just always enthusiastic.

"It's—" Jackson and I both start to answer at the same time. We laugh, and he leans in to kiss me, telling me to go first.

"Oh my God, you guys are adorable." Cici says.

I can feel the heat in my cheeks. I've discovered that Jackson isn't shy about PDA. He doesn't get carried away, but he has no problem touching or kissing me in front of anyone. Admittedly, I sort of dig it.

"It's way different than San Diego, that's for sure. I don't know if I could get used to it, but it's charming. I think I like my palm trees too much," I tell Cici.

"I do miss the foliage from back home. It's sad not having all the fruit trees around. But how cool is it to be surrounded by Christmas trees all year?"

I laugh, "That's one way to look at it."

"What about you, Jackson? Besides the amazing investment opportunities there are, what do you think about the city itself?" She's pushing him hard to purchase something here. I think she misses her brother more than she admits. I wonder why she moved away.

"City might be an exaggeration. Like Mia said, it's charming, and I can see why they call it the Big Sky State. Being surrounded by mountains is cool, but I couldn't live without the ocean. There's something about the salty air that just resonates with me. I'd miss that. It suits you, though, and that's what matters. I'm glad you're happy here."

Christ almighty, I already liked the guy way more than I should, but seeing him with his sister, I'm practically in love with him. It's surprising how strongly my feelings have grown in such a short amount of time. Although, looking back over the last couple months—not at our interactions, but who Jackson was otherwise—I can see how my feelings morphed so quickly. He's proven himself a man of integrity. Someone who's kind and considerate to his staff. I need to remind myself of this when I start panicking about falling for him because what *should* be happening versus what *is* happening scares the daylights out of me.

Jackson

Cici dropped us off to get ready for dinner once we finished the longest day of property showings in history. After ravaging Mia in the hallway outside her door, she asked for space to get ready—alone. She insisted on needing extra time, saying it would be worth it, which had me agreeing to leave her.

The day couldn't have gone better. My sister and Mia hit it off, bonding by giving me enough crap to bring my ego down a few notches. I love it. Cici is the most important person in my life, and it may be considered too soon, but Mia is right up there with her, so having them get along means the world to me.

I'm a lucky bastard to have received a chance at redemption after treating Mia so badly. She didn't have to give me the time of day after my behavior, but the fact that she did speaks volumes about the kind of person she is. Mia is good through and through. She can hold her own yet be vulnerable enough to let someone in. That someone being me.

I'm anxious to get her alone tonight. I'm already addicted, and after the fantastic night at my place, I'm more than prepared to take things further—as in, I will be balls deep inside of her before tomorrow morning… multiple times. She's made it clear she's ready, and I don't plan to hold back any longer. Besides, my dick has been protesting my decision to wait for long enough.

Ever since her revelation, my conscience has been kicking in, giving me hell for corrupting her. I'm not exactly the most vanilla guy out there when it comes to sex. Not that I'm outrageous, but I've definitely become more intense since a particular night a year ago.

I alluded that I'd been in the position of walking in on someone, but I didn't elaborate that I watched the entire fucking scene—literally. I'm not sure what compelled me at the time, but looking back, part of me was intrigued, all of me was turned on, and fuck if it didn't end up being the hottest experience I'd had.

After, I started looking for the next high, you could say. Some of the credit goes to Sebastian, who was the star performer along with his fiancé Lily, and the shit he spewed during their encounter. I wasn't much for talking during sex before, but fuck, now I can't get enough, and the dirtier the better.

Judging by the other night, I'd say Mia is on board. But that doesn't stop me from debating with myself over whether she should be with someone who ruins her right out of the gate. Unfortunately, my inner selfish bastard is winning the argument.

That's where my thoughts are as I knock on Mia's door to get her for dinner. This time, we're meeting Cici in the lobby since I made it clear when she dropped us off that we would see her there, knowing I wanted a taste of Mia before we left. And when the door opens, I couldn't be happier with that decision, as my jaw drops at the vision before me.

"Holy hell, could you be any sexier?"

She smiles with the familiar blush adorning her cheeks. She's wearing a black skintight dress that stops just below her ass, with a tie behind her neck, holding the top up with no bra underneath. Such easy access, and if we weren't due downstairs, I'd already be untying it.

"Your sister is fricking gorgeous, and I'll be next to her, so I pulled out all the stops. And since this is technically our first dinner out together, I wanted to make an impression." She moves aside for me to enter.

"Impression made. And my sister has nothing on you, sweetheart."

"Right… now I know you're full of crap. But I appreciate the compliment."

I push the door closed and cage her up against it. "You are gorgeous, Mia. Why do you think I'm constantly touching you in public? I want every man out there to know you're mine. Got it?"

"Uh-huh," she says breathlessly.

"Good. How about the part where I said you're mine? Are you mine?" I lift my knee and spread her legs, rubbing it against her pussy.

"Yes. I'm all yours."

Fuck it. I take her mouth hard and fast and pull the tie holding her dress in one second flat. I want her like I've never wanted anyone before. I'm a goner. I grab both breasts, one hand on each, kneading and squeezing. I fucking love these things. We're both grasping at each other, taking what we can, and are seconds from tearing at clothes when my phone dings, drawing us from the haze. I straighten up and take a deep breath to calm down and attempt to get myself under control.

"You should check that while I make sure I'm still presentable," Mia says, referring to my phone. When she tries slinging away, I stop her by bringing my mouth to her nipple, sucking it in. She mewls and arches into me for more. I'm just reaching between her legs to feel her heat when my phone dings again, making me pause and come up for air.

"Dammit. When we get back tonight, Mia, nothing will stop me." She brings her dress up and holds it there as I take a step back and let her around me.

"Is that a promise?" she asks seductively, then closes the bathroom door. Good idea, or I might have been tempted to follow.

I pull my phone out to see two texts from Cici: one, that she's here, and two, on her way to my room. A second later, there's a knock at the door. *Son of a bitch.* She seriously cannot follow directions. I open the door to her hand still up in the air.

"I texted that I was on my way up. I figured you'd be here when you didn't answer your door," she says as she barges into the room.

"You could've followed my instructions and met us in the lobby." I scold.

"Yeah, right. We'd have never left." Cici rolls her eyes.

"Alright… sorry I took so long. Are we ready to go?" Mia says, coming out of the bathroom as if she's been in there the whole time getting ready.

"Who's ready to have some fun?" Cici asks, rubbing her hands together.

I open the door and hold it for the ladies to exit, giving Mia a pinch on her ass and whispering in her ear, "that was more than a promise."

The restaurant Cici takes us to is hip and trendier than I expected. It's obviously a hotspot, with the who's who of Bozeman in the house. My sister seems to know the whole town, as evidenced by being stopped more than once on the way to our table.

Once seated, I order a bottle of wine with three glasses, but the waiter asks to see Mia's driver's license. I forgot how young my new girlfriend is—she's not old enough to drink. I'm about to backtrack, but before I get the chance, she digs in her purse and pulls it out. *Okay then.* My eyebrows go up in question as soon as he leaves.

"Never heard of a fake ID? Didn't we already have this conversation about you behaving like an old man?"

Cici starts cracking up. "Oh my God, Mia, I love you. Please marry my brother so we can be sisters 'cause my best friend slot is taken."

"Ha, ha. I'm not that old. You just didn't strike me as the type to have one."

"Playing in poker tournaments didn't give it away, huh?" Mia quips.

"That's a pretty smart mouth. Does it need to be taken care of?" I wag my eyebrows in jest.

At that, she turns bright red, probably thinking about how I handled it last time. It's certainly what I'm thinking about.

"Okay, you two, behave yourselves," Cici says.

"So, why did you leave San Diego, and what brought you to Bozeman?" Mia asks her, changing the subject.

"It was just time. My best friend, who happened to be my roommate, moved in with her boyfriend, so there was that. But I'd also decided

I didn't want to work for my parents and thought it would be easier not to if I lived somewhere else. There were some other things going on, and I guess I just needed a change. I went with Bozeman because it was still on the western side of the states, not too far away, and had heard it was booming. I figured if it didn't work out, then moving back was the worst that could happen." Cici shrugs at her last statement.

The waiter returns with the wine, giving me a moment to let that sink in. It was more information than I'd ever gotten from Cici about why she left, and it all came pouring out with one question from Mia. There's something so genuine about her that it makes a person want to open up. I'm not the only one to see it.

"So, since it worked out, do you think you'll stay for good or return to San Diego eventually?" Mia prompts.

"I'm not sure long term, but I do like it here. Real estate is going well, and I've made some good friends. But I'd be lying if I said I never missed home and the people I left behind, like Lily and Jackson. I guess we'll just have to see what the future holds. How about you? I heard you graduated from high school early. What's next?" she asks Mia, directing the attention away from herself.

"With a full-ride scholarship to SDSU, I'll start there in the fall for accounting. Cindy comes back in July, so I'm not sure what I'll do over the summer. I'll probably find another job to keep me busy." Mia responds and takes a sip of wine.

"Mia, you can stay on with us until you start school," I interject immediately. I don't want her going anywhere.

We're interrupted to give our orders, but when the waiter leaves, Mia addresses my comment.

"Jackson, you won't need me when Cindy gets back. And anyway, it might be easier to find something near campus while everyone is still gone for the summer." She shrugs like it's no big deal. But it is a big deal because… *I* will still need her. I don't think I'll ever stop needing her.

The rest of the dinner went well, with all of us getting to know each other better. Although my sister and I grew up together, it's different now that she moved away to start a new life for herself. It was also convenient to learn more about Mia with someone else asking the questions. All in all, this trip couldn't have worked out better.

I'd still like to dig deeper into what's going on with Mia, but I decided not to while we're here and to focus on developing whatever this is between us instead.

I'm done signing the bill, and we're about to head out when some guy stops at our table. He's trying to convince Cici to go out for drinks since it's Friday night. Mia and I look at each other, and I'm pretty sure we're on the same page.

"Cici, why don't you go ahead? Mia and I can catch an Uber back to the hotel. It's been a long couple of days for us." Mia looks at Cici and nods in agreement.

"Are you sure?" Cici asks.

"I'm positive. Go have fun, and we'll see you in the morning." I stand up, prompting them to follow.

Cici comes over and hugs me. "Thanks, Jackson. You're the best. Love you."

"Love you too. Stay out of trouble."

Cici and Mia say their goodbyes, and I'm leading Mia out the door at last. I'm beyond ready to get her alone and, finally, into my bed.

18

HAPPY

Mia

MY NERVES ARE SKYROCKETING AS WE MAKE OUR WAY TO Jackson's room. It was quiet in the Uber on the way here. I was too busy imagining how the rest of the night would go, and I bet Jackson's thoughts weren't far off. I'm more than ready for what's about to happen—I just hope he is, which is hilarious, considering I'm the virgin here. I almost laugh out loud at the absurdity.

"What's so funny?" Jackson asks as he opens the door.

Hmm… I didn't *think* I actually laughed. "What do you mean?" I ask, playing dumb.

"You were smiling. What were you thinking about?"

Maybe honesty is the best approach here. "What's funny is that I'm the one who's never had sex, but you've been the one stopping us," I say matter-of-factly, setting my purse down on the counter and turning to face him.

"Is that so? Tell me, do you think what we did on the way to the zoo was funny?" he asks as he stalks toward me.

"No." *Gulp.*

"Do you think what we did on your birthday was funny?" He's inches from me at this point.

"No," I breathe, lust taking over.

"And do you think it's funny that your pussy's about to know what it feels like to have my dick so deep inside it'll never be the same?"

"No," I whisper, barely able to breathe at this point.

He closes the distance, backing me against the desk, and places his hand at my throat, extracting a whimper. "Good. Because there's nothing funny about the way I plan to fuck you until you're begging me to stop. Is that what you want?" His hips are angled perfectly, his bulge pressing hard on my clit, driving my desire through the roof.

"Yes," I pant.

"I knew you were my dirty little girl, Mia. Let's see how messy we can make you." He moves his hand from the front of my throat to the back, bringing me in for a sensual kiss that doesn't last long enough before leading me toward the king-size bed.

I'm so aroused I can't think straight. I want him naked. When we stop, my fingers immediately start undoing his buttons, not giving him a chance to make the first move. Removing his shirt, my hands roam his chiseled chest while he remains still, giving me plenty of time to explore. Leaning forward, I lick his nipple, tasting the saltiness before flicking my tongue over it to see his reaction. He doesn't disappoint, hissing through his teeth and grabbing my hair for more.

"Fuck, that feels good," he groans.

My halter is untied at the same time I go for his pants, both of us eager to get the other undressed. But before I can push them down, he wins the battle as the top of my dress falls, and he fervently attacks my chest. A minute later, he's picking me up like a baby and tossing me onto the bed. Standing there with his bare chest and that sexy V showing from his open jeans makes my mouth water, almost enough to beg for him to take me. Instead, I simply stare, biting my bottom lip in desire.

"So we're clear, I'm going to fuck you until morning comes or you can't take anymore, whichever comes first, Mia. But to do that, we need to go over the basics."

"Jackson. I know the basics." I roll my eyes.

He climbs up and crawls over, straddling me on his hands and knees.

"Oh you do, do you?" He dips down to bite my nipple, making me squeal. "How about birth control? Are you on it?"

Ohhhh… those basics. "Yes. I got the shot right after making my online dating profile."

He immediately pops his head up and glares at me. "You were looking for someone to fuck?"

I'm afraid to answer but manage to squeak, "Maybe."

"Your ass deserves to be spanked so hard right now."

"O-Okay." I'm clenching at the thought of it.

He hangs his head in exasperation and shakes it. "You have seriously ruined me for anyone else. You know that, right?" I can't stop the smile that appears.

Lowering his body so it's flush with mine, he takes my mouth passionately. I start undulating beneath him, needing friction. His jeans are still on, along with my dress on the lower half of me, but that doesn't stop him from snaking his hand underneath to grab my bare ass. In seconds, we're both panting, ready for more.

Pulling back, breathless, he continues. "Next issue. Since you've never had sex, I'm assuming you're free of STDs?" I nod. "I haven't been with anyone in weeks, and I've tested clear since. I don't normally skip condoms, but going bare in your tight little pussy would make me the happiest man alive. But I'll still be the happiest man alive with a wrapper on, so I'm leaving it up to you."

"I know we're supposed to, but I don't want to use one." It was drilled into us in school: *never have unprotected sex.* But if we know we're both safe, then what's the problem?

"We decide what we're supposed to do, Mia, but are you 100 percent sure? Because that's all that matters."

"I'm sure. Can we stop talking now?" I say with a smirk.

"You're so fucking impatient."

"Seriously? All I've *been* is patient. I'm sick of—"

I'm cut off as he slaps his hand over my mouth. "You wanted to stop talking. Remember that," he tells me firmly as he leaves his hand in place and dives down to my breast, squeezing it hard while flicking the nipple with his tongue. I buck underneath him, squealing into his hand.

"Are you ready to be a good little girl and keep your mouth shut while I get you ready for me, or do you need your panties stuffed inside that sassy mouth again? Hm?"

He keeps his mouth on my chest while he slips his hand under my dress. His fingers push aside my panties to the surprise waiting there.

"Fuck me. Is it my imagination or are you lacking something you weren't last time?" He's referring to my prep work this morning, and the excitement on his face is evident.

"Goddam, Mia, I can't wait to get my eyes on you. But first…" He shoves his fingers inside, and I jerk my hips as I scream into his palm.

"You're so fucking wet. Your pussy's begging for it." He plunges them in and out of me, fucking me with his hand. It feels so good, but I need more.

"You've had two fingers, sweetheart, but I'll hurt this sweet pussy if I don't stretch you some more. Are you ready for it?"

With his hand still covering my mouth, I nod frantically, willing to take whatever he'll give me. I'm desperate for more, craving it. I don't have to wait long before he slowly pushes in. This time, it does sting, but only slightly and not enough to make me stop.

"Is this okay? If it's too much, I can slow down."

I shake my head.

"Are you sure?" he asks.

Frantically, I nod and thrust my hips to prove it.

He chuckles. "Okay, settle down. I just don't want to hurt you, and if this gave you pause—" He wiggles his fingers, causing me to moan. "—then I guarantee what's next will be a lot more shocking. Let me loosen you up and see if I can pull an orgasm out of you."

God, yes.

His hand starts to move in and out, every thrust going a little deeper than the last. Each time he pulls away, I'm dying for him to push back in, the feeling becoming addicting. It's not enough.

He senses my frustration and smiles. "You are one insatiable little girl, aren't you? Let's see what I can do about it. Your mouth stays shut, got it?"

I nod.

"Good girl." He removes both hands from my body, and I immediately start to protest but stop when I see the death glare he delivers.

"Really? You're going to make me stuff your mouth again, aren't you?"

I'm not sure whether I want to shake my head or not, causing him to chuckle at my obvious indecision.

"Oh, Mia. What am I going to do with you? I think I've created a monster."

At that, I nod, and he laughs as he stands up and works his pants off. I'm salivating at the sight before me. It's the first time he's had all his clothes off at once and holy shit. His body reminds me of those marble statues of the Greek gods. I could stare at it for hours.

After tossing his pants to the side, he reaches for the dress still around my hips and slides it down, leaving me naked except for my panties. Good, I didn't go lingerie shopping for nothing.

"My, my, my, look what we have here. Those are different than the white cotton ones you wore last time. I can't say which ones I like better, but fuck if I'm not a lucky bastard either way. Though, as much as I love those pretty panties, I'm dying to see underneath." He pulls them down but freezes after I'm revealed, his eyes shining with lust.

Jackson

"Holy shit, Mia. Do you have any idea what you're doing to me? This bare pussy is mine."

Without another word, I rip her panties off and climb up between her legs before assailing her luscious mound. Her hips buck until I bring my hand to her stomach and hold her down. I give no warning before spearing her pussy with my fingers, producing a scream of pleasure. I'm fucking her relentlessly with my hand while tonguing her clit and I feel her walls start to pulse, signaling that she's close.

"Come on, baby. Give it to me, so I can finally fuck my filthy little girl."

"Ahhh… Oh my God! Jackson!" She screams out as she finds her release.

I knew that would send her over the edge because damn, she is my filthy girl. I'd love to stay and savor everything she gives me, but it's more important to take advantage of the moment and give her what she's been waiting for—while she's ripe for the taking.

"That's it, Mia. Let it go," I encourage as I move to claim her mouth with mine, distracting her while I line myself up, stroking up and down a couple times before thrusting forward, breaching the tightest pussy I've ever had.

"Jackson!" She yells as her eyes squeeze shut.

"Shhh. Just breathe, Mia. You've got this, baby," I say, resting my forehead on hers. "Fuck, you're so damn tight. You doing okay?" The willpower to remain still is only so strong.

"Yeah, it was just the initial shock." The look of doubt I give her has her continuing. "It barely stings. Just keep moving and I'll be fine. Please just—"

"Shhh… I will, baby. Let me take it slow. I want this to feel good for you."

"Just *stop* talking and move already."

"Fuck, woman, where are those panties when I need them?"

I pull out, watching her face for signs of pain. When there are none, and she responds with gasps of pleasure instead, my resolve crumbles. I hammer into her, withdrawing slowly, repeating this a few times until I lose all control and begin to pound her hard and fast like I've been dying to do for weeks. It feels fucking phenomenal.

"Damn, Mia, you were made for me—I'll never be satisfied with anyone else again." No truer words were ever spoken. I'm done, ruined for the girl who's stolen my heart, my body, and now my soul.

"Jackson, yes. God, it feels so good. Please don't stop."

Christ almighty, I won't last long. I reach between us and bring my thumb to her clit, wanting to bring her over the edge with me.

"Come on, can you give me another one?" I grip the back of her neck and plunder her mouth. We're lost, drowning, consuming each other's moans when I feel her walls tighten.

"Yeah, that's it. Come for me, baby. Milk my dick and I'll fill you up."

She screams her orgasm, sending me over as I give one final hard thrust and lose myself.

"Oh God… yes. Fucking take it, Mia. Yeah. Fuck, just like that," I grunt out between short thrusts as I come undone, shooting inside her for what seems like forever with the most epic orgasm of my life. I'm positive it can't be topped.

I collapse, resting my head between her neck and shoulder. We're both panting like we just ran a marathon and are still trying to catch our breaths while sated and slick with sweat.

"Wow. It keeps getting better," she whispers.

I huff in awe. "Fuck yeah, it does," I respond while nuzzling her neck before raising my head to look at her. "How are you feeling? Did I hurt you?"

"Not at all." She pauses. "I feel… happy." Then she *laughs*.

And that's the moment I realize I want to make her happy for the rest of my life.

Mia

Our *activities* throughout the night finally caught up to me. My body is so sore this morning that it's reluctant to move. It protests as I turn to snuggle into a still-sleeping Jackson. The night couldn't have gone better. I'm still shocked by how perfect it was, afraid it's too good to be true. I wonder if sex is always like this or if it's rare to be so… I don't know… in sync with each other.

It didn't feel like my first time at all. I'm sure it has something to do with Jackson and how he didn't treat me as if it were. I think we were both so pent up by the time we made it to that moment there was no slowing down, even though he did try, until I put the kibosh on it. His sweetness is appreciated, but I've discovered it's not what I want in the bedroom. Outside of it is a different story, and where I revel in that side of him.

It's scary how fast I'm falling—or maybe *fallen* might be the better word. I'm glad his sister accepted us so quickly, and even my mom is on board, but how will his parents react? I'm still the housecleaner's daughter and a decade younger than their son. I'm just starting college. How is this even going to work? He's so far beyond where I'm at in life. How long will he be okay with the disparity between us?

I'm lost in my thoughts, staring at his beautiful face, when his eyes slowly peel open. His lips curve up, putting all my concerns back in their box.

"Good morning, gorgeous. How are you feeling?"

"I'm a little sore. It feels like I worked out for the first time in months."

"Unless you've been going to the gym, you sort of did. You got legs in while you wrapped them around me, abs while you rode me, and arms while you held yourself up as you took it bent over in the shower. I'd say that's a full-body workout." His smile is contagious.

"Hmm… yeah, I guess you're right. Maybe you can be my personal trainer and work me hard every day." *Like right now.*

He slides his arm around my back and hugs me, kissing my head. "Damn, Mia, you start talking like that first thing in the morning, and I'm going to be fucking you in a minute. Or should I say training?"

"I'm not opposed to that." *As in, yes, please.*

"You just said you were sore, sweetheart. I think you need a break. How about some pain pills and a hot bath while I get coffee going and call for room service."

"That'll have to do since someone can't meet my needs."

He flips me onto my back and hovers above. "You are an insatiable little girl, you know that? Is your pussy already begging to be filled this morning? Because I guarantee I *can* meet your needs." His dick is already at full mast between my legs, and I'm clenching in anticipation.

"It is, and I need my workout today, Jackson," I say in the poutiest voice I can.

"Oh, I'll give you a workout. Get on your hands and knees, baby."

I do a victory dance in my head while complying.

"Good girl. Let's see if you can take me." He rims my opening with his finger before entering. My moan is deep and throaty as I push back for more.

"Fuck, Mia, you're so wet already. You weren't kidding about needing it." He pulls his hand away and positions himself behind me, putting the head right where I need it.

"All right, remember you asked for it." He grabs my hair and tugs while squeezing my hip aggressively with his other hand as he slams into me, giving no reprieve before he starts to fuck me. I cry out in ecstasy with each thrust. Hopefully, the walls are thick.

"Is this what you wanted?" he growls.

"Yes, more."

If possible, he goes harder, grunting along with the rhythm. He continues squeezing my hip to the point of delicious pain but releases my hair and pushes my upper body down to the mattress.

"That's it, Mia. You're such a good fucking girl, taking what I give you." His hand leaves my hip to smack my ass right before I feel pressure at my back door. His thrusts slow down.

Oh shit, what is he doing? "Jackson, wha—"

"Don't worry, Mia. Do you trust me?"

"Yes…" I say tentatively.

"Then relax. You're about to have your mind blown. Ready, baby?"

This time, my answer is more of a plea. He slows his movements, and I feel a drop of something land on my asshole. *Did he just spit? What the…?* He applies more pressure, and I brace myself for what's next.

"This ass is mine, baby. I'll own every part of you someday."

Oh my God, between his hand holding me down, the pressure at my back door while he continues thrusting in and out of me slowly, along with his filthy words, I am lost in sensation. My moans grow louder, and I start to feel the now familiar pull toward my release. Suddenly, his finger breaches the rim, making me jolt.

"Good girl. You've got this, Mia. Relax and let me in."

I take a deep breath and feel the slight sting as he slowly enters, stretching me open. And that's only one finger. I can't imagine anything more than that.

"That's it, sweetheart. You're doing so good." Another drop of moisture lands where his finger is, and as he starts to withdraw, the most incredible sensation suddenly hits me, making my entire body come alive.

"Oh my God, Jackson," I plead.

"Yeah, baby. Your ass is loving this. I can feel it." He picks up his pace again and pounds into me like before, but this time his finger matches thrust for thrust, fucking my ass. I'm lost in the moment, tears leaking from the intensity. I almost can't take it.

"Fuck, Mia, that's it. Your pussy was made for my dick, just like you were made to be fucked hard, weren't you?"

"Jackson! Oh my God, I can't… I… I'm right there. Oh shit, I can't!" I cry out, scared of it this time.

"You can, Mia. Let it go. I'm right here, baby. I've got you."

I scream at the top of my lungs into the bed as the most intense orgasm takes over my body. His finger pushes deeper, bringing on a second, more powerful wave of pleasure. I'm convulsing with each contraction, unable to stop.

"*Fuck…* your pussy feels so good. You've got it, baby. Don't stop."

I couldn't stop if I wanted to. It just keeps going while he finds his own release and empties inside me, his climax matching mine in ferocity. He grunts and groans with each stroke, reaching new depths each time. My climax continues until he stops moving and slowly withdraws his finger when I go limp in pure exhaustion.

He inhales deeply. "Fuck, that was incredible," he says on the exhale.

"Holy shit," I mumble. My body is fully sated.

He pulls out and flops us to our sides, spooning me and kissing my head. "Maybe that'll teach you to be careful what you wish for next time."

"All that taught me is to never give up on getting what I want… and right now I want a nap." I yawn loudly, making him chuckle.

"Brat." A smack on my ass jolts me. "Too bad. We have plans with Cici, remember?"

I groan in response, earning another laugh from the beast behind me.

"I'll go run a bath for your sore pussy—and ass. How do you feel, by the way?"

"You need to stop asking me that. I'm fine."

"And you need to stop saying 'fine' and tell me how you really feel. I care about you, Mia. I want to make sure you're okay with this or if there's anything you're not comfortable with."

I turn around to face him while I respond. "Okay, I'll stop saying 'fine.' How about 'uh…mazing'? I'm amazing. Amazingly happy, amazingly sated, and amazingly in—" *Shit.* I catch myself and quickly say something to cover up my blunder. "Amazingly entranced by you." I can't believe I almost said—wait, is it even possible? It seems like it's too soon, but then… why does it feel so right?

"Is that what you were going to say? En…tranced? Or was there something else?" He caught it. What does he want the answer to be? I don't want to scare him away.

"It wasn't a hard question, Mia. Tell me what you were going to say, so I know I'm not the only one."

Oh. My. God. I can't stop the lone tear from falling, shocked at its rare presence.

He gently wipes it from my eye, bringing it to his mouth. "Are you going to dive in with me, sweetheart? Because if you go, I'll go. I know it seems fast, but I'm all in, Mia. I love you."

"I love you too. It's crazy, but… I do." More tears escape, a little from fear, a little from relief, but mostly from the joy of giving in to these feelings, no matter how insane it seems.

"It is crazy. Holy shit. I didn't see you coming from a mile away, but Christ, woman, you hit me like a Mac truck." He kisses me then, long and hard, branding me with his love. With each stroke of his tongue, I feel him reaching for my soul as he stakes a claim on my heart.

He pulls back with a huge grin on his face. "As happy as I am to be in sync with you, I'm going to go run that bath now before I'm deep in you instead." He thrusts his pelvis forward, showing his current state of arousal.

"And you call me insatiable?"

"I never said I wasn't just as bad." He winks before sauntering into the bathroom, giving me a great view on the way there.

I take stock of myself and realize how incredible I feel before doing a glorious full-body stretch while giggling at my giddiness.

"I'll never tire of that sound," Jackson says, returning and gently kissing my lips before hoisting me from the bed. "Now go take a bath while I get us some food." He swats my ass as I walk away, making me squeal in delight. Is it possible to be this happy?

19

BAD NEWS

Jackson

IS IT POSSIBLE TO BE THIS HAPPY? I'M ON CLOUD FUCKING NINE RIGHT now. I don't know how I got so lucky. It's as if we were meant to be, like the universe brought her to me and didn't give up until I opened my eyes. I think these feelings were slowly growing all along, rising to the surface, and once they did, the sunlight took it from there. All I can say is that it feels fucking fantastic.

I make our coffees and order room service with a smile that refuses to budge—until I check my phone and see the text from Mia's security detail.

> Security Sam: We finally got a match on one of the guys coming from Mia's house. It's not good. Call me.

Dammit. This had to come over now of all times?
Since Mia's in the bath, I might as well get it over with.
"Jackson, hey," he answers immediately.
"Who is he?" I cut straight to the chase.
"His name is Jay. He's a collector for the loan shark Bambino, who also runs a gambling ring in town. He's connected to a local crime syndicate.

Not sure why they'd be hanging around a girl like that, but it can't be for anything good."

"Fuck. How bad are these guys?"

"Do you want me to sugarcoat it?"

"Just spit it out."

"I haven't heard of anyone dealing with them and coming out unscathed, and that's of the ones who made it out at all."

"Goddammit. And you can't find a connection, I assume? Does it have anything to do with her dad?"

"Couldn't tell you, and these aren't the kind of guys who are open to a question-and-answer session. Sorry to be the bearer of bad news."

"Fuck… Okay. Thanks for letting me know. Keep a closer eye on her from here on out. I don't want her unprotected. I'll let you know if I find out anything. It might be time to pry some answers from her."

"Good luck. We'll talk soon."

"Okay. Bye, Sam."

After hanging up, I stand silently by the minibar and run through my options. Either I come clean to Mia and tell her I've been having her watched or maybe bring up poker again and try to coax it out of her. I just want to help the woman I'm in love with, for fuck's sake.

"Jackson?" I hear Mia call from the bedroom. She sounds upset.

What the fuck? "Mia, why are you packing?"

"I need to go home. Something's come up, and I need to get back." She's frantic, throwing clothes in her bag haphazardly.

I go over and grab her shoulders, turning her to face me. "Slow down, sweetheart. Breathe. Tell me what happened and what I can do to help."

"Nothing, I just really need to get home. I forgot I had something scheduled tonight, and I can't cancel it. I'll pay the change fee to switch my ticket and Uber to the airport." She tries returning to her bag, but I wrap my arms around her in a hug.

"Mia, please tell me what's going on. Let me help you. I'm not letting you leave without me. I'll go with."

"Jackson, no. You can't cut your visit short with Cici. I'll be fine."

I pull back and give her a stern look. "If you use that goddamn word one more time, I'm going to lose my shit. I know something bigger is going on and has been since I saw those bruises. Don't shut me out, Mia. Let me help. You can trust me."

"I do trust you. That's not the issue. It's just… you can't help me. No one can. I don't want to get you involved. Please just let it be."

"That's not going to happen, and the sooner you come to terms with that, the sooner we can work toward finding a solution. Now spit it out, Mia. What the fuck is going on?" I see her warring with herself, deliberating whether to come clean, and I know she's close to cracking.

"Sweetheart, look at me." I tip her chin up to see tears pooling in her eyes. *Fuck.* "Whatever it is, we'll handle it together. You're not alone anymore, Mia. I've got you." I see the moment she caves, her shoulders sagging in defeat.

"My dad… he ran away with a lot of money that he borrowed from some really bad people, and they came to get their money back, so I've been playing poker to work off the debt."

"Why the fuck are they coming to you instead of your dad?"

"They can't find him, and he mentioned at some point that his daughter was a card shark, so they figured they could use me to get the money back by having me play tournaments."

"So what am I missing? Why is it so important that you go back tonight?"

"Because they dictate when and what games I play in. They texted me about one tonight, and even though I told them I was out of town, they didn't care. They've been threatening to hurt my mom or worse if I don't do what they say or find out I told anyone. That's why I couldn't tell you. Why I shouldn't be telling you. Jackson, you can't say a word to anyone." She's bawling at this point, and all I can do is hold her tight while she lets herself go.

Dammit, this is bad, and I don't know what the fuck to do. I'm at a loss and feel like my hands are tied. What I do know is that there's no possible way I'm letting her out of my sight or handle this shit alone anymore.

"You're not going to that game without me. Tell me where it is, and I'll have Eli get me in. I'm not risking what happened last time."

"Jackson, first of all, you're here to visit Cici, not babysit me. Second, I can't risk them finding out that I told someone. If you show up again, they might figure out that you know."

"It's not called babysitting—it's called taking care of someone I love. As for going with you tonight, it's non-negotiable. The only thing they'll figure out is that you have a protective boyfriend. It doesn't point to you telling me anything other than where you're going."

"I don't want Cici mad at me for shortening your visit. And besides, they don't give me the address until an hour before the game."

"She won't be. I'll take care of it. Tell me the buy-in amount and what time the game is so Eli can track it down. If that doesn't work, we'll figure something out."

"It's at seven tonight, and it's another big one—three thousand this time. That's why they wouldn't let me miss it." She looks down in shame, but I lift her chin gently.

"Hey, I'm all in, remember? You're not alone anymore, sweetheart. I'll go pack my things and switch our flights. Don't worry, everything will work out. I love you." I lean in to kiss her forehead, and she releases a shuddering exhale.

"I love you too. I'm sorry."

"You have nothing to be sorry for, Mia."

I'm already dialing Eli as I close the door to her room. He answers within seconds.

"Hey, buddy, sorry to do this again, but I need another favor."

"Don't worry, I'm keeping track. Just remember you owe me when I come to collect. What can I do this time?"

"You got it, man. Mia has another game tonight, and I need you to track it down and see if you can get me in. It's a three-thousand-dollar buy-in at seven o'clock. Think you can find it with that?"

"Shouldn't be too hard with that dollar sign. There are only so many to choose from. But I thought you guys were in Montana this weekend. What's going on?"

"Yeah, we're headed back early. Long story, but basically Mia's wrapped up in some shit she shouldn't be at no fault of her own. I can't go into details."

"Sounds like trouble to me. Speaking of, how's your sister?"

"She's doing good. Seems to like it here, although personally, I couldn't handle the small-town vibe for long. She was right, though— there is some great potential here."

"Really? Maybe we'll have to take a look."

"Back off, man. You can have my sloppy seconds. I'll let you know when I'm done. Then you can look all you want."

"Don't worry, I wouldn't knock you out. We're more into commercial shit anyway. It's a completely different ballpark."

"Yeah, well, I'd offer to pass on Cici's number, but something tells me you already have it."

He laughs. "Not sure she'd accept my call, but maybe I'll have to check Bozeman out sometime if it's as ripe as you say it is."

"I'm not wishing you luck on either count, but I do hope you find my game tonight. Anyway, I've got a flight to switch and a sister to piss off, so I'll talk to you later."

"Oh fuck. I'll wish you luck with that one, man. I'll get to work on this and text you when I've got something. Talk soon."

"Thanks, Eli."

With that out of the way, I do a quick flight change on the app and then steel myself for the call I'm not looking forward to.

"Hey, Jackson, what's up? You guys about ready for me to come grab you?" Cici asks.

"I have some bad news. Mia got a call this morning, and something came up that she needs to head back for, so I switched our flights to early this afternoon. I'm sorry."

"Seriously? Can you send her back without you?" She's not asking maliciously since she likes Mia, but I know she was looking forward to spending time with me.

"Mia's caught up in something and needs me right now." I sigh. "Christ, she's needed someone in her corner for a while now. She means a lot to me, Cici. Hell… I might as well tell you—I'm in love with her."

"Yeah, doofus, I know. I saw it on your face the minute she opened the door. I'm happy for you, Jackson. She's sweet. I like her a lot, but I'm not happy you're leaving."

"I know. I wish we didn't have to either, trust me. But I'll make it up to you somehow. Maybe if we end up with a couple properties here, I'll have to show up more often. Speaking of, I told Eli about the place, and he might be interested in checking it out."

"What? Why would you do that?" I hear the panic in her tone. I'd love to know what went down with those two.

"He knew I was in town, scoping stuff out, and mentioned taking a look since I said you were right about the potential here."

"Ugh, thanks a lot. Whatever, I'm sure he's all talk. Anyway, can I come over and hang out until you catch your flight and give you a ride to the airport?"

"Absolutely. Get your butt over here so I have time to remind you why you don't want to live in the same city as me." We laugh together.

"Trust me, I haven't forgotten. It doesn't mean I don't like you visiting every so often, though."

"Goes both ways, sis."

"Yeah, yeah. I'll text you when I get there. See you in a bit." She hangs up.

I flop on the bed and take in the last twenty-four hours. It went from paradise to a shitstorm in a matter of minutes. I should have confessed that I'd been having her followed the second she came clean about everything. Why didn't I? *Fuck if I know* is my initial response. But deep down, I know exactly why. It wasn't worth risking a negative reaction from her under the current circumstances. She needs me by her side more than I need to clear my conscience.

When I get her through this mess and out of it safely, we'll have that conversation, but right now, what she doesn't know won't hurt her. I just wish my subconscious believed that. The most important thing at the moment is to keep her safe, which means protecting her in every way possible. I just found the woman I love—I'm not letting her go that easily.

Mia

After landing, Jackson dropped me off at home to regroup and let my mom know I was back. We thought about going to his place as if we were still out of town, but it didn't feel right, and honestly, I needed time to reflect.

Mom was surprised to see me, but I had my story ready and told her Jackson had to return for a meeting tonight that I'd be attending as well. She didn't bat an eye and even said to let her know if I would be back tonight or not. Apparently, I don't need Walker as an excuse anymore—being eighteen has its benefits. She asked how the weekend went and was happy to hear that Jackson and I had a good time with Cici. It's good to have our relationship out in the open and be able to talk about it with her.

Telling Jackson about my situation is a different story. It was a relief to share what I've been going through, but it opened the door to a host of new fears. I was nervous before, but now I'm terrified. Not only do I risk them finding out I told someone, but involving another person in this mess isn't fair. Especially since it's the man I've fallen head over heels in love with.

I still can't wrap my head around the last twenty-four hours. Being with Jackson is intense. He brings me to levels of pleasure I didn't think possible. The things he says and does weren't even conceivable before, and now I can't get enough. That he said he loved me before saying the words myself chased away any remaining doubt I had, allowing my complete surrender.

His desire for my safety makes me feel cared for in an unfamiliar way, and I'm relishing this new scenario. The dynamic of our relationship started on equal footing, but having him assume the role of protector is comforting. The future is less scary knowing he's by my side, but at the same time, it freaks me out. I've never depended on another person for peace of mind, so it's hard to be vulnerable. Is that what love does to a person?

My mind is spinning in circles while I get ready for tonight, and I decide a distraction might be necessary for a minute while I finish up, so I finally call Walker to fill him in on everything. He's sent numerous texts over the last few days, to which I've responded with short, hurried messages telling him I'd call when I had time.

He listens patiently as I recount the events since my birthday. He gasps, oohs, and aahs as I tell the entire story. After I make it to tonight—minus the real reason we came home—I finally go silent, giving him a chance to speak.

"One week is all it took. I knew it. Damn, girl, you scored yourself a man."

"Walker, seriously, you gotta give me more than that. Honestly, though, what do you think? Am I crazy? Is it too fast?" I'm looking for reassurance. Hopefully, it doesn't backfire.

"Mia, there's no time limit on love. It just happens. And, girl, I saw it in his eyes that day. He was already in love with you. I'd say if you're happy—and I can tell you are—*and* you're having mind-blowing sex, then you go, girl."

"Ugh, it would be about sex for you. It's not just that, though. He makes me feel… I don't know how to explain it… special. Important. Like I'm his number one priority and I'm worth it. God, that sounds vain. But it's not only how he makes me feel. It's him, how smart he is, how he holds himself, and you should've seen him with his sister. He's… everything."

"Mia, are you trying to convince me or yourself? Nothing you've said screams 'too soon.' Stop worrying about what you think is normal and just go with it. He's supposed to be older and wiser, right? Well, he's on board, so stop questioning things and enjoy the ride."

"Okay, you're right. That's exactly what I needed to hear. Thanks, Walker. I love you."

"I love you too. Now go have more sweaty sex tonight and give me details later."

"Walker!"

"I may be gay, but I'm still a guy. Later, babe."

"Ugh. Bye, Walker."

20

THE GAME

Jackson

W E'RE SILENT AS I HOLD MIA'S HAND ON THE WAY TO POKER. I texted her earlier that Eli had got me on the list. Fully understanding her situation made it hard to pull away when I dropped her off earlier. And even though her security detail gives me peace of mind, having her with me again puts me at ease.

My chat with Sam didn't alleviate my concerns, considering they can't do anything other than keep a closer eye on her. But that doesn't make me feel better knowing she was being assaulted while he was stuck outside last time. I'm planning to talk with Mia about having a full-time bodyguard, thinking it won't be necessary to tell her that I've already had someone in place if she's willing to accept it moving forward.

"I think we should go in separately so it doesn't seem like we're together. I don't want to raise any red flags," she says, pulling me straight from my thoughts to pissed off in two seconds flat.

"Mia, we are together, and I plan on making it obvious to everyone there. I won't have some creep coming on to you."

"See, this is exactly why I shouldn't have told you. This is serious, Jackson. It's not about you and me. It's bigger than that, and you know it.

If I give these guys any ammunition, who knows what they'll do next? I just need to ride it out, and eventually, I'll pay them off and be done with this. But until then, you and I both need to play by the rules and not stir the pot."

"Goddammit. I hate this for you. Wait, how much do you owe them?" *Fuck, why am I just now thinking of this?*

"A lot."

"What's a lot?"

"I'm down to $180,000."

"You're paying them off tomorrow."

"What? No, absolutely not. I get that you want to help, but there's no way you're doing that. No." She's shaking her head, as adamant as I've ever seen her, but she won't win this argument. I'm half tempted to turn this car around right now and say fuck it, but I don't want to put her or her mom in jeopardy before they have the money in hand.

"Mia, our company brings that amount in every week. I'm not taking no for an answer. Your safety is more important to me than your pride."

"You have no right to demand that. Being in a relationship doesn't mean you get to make decisions for me."

"Dammit, Mia, that's not what I'm doing. I care about you. I love you, for Christ's sake. If you're in danger, I'm in danger along with you. Everything that happens to you happens to me now, sweetheart. If you get hurt, I hurt. If you feel threatened, then I've been threatened, and if you have a burden to bear, I'm right there with you, carrying the other half. That's what it means to love someone." I bring her hand to my mouth and hold my lips against it, needing any part of her I can reach.

"We can talk logistics later," I continue. "Whatever is holding you back from letting me do this, forget it right now. We'll figure out the rest after you're safe and out from under these assholes. If you want to keep playing poker and pay me back, then do it. If you don't want to play anymore but still pay me back, you can do that too. I'm not taking away your independence—I'm trying to get it back." The tear running down her cheek pierces my heart, and I pull over.

I reach over and undo her buckle once the car is in Park. "Come here, sweetheart." I urge her into my arms and cradle her on my lap sideways, with her back to my door and legs hanging over the center console. She nuzzles into my neck as I hold her tight.

"Will you please let me take care of you?" I plead with her.

"I just… It's too much. And it would take too long to pay you back. And what happens if we broke up—"

"You're already planning for our breakup?" I ask, chuckling. "That's not giving me much confidence here, sweetheart."

She swats my chest. "I don't mean it that way, but you don't know what the future looks like. There's already a huge disparity between us. You're way older, you have more money, you're further in life, and one day, you might wake up and realize I'm not good enough for you."

"Mia, if anything, *you're* too good for *me*. I don't know what I did to deserve you, but nothing about you is less than. You're it for me. I don't want to scare you off with that statement, but it's true. If society didn't dictate what's normal and what you should or shouldn't do, I'd make you officially mine right now."

"You can't say things like that."

"Why, because it's too soon? Fuck that. Look, I'm not asking for marriage, and I'm not expecting you to feel the same, but I want you to know that's how serious I am. And if I do this, I don't care if you ever pay me back. I just want to know you're safe. God forbid we break up, but if that happens and it makes you feel better, we can write up a contract. Whatever it takes to have you accept my help."

She sighs. "Okay, fine, but I do want it in writing that I owe you with conditions on paying it back."

Thank fuck.

"Damn, you're a stubborn woman. I do like the sound of these conditions for payback, though. Can I negotiate a few of them?" I say seductively to lighten the mood and bring a smile to her face, and it works like a charm.

"You're awful. And there's nothing you could put in there that I wouldn't do anyway."

"Oh, I know, but you being forced to do things is fucking hot." And I'm not kidding, given the state of my growing erection.

"Oh my God, Jackson, seriously, you cannot turn me on right now. We need to get to the game." She sits up, ready to scoot back over to her seat.

"All right, but one kiss before you go."

While she's busy with my mouth, I sneak my hand up her skirt, unable to resist. Making quick action of moving her panties aside, my fingers slide into her already wet pussy, while my thumb teases her clit. I'm dying to pull an orgasm out of her before we go since pleasing her has quickly become an addiction.

She moans into my mouth, bucking and rubbing her ass on my dick. Fuck, I might come from that alone.

"Give me one orgasm, Mia. Let me feel it." I curl my fingers deep inside, moving back and forth against her walls, knowing it'll send her over. Immediately, I feel her tightening.

"Yes, more." She bucks harder, desperate for release.

I push deeper, my words coming out in time to each thrust of my hand. "This right here, Mia? This is what I want… every day… for the rest of my life. For you to be mine. To fuck, take care of, and pleasure… whenever, however, and wherever the fuck I want. Come on, give it to me. Now, Mia."

She wails into my neck, riding out her release. The minute she stops pulsing, I bring my fingers up, sucking them clean before plunging my tongue into her mouth.

I pull away and look her in the eyes. "I love you, Mia."

"I love you too. Thank you. That was… nice."

"You better go back to your seat before I decide to keep going until you have something better to say than 'nice.'" She giggles as she climbs over, a sound I can't get enough of.

"Nothing you do is just nice. I think you know that already, and the last thing you need from me is an inflated ego." She buckles up, and I pull back onto the road, smiling.

"You are one sassy little girl, Mia. And I fucking love it, so don't ever change."

Mia

Jackson ends up winning the battle, and we enter together. His erection still hasn't disappeared, making me giggle on the way in. Tonight's game is in an office building downtown, a much nicer location than last time. Looking through the large glass windows while we're paying, I see three tables with eight seats at each. It's another large pot, and if I can finish somewhere in the top three, I could make a nice dent in the amount owed. Although big money attracts better players, so we'll see.

All games have some system to choose your seat upon arrival, and this one has face-down seat assignments. We both choose one, ending up at different tables, which doesn't make Jackson very happy, but I'm relieved. Usually, my game face is one of my biggest strengths, but Jackson has made all my walls come down, and I'm not sure I can separate that while playing. It's best to have some time to get back in the groove before testing myself.

Going all caveman, he walks into the room with his arm around my shoulders, staking his claim. After sealing the deal with a kiss, he wishes me luck before we take our seats. Knowing we're paying them off tomorrow relieves my concern about being here together, and honestly, I feel safer having him with me.

As always, I'm met with skepticism as I take my place at the table. Oh well, it's fun to take them by surprise. It gives me a sense of satisfaction to shock the shit out of everyone and makes taking each one out that much sweeter.

We make introductions and organize our chips until the cards are dealt. As I pick up my first hand of the night, the familiar hum of excitement makes its way through me.

I try not to look at Jackson during the game, but the pull is too strong, and I end up caving between hands. His eyes are always on me, staring so intensely that I blush. He winks occasionally if both tables are mid-shuffle; otherwise, someone would think we were cheating if we had cards. I'd wink back, but oddly, it's not something I've ever been able to do. One eye just won't close without the other.

Only four players have been knocked out by the time the first fifteen-minute break rolls around, proving how fierce the competition is. Jackson motions me to the door, then grabs my arm and guides me down the hallway at a frantic pace.

"Jackson, where are we going?"

"No words. I need you to be a good little girl for me right now."

Oh God. I'm immediately turned on.

He pulls me into a single bathroom and locks the door behind him, backing me up against the wall and pinning me in place with his body. "Do you know how fucking hot it is seeing you sit at that table and win hand after hand, seeing the look of awe on all those men's faces, knowing you're all mine? All mine to take advantage of. Mine to do with what I want." All this is whispered in my ear seductively, making me shiver with anticipation.

He steps back, whips his coat off, and lays it on the ground before him. "Down on your knees. Now. This is going to be hard and fast."

I'm drowning in lust, ready to do whatever the hell he tells me as I lower to the ground, watching as he undoes his pants and starts stroking himself.

"Open that smart mouth for me and stick your tongue out." He rubs his tip on my tongue, then paints my lips with the moisture before repeating the motion.

"Need you nice and slick for me. You ready, little girl?" I groan and nod. "Open wide and relax your throat." He holds the back of my head and guides himself in slowly with his other hand.

"Fuck yeah, just what I needed. This won't take long, I promise. Breathe through your nose, baby." With that, he grabs my head with both hands and jerks into me fast and deep.

I gag immediately and glance up at him. Holy shit, I could climax from the look on his face alone. He's lost in the chase for his release, his eyes fixed on his dick sliding in and out of my mouth, feral.

"Deeper. Yes, just like that." He continues thrusting into me at a speed so fast that all I can do is try not to gag.

"Look at you sucking my dick like a good girl." My panties are pooling by now, and I can't help reaching down to rub myself, already on the verge.

He suddenly pulls out, giving me a reprieve. "My filthy girl needs another orgasm? Are you going to come while you choke on me?"

I nod before he plunges back in.

"I love seeing you on your knees. You're such a good little girl." My eyes close in ecstasy, and I moan at the combination of his words, along with my fingers working my clit.

Suddenly, he pushes in hard and stills. "God, yes. Fuck, Mia, I'm coming. Swallow it for me, baby. Take it all. *Oh fuck… yesss… agh.*" He throbs deep inside, shooting down my throat as I tip over the edge with him. Choking, I take as much as possible, while the rest spills out. After the last pulse, he drops to his knees, devouring me with his mouth, unconcerned with the mess around mine as he plunges his fingers into me, causing my orgasm to reach a whole new level.

He pulls away after it finally subsides and looks at me. "Holy shit, Mia, that was fucking hot. God, I needed that. Thank you."

"I think you should always have to pleasure me on our way somewhere if this is what happens," I say with a smirk.

He kisses me again. "God, I love you. How did I get so damn lucky?" He stands, helping me up with him. "Let's get cleaned up and back in there before we get forfeited." He must see the panic in my eyes because he immediately smirks and says, "Kidding. I'm kidding. We still have five minutes. You're okay."

We enter the room on time, and my cheeks go scarlet, feeling like everyone knows what we did. Jackson kisses me and wishes me luck again before we sit. Oh well, I'll never see these people again anyway, I suppose. I just hope a few more of them go out quicker than they did in the first session. It's time to step up my game.

Another hour goes by until three big chip leaders are at our table, me being one. Two of the small stacks go all-in by all their chips forward, and lucky for me, I'm on the button—the last player to place a bet. They probably think I won't call, each one hoping to double their stack by taking the other guy out, but too bad for them—I happen to have a pair of kings.

Now I need to decide how to maximize this play with the other chip leaders. Or maybe I just want to bet high and force them out, leaving only the short stacks to compete with. *Decisions, decisions.* I settle on luring them in for another turn by simply calling the all-in amount. It works, and after two of them place another bet following the turn, I decide to raise, causing them to fold and adding a few more chips to my stack.

The three of us remaining flip our cards over since no more betting can take place with all their chips already in play. They both groan when they see my hand, but in my mind, it's never over until the last turn. Seeing one guy with a low pair means that if that card or any of his other cards come up, my kings will lose to a three-of-a-kind or two pairs. It wouldn't significantly affect me, but I'd certainly rather take both players out. One guy stands, anxiously awaiting his fate. The dealer flips it, and I sigh in relief while the guy standing pounds the table with his fist.

"Fucking hell. Who is this damn chick, and who let her in? This is bullshit!"

Jackson is out of his chair and in the guy's face in two seconds flat. "I'd shut your fucking mouth if you know what's good for you."

"Jackson, don't," I plead. "It's fine."

"What did I tell you about that word, Mia? It's not fine; he doesn't get to disrespect you just because he's a sore loser."

"Listen, asshole, mind your own business," the guy snaps.

Jackson whirls on him. "She *is* my business, so why don't you tuck your tail between your legs and leave before I drag you out myself."

"Whatever, man, settle down. I'm out of here. Your bitch isn't worth fighting over."

Thwack! Jackson punches him square in the face.

"Jackson, stop!" I yell, even though, based on the rage in his eyes, I'm pretty sure it goes unheard.

"Son of a bitch! You broke my nose!" the guy shouts.

Two guys hold Jackson back. "I'll break more than that if you say another fucking word," he snarls.

The other players urge the guy to leave, distracting him from provoking Jackson further. After a few tense moments, he starts walking away. "You can all fuck off" are his parting words as he leaves the room. My shoulders sag in relief.

The room settles down, and some guy tells Jackson that he'll be asked to leave if there are any more problems. Jackson answers that there won't be if no one else disrespects his girlfriend, making me roll my eyes. Luckily, with those two out and some others around the room, it's time to choose new seats and consolidate down to two tables, giving us a ten-minute break.

As soon as Jackson and I reach the hallway, I lay into him. "You can't punch everyone who says something bad about me. I deal with jerks like that all the time. I'm used to it."

"You shouldn't have to be used to it, Mia. It's not okay, and it won't happen on my watch."

"I don't need you to come to my rescue. Outside of our bedroom fantasies, I'm a big girl, Jackson, which means if I need your help, I'll ask for it."

"Mia, it's my job to protect you."

"No. It's my job to protect myself. Now behave in there. Otherwise, *I'll* be the one making you leave. Those guys will probably hear about this now and add more to my total. Don't make it worse."

"Fuck them, I'm paying it off anyway. I won't stand by while someone treats you like shit. Sorry, sweetheart." He leans in and kisses me on the lips before walking back in.

I blow out a breath of frustration as I follow, wondering how I missed it that he's just as stubborn as me but seems to have the upper hand.

Ugh. Here's to hoping no one else says any shit about me.

Luckily, no one does, and the remainder of the night goes smoothly. Jackson and I end up at the same table for the second round, and just like last time, he's having good luck tonight with the cards. We try to avoid playing the same hands because neither wants to take the other out, so we dance around, watching for any signs of who has the better cards. It's affecting how we play but has no major impact other than failing to grow my stack as quickly as I could otherwise.

At the third and final break, before we combined into the final table, Jackson pulled me aside and told me to stop worrying about him and play as if he were any other player, telling me to take him out if it came to that. He said if he noticed I wasn't playing to win against him, he'd make me regret it later. The way he said it almost had me do the opposite just to see what he had in mind.

But in the end, I did play to my full capability, and as usual, the players at the final table witnessed me play enough that I'd earned their respect as a worthy opponent. Jackson finished in fourth place, winning double his buy-in, and proceeded to watch while I finished my best night yet and came out victorious.

I'm excited to be able to use tonight's winnings to reduce the amount owed before we settle up tomorrow. I'm on a poker high as we reach Jackson's place. Watching me in action apparently got him all sorts of worked up, and after mauling me in the car, he promised there was more to come. I'm very much looking forward to that.

Jackson has me up against the wall as soon as the door closes. His hands are everywhere, his mouth on mine, and all the pent-up lust comes pouring out at once. He hoists me up and turns to carry me to the bedroom when a loud knock sounds at the door.

"Who would be here at this hour?" I ask.

"No fucking clue, but it better be good." He sets me down and adjusts himself before going to answer.

Suddenly, it dawns on me who it might be. "Wait! Don't open it. Check who it is first. What if they followed me to your house?"

There's another knock, louder than the first, along with someone's voice. "FBI, open up."

21

CHOICES

Jackson

"WHAT THE FUCK IS THE FBI DOING HERE?" I ASK MORE TO myself than anything.

"I don't know, but hurry and open the door. You can't leave them out there," Mia says frantically.

Through the peephole are two agents, a man and woman in suits, standing like statues while holding their badges up. I open the door and take a closer look at each one. They seem legit to me. I'm about to ask what this is about but get the answer before having the chance.

"I'm Agent Roger Bale, and this is Agent Liz Wallace. Agent Wallace and I would like to speak with Mia. May we come in?"

"I'm assuming we don't have a choice," I say, moving aside for them to enter.

"You always have a choice, but cooperating makes our jobs easier." They walk in and see Mia standing off to the side.

Her face is pale, and she's shaking like a leaf, which prompts me to shut the door quickly and go wrap her in my arms. "Shhh. It'll be okay. I'm here, sweetheart." She seems to calm as I rub her back.

"Mia, I'm Agent Wallace. Would you mind if we ask a few questions?"

Agent Wallace is the softer of the two, which is probably why she's the one to address Mia.

"Sure." The fear in her voice pierces my heart, and I wish I could carry her off and make all her problems go away.

"Let's sit down at the kitchen table," I suggest. "Can I get you water or anything?" They both respond no as they take their seats. "Mia?"

"No, I'm fine."

I give her the look and see the tiniest hint of a smile. If my only job in life were to bring a smile to her face, I'd be content.

We sit across from the agents and I hold Mia's hand in mine, squeezing it in encouragement.

"First, are you okay with Mr. Soloman being present for this discussion?" Agent Wallace asks. "So far, this matter is strictly related to you, although we'll get to Mr. Soloman in a moment."

What the fuck is that supposed to mean?

Mia doesn't even hesitate. "Yes. I want him to stay."

"Noted. Is it okay if we record this?" Mia nods. "Your answers will need to be verbal from here on out."

"Yes, you can record it." She states firmly.

"Great, thank you, Mia. Let's start by telling you what we know. You've been receiving visits from two men, one of whom you know as Frank and the other as Jay. Is that correct?"

"Yes?" Mia answers with the accent of a question.

"Good. So, here's what we've learned so far. They've been coming to collect a debt resulting from your father, Roland Marcos, who took a loan to finance his gambling habit and skipped town with the money. How are we doing so far?"

"That's correct." The anxiousness is present in her voice. My hand squeezes hers, reminding her that I'm by her side.

"Then somehow, they discover you're a poker genius, and decide to pimp you out, so to speak, to play at their organized games and win, essentially racketeering their own system. And each time you win, the amount goes toward your father's debt. Are we still on the right track?"

"Yes, but—" They cut her off and continue.

"So, they text you where to be and when to be there, and after you win, you leave it near your front door so they can grab it the next day. Still tracking?"

"Yes, but how do you know all that?" Mia asks.

"We'll get to that soon. Here's where we need help filling in the blanks. Can you explain how they learned about your particular skill and how they *persuaded* you to cooperate? We're also unclear as to the extent of the amount owed. We have more questions, but this will complete the narrative to date."

Enough is enough. I'm not letting Mia talk until we know why they're here. "How about before she answers your questions, you tell us your intentions and why you're here. And how about whether she should have an attorney present."

"See, when people start throwing around the word 'attorney,' things generally go south, especially when we're here to help you, Mia," Agent Bale pipes up. They're clearly going for the good cop, bad cop routine, trying to play Mia.

"Then prove it and tell me why you're here," Mia responds, filling my heart with pride. God, she's so strong. I don't give her enough credit.

"Alright, let's cut to the chase and see if we can move this along. We've been after this group of criminals for a while. They have worse operations than loan sharking and illegal gambling, but until we pinpointed you and your situation, we didn't have anything solid to bring them in on. Now we do. If we can take them down on this, it could halt their more serious crimes while we're at it."

"How did you find out about me?" Mia asks, still bewildered.

"That's where this guy comes in," Agent Bale says, pointing to me. *Fuck, I think I know where this is going. Goddammit.* "If it weren't for this guy, we might still be chasing our tails, but when a security firm started poking around, looking into the same guys we were, we decided to see why. Turns out, it was you."

Fuck me.

Confusion is written all over Mia's face. "What are you talking about?" she asks Agent Bale, then looks in my direction, turning the question on me and yanking her hand from my hold.

"Mia, I was going to tell you. I wanted to protect you, and since I didn't know what was going on or how to do that, this was the only way I could think of."

"What did you do, Jackson?" Her voice is filled with accusation as her eyes start to go glassy.

"They hurt you, Mia. I saw the bruises myself, and I knew something was wrong. I couldn't leave you vulnerable and risk your safety, so I hired a security firm to watch over you. I was trying to help, Mia." I'm frustrated that I'm not getting through to her.

"By having me followed? Are you insane? You can't just violate someone's privacy like that. How dare you?" She scoots her chair farther away, putting enough space between us that I can't reach her.

"You were in danger, Mia, and you wouldn't tell me what was happening. If you had just told me up front, I could've paid these guys off right away, and this whole mess would've been over by now."

"Oh, so this is *my* fault? Right. I should've just told *you*, the asshole who made my life fucking miserable for two whole months. Just asked for help from the guy who hated my guts. How stupid of me, huh? No, what's stupid is that I trusted you. What's stupid is that I let you fool me."

Her tears fall, breaking my heart, while both agents observe the conversation with intrigue. How can my world come crumbling down in a matter of minutes?

"Mia, I'm sorry. My hands were tied, and I did what I thought was necessary to keep you safe. That's all I ever cared about. You were important to me long before I admitted it to myself. You need to understand."

"No—we're done, Jackson. I can't trust you. Not only did you lie to me, but you put my mom in danger with your actions. You may have been trying to protect me, but you risked the most important person in my life. If Frank and Jay had found out about this like the FBI did, then she might be dead right now."

Fuck, why didn't I tell her when I had the chance? She might have taken it differently instead of being blindsided. I'm such an idiot, not to mention the reason the FBI is here at all.

"Mia, wait. I thought I was doing the right thing. I would never hurt you. I was only trying to protect you. You have to see that." How can she not?

"All I see is someone who lied to me and kept secrets from the person he was supposed to be in love with." She turns toward the agents. "Is there somewhere else we can finish this? I'd like to leave now."

"Cer—" Agent Wallace starts to respond, but I'm not ready to give up yet.

"Mia, you know I love you. Please don't leave. Let's work this out so I can help you through this."

She stands up, and the agents follow. "You've done enough to help, Jackson. You know, since you brought the FBI in, I don't need you anymore."

It's the final blow. The air deflates from my lungs as I accept defeat.

She grabs her bag and walks out the door, and just like that, she's gone, taking my heart with her. I'm not sure how to describe this ache in my chest. It's like nothing I've felt before, and knowing I'm the only one to blame is the final nail in the coffin.

Mia

I rush to the elevator, not caring if they're behind me. I'll wait in the lobby if necessary, but I need to walk away before my resolve crumbles. I'm sobbing as I enter, pressing the button frantically, but before the doors shut completely, they stop them and step in. Agent Wallace hands me a tissue.

"I'm sorry," I say through my sniffles. "I'll be fine in a minute. Is there somewhere we can go other than my house? I don't want to worry my mom." My eyes widen from my sudden thought. "What if they find out about this and they go after her? She's home alone. Is there anything you can do?" I'm panicking.

"It's okay, Mia, she's safe. We have someone watching your house 24/7 right now."

"Thank God. So, can we go somewhere else, then?"

"Sure. Would you like something to eat or some coffee?" she asks as we make our way out of the building.

"Yeah, coffee sounds good."

They remain silent the entire way, leaving me to cry it out while they drive. Looking back, my reaction may have been harsh. I know he was trying to protect me, but it's hard to come to terms with him doing it behind my back. Even at the time of my own confession, he said noth-ing. Would I have been mad if he had told me then? I'm sure finding out this way made it worse.

My phone has been pinging with texts from Jackson, telling me he's sorry, that he loves me, that he'll do anything to make it right. God, I said some terrible things to him. The fact that he's still trying after that is a testament to his desperation. I'm tempted to respond but decide to get this over with first.

After arriving at the coffee shop down from my house, Agent Wallace starts in as soon as we're seated with our drinks. "We're going to start where we left off, all right?" I nod, staring down at my cup, my mind numb from the last hour. "So, as we put the pieces together about your situation, it became clear that you could put these guys behind bars by bringing them in for extortion, money laundering, illegal gambling, and why not tack on assault of a minor. We start there, then go after their boss who's giving the orders."

"Yeah, they mentioned their boss quite a bit, but never by name. It was always just 'boss.' So, how does this work exactly? Do I just give a statement, press charges, and then testify when the time comes?"

Agent Wallace has been nice, but I'm starting to lose my patience as she answers. "I wish it were that simple, Mia. This is where it gets tricky. First, you need to understand that you're dealing with a very powerful crime family whose reach is wide. They have people on the inside ev-erywhere, from the police to the government and even the courts. They also have handlers, like Frank and Jay, who make sure those individuals do what they ask by issuing threats and following through on them. It's a dangerous organization to go up against and takes special precautions."

"Okay, so what do you need me to do?" I just want her to get to the point already.

Agent Wallace continues, "Before we get to that, it's important for you to know that these things take time. Pressing charges, gathering evi-dence, filing motions, and getting through a trial, if it comes to that, could take years. While this is all happening, these guys still have connections, meaning they can often eliminate the proof against them before it ever makes it to court, essentially ensuring their freedom. In this case, you're that proof."

I scoff. "So, you're saying my life would be in danger even more than it is now if I were to help you? Why would I do it, then?"

Agent Bale takes a turn. "Were you aware that you've been participating in illegal gaming in the State of California and that the penalty is up to six months in jail and a fine of up to a thousand dollars per occurrence? You've been to four, maybe five games, so let's see, that would be two years for good behavior and five thousand dollars. Or we could take your testimony and call it even." I've decided I don't like him—at all.

I cross my arms. "Which is only helpful if I'm alive, and from what it sounds like, that wouldn't be for long, so I think I'm better off going to jail. You're not selling your case much."

"What if we offered you a place in our witness protection program? New identity, a new life—safety. You can choose where to live from a list of locations and, after the trial's over, decide if you want to return to the life you have now or remain in your new one."

"Let me get this straight: I can either let you put me in jail and fight charges for illegal gambling with money I don't have or agree to testify for you and be placed in the witness protection program. Are there any other options?" Is this seriously happening right now? I can't believe my life just fell apart in under an hour.

Agent Wallace answers, "I hate to be the bearer of bad news, but no. Remember, you would be an integral part of bringing justice to hundreds of people who have suffered at the hands of this organization. You'd be saving lives, Mia."

"Exactly how does this protection thing work? Can I stay in contact with my family? Friends? Anyone? And what about money, a job? Where would I live? And my mom? I can't leave her. Would—"

Bale puts his hand up to stop me. "Listen, there are a lot of details to work out, and we do all that while you're safe at a secure location, which is our number one priority. As for your mom, she can go with you, but you both leave everyone behind. Not a single person will know where you are. The smallest tip can be traced. A noise in the background can give it away. No contact is allowed in the program."

How can they be so matter-of-fact about this? They're discussing uprooting my whole life like it's no big deal.

I shake my head. "This isn't something I can decide overnight."

"Unfortunately, that's all you have. Your window closes tomorrow at noon, and then we'll decide for you," Agent Bale says sternly.

"Meaning you'll arrest me."

"The choice is yours, Mia." He says.

Some choice. "Gee, thanks, that's so generous of you."

"Think of the good that will come from this. I'm sorry you're in this position. It's a shitty hand you were dealt." Agent Wallace's pun doesn't go unnoticed but isn't appreciated under the circumstances.

"Can I go home now?" My reasonableness has worn off, and any more jokes and I just might lose it.

When it sinks in that yesterday was real and not a dream, I want to close my eyes and never wake. Mom and I stayed up late into the night while I confessed everything that had happened since Jay and Frank showed up. There were tears and apologies on both sides, hers from thinking I bore the burden alone and mine from keeping it from her.

We went over both options round and round, back and forth, weighing the pros and cons of each. The pro side had less to do with actual pros and more with what made one choice better than the other. The way I see it, there are no positives other than bringing this guy down and preventing him from hurting anyone else, which ultimately weighed heavily in our decision.

Mom was worried about the impact on me in both scenarios, considering it would be my jail time on one hand or saying goodbye to friends on the other. Finally, we did the only thing that made sense, so I texted the number they gave me, solidifying it before we changed our minds. The only thing left is to say goodbye to Walker, who will be here in the morning—he just doesn't know why.

After we exhausted that discussion, she held me while I broke down and recounted what happened with Jackson. She assured me that it would all work out, saying there would be many other loves in my lifetime.

Unfortunately, I know better. He ruined me for any others. How do you move on after having Mr. Perfect? God needs to make up his mind on whether I deserve happiness or not because this back-and-forth is killing me.

The things I said at the height of my anger have been on replay, and as badly as I want to call and take it all back, I know that would only result with me in his arms. And seeing him before I go would make this decision impossible. There's no way I can walk away again, so this will have to be how it ends.

I wish I'd known it was the last time I was going to see him. I would have taken a moment longer to memorize every feature, scent, and feeling, ingraining it all to my memory the same way my love for him is embedded into my soul.

Instead, my last memory is painful, heartbreaking, and filled with guilt. The look in his eyes at my final jab when I told him I didn't need him anymore will haunt me forever. The worst part is that it was a total lie. I can't imagine a world where I don't need him in it. Not to protect me but to make me smile. To make me laugh. To make me melt. No one can check all the boxes Jackson did—hell, he created the damn things.

I hate that I can't say goodbye, and I'm warring with myself about whether I'm making the right decision, but I think it's better this way. To leave him with bitterness so he has an easier time moving on. God, just imagining him with someone else wrecks me. How long will it take? Will he be married when I see him next? The thought guts me.

Finally forcing myself from bed, one look in the mirror confirms everything. My eyes are red and swollen from crying for hours last night, and I'm sure there are more tears on the way since Walker is coming over to hear the bad news. I didn't trust Jackson not to come knocking on my door, so I texted him that I needed more time before we talked, knowing we wouldn't get that chance.

I try to put myself together and decide to fix some coffee while waiting for Walker to get here. When I enter the kitchen, Mom is there. "Morning. Any change of heart today?"

"No, I think we made the right decision. I know this is going to be hard for you, sweetie. I wish there were another option."

"Me too. Walker's on his way over, so I guess I'll be saying goodbye in a minute." I feel the tears threatening again.

"Oh, mija, come here." She wraps me in her arms. "We're going to be okay. We've already had to start over once and we can do it again. We're tough cookies, you and I. We'll get through this, Mia."

There's a knock at the door, signaling Walker's arrival.

"I'll give you some privacy and go pack some of my things. You've got this, honey."

"Thanks, Mom."

I open the front door, and even though I prepped myself and swore I wouldn't do this, a sob breaks out the minute I see him.

"Holy shit, Mia. What's wrong? Is your mom okay?" he asks, encircling me in a hug.

"Yeah, she's fine. I'm sorry. Here, come in so I fill you in on everything. Let me get you some coffee." I take a minute to collect myself while I pour two mugs.

Sitting at the kitchen table, I explain as much as possible without giving any information that could put him in jeopardy. When I get to the part about going into the witness protection program, he shakes his head in disbelief, refusing to accept it.

"Walker, it's the only choice, trust me. We've been all over the board trying to come up with other options, and there are none. It has to be this way, but like I said, it won't be forever. Who knows? I might be back in a couple of years." Here I am highlighting the positives when all I've been focused on are the negatives.

"There's no guarantee on that, and we can't even talk while you're gone. It's crap that they're forcing you to do this. What does Jackson have to say about it?" I left out the part about Jackson, but it looks like I won't get away with it.

I sigh heavily before explaining our final moments. "We didn't exactly end on good terms. I'm not going to tell him what happened after I left."

"He doesn't know you're leaving? That's not right, Mia."

"It would only make it harder on both of us. Since I basically broke things off, being gone will just seal the deal. And this way, he'll have something to be angry about and have an easier time moving on. There's no sense in both of us being this miserable."

"You think he won't be miserable thinking this was all his fault and blame himself? He should know how you feel and the truth about why you're leaving so he doesn't beat himself up over it."

"Gah! I don't know what the right answer is, okay? But I can't say goodbye to him. Please, Walker, let it go. This is what I need." My tears are back in full force.

"God, Mia, I just can't believe this is happening. I'm gonna miss you like crazy."

"I'm going to miss you so much." We stand, throwing our arms around each other and staying like that long enough for me to soak his shirt.

"I love you, Walker. I'll get ahold of you the second I'm allowed. Don't change your number. And don't forget about me."

"Mia, stop it. You're like my sister. We'll be back together in no time. You know I love you, and you better not replace me with some other best friend because no one is as awesome as me."

I laugh, grateful for the distraction. "Never. I'm definitely going to miss your humor. Something tells me I'll be needing it."

I walk him to the door, struggling to keep from breaking down until his car disappears, and then start sobbing for what feels like the millionth time.

Two more hours until my life changes forever.

22

INCENTIVE

Jackson

WHEN I GET TO WORK MONDAY MORNING AND SEE AN unfamiliar face at Mia's desk, I come to an abrupt halt.

"Who the fuck are you, and why are you at Mia's desk?"

"Oh, um, I'm Rebecca. The temp agency sent me over. I'm sorry, am I at the wrong desk? I was told I was filling in for Cindy, and they led me here." She starts to stand up.

"No. Just… stay there for now. Let me figure out what's going on. I'll be back."

I slam my office door and call the agency. "This is Jackson Soloman with Soloman Management. Who ordered the temp you sent over?" I bark into the receiver.

"Mmmm, let's see… Hazel Soloman called in. She requested a full-time executive assistant for four months. Is there a problem with who we sent over?"

"No. Thank you for the information." I hang up and immediately call my mom.

"Good morning, Jackson. How is the new assistant working out?

I'm sorry, honey. You were right. We should've just gone with a temp service to—"

"Mom, what's going on? Where is Mia?"

"Oh, I figured you knew. I got a call from Sofia yesterday telling me they were leaving town and that Mia wouldn't be able to work anymore starting Monday. I felt bad since it's my fault for putting her there in the first place, so I called in a favor to have someone in place before you got there this morning. I am sorry, honey."

"Dammit. Did she say where they were going or why?" I ask desperately.

"Jackson, what's wrong? I figured you'd be happy about this."

"Mom, just tell me everything she said. There's a lot you don't know, but I don't have time to explain right now. Please…"

"She didn't go into details, but I assumed they had a death in the family with how sad she sounded. I asked if I could help, and she told me that nothing could be done and that they'd be fine."

I growl into the phone. "That sounds familiar. Okay, I've gotta go. Bye, Mom."

"Wait! Jackson, please tell me what's going on."

I inhale deeply, preparing myself for what I'm about to say. "Mia and I… we were… together. I love her, and I fucked up. I need to find her and make things right between us."

"Jackson, she's so—"

"Yeah, I know, Mom. She's young. It doesn't matter—she's the one. She makes me happy. She's perfect for me, and when you meet her, I know you'll see that, but first, I have to get her back."

"Oh, wow. I didn't see that coming. I'm sorry, honey, I'm sure it'll all work out, though. Will you keep me posted?"

"Sure, but I need to go. I have to make some calls. Bye, Mom."

"Bye, honey. Good luck."

This is the last straw. I tried to do what Mia asked and give her space before doubling my efforts, but I won't let her throw away her job—her life—because of me. She hasn't answered any of my calls or texts other than to send that single message asking for time. Well, time's up.

I dial her number expecting voicemail, which I've memorized by now, but in its place is the disconnected service message. *What the actual fuck?* She can't be serious.

Grabbing my keys, I storm out of the office and fall short when I remember the new assistant. I walk up to the desk to apologize for my behavior.

"Sorry for the rude introduction earlier, Rebecca. I'm Jackson." I shake her hand. "Everything you need to know is somewhere on the desk or in one of the drawers. If you could just find the folder with instructions and do your best today, we'll work through the rest tomorrow if that's okay."

"Thank you, Jackson. I'll be good here. Go do what you need."

"Thanks."

I walk away, already sick of this bullshit and intent on getting my girl back. I strategize on the drive, trying to decide where to start and how to get through to her. I've been beating myself up over not telling her the minute she confessed what was going on. My instinct says she would have reacted a lot differently, and I know I'm a coward for not telling her. This is my punishment, I suppose, but enough is enough. You don't walk away from a connection like ours; it's that simple.

There's an ache in my gut pulling up to Mia's. Something's off, but I can't place it. After two attempts at knocking, I determine no one's home, or she's painstakingly trying to avoid me. A sense of foreboding hits me, urging me to peer through the front window, immediately discovering what's off—the house is empty. Standing in shock for a minute, unable to comprehend what I'm seeing, it hits me where to go for answers.

The agents left a card and said to call if I thought of anything helpful before following Mia out the other night. The last thing I'd do is help the assholes who ruined my life, but maybe they can shed some light on what the fuck's going on and where my woman is. I pull the card from my wallet when I get back in the car and dial the number.

"Good morning, Jackson. How can I help you today?" The pretentious fucker. He knows exactly why I'm calling.

"Cut the bullshit. Where is she?"

"I'm afraid I don't know what you're talking about. Did you lose your girlfriend?"

"Listen, motherfucker, I'm two seconds from showing up there to get answers any way necessary, so start talking."

"Threatening an FBI agent is a criminal offense. However, I'd be happy to have a civil conversation if you'd like to come in. Who knows? Maybe we can help each other out. Say around one?" I'm not sure what this guy's angle is, nor am I waiting that long to find out.

"I'll see you in twenty minutes." I hang up, seething.

Fuck, this is all my fault. Can she forgive me? Will I be able to forgive myself? That's a hell no. But I'll spend forever making it right and do whatever it takes to win her back.

Exactly twenty minutes later, I'm at the reception desk in the FBI field office. "Jackson Soloman to see Agent Bale."

"Great, follow me, Mr. Soloman."

I'm taken to an interrogation room like the ones you see on TV, boasting a lone metal table with a chair on each side and a darkened window to the observation room. Nothing else is inside the baren space other than a camera in each corner of the ceiling. Why am I in a fucking interrogation room in the first place, and what the hell is taking so long?

Fifteen minutes later, the door opens. "Jackson, good to see you again," Agent Bale says, strutting in wearing a boring suit similar to the last one.

"Just tell me where Mia is so we can stop wasting each other's time."

"Well, now, I'm not at liberty to disclose classified information. Mia's under our protection now, and we take that very seriously." He sits in the chair across from me and folds his hands on the table as if this is just another ordinary day.

"What do you mean, under your protection? Why has her house been emptied? Are you hiding her until you track these guys down? Is she pressing charges against them?" I fire off some of the questions flooding my mind.

"One thing at a time, okay? First, you must not know who we're dealing with if you think it's as easy as pressing charges, so let me educate you. Frank and Jay are only the lackeys for the man pulling the strings. We bring those guys in and there will be two more to replace them, and I guarantee their replacements won't have orders to collect money. Are you following so far?" He's a smug fucker.

"Just get to the point. I'm not an idiot. I know who's involved. All I want to know is where my girlfriend is and how you plan to keep her safe."

"Hmm, it didn't sound like she was still your girlfriend by the time we left the other night." The bastard smirks at me. He's trying to goad me.

"Good to know you're an expert at relationships. Now quit fucking around and tell me what I came here for because I'm losing patience."

"I don't think you're in a position to be making demands, but since I have a soft spot for love, I'll let it slide."

The fuck he knows anything about love. I decide I'm done talking, filling the room with silence and forcing him to continue.

"The point is, we have a bigger problem than Mia's, and until we have that handled, she has voluntarily entered our witness protection program until the threat against her has been detained."

Voluntarily my ass. "What the fuck does that mean? Did you give her a choice? She wouldn't have left her mom."

"Her mom entered the program with her. She did have a choice, but unfortunately, would've been facing charges related to illegal gambling if she decided to deal with the situation herself." He has the audacity to shrug like it's no big deal.

"You son of a bitch!" I slam my fist on the table. "That's not a choice. You fucking blackmailed her, asshole."

He holds his hands up, palms facing me. "Now, let's just calm down. I'd hate to arrest you for disorderly conduct."

Taking a deep breath and sitting back again, I try to calm myself, knowing I need to keep this guy talking so I can figure out how to fix this fucked-up situation.

"How long are you keeping her for?"

"As long as it takes. These things can go years before a trial, and that itself could take months longer."

"Did you allow her to tell anyone?" I've got to be missing some piece of the puzzle.

"Mia was allowed to say goodbye to whoever she wanted, along with a vague explanation. In fact, a boy her age stopped by this morning."

Fuck this guy. I'm sure he knows everyone who's been in and out of her place for weeks. I'm betting her phone was tapped, her every move-ment tracked. And I'm positive it's no coincidence that they pounced after her eighteenth birthday so they could talk to her without an adult present and take advantage of a vulnerable young woman who would play right into their hands. And because I fucked up, I wasn't there to help.

She said goodbye to Walker but didn't feel the need to tell me. That's how pissed she is. It's not rocket science knowing this is my fault. Had I not had security digging, we would have paid the debt yesterday as planned, with the FBI having no idea she even existed. Now she's in so deep, there might not be anything I can do to pull her out. *Fuck!*

"Are there any other options? There must be another solution without endangering or compromising her whole life." This can't be the end.

"Now you're asking the right questions. It just so happens that there's an angle we were working, but we kept hitting dead ends. What do you know about her dad, Roland Marcos?"

What the hell?

"I'm betting less than you do, considering I didn't even know his name until you said it the other night. He left them a few years ago to feed his gambling addiction. Like you said yesterday, he ran off, and Mia got caught in the crosshairs."

"Where do you think he got that loan? Those usually come from the top, which means he has a direct connection. I reckon his testimony would be better than Mia's. I would also think a father would take his daughter's place if he knew she was in a bad situation. We wouldn't need Mia's testimony if we had his."

"So why don't you focus on finding him?"

"We did, but we don't have unlimited resources or time, and with Mia practically served up on a platter, we didn't need to anymore. However, if someone were to bring us a better option, we'd have no reason to turn that down, now, would we?" The asshole knows exactly what he's doing by drawing attention to my fuckup. This was his plan all along.

"Is this what it sounds like? If I find her dad, you'll trade him for Mia?"

"That's the smartest thing you've said all day." The desire to break this guy's nose is overwhelming, but I keep myself in check for Mia's sake.

"I wouldn't know where to start. If you haven't found him with your *limited resources*, what makes you think I stand a chance?"

"Your incentive." The fucker's finally right about something.

"So, let's pretend I succeed and show up on your doorstep with a present. How do I know you'll keep your end of the bargain and release Mia?"

"You don't, but I'll give you my word that if you deliver, I'll present you with a gift in return. Shake on it?" He holds his hand out, but I remain still, causing him to drop it while raising his brows in question.

"What about those bogus gambling charges? If I agree to be your pawn and succeed at bringing him in, I want those off the table." This time, my hand is out first.

We have a deal.

23

NEWER BEGINNINGS

Mia

PROGRESS. YESTERDAY WAS MY FIRST FULL DAY WITHOUT CRYING a single tear. So far, it's been sixty-five days—well, sixty-six now, but who's counting…? If it weren't for signing up for online classes over the summer and starting college early, the transition would have been worse. As it is, I've been pretty distracted by all that, along with my part-time job, leaving not much room for wallowing.

But when I turn the lights off and climb into bed, I can't seem to hold back—until last night. Sure, I stayed up until I was a zombie finishing an essay, but the point is, I did it. I was so exhausted that I fell asleep with no tears. There's hope for me yet.

When I go into the kitchen for coffee, I'm surprised to see Mom there. "Good morning. Why are you still home?"

That's what we're calling it, even though this feels nothing like home, because what else are we going to do? They gave us a list of places to move that were easy to stay hidden and good for integration into the community. I chose the farthest option from San Diego, which happened to be Presque Isle, Maine—literally the farthest place save for Alaska.

"My first job was canceled. I'm leaving soon, but it was nice to relax and take my time this morning. Did you sleep well?"

"I did, actually," I answer, grabbing coffee and plopping on a stool at the bar. This house is so different from our old one. It's one level instead of two, and we didn't have a kitchen island, which I've grown fond of. The place came furnished, and everything was nicer than what we had before. I'm not sure when it'll start feeling like home, but we'll have plenty of time to find out.

"Good. You look… better today. It's nice to see you adjusting. How's work?" What she means is that I usually look like hell in the mornings because I cry every night, but she doesn't need to say it. I know she's been worried about me, and I get it—she's my mom, it's her job. But worrying about it doesn't do any good.

"It's work. Just something to keep me occupied." I shrug in response and see the sadness in her eyes. She knows I'm unhappy. I stopped hiding anything from her after everything happened, and that included my depression. Look where it got me last time I tried to keep things from her. Now, I just let it all out. The good, the bad, and the ugly—it is what it is.

"What about your coworkers? Are you going to hang out with anyone? Maybe go do something fun." She means well.

"Mom, I'm fine. I'm busy with summer school anyway. I could have my degree in two years if I keep this up. I think that's a better way to spend my time." And the only way I want to spend it.

"Mija, making new friends doesn't make your old ones any less important. You can have both." How wrong she is.

"I don't have any old friends, Mom. If I did, I'd call them, send postcards, and message them. Except I'm not allowed to, and I don't even have social media accounts. Do you know how weird people think I am when they find out I'm not on social media? They look at me like I'm from another planet."

"Now you're just being ridiculous. Lots of people don't have social media."

"Mom, I'm eighteen, not fifty. At my age, everyone has something." I sigh. "Look, seriously, it doesn't matter. Like you said, I'm adjusting… but I'm just not the same girl I was in San Diego. I'm the new Mary, just like you're the new Sara. We're both adapting."

She gives up after that and leaves me alone. I may look better this morning, but it didn't take her long to see my attitude wasn't. I tried to be resilient and keep an open mind for the first few weeks we were here. For my mom's sake, I attempted to look at the bright side, to be positive—and then, suddenly, it hit me like a ton of bricks. This is my life. But it's not… and it fucking sucks.

Jackson

It's been sixty-six days—and you can bet I'm counting. I'm no closer to finding Mia's dad than I was on day one. I've been through three private investigators, and not one has found a single lead. I'm about to call a fourth when the answer stares me in the face. I'm no detective, but something Agent Bale said resonates with me: I'm more incentivized than anyone.

If there's one person who will move mountains to find Roland Marcos, it's me. I don't know how the fuck to do it, but I have an idea where to start. I grab Mia's personnel file from my desk to see which high school she attended. Bingo. It's almost lunchtime, which means I'd better get a move on.

I'm just in time to see students filing out for the off-campus lunch. I hurry toward the front of the parking lot and stop the first kid I see.

"Hey there, I was hoping you could help me find someone. He's a senior, his name is Walker, gay, tall, good-looking…"

"Yeah, he usually leaves for lunch. He'll probably be out any minute—oh, there he is. Hey, Walker!" the guy shouts. "This guy is looking for you."

He spots me, and I see his eyes widen in surprise. I walk over, relieved at having found him so quickly.

"Hey, are you free for lunch? I thought we could go somewhere to talk," I say as he approaches.

"Wow, I didn't think I'd see you again." He's skeptical, but there's curiosity there.

"I think we have some catching up to do. What do you say?"

"Yeah. Damn, it's just… you bring it all back. It sucks, you know?"

Boy, do I.

"Yeah, come on, I'll buy." Fuck does it bring it back. But if it gets me closer to bringing *her* back, that's all that matters.

We make small talk on the short drive, waiting to bring up Mia until we sit down with our food. We pick an outdoor table and take our first few bites before diving into the difficult topic. But even talking about her is better than nothing.

"So, how have you been? You were close to Mia. Did you know you were the only person she said goodbye to?" I shake my head in disbelief as he sighs.

"Shit. Yeah. I'm sorry about that. It sucks not knowing how she's doing, not being able to call her. I'll go to send her a text out of habit sometimes, and then, bam, it hits me all over again. What about you? Honestly, I figured you'd move on right away. No offense."

"None taken. But no, there's no moving on for me. I'm not letting her go." *Ever.*

"You don't have a choice. She's gone. You plan on staying celibate for the next two to three years? And what if she decides to stay in her new life instead of coming back? Did you know they give her that option?"

"I'll wait however long it takes. I'm not giving up on us. I'm assuming she told you what happened?" He nods. "It's my fault she's gone, but I *will* fix this and then pray she forgives me. When I said I was all in, I meant it."

He shakes his head. "Damn, you're worse off than I expected. For what it's worth, I tried to get her to talk to you before she left. I told Mia this would happen, that you'd blame yourself. I didn't think you'd still hold a torch for her, though."

"It's not just a torch—it's a fucking inferno. Listen, Mia's it for me. I can't believe I let her slip through my fingers. I just wish she would've let me explain before she left or… I don't know, at least tried to see where I was coming from." I put my head in my hand and shake it with a growl.

"Dude, are you okay?" Walker asks.

"Yeah, it's just… fuck, I wish we could've talked. Those assholes took advantage of her by pushing that decision. She shouldn't be gone, for Christ's sake!" I'm no less angry than I was in the interrogation room with Agent Bale that day.

"I agree, but there's nothing you can do."

"There is, which is why I came to see you. But then… I never get to talk about her anymore, and it was good to hear her name again—to speak her name again. Thank you for that." I take a drink, giving myself a moment. "But the real reason I'm here is that there *is* something I can do to bring her back. I need to find her dad."

The shock on his face is instant. "Her dad? Why? What good will that do?"

"He's the one they need. His testimony is more powerful than Mia's since he dealt directly with the head of the organization. So if I can find him, he can take her place."

"You're kidding me. That's all it would take?"

I shake my head in exasperation. "Sounds easy, doesn't it? If the FBI couldn't track him down, though, how am I supposed to? So far, I haven't found a single lead, but I won't give up until I do. I'm grasping at straws here, trying to find something—anything. You were Mia's best friend. She had to have talked to you about him, maybe mentioned his family, favorite cities, gambling habits—anything?"

"Damn, that's heavy. I wish I had something for you, but Mia hated talking about her dad. She never forgave him for walking out on her mom. That's Mia, always putting everyone else first. She never said how shitty it was that he walked out on her too."

"She's definitely a caretaker, which is all the more reason to do whatever I can to take care of *her* this time. Is there anything you can think of? The smallest detail could help."

He hesitates for a moment, like he's thinking it over, then huffs. "Look, the only thing I know is he had a gambling problem, and we both know that. She never said a thing about him. I got nothin', dude. If something pops in my head, I'll get in touch, but I wouldn't hold your breath."

"Yeah, okay. At least I can check this off the list. What's your number? I'll text you so you have mine, and then I better take you back."

We make small talk in the car as I drive him back to school, discussing his classes and my business. After I drop him off, I head straight to my place, preparing myself for the next item on the list.

Grabbing my phone, I call my sister.

"Hi, Jackson, what's up?" Cici answers.

"Hey. I need your help with something."

"Okay." *She would do anything for me—until she hears what I'm about to ask. It won't be easy to convince her.*

"I need to go away for a while and won't be able to run things while I'm gone. I know it's a huge request, and I wouldn't if it wasn't important, but can you come home and take my place for a couple of months?"

"What the hell, Jackson? What's going on? Where are you going?"

"Remember when I told you Mia had family issues and had to move away?"

"Yeah, how could I forget? You've been miserable ever since." *That sounds familiar.*

"Well, there's more to the story." For the next few minutes, I tell her everything, starting the night Mia walked out, to my meeting with Agent Bale, finishing with my revelation this morning.

"Holy shit, why didn't you say anything before? It would've explained a lot about your attitude over the last couple of months. God, Jackson, I'm so sorry."

"I didn't think it would go on this long. I figured I'd find him right away, and she'd be back by now, but I've gone through three private investigators. I'm hiring the last one now to track some information down so I can take over the search. I need to get her back, Cici, and it's going to take my sole focus to do it."

"I get it, I do, but Jackson, you know this is a big ask. What about Mom and Dad? Have you talked to *them* about this?" *I knew this would be the sticking point.*

"They're still on their monthlong cruise. Besides, I'm running this company, Cici—they're not. It's my decision. You know this business just as well as I do, whether you'll admit it or not. You're the only one I can count on. I wouldn't be asking otherwise. Plus, you were planning to come for Lily's wedding, and this way, you'll be here early to help. Please just think about it. Give me a couple of months to dive in, and when I find him, you'll be free to go." *I'm practically begging at this point.*

"What about the closings we have coming up? You're buying two projects here that'll need your attention."

"*We're* buying two projects there, and it's not like I'll be off-grid. I just can't be around all day, every day. I'll be available for things if necessary and can sign documents from wherever. It's just your presence in the office that I'm asking for."

"You're asking for more than that, and you know it. Mom and Dad are coming home eventually, and then I'll be forced to deal with them."

"Have you ever thought that maybe it's time for you to?" I gave up trying to solve their issues a long time ago.

"You're not helping your case with comments like that," she snaps.

"Sorry. I'll do anything, Cici. What's it going to take? I'll pay your rent in Bozeman. You can live in my condo while you're here—it was always better than yours anyway—and I'll even buy you whatever purse your heart desires."

"A purse? Think bigger, Jackson—a *lot* bigger. And you're damn right you're paying my rent."

"Does that mean you'll do it?" I'm afraid to get my hopes up.

She sighs. "Ugh… fine, I'll do it. Only because I like Mia, though. It has nothing to do with you."

I laugh for what feels like the first time in weeks. "God, you have no idea how much this means to me. I love you, sis. Seriously, thank you."

"All right, all right. I must love you, too, if I'm agreeing to this. When do you want me there? I have to wrap up a few things before I leave."

"That's okay. I'm sure it'll take a couple of days to track down the information, and then I'll need to make arrangements. Is two weeks enough?"

"That should work. You owe me. And Jackson—don't worry, you'll find him."

"I will. It's just a matter of time."

The information for my search came within a week. I'm starting at ground zero with Sofia's family in Puerto Rico. They had to have met her husband at some point; maybe they'll remember something about him that could help. I'm not leaving any stone unturned. I wish I could have gone right after receiving everything, but I waited for Cici and spent another week refamiliarizing her with the office and all current transactions. Now, I'm ready to get the hell out of here.

I'm looking forward to meeting the guys once more before taking off. Unlike my family, they've known everything from day one and are up to speed about my plan to find Roland. Braden helped by giving me two private investigators early on, but both came up empty-handed. I'm sick of relying on other people only to be disappointed.

"Hey, guys." I greet the three men sitting at the table.

"You all set to head out tomorrow?" Braden asks.

"Packed up and ready to go. I've wanted to leave all week, but I had to get Cici up to date first."

"I can't believe you convinced her to come back. What did you bribe her with, because I know she doesn't love you that much." Eli chuckles.

"I'm pretty sure it has more to do with how much she and Mia hit it off, but there might be a purse involved. I would've offered more. I'm just glad she pulled through."

"I can't say the same since I've seen Lily less this week than I have all year," Sebastian says sullenly.

"I think that's the only other reason Cici agreed to come. She's excited to be here for the wedding. How's it going, anyway?" I ask. He and Lily are finally tying the knot in September. They had to wait for the venue they wanted. You'd think they could buy anything with all the money the Dubrees have, but what do I know?

"I try to stay out of it as much as possible. The wedding planner I hired has pretty much saved my sanity. Worth their weight in gold." Sebastian says, holding his beer up before taking a sip.

"Do you have a time limit you're setting for yourself or a plan for failure?" Braden asks out of the blue, bringing the conversation back to me. He's the skeptical one of the bunch. Surprisingly, Sebastian has been the most supportive. The scare he had with Lily gives him a level of understanding the others lack. And I'm sure it doesn't hurt that his onetime competition has a new obsession.

"You don't tell someone to plan for failure, dumbass," Sebastian quips.

I answer anyway. "I'll keep searching until I find him. Failure isn't an option."

"Does your sister know that? I thought you told her it would be for a couple of months tops?" Eli asks, concerned.

"If everything goes my way, it *will* only be a couple months. She'll be fine with Lily here, even if it takes longer. I'm sure some shit's going to come up with my parents when they get back, though. Keep an eye on her for me. I want to make sure she handles it okay."

"I'll check on her and let you know," Braden offers.

"Definitely not. Stay focused on your next piece of ass, and leave Cici alone. The last thing she needs is a ride on the Braden train. I can keep an eye on her. I'll see her more than Braden anyway since she's always with Lily," Eli is quick to add. He can come up with any excuse he wants, but we've all figured out there's more to the story by now.

"Hey, you know she liked me there for a while. Right after I broke up with Layla. If I weren't so fucked over the breakup, I probably would've moved in on that." Braden's goading him at this point.

"Shut the fuck up, Braden. That ship sailed. Leave her alone." Eli takes the bait, making the rest of us laugh. And joking or not, I decided to add my two cents.

"I second that. You know I love you, Braden, but keep your dick away from my sister. I know some of the places it's been. Eli, I'll take your offer if you stay alive long enough in between all the crazy shit you do. Keep me posted if she gets into it with my parents." Eli's been obsessed over chasing his next adrenaline high. His motto of living life to the fullest is getting a little reckless if you ask me.

"I'll second that one," Sebastian adds while giving Eli a look of admonishment.

"Do they know she's here yet?" Eli asks me, ignoring our comments.

"No, I left a letter on the counter. They'll get it when they get back. They're still on the cruise, but they have a message to call me on their way home so I can at least warn them what they're coming home to."

"Well, I hope you're more successful than the FBI, not to mention all the PIs you went through, but come on, man, you must know this is a long shot. I don't want to see you lose your mind if you can't find him. That's all I meant earlier. I know you feel guilty, but it's not worth throwing your life away."

"Braden, I'm going to let that slide because I know you're coming from a good place, but she *is* my life. I thought I made that clear. Even if it's not until the end of the trial, I'll get her back, and if her dad is the way to make that happen sooner, then I'll find him."

"Well, then, I hope you succeed sooner than later 'cause I'm gonna miss my best friend. These douchebags aren't as fun." He lifts his beer, and everyone follows suit.

"Good luck, man," Eli says.

"Bring him in," Sebastian adds as we clink our glasses in a final toast.

24

THE SEARCH

Jackson

It's been three weeks since I arrived in Puerto Rico, 108 days without Mia, and I'm no closer to finding her dad. I've just finished making the rounds with Mia's extended family after visiting each one in person. People tend to remember more when you're face to face. Also, it allowed for more time so if anything came to mind, they could tell me then and there. If I only made phone calls, the chances of them getting in touch after are less likely. It doesn't mean I won't follow up with everyone, though. Not only to see if anything came back to them but also to thank them for their hospitality.

They were all generous, showering me with meals and excited to spend time with someone who had ties to the family they lost. I tried not to explain why I was looking for Mia's dad but gave them enough to stress the importance of my search. I came up mostly empty-handed, except for finding out where her parents met.

Interestingly, Mia's mom was on vacation in the US, and during a stop in Las Vegas, she met Roland, who lived there. According to Sofia's account of the story, it was love at first sight. I asked why they didn't stay in Vegas, and from what they'd heard, she didn't want to raise her daughter there, so they somehow ended up in San Diego. They knew about his gambling habits from Sofia, who would call often and confide in her sister about their problems.

Sofia knew he was playing too much before he left and was always worried his habits would get them in trouble at some point. She assumed he stuck around San Diego, but she never knew for sure. They gave me the most recent picture they had of him, so I have something tangible to go on. I see similarities between him and Mia, but she takes after her mom more so.

It was a success for the picture alone, but the information about Vegas might also be helpful. My next stop on the Roland Marcos tour is his own family. There aren't many—an uncle and a few cousins—but maybe they've heard from him recently. It'll take me a while, even with his few relatives, since they're so spread out. Luckily, I have plenty of time now with Cici running things back home. Speaking of, I decide to call and check in and give her an update.

"Hi, Jackson. Are you still in Puerto Rico?" Cici answers.

"I'm at the airport, ready to fly out. I made it through everyone here, and now I'm headed to Arkansas to talk to Roland's uncle."

"Did you learn anything?" she asks eagerly.

I fill her in and ask how things are going there.

"Everything's good. Rebecca and I are holding down the fort. It took a while to get back in the swing of things, but it all came back to me eventually." She stepped right in and handled it like a champ. She might not like the family business, but she's good at it.

"It seems like you never left with how good you're doing. Have you heard from Mom and Dad yet?"

She laughs. "No, but they've been checking in with Rebecca. They're too stubborn to talk to me, you know that."

"You know you're their daughter, right, smart one? As a neutral observer, you all play a part in this, but it only takes one of you to admit it first. That's the problem with the Soloman stubbornness."

"Okay, Obi-Wan Kenobi, are we done here?"

I chuckle. "Yeah, I'll talk to you soon."

"Later, Obi-Wan."

I'm laughing as I hang up. Thank God. I wondered if that sound would ever leave my mouth again.

Mia

My eyelids are like lead weights this morning. I need to limit my reading at night. It's lasting longer and longer until my eyes start closing on their own. After weeks of going to bed with Jackson on my mind, always resulting in tears, I took up reading. A good distraction became a bad habit. I'm hoping to counter it by adding a good habit to the mix.

I don my sneakers and head out the door, trying to decide which way to go on my run today. Never in my wildest dreams did I think I would ever be one of those crazy people who ran by choice and weren't being chased by an axe murderer, but here I am. The counselor suggested it— go figure, at least something she said actually helped.

When my mom saw me spiraling, she asked our handler to find a counselor. I guess it's common for some to have a more difficult time with the transition into the program. I'm one of them. But other than my new running ritual, I don't think I've gotten anything from therapy. Whoever thinks bringing up your problems every week is the answer to solving them is more messed up than me. Makes no sense, but if it satisfies my mom and makes her feel better, then so be it. Hence, the reading habit.

Once I started to talk about everything wrong in my life, the floodgates opened. The thing is that my issue isn't with my past or some trauma I need to work through—it's happening *right now*, and nobody can fucking fix it. How am I supposed to deal with being stuck in a life that isn't mine, using a made-up name, with people who have no idea who I really am and never will?

The counselor who specializes in cases like this says I should allow myself to make friends and live here as if we decided to move and start over. That I'm not diminishing my old life but accepting the possibility of two, and if I ever decide to go back, my life will be that much richer from the added friends and experiences. Seriously? I may have puked in my mouth a little. Did I mention that she works for the FBI? What a load of crap. She gets paid to say that shit.

How about we take you away from the love of your life and see how it goes. See how long it takes until you start picturing him moving on and wondering how long it took. See how it feels to lie in bed at night and imagine he's on a date, what she might look like, if he thinks of you when he leans in to kiss her.

I stop and bend over with my hands on my knees, catching my breath. I may have gotten carried away during that rant. I've been better recently, but I had a session yesterday. And they say counseling helps. Whatever.

"Mary?" I hear my name being called.

I straighten up to see Jeff, one of my coworkers from the coffee shop, coming to a stop in front of me. "Oh, hi, Jeff."

"I wasn't sure if it was you bent over like that. Are you okay?" I can't blame him for being concerned since I'm acting like I just finished a marathon.

"Yeah, just overdid it for a minute there. I probably should've had some more coffee. I'm too tired for this."

"Don't worry, I have days like that too. I haven't seen you on this trail before. Have I just missed you, or is this a rare thing?"

I laugh. "It probably looks like that, but I've been consistent for a few weeks. I run in different directions every day so I don't get bored. I take it this is your regular route?"

"It is. I like knowing how much farther I have. It keeps me going."

"That's not a bad way to look at it. On the other hand, if you don't know where you are, you're forced to keep going until you make it back."

This time, he laughs. "Very true. We're both just trying to make it in our own way."

"As is life." Maybe *I* should be the counselor.

"Since you said you needed more coffee, would you want to grab one with me and continue this profound conversation?" He smiles in jest. "I feel like this is the most we've talked, and we've worked together for months now."

"I know, crazy. I would, but I have a big paper due and put it off until the last minute. Sorry."

"No worries. Procrastination is my middle name. Maybe another time. I'll see you at work."

"Bye, Jeff."

We jog off in opposite directions, and my heart is already going at a speed far beyond what my run is causing. I can't believe he asked me out. Not that it was for a date, for crying out loud. Coffee isn't a date, right? I didn't even say yes, yet I feel like I just cheated on Jackson. Ugh, I'm not even *with* Jackson anymore. Well, he's not with me, at least. My heart hasn't decided to let him go yet, but that doesn't mean I should be getting so worked up over this. If only I could stop thinking about him constantly, but it's become habit after 108 days of doing it.

I need to focus on the tasks at hand: get home, shower, and make up a topic for this fake paper I'll not be working on in case it comes up. After that, I should make a list of excuses to have in my back pocket if this happens again. It's hard enough being around people at work who think I'm someone I'm not; I can't imagine a relationship with someone who doesn't even know my name.

Jackson

Well, fuck. Both families are now checked off my list at 125 days without Mia, and I'm still at a loss. I'm not sure what kind of man can win the heart of a woman like Sofia after alienating his entire family by being a prick. No one has heard from him in years, and the last they knew, he'd left to become a poker pro in Vegas. It's safe to say that all signs point to Las Vegas, where I'm currently headed, waiting to board a flight from Kentucky. To pass the time, I call Eli to check in and hopefully pick his brain.

"Jackson, what's up, man?" he answers.

"Hey, Eli. Just sitting in another airport, getting ready to fly to Sin City."

"No kidding. What did you find out?"

"Jack shit, but so far, Vegas has been brought up by everyone. Now that I've eliminated the possibility of family knowing where he is, the only thing left to do is play the poker circuit and look for him directly. I figure I'll ask around and flash his picture."

"Sounds like a plan. Where are you going to start?"

"That's why I called. Since you're in the know, I was hoping you could poke around and see if you could get me into some lesser-known games outside the mainstream. I'll visit the poker rooms but will probably have better luck in the smaller circuit, especially given his history of being on the run." What that translates to is that I have no fucking clue what I'm doing and grasping at straws.

"I'd be surprised if he was playing in Vegas, where more people are watching. Not to discourage you, I get you need to start somewhere. And who knows, maybe the guy has friends who have an idea where he might be."

"Think you can do some digging for me?" I ask.

"I'll see what I can find. Quite a few guys go there to play, so I'll ask if they can get you on the list for a few tournaments. Also, put some feelers out while you're in the card rooms and give hints that you're interested in private games. You might be surprised what doors open."

"I'll do that. Thanks for the tip. I had the same thought about him not being in Vegas, but you're right, I need to start somewhere. Change of subject—how's Cici? Have you seen her lately?"

"I see her all the time. She's become a permanent fixture at Sebastian's, and I live in the same building. She seems good, excited about the wedding—it's all they talk about these days. I haven't seen anything out of the ordinary."

"The last we talked, my parents still hadn't spoken to her and were only talking to the assistant. She doesn't seem down at all?"

"I don't think it's possible with the wedding coming up, but if it makes you feel better, I'll pay closer attention and ask about work when I see her next."

"I'd appreciate that. I just want to make sure she's not putting on a front for me and then find out later she was miserable the whole time. I don't want anyone else to suffer because of my shit."

"I get it. I'll let you know if I find anything you should be concerned about. Otherwise, stop worrying and focus on what needs to be done. We're all here for you, man, and the sooner you find him, the better."

"Thanks, Eli. Text me what you find out and tell everyone I said hi."

"Sounds good. See ya."

"Bye."

I'm more at ease than I've been in a while after our conversation. For one, I know he's looking after my sister, and whatever's going on between them, I can tell he genuinely cares about her. Whether that results in a relationship or being good friends, I'm on board. I'm also grateful to have his help with my search in Vegas. I'm at a loss with this whole thing, and having someone on my side is refreshing.

I've made some headway over the last couple of months in Sin City. The circle of players I've worked my way into have connections far beyond. I've also met some friends I might share the truth with who could become additional allies. I'm inserting myself into higher-stakes games to see if any of those guys have heard of him. If I strike out there, I may move to another market.

Now that the FBI has arrested the puppeteer of the operation, time is of the essence. That means they intend to use Mia's testimony, and if I don't find Roland in time to replace her before she's named as a key witness, then this will all have been for nothing.

But before I do anything else, I need to make it through Sebastian's bachelor party tonight.

"God, it's good to see you guys. I didn't realize how much I'd missed this. I can't believe you all flew in for the weekend." Sebastian, Braden, Eli, and I are sitting at a VIP table at the club in our hotel after dinner with the ladies. Lily, Cici, and two other women who came are on the dance floor. We're seated where we can watch them while they let loose and have fun. Speaking of, I'm doing a bit of that myself.

"It was Lily and Cici's idea. They insisted that a bachelor party isn't a bachelor party if it's not in Vegas. I told them I'd only do it if we combined it with the bachelorettes, so here we are. It's safe to say that your being here had a lot to do with it." Sebastian looks at me momentarily, but his focus remains on Lily.

"I'm just happy you're here." A little too happy with the way my head is spinning and words slurring. But fuck it, I don't remember the last time I allowed myself to relax. So I don't think twice as I knock back the rest of my drink.

"You've been lonely, huh? You know we're only a quick flight away. You should come home every now and then," Braden says.

"I can't. I've got important stuff happening here. Top secret… I'm an agent of love, trying to save my woman."

"Okay, buddy, I think it might be time to call it a night," Eli says while laughing.

"No way, the night'sss young. I'll just visit the lil boys' room an'be right back." That didn't sound right, even to me. I stand up and sway on my feet, grabbing the back of the couch for support.

"Whoa there, big guy." Eli stands up at the same time and grabs my shoulder. "Look, why don't I help you to your room, and you can use the bathroom there."

"S'prolly a good idea. Shit, I feel like I's roofied."

"You roofied yourself, man," Braden chimes in.

"All right, let's go, buddy." Eli leads me out and as we pass the dance floor I hear our names being called.

"Hey, where are you guys going?" We pause as Cici catches up.

"Jackson had a bit too much tonight, so I'm helping him to his room," Eli answers.

"S'all good. I can make it." I try to play it cool.

"Geez, Jackson, drink much? I can take him up so you can stay with the guys." Cici comes over and takes my other arm as the room spins.

"I'm not leaving you alone to wrangle a 180-pound man of steel to his room. What if he passes out on the way?" Eli asks.

"Then I'll get security to help. It's fine, I've got him."

"Hey, guyz, I'm right heeere." I hiccup. Great.

"Cici quit being stubborn. You can go with me or stay and dance— the choice is yours," Eli states firmly and then starts walking again, pulling me along. I'm too busy trying to stay upright to interject.

"Argh. You're infuriating." Cici stomps beside me.

"Surrry, sis. Didn't mean t'ruin yer night. I haven't drunk in a while." I start laughing. "Get it? Drunk in a while, and I'm drunk."

"How are you such a lightweight with all this muscle?" Cici asks.

"He had a lot at dinner and then pounded a couple more here. I think it's been a while since he's let his guard down," Eli explains.

"Can't let my guard down. Too important."

"Jackson, I'm sorry. This must suck for you," Cici says.

Thank God we made it to my room without incident, and somehow, they managed to get me inside and into bed. At least, that's what I'm assuming, because I don't remember anything past leaving the club, and this is where I woke up.

Fucking hell, my head hurts. What was I thinking? First night back with my friends and I took it to a whole new level. That might be one for the record books. It was a welcomed diversion to turn off my mind. I don't remember the last time I wasn't consumed with thoughts of Mia, her dad, poker, or the fucking FBI. I'm going crazy with this shit.

Dammit, I miss her so much, it hurts. I've memorized every picture of us on my phone down to the order of the images. I'm ready to have her back. I want to hold her, tell her how special she is, and how much I love her. It's been too long, 195 days since I've had her in my arms. I don't know how much longer I can take.

Arguing with my sister at breakfast this morning is the last thing I want to be doing after not seeing her for so long, but I knew it was coming, which was why I waited until the end of her visit.

"I'm sorry, Cici. I have a lead that could finally pay off. If I don't make this game next weekend, I might as well stop trying." Letting my friends down is not the intention, but I can't compromise the breakthrough I've been trying to get for months.

"I can't believe you're not coming to the wedding. What's wrong with you? You're like Lily's brother."

"Not true, considering I've made out with her, not to mention I'm the guy who third-personed her first time with Sebastian. They'll survive if I'm not at their wedding."

"Okay, you make a good argument. I'm just worried about you. Are you okay?" Cici won't let up after last night. I overdid it, but it's not an everyday occurrence; it's rare.

"Listen, I'm not going to lie and tell you I'm great just to make you feel better. I'm frustrated that the solution to my problems seems impossible to find, which is why this game is so important. I'd also rather not be at a wedding where two people are pledging their love when I've been miserable being separated from the woman *I love*. Call me selfish, but I can't do it."

"You're right, I'm sorry. You'll get her back, Jackson."

"I know I will. It's just taking longer than expected. How are you doing at the office? I know I told you only a couple months, but we're going on four now. Are you still okay with sticking around?"

"I already told you I'll stay as long as you need. It's been less stressful with the deals in Bozeman finished, so I'm good. And even though Rebecca was great, nothing compares to having Cindy back—she makes this job a breeze. Don't worry about me. You have enough on your plate."

"I want you to know that I appreciate you putting your life on hold. I'm sorry to have asked that of you." I catch the server's eye for the check.

"That's what family is for. You'd do the same for me, right?"

"In a heartbeat."

After paying, we stand to hug and say our goodbyes.

"Have fun at the wedding next weekend, but not too much—don't do anything I wouldn't do. I already sent a card, but give Lily a hug and tell them congrats for me."

"I will. Keep me posted on things, and good luck in LA."

"Bye, Cici." I walk away with a load off my chest. I knew telling her I was skipping the wedding would piss her off, but I seriously can't do it. It's probably a smart decision if last night is any indication. The game I'm going to isn't a bullshit story either.

The guys I've been talking to got me into this tournament. It's a private high-stakes game with some seedier players and might be the crowd that leads me in the right direction. The trick will be navigating a conversation without raising any red flags, causing suspicion from the wrong people.

Mia

I woke up to a panic attack this morning. The fall semester is kicking my ass, and after staying up late to finish a project, I ended up not thinking of Jackson before bed last night for the first time since we've been apart. Did we reach our expiration date?

I often wonder if he's moved on after so long. I've got to be kidding myself to hold out hope that he hasn't. He was no stranger to the ladies before I came along, so I don't know what makes me think he would be celibate other than wishful thinking. And that's not fair of me. He deserves happiness—we both do. I just wish it could have been together.

Between school, my newfound passion for running, and my job at the coffee shop, I'm spending less time obsessing over the past. It's refreshing to feel somewhat normal again, even if it did take over six months for it to happen, but I still have my moments.

Not only am I exhausted from lack of sleep, but Mondays suck in general. It's my longest day of classes, which means sitting in front of the computer for hours before the afternoon shift at work. I might have been a little ambitious with this semester's class load, trying to squeeze in as many credits as possible while the government pays for it. And since the government is paying, I chose one of the top online degree programs in the country, which means it's no joke.

I could have chosen to attend a local university, but don't want to lie to even more people and introduce myself as someone I'm not. Plus, there's always a slim chance someone from San Diego ends up at the same one, and then we'd be forced to start over. No, thank you. Online school is great.

One of the benefits of working at a coffee shop is being able to make an energy drink at the start of my shift—highlight of my day right here.

"Those are terrible for you, you know," Jeff says as he's clocking out.

"Says the guy who drinks triple-shot espressos on the daily."

Jeff and I have been talking more at work. It's getting more personal with questions about family, childhood stuff, and talk of the future. It scares me but also feels good at the same time. I haven't had someone other than my mom to talk to in forever.

At first, I was constantly previewing my answers for anything I wasn't supposed to say, but it's become easier. At night, though, I always feel guilty for enjoying our conversations. I'm starting to wonder if that will ever go away with not receiving closure with Jackson.

"Touché. Did you get that paper done over the weekend?"

"Yeah, barely. I submitted it at the final hour last night." This time, when I told him I was busy with homework over the weekend, I wasn't making it up.

"Damn, if your sophomore year is that difficult, I can't imagine how much worse it'll get. The business program I'm in isn't that hard, and my junior year is still kicking my butt."

"The minor in criminal justice might have been a bit much, but if I can use my accounting degree at a major law firm, it could mean good money down the road. It'll be worth it in the end." *I hope so, anyway.*

"Since you got your paper done, how about you relax for once and come to a Halloween party with me on Thursday night? Not a date, just something for you to let loose at. Come on—I'm offering a zero-pressure option this time. What do you say?"

Asking me out has become a regular thing these days, but he knows I'll say no, so now it's more of a running joke. It usually goes something like this: "I know you have to clean your room tonight, but I'd love to take you to dinner if you want to put it off?" Or "I'm sure you're already going grocery shopping, but would you want to grab a bite to eat beforehand so you're not hungry as you walk down the aisles?" It's cute, and recently, I can't tell if he's really asking me out or keeping the joke going—which doesn't matter, I suppose, since I don't plan on saying yes.

This party, though, has me considering. "I don't remember the last time I was at a party," I muse.

"Exactly, which is why you should go. It's a costume party, so you can pretend to be someone else for the night. That's always fun, right?"

Ha. If he only knew I do that every day. "How big is the party?"

"I'm scared to answer that without knowing what you're hoping for. This is the first time you haven't come back with a no right away, and I don't want to risk it."

I laugh. Jeff's gotten good at pulling those sounds from me. "You said it wouldn't be a date, so I figured if it were a big party, that would make it seem less date-ish." I don't want to lead him on by going, and if there were only three couples or something, that would be awkward.

He looks relieved. "I wasn't sure if you were crowd averse, but it's a big party. It's at one of the frat houses, and they practically invite the entire student body. I even have a buddy staying sober to drive, so we would have a chaperone. See? Not a date." I roll my eyes as he leans his hip on the counter with his arms crossed, smiling while he waits for my answer.

"Okay, fine, I'll go. Just as friends," I point out once more.

He grins. "Friends. Scout's honor." He does the salute, and I blanche.

"No, wait. Never mind, I—"

"Mary, what did I do?" Jeff asks in a panic.

"Nothing. No, I just… I'm sorry. I'm not ready." I look up to the ceiling and breathe deeply.

"Okay. Mary, I like you, I think that's obvious. But it seems like you're trying to get over someone and if you need me to back off, I will."

"Please don't. I like what we have going. It's just… I can't promise that I'll ever be able to say yes. That doesn't mean I want you to stop what you're doing, though."

"Then we'll pretend today didn't happen, and I'll try again tomorrow. Maybe you should tell me what I did, though, so I don't do it again?"

My cheeks go red. "The Scout's honor thing," I say, turning away and busying myself by wiping a counter. Just saying it sounds ridiculous, but I swear it was a sign.

"Good to know. Won't happen again." He goes to raise his hand to do it but stops abruptly. "Aaand… I'm going now."

Once he's gone, I sigh in frustration. I'm so confused. When Jeff said I was trying to get over someone, it hit me—that's not what I've been doing at all. I've been trying to hang on to someone. I don't want to let Jackson go, but maybe that's the problem. When he made that motion with his hand, all I could see was Jackson, and it felt like a sign, like the universe was telling me to remember.

But you know what? Fuck the universe, because for the last 230 days, it's done a pretty shitty job of things.

25

CLOSING IN

Jackson

AFTER MOVING TO LOS ANGELES A COUPLE OF MONTHS AGO, I finally feel like I'm on the brink of finding Roland. One of the Vegas tables eventually paid off, and a guy knew who he was. He'd heard that Roland left Sin City to try his hand in a more lucrative market and assumed he went to LA, where the big money was. By no means was it solid evidence, but at that point, I would have gone on less.

It turned out to be a wise decision because I've been talking to other players about the transplants coming in recently, and there's a good chance Roland is around. I've become comfortable enough with one of the guys to have him join me for a pregame drink. He seems to be in the know around here and not on the wrong side of the fence. I've been buddying up to him for weeks now, and I'm ready to divulge why I'm here and show Roland's picture.

"Hey, Jackson, thanks for the invite," Darryl says as he reaches me.

"Yeah, I'm glad it worked out. I thought having a beer somewhere away from the poker table for once would be nice."

As he sits, the waitress brings our drinks. "I ordered one for you, hope that's okay." I say to him.

"Never one to turn down a beer. Cheers."

"Cheers." We each take a sip, and then I dive right in. "So, I've been around for a couple months now and noticed you're pretty connected with the poker circuit. Seems like you've been playing a long time and have things dialed in with who's who."

"When it's your full-time job, that tends to happen. I wouldn't be any good if I weren't paying attention."

"Right, so I imagine you're the right person to ask about a guy I'm trying to find, and you seem like someone I could trust to keep this confidential." So far, he doesn't seem put off.

"As long as you're not looking to start any trouble or do something illegal, I don't see why not. Are you working for the government or some shit?" He sounds a bit skeptical, so it's now or never.

"Yes and no. I'm not working for the government, but I'm trying to find someone for them."

"Like a bounty hunter?" he asks, making me laugh.

"Huh. Now that you say that, I guess, in a way, I am. But instead of getting money for the guy I'm looking for, I'll get my girlfriend back." His eyes go wide as I take a swig of my beer.

"Okay, you're gonna have to explain that one." He laughs.

"The FBI has my girlfriend in a witness protection program. If I bring her dad in, they'll trade her testimony for his. They gave up looking for him when they landed her, and I've been trying to find him for over eight months now."

"Fuck, that's some fucked up shit," Darryl says, sighing.

"You're telling me."

"What will you do when you find him? Have the FBI pick him up or what?"

"I was thinking of paying him a visit to tell him how he fucked up his daughter's life, and if the asshole doesn't feel like manning up and making it right, then I'll cuff him myself and bring him to their doorstep."

"Jackson, the fucking bounty hunter. I like it. So, what's his name, and what does he look like?"

"Glad you asked." I pull the picture out and set it in front of him.

"That's Ronny. I know the guy." Darryl shrugs like it's no big deal. Meanwhile, I about fall out of my chair.

Fucking A. After 270 days, I'm closing in.

Mia

It was a date; nothing happened, but it almost did. When Jeff started closing in for a kiss goodbye, I opened the door and bolted inside. My mom was there to hold me as I broke down in her arms. It's the first time in 270 days that I was completely honest about where my head was and my struggle since being here.

It was liberating to confess everything. Mom had no idea Jackson and I had become that serious in such a short time and felt terrible for not helping me through it. It was my fault for not confiding in her to begin with, but my absolving her of guilt didn't make her feel better. She tried insisting that we pack up and exit the program, dealing with the fallout.

I almost filled my suitcase right then, but after thinking about it more, I knew it wasn't the solution. Yes, I'd have Walker in my life, but going home at the risk of seeing Jackson with someone else would break my heart all over again. So, after talking it through, we both decided the best thing was to stay.

I've made progress. I downloaded all my pictures of Jackson to a separate file on my computer and deleted them from my phone. That way, my temptation to look throughout the day was taken away. Jeff finally convinced me to go on a date, which ended up being fun. It wasn't much different from work, just a change in environment.

If I stay the course and continue taking baby steps, the gaping hole in my heart will eventually heal, right?

Jackson

After having beers with Darryl last Friday, executing a plan for Roland took a week. He did me a solid and organized a fake game set up in a hotel room so Roland would walk right into my hands. I'm glad for the extra few days to prepare because it turns out that Mia's dad is a piece of shit who couldn't care less about his daughter.

Once I let him in the room and he realized he'd been duped, he tried to make a run for it. The fucker didn't make it far before my gun came out, and he quickly decided his life was more important than bolting.

I ordered him to sit the fuck down, pointing the gun in his direction, and it's been trained on him since.

Now, here I am explaining to him what's going on and what's about to happen. After I finish, he pauses for all of thirty seconds and goes straight into "save his ass" mode.

"I've been hitting some big pots. Name your price, and we'll pretend this conversation never happened," he says coolly.

"You'd seriously let your daughter take the heat for you? Ruin her life so you can keep playing poker? What the fuck is wrong with you?" I'm seething.

"She's being taken care of, isn't she? They're fine living off the government for free while waiting for a court date. I don't see what the problem is."

"There's a reason they're in the program, dumbass. They're in danger because you ran. They're hiding, giving up their lives because of your shitty decisions."

"You don't think *I'm* in danger? I'm hiding from the same guys they are."

Who the fuck is this asshole? Mia is better off without him.

"Then go in and give your testimony. Take Mia's place and let the FBI protect you. Do it for your daughter."

"The best thing for her is to have me out of her life. This way, it stays like that. Tell me how much to make you go away so you can pick up the next guy on your list."

While we agree that he should stay out of her life, I think it's time to make clear what's about to go down and that it's nonnegotiable.

"I think you've got the wrong idea. I'm not here for the FBI. I'm here for Mia, and the only payment I'll accept is you." I stalk toward him.

"Let's talk about this—work something out." He's got his hands up in the air facing me, trying to stop my advance.

I've already had enough of this asshole and his begging, so I knock him out with the butt of my gun and cuff him. It was intentional to pick a motel with exterior doors. It's not hard to drape him over my shoulder and load him into the back seat of my car, which is already packed for my return to San Diego.

Two and a half hours later, and 277 days since I vowed to deliver this asshole, I drag Roland into the FBI's office, demanding to see Agent Bale.

"Well, well, well, look what the cat dragged in," he says when he sees us. "If it isn't Jackson Soloman. And I assume this is the one and only Roland Marcos? I gotta hand it to you… I didn't think you'd be able to find him, but here you are." He turns to another agent walking up. "Put him in room one. I'll be in shortly." The guy leads Roland away.

"You've got your man. Now tell me where Mia is."

"It doesn't work that fast around here. We need to sort this out first—take Roland's statement, ensure he'll cooperate, then talk with Mia and Sofia to review their options. It won't happen overnight, Jackson. These things take time."

"Yeah, well, I've waited over nine months, so I'd appreciate you speeding that up." I'll go crazy if they make me wait much longer.

"We'll do the best we can. Give us a couple days to figure things out. I'll reach out when I have some answers for you, all right?" He holds out his hand to shake, and I take it.

"I'll be waiting."

Mia

"Hello?" My greeting sounds skeptical. Caller ID showed Agent Wallace's name, but I haven't heard from them for months, so the call has me nervous.

"Hi, Mia, it's Agent Wallace. Is now a good time to talk?"

This is so out of the blue. Hearing the voice from my past again gives me butterflies in my stomach.

"I'm home, and my mom is the only other person here, so we're good."

"Great. I have some news for you. Can you put me on speaker so you can both listen in?"

"Um, sure. Let me just go to the other room. Hang on." I press Mute and go into the kitchen, where I find Mom.

"Agent Wallace is on the phone and has something to tell us. I'll put it on speaker, okay?" I sit on a stool at the breakfast bar.

"I wonder what it is," she says, taking the seat next to me.

I unmute the call. "Okay, we're both here, and you're on speaker."

"Great. We just had a new development. As you know, we've been building our case against not only Frank and Jay but also their boss, whom you were fortunate enough not to meet. Unfortunately, your testimony was only enough to bring in Frank and Jay. Our goal was to use their cooperation to go after their boss, but it's been somewhat difficult to navigate."

"Are you any closer to reaching a trial?" I ask.

"We're not, and because of that, your name hasn't been submitted as a witness of record, which is good news considering we have another key witness who came in having had direct contact with all parties, not just Frank and Jay. That means you aren't essential to the case since he's willing to testify. We'll only use your testimony if jurisdiction allows us to submit you as an anonymous witness. Either way, you're in the clear. You're being released from the program and are both free to return to your previous identities if you choose."

"What do you mean, if we choose?" I'm seriously shell-shocked right now, but not enough to have missed that last part.

"In cases lasting an extended period, people tend to settle into their new lives, and sometimes it's more appealing to stay where they are. Each situation is unique, and we leave it up to the individuals to decide what's best for them before we help facilitate whichever direction they go."

"So, you're saying we're being released from the program, but if we want to stay, we can? What if we stay, can we still contact our family and friends?" I have so many more questions.

"Yes, Mia, that's exactly what I'm saying, and yes, you are free to call anyone from your past after you're officially released. The next step would be making any final arrangements to help you transition out of the program and processing the paperwork for whichever location you choose. We realize it's not always an easy decision. Take some time to talk it over and call me in the next day or two so I can get the ball rolling. Reach out with any questions that come up. I know we have some details to work out regarding school and living arrangements, but we can tackle those items once you've decided where to park yourselves."

"Wow, okay. I guess we have a lot to talk about, then. Thank you, Agent Wallace. I'll let you know what we decide."

"Good luck, ladies. Bye."

"Wait! What about our names? Can we go back to our real ones?" I ask.

"Yes, but if you stay where you are and want to keep your new ones, you can also do that. We'll take care of all the logistics during the exit protocol."

"Okay. We'll decide soon."

"Sounds good. Bye, ladies."

I hang up, and my mom and I sit in silence, staring at the phone. Why now? Wasn't 278 days long enough to be tormented? Nope, now I'm faced with one of the most difficult decisions yet. The hole that finally started to close just opened wide again.

Jackson

"We made a deal. I expect you to hold up your end of the bargain. You can either bring her to me or tell me where the fuck she is so I can go get her myself." I'm in the interrogation room at the FBI office in San Diego, 280 days after my life fell apart and two days after I made a delivery to put it back together. I came as soon as I got out of the shower to a fucking voicemail from Agent Bale saying that Mia was staying put.

"Look, Jackson, we talked to them and explained the situation. They know we have another witness in custody and that we're taking his testimony in place of hers. We told them they were free to return but could also choose to stay where they were. They chose to stay."

"And where is that?" I ask, barely keeping my anger under control.

"That information is classified. It's their decision to reintroduce themselves to their previous life if and when they choose. She knows she can contact anyone from her past immediately after the paperwork is filed."

"That's not good enough. I want a way to contact her." This is unacceptable.

"Did you know we keep a close eye on the people in witness protection, especially within the first year?"

"What's your point?"

"My point is, she's made a new life there—new job, new school, new… *friends*. She would've come back if she wanted. Maybe you should respect her decision and work toward moving on like she has."

That can't be true. Did I take too long? It can't end like this.

"Fuck you, and your advice. You owe me a location, asshole. I'm going to become your worst nightmare until I get it. If what you said is true about her new *friends*, I'll leave her alone, but I'm not backing down until I see for myself. Either take me to her or tell me where I can find her. It's the least you can do since I spent the last nine months of my life tracking down your key witness."

He sighs and looks toward the two-way mirror like he's listening to someone. "All right, if that's what it takes to get you off our ass, you can see for yourself. No contact, though, just observation. Do we have a deal?"

"Deal." *Thank fuck.*

"Give us a week to make arrangements with the local handler. We'll have him escort you to a surveillance point."

I'm dialing the number I should have called days ago as I walk out of the building.

"Hey, Jackson, long time no talk," Walker answers.

"Yeah, I figured it was time for an update. I finally found Mia's dad and made a special delivery to the FBI on Friday. They told me today that Mia decided to stay where she is. They won't give me a way to contact her and said it's her choice whether to reconnect. It's fucking bullshit."

"Damn, that's harsh, considering you're the reason she's free. I'm sorry. Especially since you wasted almost a year for nothing."

"If it helped Mia, it wasn't wasted. They told me she's moved on and implied that she's dating someone. They're allowing me to see for myself but just to observe and prove she's okay. At least it's something. Who knows, maybe it'll give me closure."

"Ouch."

"Yeah. Will you do me a favor and let me know if you hear from her?"

"Sure, if you call me after seeing her and let me know how she looks."

"I will. Talk to you then."

I hang up and drive home, almost wishing I hadn't found Roland last week. At least then I'd still be under the delusion of holding Mia in my arms again. How the hell am I supposed to just walk away after this?

Mia

Dredging myself out of bed, I head into the kitchen for coffee before attempting my morning run. I need all the help I can get for that.

"Good morning, mija. Did you sleep well last night?" Mom asks from the living room.

It's nice seeing her relaxed on her days off, which has been more often since we've lived here—yet another reason our decision was a good one. We're still working out the details of our exit from the program, so I guess we'll see if that remains the case.

"Okay, I guess. Did you?" I ask in return.

"I always sleep better on Fridays, knowing I can rest the next day." She hesitates a moment. "So, it's been a week since we decided, and we haven't talked about it since. How are you feeling? Are you still sure it's what you want? We can always change our minds."

"I'm sure. We've settled in here, and like I said, going back could be an emotional setback." One I can't put myself through again.

"You're right, it could be, but what if there's a chance it wouldn't, and you're missing the opportunity to be with him? Are you willing to take that risk?"

"I don't know what to say. I'm not sure what the right thing is, but I can't start over again. It took me so long to even think of him without crying. If you'd asked me that question a month ago, my answer may have been different, but I've felt like I can breathe again recently."

"Does that have anything to do with another certain someone?" she asks with a smile.

"Maybe…" I'm still undecided on that. I've been wondering recently whether I could really see Jeff as more than a friend or if I'm just using him as a distraction.

"All right. Well, don't be surprised if I check in now and then. I just want you to be happy, Mia. Have you decided if you're going to use your real name here?"

"Yeah, I think it would be easier and more natural."

"I'm glad. I think that's a good decision, mija."

"I hope they give us the okay to call people soon. It would be nice to wish the family a Merry Christmas next week. Plus, I'm dying to call Walker."

"I bet it'll be any day now. Fingers crossed." She makes the gesture.

"I better change for my run so I have time to get ready for work. Love you."

Running has turned into a lifesaver for me. It's the best time to dive into my thoughts and figure out what the heck I'm doing. This past week was rough, making such a big decision and second-guessing myself every five minutes. I can't wait to fill Walker in on everything and be able to talk like we used to. He always has the best advice.

I've had plenty of time to move on, so why haven't I been able to? Maybe this decision is what I need to make that happen. Jeff has been patient in coaxing me out of my shell, but if it's so difficult, maybe it's not meant to be. Time will tell, I suppose, and since I have an infinite amount of that now, perhaps I need to move forward and find out.

Saturdays are generally busier in the coffee shop, making it the only day Jeff and I both work instead of passing during shift changes. We do well together, as he tends to take the register, leaving me to stay busy making the drinks. I love working, having my mind quiet down, too occupied with the task at hand. Also, Jeff would agree that I make better drinks. I've developed a cult following for my lattes, with perfect temperatures, flavor, and just the right amount of foam.

We've been slammed all afternoon because it's one of the last shopping days before Christmas, but we just got our first reprieve of the day. I'm sore from the number of coffees I've made and stretching my neck as I wipe the counters.

"Here, you've been a madwoman today. Let me help." He comes up behind me and begins massaging my shoulders.

"Oh my God, that feels sooo good. I think that's a record for the most drinks I've made in a day." He continues massaging while I stand there and melt. He's good. "How did I not know you could do this? Wow, I'd be paying you after each shift had I known."

"You'd never have to pay me to put my hands on you, Mary. I'll happily do this every day for free." Hearing my name from his mouth reminds me that I haven't told him anything yet. I don't think that's a conversation to have at work, though, so maybe I should suggest we do something.

"Keep going and I might hold you to that." Unfortunately, a customer comes in, and I groan at having to stop, making him laugh.

"There's more where that came from, don't worry." He rubs up and down each arm before going to the register.

"What do you think about hanging out next Friday after my shift? We could grab dinner or something… unless you'll still have family in town. Then we can do it another time," I ask when we're alone again.

He picks up my hand and starts massaging my forearm. "Seriously, wow." I moan as my head slumps down.

"If I'd know this was all it would've taken to get you to go out with me, I would've been doing this all along. I must be good if you're asking *me* out now."

I playfully shove his shoulder. "It's not the massage. I was going to see if you wanted to do something anyway. I figured it was my turn after last time. I know you've had family in town, so I was waiting."

"I would love to have dinner with you next Friday. It's a date." He kisses my hand before switching to the other arm.

Is that what it is? Did I seriously just ask him out on a date?

My head turns toward the door at the sound of another customer coming in when something out the window catches my eye. Not something, but someone. Across the street, between two buildings, I see two men walking away. The movement from the corner of my eye was of them turning before going down the alley.

My heart is thumping like crazy. Am I manifesting him because of what I just did, or was seeing Jackson's doppelgänger the universe trying, yet again, to tell me something?

Jackson

I was frozen, unable to move my feet, when the agent escorting me to see Mia physically turned my body and pushed me down the alley.

"Sorry, buddy, time's up. You saw what you needed to and almost blew it in the process."

I'm numb. No words can describe the despair at seeing someone else's hands on her. The banter between them, the way she smiled at him… it was like a knife in my heart. I needed this, though, to be sure they were telling the truth. I wouldn't have taken anyone's word without seeing it firsthand.

But now that I have…

26

TRUTHS

Mia

IT'S AN EXCITING DAY, NOT ONLY BECAUSE IT'S CHRISTMAS, BUT WE found out yesterday that we can finally contact our family and friends and waited until today. I'm dying to talk to Walker, but we decided to open presents first and then start reaching out to people. We both splurged a little more this year, our way to make the crazy shit we've been going through a little lighter.

Mom insisted that I call Walker while she starts with the family. As I wait for him to answer, my smile is the biggest it's been in months.

"Hello?" Hearing his voice again makes my smile even bigger, if possible.

"Walker, it's Mia." The words burst from my mouth.

"Holy shit."

"Oh my gosh, it's so good to hear your voice. I've missed you so much."

"You have no idea. I just can't believe it's really you. Wait, are you back?"

"No, I'm not coming back. I mean, I could, but we decided to stay here. But I can tell you where I am now, and you can come visit when-ever you want."

"Hold up. Why aren't you coming home? Are you still in the program?"

I filled him in on the last week and how we were released. "Now that we don't have to hide anymore, we can talk all the time."

"Then tell me why you're not coming home. You have friends here, a full ride to SDSU…" The hurt in his voice is something I didn't prepare myself for.

"They said some people in the program decide to stay in their new life instead of returning to their old one because they've settled in, and my mom and I decided to stay.

We've made a life here. I'm doing university online, and I love my job. Mom has more free time. It just made sense."

"Okay, but what about Jackson?" Knowing this was coming doesn't make it easier.

"What about him? It's been almost a year, Walker. I'm sure he's moved on by now."

"So, let me get this straight—the FBI told you they have someone else to testify, but they didn't tell you who or how they found him?"

"I'm sure they can't disclose that information. And it doesn't mat-ter." What is up with him?

"It definitely matters."

I hear him sigh loudly, and I picture him shaking his head. Tears start pooling in my eyes at the thought of not only being too late for Jackson but also for Walker.

"I don't see why. I'm out. Who cares how? All I care about is that I'm not in the program anymore, and we can talk again. Why are you acting like this?" I'm sure he can hear my tears through the phone.

"Mia, you have no idea… Not a day went by that I didn't think of you. I've missed my best friend, and I'm so happy to hear your voice. I'm upset because there's more to the story than what they told you."

"How would you know?" I'm lost. This is not how I thought our first conversation would go.

"Dammit, I can't believe those assholes didn't tell you anything."

"Walker, what are you talking about? What didn't they tell me?"

"Mia… your dad took your place. He's going to testify against the boss because he dealt with him before he ran off."

"What? Did he turn himself in for me? And how would you know this and I don't?"

"Mia, what did you think Jackson would do when you left? Did you honestly believe he would just take it lying down and not try to find you?"

Talk about a one-eighty. "Can we talk about that later? Explain how you know about my dad."

"Jackson *is* the explanation, Mia. Your dad wouldn't turn himself in because he's exactly the piece of shit you thought he was."

"Then how did they get him, and what does Jackson have to do with it?"

"Jackson is the one who found him. He spent the last nine months looking for your dad. The FBI tried to find him before they had you, and they couldn't, so they made a deal with Jackson."

"Walker, tell me what's going on. Why would he do that?"

"Because he never let you go, Mia. He went straight to the FBI after you left, knowing they were involved. They wouldn't tell him where you were but said if he brought in your dad, they would trade you for him. He's been searching ever since, and it took him this long to find him."

"Oh my God!"

"Yeah." Walker sighs, letting it all sink in for a minute.

"Wait, how do you know all this?"

"Because Jackson came to me two months after you left, asking if I knew anything about your dad or where he might be. You never talked about him, so I wasn't any help. He was in bad shape, Mia."

I'm speechless, tears falling while I try to articulate words. Luckily, Walker keeps talking so I don't have to.

"Anyway, he finally found him a couple of weeks ago and dragged his ass in. Instead of the FBI releasing you like he expected, they told him you weren't coming back. They refused to tell him where you were, but he caused enough trouble that they agreed to let him see you."

"When? I haven't heard from him. Is he coming here?" I can't believe I'm going to see him again.

"He was already there. An agent escorted him to your work so he could see for himself that you were okay. That was last Saturday. They told him you'd moved on, and whatever he saw through the window con-firmed it."

I'm thinking back when it hits me—it wasn't his doppelgänger I saw across the street; it was Jackson himself. I'm picturing what he would've seen between Jeff and me: the laughing, massaging, kiss of my hand. Crap. It was the day I decided to try harder to move on.

"Oh my God, Walker, it wasn't what it looked like. We've only been on one date and didn't even kiss—I couldn't bring myself to do it. I was forcing myself to try because I assumed Jackson had already moved on. The only reason I wanted to stay here is because going home to see him with somebody else would've killed me."

"Now that you know the truth, what are you going to do about it?"

"I don't know. I'm so confused. You don't know how hard it was to make this decision. I was trying to take a step in the right direction. I'm so lost right now."

"I'm sorry, Mia. I can't imagine what you've had to deal with. I'm sure it isn't easy to have a whole new reality thrown at you. All I can say is, I've talked to Jackson enough to know that he would never have given up until he saw you last Saturday."

My mind is spinning after the phone call with Walker. We talked for a while longer about his life and what was happening, all while still in a daze. He said he'd plan a trip to visit after graduation. My stomach is in knots as I wait for Mom to finish the phone call she's on. Right when the word "bye" leaves her mouth, I walk around the corner.

"Mom, the witness who took our place was Dad." I blurt, needing to get it off my chest.

"I figured as much." She sighs. "That was Carmen. She said Jackson was there looking for information about your father."

"In Puerto Rico? When?" Walker didn't tell me how Jackson found my dad, only that it took a long time. I didn't think about everything he went through.

"Not long after we left. He visited every one of our relatives to see if anyone knew anything about your dad and where he might be. They said he was desperate."

"Oh my God. I can't believe he went there. He could've just called."

She smiles softly. "Maybe you're not the only one who hasn't moved on, honey."

"I'm not. Walker told me he thought the FBI would bring me back if he brought Dad in, but they didn't tell me that. I'm so mad. Why would they keep that from me?"

"I'm not sure, mija, but now that you know, what do you want to do?"

"I need to see him, tell him how I feel… I need to apologize."

"Well, then, let's find you the next flight home." She reaches for her phone.

Home…please tell me I'm not dreaming.

Wait—did she just say… "Now?"

"What is there to stop you? Mia, this is the most hopeful I've seen you in months. Do what you need to do. I'm not going anywhere, and I want to see you happy. Do this for me."

Jackson

I'm at my parent's house for Christmas, trying not to make everyone else miserable as we sit around the dinner table. Since Lily is practically family, and Sebastian and Eli don't have any left, they're also here. Seeing the couple in their newlywed bliss makes me want to stab my eye out with a fork while trying to maintain the smile I've got pasted on. I'm tempted to have a repeat of my night in Vegas, but the worry on Cici's and Mom's faces stops me.

One bright spot to being home is seeing my parents and Cici in the same room together. At least something good came out of the last nine months. It didn't happen quickly, but it sounds like Cindy had a hand in getting them to reconcile. I'm glad they've mended things; having people you love on opposite sides of the fence is rough.

"So, what's your plan now that I'm back? Are you sticking around for a while or heading back to Bozeman soon?" I ask Cici.

"Are you trying to get rid of me already?" she quips.

"No, but I feel bad for keeping you here so long. I figured you'd be ready to go home." I notice she looks not only at my parents but in Eli's direction.

"I'm not sure I'm ready per se, but I do have to go back at some point since all my stuff is still there, and I still have my condo. Even though I was subleasing, I renewed my lease for another year four months ago, plus I like my job there."

"You can do real estate anywhere, honey. San Diego is a good market, and you know so many people here," Mom chimes in, which surprises me, considering the last time I saw that happen, it ended in fireworks. They've come a long way.

"I know. I'm not sure what I want to do." I don't miss her subtle look in Eli's direction once again, and I plan to ask him about it later.

I let my mind wander from the conversation, imagining what it would be like having Mia here—the stolen kisses around the corner, showing her my bedroom… my bed. My gut churns when reality rears its head, knowing she's doing that with someone else.

A vibration in my pocket interrupts me from continuing down that rabbit hole. Odd, since anyone who would call me on Christmas Day is currently seated at this table. Pulling my phone out, I see Walker's name on the screen.

"Sorry, I need to take this," I tell the room as I leave to go somewhere private.

"Walker?" I answer once I'm alone.

"Hey, Jackson." His voice tells me why he's calling.

"You heard from her, didn't you?" Another knife to the gut, knowing I didn't—won't.

"Yeah, I just hung up."

My silence speaks more than words.

"It's not what you think. Listen, they didn't tell her whose testimony they were taking in place of hers, and they didn't tell her how they got it." His words sink in slowly.

"What do you mean, they didn't tell her? Are you fucking serious right now?" My blood is boiling.

"She had no idea. Not a clue that you spent the last nine months tracking the son of a bitch down."

"Did you tell her?" I ask, hoping he did.

"Of course. She deserves to know. It shocked the shit out of her. Not only about her dad but about you being the one who found him. She's confused about the whole thing."

"What is there to be confused about?"

"All this time, she assumed you had moved on and were probably with someone else by now. She was trying to do the same but had only been on one date with that guy, and nothing happened."

"So what are you saying? That she hasn't moved on? Because if that's the case, I'll go clear up her confusion right now."

"I figured you'd say that… which is why I got her address for you. Merry fucking Christmas."

I'm in a daze as I rejoin the table after hanging up with Walker.

"Jackson, who was that?" Cici asks when I sit down.

"It was Walker, Mia's best friend. She called him today." Pity fills everyone's faces at once.

"I'm sorry, honey," Mom says.

"No, it was good." I shake my head. "I still can't believe it."

"Believe what? What did he say?" Eli asks.

"They didn't tell Mia who replaced her or how. They simply told her she was being released because they had a better witness. She had no idea about her dad or that I was the one to track him down."

"That's crap," my dad says angrily.

"Did Walker tell her? What did she say?" Eli adds.

They all fire off questions, but Cici has the most important one. "But, Jackson, does it matter? I thought she was with someone else."

I repeat what Walker told me.

"Now that you know, what are you going to do?" Eli asks.

"You need to go talk to her. Show up at her work and tell her how you feel. Get her back," Lily chimes in, surprising me.

"Walker got her address for me, so I'll be showing up on her doorstep," I tell them.

"Then go. What are you waiting for? Oooh, I'm so excited!" Cici claps her hands, beaming.

"I don't need to leave on Christmas. She's not going anywhere. I've waited this long. I can handle one more day." Not really, but I can't walk out on Christmas.

"Jackson," my mom interjects, "you've waited long enough. Go."

That's all I need to hear to get my ass moving.

It took twenty minutes on the phone with the credit card concierge to find out I wouldn't arrive until tomorrow afternoon, whether I left on tonight's flight or the one in the morning. The city Mia chose, Presque Isle, is literally the farthest airport possible from San Diego, if we're not counting Alaska. Not to mention, only one airline flies in and out.

I was deflated, but it allowed me to finish Christmas Day with a few smiles making an appearance. All night, my head was occupied with what I would say, how to apologize, what it would feel like to hold her in my arms—whether she'd let me.

The dark circles under my eyes this morning prove I didn't sleep. I'm walking to my gate two hours early with only my wallet and the clothes on my back after Cici dropped me off. I'm usually the guy who's rushing through security, arriving right before boarding, but I was too eager to get here. Today, I'll happily wait for the chance to see Mia again. After 291 days, what's a few more hours?

Mia

We found a flight out late that afternoon, which is a miracle considering only one airline services our small area. The bad news is that it was an overnight layover with a flight so early in the morning that I decided to stay at the Newark airport and wait it out. It was a long night of head bobbing.

It gave me time to call Jeff and explain what was happening. I felt terrible, but he was more understanding than I expected. He was blown away by the whole story and sympathized with what I had been through. Having witnessed my behavior since I'd arrived, he said it made a lot of sense now. Hanging up the phone was like ending a conversation with a good friend, and I see us continuing that way.

All night, I recited lines about what I'd say to Jackson. How I needed to apologize in person before anything else and then tell him thank you, which isn't nearly enough. I still can't comprehend how he gave up so much time, his entire life, to find my dad, and that he did it all for me. Could it be because he still loves me? Or maybe that's wishful thinking.

What if Walker misread him, and he only did it because he felt responsible for the situation in the first place?

Questions like that have been swirling in my mind the entire way here, and now that I've finally arrived in San Diego, I'm about to get the answers I'm desperate for. It's surreal being back. The last time I walked through this airport was with a sense of hopelessness, and now it's with hope. The anxiousness, though, remains the same.

I'm so close, taking the last moving walkway before exiting security, when my heart stops as I spot someone on the left side, freezing me in my tracks. The guy behind bumps into me and yells, "What the heck, lady? Can you move over if you're just going to stand there?"

He's so loud that it causes everyone to look over, and that's when I lock eyes with Jackson for the first time in 291 days.

27

FULL CIRCLE

Mia

"**M**IA?"

We're moving in the opposite direction, our shocked gazes following each other until he jumps the handrails to my side right after passing.

"What are you doing here?" he asks when he reaches me.

Before I can answer, he puts his hands on my waist to turn my body, guiding me off the walkway out of traffic. The minute his hands touch me, all thoughts vanish. I throw my arms around him the second we stop, tears already falling as I bask in the feeling I've missed so much.

All of my prepared statements fly out the window as I blurt the first things that come to mind. "Jackson, I'm so sorry for leaving you like that. I'm so sorry. I've missed you so much, it hurts." My tears soak his shirt as he rubs my back up and down.

"Shhh. Mia, it's okay. I know, sweetheart. My heart's been empty without you." His lips touch my head, and his hand comes to my cheek, wiping the tears.

"I can't believe you're here. Did you come to see Walker?" he asks, and it breaks my heart that he doesn't think I'm here to see him, still thinking I've replaced him.

"No, I came to see you. To explain why I didn't come back right away. I didn't know, Jackson. I didn't know anything. I'm so sorry." I give up trying to talk through my tears.

"I know, Mia. It's okay. Shhh. Walker told me." He continues to caress my hair in slow strokes that calm me. "You don't have to apologize. It's not your fault, sweetheart. I'm the one who's sorry." I shake my head vehemently and am about to protest, but he stops me. "Why don't we go home so we can talk."

I nod against his chest and slowly pull away. He brings his hand to my other cheek and angles my head up. "Twenty-four hours ago, I didn't think I'd ever see you again, and now you're here. I've missed you so much, Mia. You have no idea how many times I've dreamed of holding you again."

"I do because I've done the same. I love you, Jackson. I never stopped." I couldn't wait a second longer, needing him to know.

"God, hearing you say that is like waking up from a dream. My heart was made to love you, Mia." He leans in to kiss me softly, pulling away too quickly. "Let's go before I end up making a scene in the airport."

My heart is full, bursting with happiness, and it feels like it's bubbling out of me as we leave. Jackson's arm is around me, holding me tight to his body as we walk. It seems unreal to be here. Knowing he waited for me seems too good to be true, and I'm scared I'm going to wake up any minute.

I stop abruptly when we make it outside and turn to Jackson. "Wait. Why were you here? Are you going somewhere?"

"Yeah, I was going to this little town in Maine to win back the love of my life. You distracted me." His smile matches mine, and I see the happiness in his eyes. "Fuck making a scene."

He cups my face as he leans down and takes my lips in a bruising kiss, months of tension pouring out of it, giving me affirmation that our hearts and minds are in the same place. It feels like hours pass before his phone dings, letting us know our Uber is here, forcing us to stop.

We talk the entire ride, catching up on our time apart and

confessing our struggles at being separated. So much heartbreak could have been avoided if we'd spoken before I left. I'm still shocked at the sacrifice he made by putting his life on hold. He's relieved that I hadn't moved on like he'd thought and feels terrible about how long I suffered thinking he had.

When he got to the part about my dad, I wasn't shocked and didn't react as anticipated. The day my dad left was the day I knew he was a piece of crap. I didn't need this experience to tell me that—it only confirmed it. Knowing he'd rather save his ass over his wife and daughter is nothing less than expected. We're both pissed about the FBI keeping things from me and making Jackson believe something that wasn't true. Knowing they almost stole this from us is maddening.

By the time we reach his front door, we've covered every detail, question, and uncertainty. Judging by our chemistry on the way here, it's as if we were never apart. He didn't let me go once, caressing me while I savored his touch.

A sense of calm sets in as I enter his condo. "Can you imagine if we passed without seeing each other? I'd be here, and you'd be there," I muse.

He reaches for my hand and yanks me into him, making me squeal. Wrapping his arm around my waist, he holds me flush. "I'm done imagining anything when it comes to you. I need the real thing. Everything I've imagined over the last nine months, I'm ready to make happen. The question is, are you?"

Oh hell yes. "Do you really need to ask? Maybe I wasn't clear enough on the way over, but I was pretty sure—"

I don't get a chance to finish before his mouth crashes to mine in another all-consuming kiss. I feel him hardening against me, and I'm putty in his hands. He fists my hair like he's punishing me for his deprivation, pulling my head back as he devours my mouth. Wetness pools below as I whimper with need, feeling just as deprived.

"Fuck, I've missed you and your sassy little mouth. I've missed everything about you," he tells me before lowering his lips to my neck, licking and biting along the way.

I reach for the top button of his shirt and work my way down until I can feel his chest, running my hands up and down, wanting more. His belt comes next before I undo his pants. I'm going insane with his hands on my breast while his mouth hits the spot that drives me wild. Leaning forward, I kiss his chest, wanting more from him. It's been too long.

I begin to lower, kissing along the way, teasing his nipple and making him moan, filling me with a desire to pull more from him. Reaching the ground with my knees, I look up to find the sincerest expression of adoration, almost bringing me to tears. I want to please him, return some part of what we lost, and bring him enough pleasure to forget that I was ever gone.

I tug his pants down, and his engorged shaft springs free, begging to be touched. I wrap my hand around it, squeezing him tight. I'm desperate to get my mouth on him.

"Fuck, Mia. You have no idea how many times I've jerked off to this picture. I need you so fucking bad."

My tongue gently licks the tip and then circles it before dipping into the tiny hole. His deep moans urge me for more, so I lick my lips and slowly take him in as I explore with my tongue. My hand continues to squeeze, moving in time with my mouth, and when I can take no more, I pull back just as slowly.

"Nothing holds a candle to the real thing. You feel so fucking good. I've missed my little girl's mouth around my dick."

My pussy clenches, and I moan around him, continuing my slow movements. I knew it was only a matter of time before I would feel his hand on my head, ready to set the pace, and I'm eager for his control.

"Are you still my filthy little girl, starving for my cum? You need this so... fucking... badly, don't you, Mia?" His words are spoken in time with his thrusts, his hand pulling my hair, pushing, getting faster each time. There's nothing to do but hold my mouth open as he slides in and out. My pussy is aching with need.

His other hand grabs my chin and holds it as he jerks his hips in and out while I'm immobile. He watches intently.

"Fuck. You ready to take me down your throat and drink my come?"

Oh. My. God. Did I just orgasm?

"Shit, yes." His face scrunches as he pushes deeper, making me gag. "I'm there, fuck... yes. Swallow it and taste what you do to me."

I gulp as much as I can, trying to keep up.

"That's it, Mia. Take it all. Fuuuck!" He shoves it in one final time and holds it there, letting out a long growl as his final pulses shoot the last of it into my mouth.

Jackson

That felt like heaven and so much better than my hand. Fuck, it's been too long. I look down and see Mia's lust-filled eyes, and I know she's on the verge. It's been too long for both of us.

"Fuck, Mia, that was so good, sweetheart. Your mouth is unbelievable." After pulling my pants up, I bend down and lift her like a baby. "Is it my little girl's turn to be pleasured?"

She rests her head on my chest and groans.

"I'll take that as a yes." I laugh, carrying her to the bedroom, laying her on my bed—*our* bed, if all goes according to plan. I'm so fucking happy to have her here again. But my subconscious is trying to reconcile with reality, afraid she might disappear any minute.

"Have you been taking care of yourself, Mia?" I ask as I sit on the edge of the bed next to her, removing her shirt and bra.

"What do you mean?" she asks innocently.

"Don't be shy, sweet girl. Tell me you've taken good care of your pussy for me."

She shudders at my words. She loves my filthy talk, and I love her reaction to it—every time. "Sometimes."

"How? Did you use your hand? Toys? How did you please that pretty little pussy?" My hands are roaming over her, squeezing her tits and pinching her nipples as she squirms beneath me. I keep my eyes on her face, watching her desire climb higher with each question, each squeeze, and each pinch.

"I used my hand. Uhhh, that feels so good."

"No toys? I'm glad. You kept your pussy nice and tight for me, didn't you? I can't wait to spread you open again, stretch you so good with my dick. Should we get you wet and ready? I wouldn't want to hurt my little girl and her tight pussy." I squeeze her nipple, causing her body to buck in pleasure.

"Jackson, yes, please. Oh God, yes…" Begging and bucking her hips now, she's right where I want her.

I lean down to suck her breast as I reach her core and press slightly. "Is this where you need it, Mia?"

"Yes, Jackson." She's practically crying with desire.

"Okay, sweetheart. Since you sucked my dick like a good little girl, I think you deserve a reward." I sit up and work her pants off, tossing them to the ground before crawling between her legs, grabbing under the knees, and spreading her wide open. I hold her on display for me, my mouth watering at her arousal. I look up at the blush on her cheeks.

"Fuck, I've missed this gorgeous pussy. Can you be a good girl and keep your legs just like this?"

She nods, barely holding back from touching herself, her hand inching closer.

"It's been too long, sweetheart, and I'm making up for lost time. Be a good girl for me." I have a bird's-eye view, so I catch it right as she clenches from those last words. I love how fucking filthy she is.

"Keep them spread, okay?"

She nods again as I get up. Her protesting whimper is precious.

I stand at the end of the bed and stare at her, watching as moisture continues to pool at her core. I slide my shirt to the ground, keeping my gaze trained between her legs as I remove the rest of my clothes. I stand there like a statue with my legs parted, still staring at the same spot. My hand fists my dick and slowly pumps it up and down.

I chuckle as she whines. "It's all yours, Mia, I promise. But first, you're going to show me how you took care of my pussy." Her eyes go wide, eliciting another chuckle.

"Come on, Mia, you've been dying to touch yourself. Show me how you make yourself come so I can taste it. I need my meal before dessert, baby."

She's so turned on that it's mere seconds before her hand snakes down to touch her clit. I pump myself as I watch, ready to shoot my load again and spill all over her. That will have to wait, though, because today, I'll be putting it deep inside her tight channel where it belongs. Her hand moves down to moisten her fingers at her entrance before returning to her clit. She rubs it in a tight circular motion while she watches me rub off. After a few minutes, her eyes go glassy, and her tight channel starts to pulse.

"Stop," I demand, making her freeze wide-eyed. "You right there, baby?"

"Yes. Why did you make me stop?" Her poutiness causes me to smirk.

"Because I'm in charge of your pleasure now, Mia. You're all mine. It's my job to please you, show you what it means to love you, and satisfy your every desire. Your every need. Your every craving. Anything your body wants will come from me, today and always."

Already between her legs, I lower my mouth to her pussy and, starting low, lick up to her clit, repeating the motion twice more. She moans in response. I thrust my tongue into her delicious channel, searching for more, reaching in as far as possible. Her hips try to buck as I hold her still.

My chin is soaking from the juices leaking down to her ass, and I bring my finger to her tight pucker to feel how much liquid is there. It's a lot. So much that I can't refrain from pushing in. Her ass pinches my finger, causing my dick to pulse. It's so fucking tight, and the sounds it's causing her to make are driving me mad.

"You like my finger in your ass? I can't wait to fuck you here, Mia, make you scream with pleasure while you hold me in a vise."

Her pussy squeezes my tongue as I take everything I can. Withdrawing my mouth, I look up, and she shoots me an evil glare at stopping her climax again.

"Sorry, sweetheart. You'll thank me later, though. We need to get you stretched out again to take me. I don't want to hurt you."

"Grrr. You're driving me crazy. Please don't make me wait anymore. I'll be fine."

"Patience, Mia. I can see why edging is a thing. This is sort of fun." I smile, wiggling the finger in her ass.

"Not for me. Please, Jackson, I need it," she whines.

"Don't worry, my dick won't wait much longer, so let's get you ready. Give me a close-up and rub your clit for me."

She does with no hesitation this time. It won't take her long, so I need to get moving. My other hand finds her opening, and I slowly push one finger inside. Fuck me, she's tighter than I remember. Her hips buck without my hand holding her down.

"Keep still for me, sweetheart. That's it. Spread your legs wide. Good girl." She follows every instruction I give her. I can tell she's not far from the edge. "Slow down or I'll make you stop, and I know you don't want that, do you?"

She shakes her head vehemently. Fuck, I love seeing her so needy for me.

I add a second finger and see the strain on her face as I push in slowly. When I'm all the way, I start pumping, moving in pace with her fingers, watching as the strain turns to pleasure.

"That's it. You're stretching so good for me. Are you ready to finish, Mia?"

"Yes, please. Let me."

"Then show me how you come."

I add a third finger while she's focused on her clit and begin to pump hard while she writhes on the bed. The finger in her ass becomes two, and as I push them in farther, she explodes. She screams as her climax hits her, and both her ass and pussy start pulsing.

She is glorious. I remove my hands and dive in with my tongue, lapping up everything she gives until her body shudders her last ounce of pleasure and melts into the bed.

"Oh. My. God. How did I live without that?"

I move up over her, resting on my arms, my face inches from hers. "Whoa, try that again. How did you live without that—or did you mean without me?"

"I for sure meant without you. That's not normal, is it?"

"Sweetheart, if I can make you scream like that every day for the rest of my life, then it's fucking normal." I lean down to kiss the tip of her nose. "I missed you, Mia."

"I missed you, Jackson."

"I love you, Mia."

"I love you, Jackson. Now, are you going to make love to me or make me wait another two hundred and—"

"Ninety-one days? Hmmm, that could be arranged." I finish her sentence, knowing exactly how long I've been waiting.

"Jackson—"

I can't hold back anymore. I fuse my mouth to hers and go balls deep in one hard thrust. Catching her squeals in my mouth, I continue driving into her with reckless abandon, releasing all my fear, anxiety, and angst from the last nine months. Having her in my arms beneath me is a dream come true, but knowing I was almost too late is almost more than I can bear.

Mia

"You're my greedy little girl, aren't you, Mia? Did you miss this as much as I did, baby?"

"Yes! God, yes. More. please."

Suddenly, he withdraws and flips me over. "On your knees, Mia. Grab the headboard. You want more? I'll give you more. Just remember that you asked for it." He smacks my ass hard. *Ouch!*

He grabs my ass cheek and spreads it while rubbing his dick up and down before stopping at my forbidden hole.

"Jackson, what are you doing?" It felt good when he had his fingers there, and rubbing like that feels good, but I'm not sure about going in.

"I'm not taking it today, sweetheart, but sometime soon, this ass is mine." He lowers himself back to my core.

In the next second, he slams into me, my arms on the headboard holding me in place. He hammers repeatedly as he grips my hips tightly, causing me to gasp with each thrust.

"You asked for it, little girl. Now take what I give you." I'm so close… again. He reaches around and starts fingering my clit.

"Oh shit. Jackson… I'm there."

"Your pussy is gripping my dick so hard. Let go, sweetheart, as I fill you up. Fuck. That's it. Take it." He grunts through the rest of his release as my screams die down and our climaxes ebb.

I swear his orgasm lengthened mine, and it felt like he went past some barrier that brought it to the next level. I wasn't kidding when I asked him if this was normal. Why would anyone not be doing this all the time? I start laughing to myself, and he must feel it.

"Did you seriously just laugh while I'm still inside you after the best sex this century? Please tell me it's unrelated to this, and then explain how you could be thinking about something else. And it better be good, or this ass in front of me is going to be bright red in a second." He rubs a cheek in warning.

"Somebody's sensitive." *Slap!* "Ow!"

"I warned you." He chuckles.

"I was wondering why everyone isn't having sex all the time if it always feels this good."

That earns a full-on laugh as he pulls out and flops us onto our sides, spooning me from behind. "I still can't believe you're here," he says as he kisses my head.

I turn to face him. "I know. It seems surreal."

I can't bear knowing how close I was to making a decision that would have prevented this.

"Move in with me."

Wait. What?

I lift my head up to see if he's joking. Nope, he is dead serious.

"Are you crazy?"

"Move in with me, marry me, and have my babies—in that order."

"Jackson!"

"What?" he deadpans.

"You *are* crazy. You can't say things like that. Was that a proposal? We were together for a week, maybe two, before I left… for over nine months!"

"Semantics. What matters is that I don't want a life without you in it. You being gone proved that, and having you back solidifies it. I'll let you think about the second two, but move in while you do because I can't stand the thought of having you anywhere other than in my space." He's resolute.

I lean my head against his chest and groan, then quickly pull back and say, "What about my mom? I can't leave her there."

"She can move in too." I give him a look. "Okay, your insatiable sex drive and screams might make that awkward. We'll find her a place nearby, or maybe there'll be an opening in this building."

I flop my head forward again. Is this for real? Could it seriously work, or is it insane to be considering?

"What about your parents? They haven't even met me. What if they think our age difference is an issue and don't approve?"

"I've told them all about you, as has Cici, and they already adore you. You know why?" he asks as he pushes my head up to look at him.

"Why?"

"Because they know I love you and that you make me happy."

I roll my eyes. "You make it sound so simple. And really hard to say no."

"Then don't. Say yes. It *is* that simple. I'll hire a moving company tomorrow, and we'll tape your mouth shut during sex until we find a place for your mom."

"Hey!" I shove him as he starts tickling me.

"You think you can be quiet instead?" He keeps tickling me as I laugh uncontrollably.

"You know, your sheets are getting dirty."

"They're about to get dirtier, and you still haven't answered me."

"If I can be quiet or not?" I giggle.

"Mia," he says firmly. "Say yes."

"Yes."

"Yes? You will?" He's shocked.

"I think you need a hearing check, old man." He growls, making me giggle again.

"Is that so, little girl?"

I squeal as he flips us over, hovering above me. Looking into my eyes, he slowly enters, making us one. "Mia, I love you so much. My heart was made to love you. I promise I'll never let you go again."

"That's your best promise yet."

Acknowledgments

Wow, book number two. I'm sort of in awe that it's done. It's starting to feel real. When book one was published, I thought, yeah, so what? It's one book. Big deal, right? But now, with a second book under my belt and two more in the works, I'm beginning to think, huh… I might just be an author. It's quite surreal—nothing more so than the supporters and fans who read my work and love it, so a big thank you to everyone! You've truly made this a reality.

Now, let's talk about this book. Dangerous Pursuit, I love it. Sebastian from Pursuit of Innocence will always hold a special place in my heart, but this book right here? It's got me. I am so in love with this story, and I hope it excites you as much as it does me. And hopefully, like it did me, it left you even more excited for what's coming next.

There are so many people to thank, but none are more important than my husband, John. This book could not have happened without his unwavering encouragement, steadfast support, and invaluable guidance. Having him by my side to push (I'd say gently, but if you knew him, you'd know I was lying.) when necessary, have me (make me) take a break when he knew I needed it, and his word count rewards (I'll keep those to myself…) were not just helpful but crucial to completing this book.

The many times he catered to me while I frantically wrote or edited was astounding. He put up with my 'working' days when I ignored him, literally putting my hand up to silence him sometimes. His patience and understanding are beyond commendable. He is more appreciated than can ever be expressed with words.

John, you are my everything. Thank you for being by my side, believing in me, and for helping bring this book to life. I am forever grateful for your love and support—I love you.

My amazing firstborn, Cassie Rosa, has been paramount to The Pursuit Series. I don't know where to start. Without her, I would sell no books; I would have no reviews, and you probably wouldn't be holding this book right now because you wouldn't know about it. She is a-maz-ing. Her hard work and dedication to promoting me and my books allow me more time to write the next, so we all owe a big thank you to Cassie. Thank you, beautiful daughter of mine. Please give her a shout-out next time you visit one of my social media accounts; she'll be watching.

I can't brag enough about Jolene, my amazing cover artist and graphic designer. Jolene is a rock star, people. Her graphics are gorgeous—the cover says it all—and her creative energy is astounding. I'm constantly blown away by each new piece she shows me. Because of her beautiful imagery and branding, I look much more put together than I am. Thank you, Jolene, not only for your superhuman skills on a computer but also for your friendship. It means the world.

A big thank you to Abby Rosa, my second oldest amazing daughter. Without her last-minute proofreading, there would have been some pesky errors. She has an eye for things, that's for sure. I'm so proud of her natural ability to edit and improve sentences to make them sound 100 times better. She knocked it out of the park hours before the deadline, and I'm so grateful for her. Thank you, Abby, I love you!

And because I can, I'll mention Izzy and Sami, my two youngest daughters, who consistently lift me up and shower me with encouragement. Knowing they're proud of their mom is a beautiful feeling. I love you girls. Thank you for your constant praise and positivity.

Lastly, a special thank you to my vast circle of friends and family. What would I do without all of you? I'm so blessed to have a fantastic group of people rallying around me and cheering me on. Thank you to those who read through some of the early chapters, when errors were plentiful and repetitions annoying, yet still told me how great it was. You are the true heroes in my world.

And there's no bigger hero than Michele. How you continue to lift me up, listen to my woes, and handle my trivial complaints daily during your time of strife is beyond me. It truly shows the wonderful person you are, and I couldn't be more thankful. You are the strongest woman I know, and I'm fortunate to have your friendship.

I'm looking forward to our Bahamian days. XOXO

Did you miss Sebastian and Lily's story in
Pursuit of Innocence?

"I'm done waiting around. You're mine. No more games or pining over someone else when it's me you want. You won't remember his name after I get through with you."

Lily knows exactly what she wants in life. To graduate, land a high-paying job, and forge her own way. Nothing will distract her. Until the ultimate playboy, billionaire Sebastian Dubree, barges in. Not to be overlooked, Lily's longtime crush, Jackson, decides she's worth the fight.

Reluctant to succumb to either, she quickly becomes a challenge to conquer. Lily must decide between the familiarity of her childhood longing or the newly discovered passion ignited by the dominant CEO. But can she surrender without losing herself in the process, or will someone take matters into his own hands?

Boundaries blur between desire and resistance in this gripping coming-of-age romance, leaving readers yearning for more.

Visit www.bethanyrosa.com to explore other books in
The Pursuit Series

Or scan the link below:

Don't miss Lucy and Justin's story in *Holidate Pursuit,*
a holiday novella in The Pursuit Series

**Do I have a sign on my back that says,
'Love her and leave her'?
Because that's what it feels like these days.**

I thought I'd never see Justin again when he ghosted me after the best night of my life. But guess who shows up at the company Christmas party months later wanting to talk? I don't think so Mr. Burns. Burn me once, shame on you. Burn me twice, shame on me. That's sober Lucy talking. Drunk Lucy has a different idea—she asks him to stand in as my fake fiancé this Christmas. Thank God he's smart enough to say no… or is he?

One week. One bed. How could I resist?

I had my reasons for disappearing on Lucy, and I've regretted it ever since. So, when the opportunity presents itself, I can't refuse my shot at redemption. Just as it starts to feel like a second chance, the tree comes crashing down.

**Filled with humor, heart, and holiday magic,
Holidate Pursuit is a fun, steamy romance about
second chances and choosing love over all else.**

To Purchase *Holidate Pursuit,* visit www.bethanyrosa.com
Or scan below:

The Pursuit Series

Pursuit of Innocence
Dangerous Pursuit
Pursuit of Love
TBR 4/25

If you'd like to keep up with upcoming releases and learn more
about author Bethany Rosa, visit
www.BethanyRosa.com

Or Scan the QR code below to follow Bethany on her social
media accounts or purchase any other books.